PRAISE FOR ROSE TREMAIN
AND
THE WAY I FOUND HER

"One is struck, before Ms. Tremain's fine and diverse fictions, not merely by the pleasures of their prose but by the rigor of her literary risk-taking and by the virtuosic acuity with which she inhabits her characters—in short, by the formidable mind behind her work. . . . What impresses most about this highly enjoyable novel is the accuracy with which she captures the reflections of a precocious intelligence on the cusp of adulthood."

—*The New York Times*

"A touching love story. . . . What is clear—thanks to Tremain's convincingly detailed storytelling—is that the relationship [between Lewis and Valentina] is based on more than a crush. And never does the author let readers forget that this is Lewis' first love."

—*People*

"There is magic in Rose Tremain's evocation of a summer in Paris. . . . Her touch is light, subtle, and complex—just like the beautiful city at the center of her tale."

—*The Washington Times*

"Lewis' own narrative is curiously reminiscent of the nineteen-fifties, and the effect is one of pleasurable nostalgia."

—*The New Yorker*

"With consummate skill, Ms. Tremain modulates the tone of the proceedings as her young hero encroaches on ever more dangerous terrain. . . . Almost everything Ms. Tremain writes testifies to her curiosity, inventiveness, and willingness to tackle a wide range of subjects."

—*The Wall Street Journal*

"Tremain's greatest gift is a deep respect for her characters. Lewis' feelings toward his beautiful, stubborn mother and the larger-than-life Valentina are conveyed without a hint of condescension."

—*The Seattle Times*

"If impeccable tone and vocabulary, irresistible characters, a great story, humor and compassion and insight, suspense and imagination and stark-eyed reality make a great novel, then THE WAY I FOUND HER is one.... I challenge you not to love Valentina Gavril as much as Lewis Little does."

—*The Commercial Appeal* (Memphis)

"Tremain uses a magical and distinctive prose to make the exotic seem familiar, and the familiar strangely charmed. It is the rare power of her grace and imagination that make her one of the most exciting, inventive, and humane of contemporary British novelists."

—New York *Newsday*

"A classic boy-meets-world saga—lusty, acute, breezy. . . . Metafiction at its best. THE WAY I FOUND HER is less a coming-of-age novel than a novel about coming-of-age novels. . . . Tremain is a funny and perceptive writer. . . ."

—*The Village Voice*

"Tremain's new novel is a stunning mixture of mystery, romance, and tragedy. . . . THE WAY I FOUND HER is a philosophical exploration of passions expressed through the human psyche."

—*Booklist* (starred review)

"This mesmerizing and immensely affecting novel almost begs for rereading to fully appreciate the subtlety with which Tremain ties the lessons of literature and life into a haunting parable of innocence lost."

—*Publishers Weekly* (starred review)

"THE WAY I FOUND HER is a magical invention of page-turning suspense, sadness, grief, and passion, whose sure and delicate exposure of a sensibility flowering on hot Parisian summer teaches us the price of experience. Quite simply magnificent. Do not miss it."

—*The Times* (London)

"Thoroughly engrossing."

—*Entertainment Weekly*

"An adolescent world emerges here that is wonderfully complete, melding with adult preoccupations in ways both subtle and seductive. The result is riveting."

—*Kirkus Reviews* (starred review)

"Surely one of the top ten novels of the year, with Tremain more original, funny and captivating than ever."

—*Elle*

"Tremain endows Lewis with wonderful powers of imagination and curiosity. This makes his walks around Paris . . . and how the city appears from its rooftops . . . enthralling in their immediacy. You all but feel the heat shimmering on the slate roofs and hear the pigeon wings beating the air in the Parc Monceau."

—*The Buffalo News* (NY)

"Completely captivating . . . This fully fleshed, searching consciousness [Lewis'] is Tremain's most remarkable creation here . . . funny and suspenseful . . . an elegy for lost love. . . ."

—*Bookforum*

"Deliciously enjoyable."

—*The British Sunday Times*

For orders other than by individual consumers, Pocket Books grants a discount on the purchase of **10 or more** copies of single titles for special markets or premium use. For further details, please write to the Vice President of Special Markets, Pocket Books, 1230 Avenue of the Americas, 9th Floor, New York, NY 10020-1586.

For information on how individual consumers can place orders, please write to Mail Order Department, Simon & Schuster Inc., 100 Front Street, Riverside, NJ 08075.

*T*HE WAY
I FOUND HER

ROSE TREMAIN

WASHINGTON SQUARE PRESS
PUBLISHED BY POCKET BOOKS

New York   London   Toronto   Sydney   Singapore

For RH,
who navigated along the route.
With love.

This book is a work of fiction. Names, characters, places, and incidents are products of the author's imagination or are used fictitiously. Any resemblance to actual events or locales or persons living or dead is entirely coincidental.

A Washington Square Press Publication of
POCKET BOOKS, a division of Simon & Schuster Inc.
1230 Avenue of the Americas, New York, NY 10020

Copyright © 1997 by Rose Tremain

Published by arrangement with Farrar, Straus and Giroux

ISBN-10: 0-671-03570-3
ISBN-13: 978-0-671-03570-9

First Washington Square Press trade paperback printing May 1999

10 9 8 7 6 5 4

WASHINGTON SQUARE PRESS and colophon are registered trademarks of Simon & Schuster Inc.

Cover design by Brigid Pearson
Cover photo by Stephen D. Colhoun

Printed in the U.S.A.

The author and publishers are grateful to the Foundation Jacques Brel for permission to quote from "Ne me quitte pas" by Jacques Brel.

Part One

There are days when it feels really cold in here.

I'll admit, I hope it doesn't get much colder, because then I might have to move and I don't want to move. I'm OK where I am. I like lying in the dark and listening to the wind.

I've begun to believe, anyway, that the cold comes from inside me, not from outside. Moving might not change a thing. Because it's like some kind of frost has got into me. It's forming icy crystals along my spine. It's telling me that time is going along differently in me and making me old in the space of this one winter.

Not that I care, really. I don't want to talk about the present. It's Valentina I want to talk about. She's the only subject that's in my mind.

I think I'll start with something else, though. I'll start with the moment when I noticed that my mother had become a beautiful woman.

I once thought beauty was something only found in old paintings. It never really occurred to me that ordinary people could be beautiful, here and now. And then I saw – that day in July – that they could be and that my mother was one of them.

She was sitting in my room, by my window, trying to mend my Action Man, whose name was Elroy. Or at least, it *had been* Elroy. But now Elroy's torso had parted from his pelvis, so I personally knew that he was dead and finished and I told Mum not to bother with him. I never played with him any more. But she took no notice of me. She just sat there, very intent, like a lacemaker or like a mathematician, with the sun on her crazy hair, trying to bring Elroy back into existence. And that's when I noticed it: the fantastic, gorgeous beauty of my mother, Alice Little.

She was thirty-seven and I was thirteen. She'd had me when she was twenty-four. The birth had been easy, everyone said, because I was so small, such an absolute *pune*. I weighed about five pounds. In the photograph they took of me in the nursing home, I look like a piece of Play Doh. I'm amazed anyone wanted to keep me. Under the photograph, some nurse has written *Baby Lewis, aged three days*. It's embarrassing to think I started out so pathetically. Luckily, parents don't see you as you are. What they see is beauty.

It was the day before we left our house in Devon and went to Paris. I could describe it as the day before my real life began. Mum was wearing a little mauve skimpy top and a drapey kind of skirt she'd bought from an Indian shop. Elroy, in his Royal Marines uniform, lay on this skirt and his motionless blue eyes looked up at Mum's hair, which is extremely startling kind of hair, like a red thorn tree. Her arms are freckled and she told me that when she was a little girl growing up in Scotland she used to believe that freckles were in the air, like snow, and fell on your arms and on your nose when you went roller-skating on summer afternoons. She used to try to wash them off in the bath with a loofah.

She had to give up on Elroy, as I knew she would. Everything plastic is difficult to mend. Nothing bonds with it. So I kicked him under my bed to lie in the darkness and dust and I thought, that darkness and dust that he's lying in, there's something else in it too: it's the boy I was when I imagined Elroy was real.

On the plane taking us to Paris, I saw that other people had noticed Mum's beauty. They sat in their blue-and-red airline seats, watching her. Not just the men. I saw the women wondering if her thorn-tree hair was really growing out of her scalp.

The man sitting next to Mum on the aisle side had been so

disturbed by her that he was having difficulty opening the little foil packet of peanuts he'd been given with his drink. He began to tear at the peanut packet with his teeth. He tore so frantically that peanuts exploded over his drinks table and cascaded down into his silk-suited lap. He was Italian and he swore under his breath. Italian swearing sounds as if it's the dirtiest language on earth, as if the swearer's tongue is licking the grating over a drain.

Then I got out the brand-new notebook my father had given me before we left and wrote in it the first of all the things I came to write down in the coming weeks. The notebook was bought at the airport Smith's and had a photograph of Concorde on it. 'There you are, Lewis,' my father had said: 'Concorde.' 'Oh, great,' I said. 'Thanks. Brilliant.' Except that we weren't *on* Concorde. We were on some enormous jumbo plane about ten seats wide. The stewards wore draylon shirts. At the back was a gaggle of babies, mewling. It wasn't the best place in the sky to be.

'What are you writing?' asked Alice.

'Nothing much,' I said. 'Just a private theory.'

I called it *Lewis Little's Exploding Peanut Theory of Beauty*. Its first premise was: *Beauty causes alteration. I'm talking about the beauty of women. Alteration may frequently result in some accident or other. These accidents might be small and of no significance (cf. the Italian in the aisle seat) or they might be important, even a life-or-death matter. Alice Little, my mother, has come into the category of beautiful women. (NB: she may have been there for a while without my noticing.) Ergo, it's probable that she is going to be the cause of an accident of some kind in the near future. This probability is heightened by the fact that the near future is going to take place in Paris.*

Ours wasn't a family which ever did really interesting things. We would never have thought up the idea of going to Paris. We would have stayed in Devon that summer as usual and flown our bird kite on the windy cliffs and gone shrimping in rock pools.

But then came the call from Valentina. I answered the telephone one Sunday in May while Mum and Dad were in the pub and I was doing my history homework and Valentina said to me: 'Listen, darling. I must have your mother here this summer. That's it, you know. You must persuade her to come, Lewis. I'm sure she does everything you ask, because that is what the mothers of clever sons do. I'm counting on you.'

I used to be a very accommodating little boy. When I was still made of Play Doh, people were able to mould me to fit their whims and desires, but now I was going through a phase of disliking being counted on. So later I said to Mum, 'Valentina wants you to go to Paris in the holidays, but I don't want you to. Don't go, will you?'

I remember that Mum sat down and took my hand and stroked it with the back of hers, like she was trying to snow me with freckles. 'If I go,' she said, 'will you come with me?'

I'd been to Brittany once, but never to Paris. All I could remember of France was a high wind and a vast hotel and the salty smell of oysters. And I remembered Valentina. She'd been with us in the vast hotel and worn gold jewellery at breakfast. She'd been born in Russia, but had lived in Paris for thirty-eight of her forty-one years. She'd told me that her only memory of her Russian life was standing in a maize field and looking up at the moon.

'Where would we live?' I asked.

And then I was told that it was all already planned. This is what parents are in the habit of doing: they pretend to ask you a question when really they're giving you an order.

Mum told me that Valentina had a huge apartment and we would stay there with her – just Mum and me. Dad didn't want to come. He had a summer 'project'. Dad was a school-teacher and the word 'project' gave him a kind of gladness of heart. But he wanted us to go. He was all for it, in fact. He

6

told Mum that he thought it was a good idea to introduce me to a great European city.

I said: 'What will I do in this great European city while you and Valentina are working?'

Still snowing my hand with freckles, Mum said: 'Well, you'll discover things. Your French is good and now you'll be able to perfect it.'

'Who will I perfect it with?'

'I don't know. Valentina's friends. You'll meet people your own age, too. And they play chess in the parks. You could talk to the chess players.'

'Will they talk to me?'

'I don't know. I expect so.'

'Will I be able to play chess with them?'

'I can't say. You'll have to ask them.'

I looked at Alice and she was sweetly smiling, as if she were laughing at me or as if everything in the world were as easy as looking for shrimps in a pool. I wanted to tell her that I thought I'd feel stupid going round Paris begging people to talk to me or play games with me, but I didn't. And then she took the hand that she was stroking and put it to her cheek and said: 'We'll watch over you. Of course we will.'

Before we left for Paris, my father, Hugh, had told me in confidence what his 'project' was. We were sitting on a cliff at the time, watching gulls circling in the air. Hugh said: 'Lewis, I'm going to build a hut in the garden.'

He said this as if he were old Brunel about to start on the Clifton Bridge. He seemed to want me to marvel.

I don't remember what I did say. Perhaps I just looked up at the birds, trying to think of something, and then Hugh went on: 'It's a secret between you and me, OK? I'm building it for Mum. We'll put a desk and a chair in it. It'll be a place where she can sit and read or work in the summer.'

I didn't look at him. If I had looked at him, I would have seen a short, neat man with gentle brown eyes and thick hair just smartly flecked with grey. His mother, Gwyneth, was Welsh and his father, Bertie, English. With my mother being Scottish, I have the DNA of almost the whole of the British Isles sloshing round in my body, but I've wound up with the Welsh name Dad insisted on.

Dad loved the Devon cliffs. He kept pointing things out to me – tamarisk trees and standing stones and larks' nests in the gorse and wild snapdragons. He'd pointed these things out about ninety-nine times. After a while, he said: 'The thing is, I've never built anything in my life. I've got a DIY manual that makes it all look easy, but it almost certainly isn't. So listen. If, when you come back from Paris, there's absolutely no sign of a hut in the garden, don't mention it in front of Mum, OK? I'll invent another project – something to do with school. OK, Lewis? It might be because the hut has fallen down, or it might be that it's simply proved too difficult.'

I said I thought a hut ought not to be too terribly hard, but Dad said you never really knew, in life, what was going to prove hard or prove easy. People's assumptions about their own capabilities were often amazingly wrong.

I remember picturing the finished hut at the bottom of the garden, sort of red and oblong with one tiny window and a little squat roof. I thought it risked looking like a public toilet, or even a private outside toilet for us, like houses had in the old days, and I didn't think Mum would want to go and work in an outside toilet, so I said: 'Dad, wouldn't a summerhouse be better than a hut?' And he said yes, of course it would, and that maybe, in the autumn, that's what we'd find there: a beautiful summerhouse with a wooden floor and an ironwork balcony and a weather vane on the top. But it was better not to imagine it.

My Paris room was a maid's room in the roof of the apartment building. I don't know why I'd been given it, because Valentina's apartment was huge, with loads of rooms in it, but I had, and I didn't mind; I enjoyed feeling that I was up there alone.

8

You reached my room by a little narrow staircase. The thing I really liked about it was that it had a round window, looking out on to the street, which was called the rue Rembrandt. I didn't know whether, long ago, Rembrandt himself had come there and said in Dutch: 'What a nice street! Please name it after me', or whether he never set foot in it.

When I looked out of the round window, my head filled it up completely, as if the window had been measured for me by a person who made astronaut helmets. It was also positioned at exactly the right height for me, about five foot above the floor, so I could stick my face into it and examine the roofs opposite for as long as I wanted, and be perfectly comfortable.

As soon as I first saw these roofs on the other side of the rue Rembrandt, I realised they were different from English roofs. Nothing much ever seems to grow out of an English roof, but here there were dormers and balustrades and TV masts and chimney stacks and bits of ironwork and flowerpots and an ornamental gold cross, all sprouting out of the slate and jostling each other for space. So I got out my Concorde notebook and, leaving some blank pages in which to develop my Exploding Peanut Theory of Beauty, wrote down an instruction to myself to investigate the life of a Paris roof, inside and out. I put: *NB: I am well placed to do this.*

Next to my bedroom was a peculiar bathroom with a huge iron bath standing on claw feet in the middle of the floor. Valentina had said: 'I had to put this bathroom in, darling, because of course nobody used to consider that maids needed to bathe. The smell of them must have been extremely disconcerting, mustn't it?'

This bathroom was the chosen place for the overspill from Valentina's wardrobe. I counted thirty-one dresses and evening gowns and nine coats, wrapped in polythene, hanging on a movable chrome rail. I wondered whether they were cast-offs or whether Valentina would sometimes come up to my bathroom in just a satin slip or something and choose a dress for the evening.

9

While I was counting the ball gowns, I found a door. It had been hidden by the clothes rail and it was locked and there was no key. I put my ear to the keyhole. I supposed that what the door led to was another maid's room like mine, so I listened for the kind of sound I thought a maid might make; a sigh, for instance. But I couldn't hear anything at all, and at this moment Valentina called up my stairs and said we were going out to supper.

I combed my hair and went down and stood at the door of the salon. The salon had a parquet floor with a gleam on it like on the surface of still water. And it was as if, suddenly, I didn't dare to cross this water or thought I'd disturb it or muddy it or something and so I just stayed by the door, watching.

Valentina was alone in the room, sitting on a spindly sofa, smoking one of her Russian cigarettes. The cigarette was yellow. When she saw me hesitating, she held out her arm, which was plump and golden-skinned, and said: 'Come on, darling. Come and tell me all the secrets of your life!'

I didn't have any secrets. I felt like I was waiting and waiting for the day when my first secret was going to appear. And then, as I walked across the watery floor and the mingled smell of the yellow cigarette and Valentina's expensive perfume wafted into my brain, I thought, this feels like the kind of place where this famous day might happen.

We didn't go straight to a restaurant but walked into a park near Valentina's flat called the Parc Monceau.

You can't sit on the grass in Paris parks, so Mum and Valentina sat on a bench and I stood staring at the grass, admiring how green and shiny it was, as if it had been washed and combed by a hairdresser.

'Now,' said Valentina, 'you see the evening begin to come down.'

Mum and Valentina kept very still on their bench, watching the sky and the way the colour in the park was beginning to fade away. 'Look,' I heard Valentina say, 'the evening is a bird covering us with its wings.' Then she laughed and put her arm round Alice's shoulder, and I remembered this from Brittany, that she was always touching people and holding them to her, as if she wanted to keep everybody safe and near her, within reach all the time.

I was looking around now, to see if I could spot some chess players, but I couldn't see any. I decided they had their favourite bit of the park and we didn't happen to be in it.

'Valentina,' I said, 'where are the chess players?'

'Chess players?' she said. 'Oh, Lewis darling, it's almost dusk and anyway I don't think there are any chess games in this park. You must go to the Luxembourg.'

'OK,' I said.

Then I heard Valentina whisper to Alice: 'You know, Alice, I forgot about the bloody chess. But I will find him someone to play with.'

'He can find someone himself,' said Alice. 'Don't worry about it.'

Then Valentina got up. She was wearing yellow sandals, which matched her cigarettes. 'OK,' she announced, 'now we are going to walk through the park to the Place des Ternes and have supper in a restaurant there. Come on, Lewis. Are you as hungry as an anaconda?'

'Yes,' I said. 'I'm as hungry as an anaconda, Valentina.'

Valentina laughed again. That laugh of hers was the kind of laugh you imagine women having long ago, before they realised they were an oppressed category of people.

She said to Alice: 'Lewis is a good sport, you know. I hope he's going to be happy up in that room.'

When we got to the restaurant, we sat outside at a table on the pavement. I remembered this from Brittany, hundreds of tables on pavements, except that there a cold wind blew off the sea, and here the air was really hot and full of car fumes and light. Opposite the tables on the pavement was a flower seller. He was packing up his stall and I watched him going backwards and forwards, backwards and forwards, loading his buckets of flowers, one by one, into a dented old Renault van.

I think this flower seller put me into a kind of exhausted trance. Him and the neon lights in the Place, blinking on and off, and the sound of Valentina's voice. I was finding it hard to eat my meal and hard to concentrate on what anyone was saying. I kept wondering how long the unsold flowers would last and whether, in the morning, they'd all be set out again, or if some would be chucked on to the flower seller's compost heap – if he *had* a compost heap; if he didn't live in a maid's room on a top floor . . .

'So, you see,' I suddenly heard Valentina say: 'this is why I have vowed these things.'

'What things, Valentina?' I asked.

'I've just been telling you, darling. Never to be poor again. Never to be hungry. Never to live in a cold room smelling of coal.'

'Why would you have to be poor and hungry and live in a cold room smelling of coal?'

'Well, I hope I won't, Lewis. I hope all that is in the past.'

I couldn't remember what Valentina was talking about.

'Are you tired?' asked Mum.

I nodded. Valentina reached out and touched my forehead. Then she stroked one of my eyebrows with the back of her index finger. I thought, the eyebrow isn't a part of me that anybody has ever stroked before. Stroking it must be a special Russian thing. It could have a secret significance that I'm not yet able to understand.

What Valentina called her 'job in life' was writing.

Mum told me that certain writers make millions of pounds and others don't make enough to pay their gas bills, but Valentina was in the first category. The books she wrote were called *Valentina Gavril's Medieval Romances*, and all round the world people clamoured to buy them. In a survey done in the States, it was revealed that eighty-nine per cent of Valentina's readers

12

were women, but Valentina said to Alice that she didn't give a toss who her readers were, they could be orang-utans, turning the pages with their feet. She said that what mattered was that, through her books, she had become rich and so escaped from her old life and had been able to install her mother in a nice apartment near her favourite church.

I asked what her old life was and Mum told me that the Gavrilovich family was poor and that they owned something called a *café, bois et charbon* in some dismal little bit of Paris with hardly any trees. Not many *café-charbons* existed any more. They were places that opened very early in the morning, where you could have breakfast or a drink or buy a sack of coal. I said I didn't think drinks and sacks of coal went very logically together, but all Mum said was: 'Ask Valentina to tell you about it.' And then I realised she'd been *trying* to tell me about it the evening we went to the Place des Ternes, but I just hadn't been able to take it in.

Alice was Valentina's English translator. Her French was really brilliant and she'd passed a minute bit of this brilliance on to me.

Translators don't make millions; they just make enough to buy their clothes from Indian boutiques and give their hair mud baths of henna. The reason we were in Paris was that Valentina's English publishers were so keen to get their hands on her next Medieval Romance that the translation was being begun even before Valentina had finished writing the book. That's what she'd meant when she said to me that she *needed* to have Mum with her in Paris. She was going to give the manuscript to her, chapter by chapter.

I'd never read any of Valentina's books. I thought the idea of a Medieval Romance sounded drippy. And Mum told me the novels were 'all the same'. She said they all had something Valentina called her 'long-shot opening'. 'I become a cinematographer, you see,' she'd told Alice. 'I start with a wide shot of the beautiful medieval countryside of France, all unspoiled and full of forests. Then, gradually, I go in closer and we see a house or castle, its sleeping roofs, its moats and battlements. And by this time, the reader knows where she is: she is in long-ago time. She can forget the difficult present. She can relax and surrender herself to another world. And then I go in closer still and we see a window; then a face at that window. It is our heroine. We go inside the room and there she is, waiting for life and romance to start, and so last of all we see inside her heart.'

I listened to all this and didn't pass any comment. Apparently, Valentina had only one worry – that she would eventually run out of stories. What I was thinking was, maybe it wouldn't be such a bad thing if she did.

That first night in Paris, in my maid's room, I couldn't sleep, even though I was tired, so I went down, about one o'clock, and knocked on the door of Mum's room. Her light was on and she was reading Valentina's manuscript.

'Is it good?' I asked.

'It's odd,' she said. 'It's different from the others.'

'I thought you said they were all the same?'

'They were. But this one is completely different.'

Mum's bedroom in the flat was huge. She looked small in the colossal bed. There were blue curtains at her window that reminded me of the curtains in old-fashioned theatres, with gold tassles hanging off them. The street beyond would be the stage. Mum said: 'Listen to the air conditioning. It's like the sound of the sea at home.'

So then she put away the manuscript and we sat there, thinking about Devon. I was privately thinking about Dad and his tragic hut, but what Mum was thinking about precisely I don't know.

Valentina's dog was a fantastic animal. He was an Irish Setter named Sergei. His coat, in certain lights, was the colour of Mum's hair.

After breakfast the next morning, Valentina called me to her and put her arm round my waist. 'Now, Lewis,' she said, 'you are going to get to know Sergei. Sergei, come here. This is Lewis. You must show Lewis what a clever dog you are.'

We'd never had a dog at home. The only non-human creature I'd talked to in my childhood had been Elroy. I'd even taken Elroy on walks and showed him the larks' nests and the standing stones. Now, for the first time, a dog's lead was put into my hand.

'OK, darling,' said Valentina, 'Sergei has to be walked every morning and this will become your job. He will show you Paris. He knows his way right round the city. Not round the *banlieue*, of course, where we never go, but right round the centre of Paris. And he is an angel. He will find his way home from wherever you are. So off you go, Lewis. Here's the lead. Take some money.'

Sergei's lead was a string coiled inside a kind of hand-shaped box. Valentina had said: 'With this, you can let Sergei walk a long way ahead of you and then rein him in again, like a kite.' As soon as Sergei and I got down to the street, Sergei turned left towards the park. He extended his lead so far so quickly that he was at the park gates before I'd even got into my stride. I tried to rein him in, as instructed by Valentina, but Sergei was a strong dog and he didn't want to be reined in. He wanted to arrive at the park and sniff the juniper bushes and piss against the marble statues.

I made a mental note about the inaccuracy of Valentina's kite analogy. It seemed to me that she didn't know what flying a kite was really like and that it was probable she'd passed her whole life without ever flying one. I thought, perhaps, when she was a little girl in Russia, a kite was too expensive a thing for her family to buy? The most difficult thing of all with a kite is getting it to go up. Whereas the difficult thing with Sergei was getting him to come back to me. And only on certain kite-flying days, when the lift factor is very strong, is the task of winding in the kite remotely hard.

Sergei tugged me round the park. My arm began to ache.

My arms were still the puniest bits of me. I could only rest when Sergei found some smell on the dusty paths delicious enough to make him pause. He saw some pigeons and began chasing them. His long lead went whirring out like a fishing line with a shark on the end of it. Then I heard an unexpected noise. It was a long blast on a whistle, like the PE instructor at school ending a game of football. And a man in a uniform came striding over to me, shouting and wagging his finger. The pigeons flew away and Sergei sat down and looked at the man accusingly, so I just stood and waited.

The man was really angry. Under his summer tan, his face was quite red. I hoped he wasn't carrying a gun. All along the path, old people sitting on the benches began to stare at me. A jogger passed, wearing a luminous bandana, and gave me a glare. And then I understood: dogs weren't allowed in the park. The uniformed man pointed at Sergei and made an X-shape with his arms. 'Défendu,' he kept saying. 'Défendu, défendu!'

I shrugged. It was meant to be the gesture of an innocent, of the person who's landed from outer space, knowing nothing. If Valentina hadn't told me about the blow-dried grass, I might have trespassed on that too. How was I supposed to know the etiquette of the park without her help?

'Sortez, s'il vous plaît,' said the man. I could tell he thought I was an idiot. It hadn't occurred to him that I was a schoolboy from Devon. 'OK, d'accord,' I said. And I tugged at the lead until Sergei came grudgingly towards me and there we were back in the rue Rembrandt. I noticed then that on the green park gates was a little picture of a dog with a line through it, but in a strange place your eyes can skim right past important things.

I stood in the street. 'Now where?' I asked Sergei. He was shitting in the gutter, between a Renault Clio and a Volvo Estate, and while I waited for him to finish I looked all around me anxiously, hoping he wasn't breaking some invisible law.

*

When I got back, Alice and Valentina hardly noticed me. 'Later, darling, you will tell us where you've been,' said Valentina.

They were sitting in Valentina's study, talking. The subject they were discussing was medieval time. This was one of the things I'd begun to like about Valentina: you never knew what weird subject she was going to start on next.

Sergei lay down on the parquet in the salon and I got myself an Orangina from Valentina's fridge (she remembered I used to drink Orangina on that holiday in Brittany) and sat down by him, listening to this peculiar conversation coming through the open study door.

Valentina said: 'You know how they measured time in the Middle Ages, Alice? In hours of differing length. Because they counted twelve hours from sunrise to sunset and twelve hours from sunset to sunrise, no matter what season they were in. And so you see what happens? The hours of the night in summer become thirty-minute hours and the hours of the night in midwinter ninety-minute hours! But you can imagine that people might forget what kind of hour they were in, can't you? In the darkness, especially, they could measure the hour wrongly. And this is what happens to Barthélémy.'

'I see,' said Alice. I wanted her to ask who Barthélémy was, but she didn't, because she already knew.

'So,' she said, 'when he's doing his experiments at night, he forgets that the hours are getting shorter as the spring comes?'

'Yes. He is calculating in ninety-minute hours, when really an hour at that time of the year lasts only eighty-five minutes and then eighty-four and then eighty and then seventy. And this forgetting is fatal. You see?'

There was a silence at that moment. It seemed to be Mum's turn to speak, but she didn't say anything. Then Valentina went on: 'I have no difficulty in understanding the concept of the ninety-minute hour. In my other life, I *lived* ninety-minute hours. Even in summer, I don't think the hours were any shorter than seventy or eighty minutes.'

Alice said: 'Time alters as we get older.'

'No,' said Valentina, 'it's not to do with age. It's to do with *movement*. When I worked for my parents in the *café-charbon*, the places I moved between were the wine cellar and the café. Down, up. Cellar, café. Café, cellar. Up, down. That was all. To a prisoner, time is different.'

'Is that how you think of your old life – as being in prison?' asked Alice.

'Yes, of course,' said Valentina. 'Worse for my father. The places he went between were the coal bunker and the yard. All day. Coal bunker, yard. Yard, coal bunker. Fill up a sack, take it up to the yard. You know how much a sack of coal weighs?'

'No.'

'As much as a child of seven. All day, my father puts this child on his back and carries it to the yard. Perhaps one day I will write something about that. But no one will publish it.'

'Why not?'

'Because from me, from Valentina Gavril, the readers want Medieval Romances. That's all they want, Alice. A little terror, a little chivalry, a lot of fucking, a happy ending. Why not? A book can shorten an hour. But you know my last translator used to change things around. She was an American feminist and so she tried secretly to change the women in my books and make them more like feminists. She forgot my English was almost as good as hers. I had to kill her in the end.'

'What?' said Alice.

I put down my Orangina and leant nearer the study door. I heard Valentina laugh. 'Yes, I killed her,' she said.

There was a pause here. Being a Scot, Mum isn't afraid to dismiss totally bluntly everything that strikes her as untrue. She has this haughty, withering look she can give you, worse than any look the teachers give you at school.

'I kill my characters all the time,' Valentina went on. 'I decapitate them, disembowel them, poison them, burn them. I know so many methods. And I killed that translator.'

The trouble about eavesdropping is you're just left alone with

18

the things you've heard. You're marooned with them, like on a really uncomfortable rock, and all around you is a silent sea. I was trying to imagine Valentina taking off her jewellery and her expensive shoes and tiptoeing along the corridor with a carving knife, when she and Alice came out of the study and sat down with me and asked me to tell them about my morning.

We'd walked such a long way that Sergei was exhausted and he went to sleep with his head on Valentina's foot. She wasn't wearing yellow sandals today, but white ones. The colour of her toenails was dark shining red, like wine, or like blood.

I told her and Alice that I'd seen the river and the Eiffel Tower. I said the hugeness of the Tower had made me feel strange. What I meant by strange was 'happy'. The thing I used to envy in my games with Elroy were how large the world must have seemed to him.

I told them I liked it when things were vast and made of iron. And I described a courtyard I went into where there was an iron girder strung between two houses. It seemed to be holding the two buildings apart, as if one was the Capulet house and the other was the house of the Montagues. I'd had *Romeo and Juliet* on my mind lately, because we'd been studying it at school and I really liked the absolute total sadness of it, I don't know why.

I said I realised after a moment that the girder wasn't really holding the two houses apart, but making a bridge between them. Creeper had climbed up the wall of the Montague house and along the girder and hung down in tentacles, and so Romeo could have climbed out of his window and inched his way along the girder, holding on to the creeper, until he reached Juliet's bedroom.

Valentina laughed when I said all this. Mum and Dad hardly ever laughed at the things I said, but I seemed to amuse Valentina, or else she was a woman who, now that she didn't have to work in a coal yard, was easily entertained.

She asked me what else I'd done. I said Sergei had tugged me across one of the bridges over the river and that I was so thirsty by that time that I'd sat down in a café and ordered a Coke for me and a bowl of water for Sergei. Near his bowl Sergei had found a perfectly formed strawberry tart in the gutter.

Then I told them about the woman I'd seen in the café while I was drinking the Coke and Sergei was snaffling up the tart. She was old, but she had this little face like a kitten. She kept dabbing her nose with powder. It was hot in the café, so she dabbed loads and loads of times. I said: 'I felt really sorry for her.'

'I expect she was waiting for someone, darling,' said Valentina.

'Well, maybe she was,' I said, 'but no one came.'

'Then what do you think was happening, Lewis?'

I could tell Mum wasn't in the least interested in this conversation. She was looking away from both of us, staring into her own separate thoughts. Valentina put her arm through mine. She smelled of some special delicious perfume I'd never breathed before. I took some deep sniffs of it before I said: 'I think she thought people passing would mistake her for some old movie star and come in and order up champagne, or something. She kept scanning out for the one person who was going to see her former beauty, but that person never came by.'

Valentina laughed again. Then she said: 'That's really very sad, Lewis. I don't know why I'm laughing.'

'I thought about pretending to *be* that one person,' I went on, 'but I couldn't remember the names of any old movie stars.'

Valentina began to reel off a list of names of former beauties. They were mostly French and I'd never heard of any of them. I remembered one name: Simone Signoret. Valentina said hers was the saddest story of all.

When it was almost lunchtime, I went up to my room. I got out my Concorde notebook and added a Second Hypothesis to my *Exploding Peanut Theory of Beauty.* It didn't have the simplicity of the first, but all the same I quite liked it. It went like this: *Female beauty, if or when lost by the former owner of it, can cause insanity. The brain, which might have roughly the same mass as a Family Size pack of dry-roasted peanuts, 'explodes' into irrational behaviour, searching for signs — such as the passing glance of a stranger in the street — that the irretrievably lost beauty has suddenly been found again.*

It was stifling in my room. Maids weren't meant to be in their rooms during the day; they were meant to be dusting parquet or polishing the silver downstairs. I went into my bathroom and ran some cold water in the washbasin and laid my face in it, till it began to cool. It was while I had my head in the water that I remembered something my father had said to me about happiness. We were shrimping at the time. Hugh said: 'See this deep pool, Lewis, and see the little grey shrimp? Think of the pool as your life and your quota of happiness as the shrimp and then you won't expect too much of anything, and when disappointment comes you won't drown.' At the time, I'd thought this a kind of wise and fathomless thing to say, but now it seemed to me, standing there with my head in the basin, that to equate happiness with a shrimp was completely stupid.

When I emerged from the water, I heard a new sound. I dried my face and listened. Someone was whistling on the other side of the locked door.

I tiptoed across the bathroom and bent down by the keyhole of the door. I tried to see into the room beyond, but I couldn't. Perhaps the key was in the lock on the other side, or perhaps some piece of furniture had been put in front of it? But there was definitely whistling going on. It sounded like the sad song of a maid, except it was a man whistling, as if he might be reading some boring newspaper. One of my teachers at school did this, whistled while he marked dull assignments, and only stopped when he found something to interest him. He'd whistled all through my essay on *Romeo and Juliet*, right to the last full stop.

There was no sound of the whistler moving about – no footstep or anything. I imagined someone sitting on a stool, in front of a round window identical to mine, reading about all the thousands of things going on in France and in the wider world and whistling right through them.

I thought about knocking softly on the door. I then considered asking the whistler if he played chess, but I thought, it might be a maid after all and a maid could misinterpret the question. So I stayed still, just listening, until I realised how starving I was. I started to hope that Valentina had made or bought a huge strawberry tart even better than the one Sergei had found in the gutter.

Before I left England, Dad had told me about the *bouquinistes*, who sell old books and prints and cards from little stalls alongside the river, and the next day Sergei led me right to them. I reined him in tight and browsed slowly past them. The stall holders didn't seem very interested in selling anything. It was like they just enjoyed chatting there, where a breeze was coming off the water. I prefer people like that to the kind who try to stick their crappy wares up your nostrils.

I hadn't really intended to buy anything, but then I saw a copy of *Le Grand Meaulnes* bound in chalky leather and I picked it up. I tied Sergei to a plane tree and opened the book. The previous owner had written his name and a date inside it in faded blue ink: Paul Berger, 1961. I worked out that if Paul Berger had been, say, thirteen or fourteen in 1961, he was now in his late forties, about the same age as Dad. He might now be a banker or a futures trader and not even remember the name of Alain-Fournier. On the other hand, he could be a writer himself by now, the kind of writer no one has heard of but who makes a puny living writing the books he once liked to read. The favourite authors of this kind of writer are all dead, but he still tries to become like them. He doesn't notice that the world he's writing about no longer exists. Paul Berger might now be on his tenth attempt to rewrite *Le Grand Meaulnes*.

I bought the book. The stall holder looked quite miserable to part with it. He put it in a used brown paper bag and handed it to me carefully, with a kind of solemnity. Sergei, when I unwound him from the tree, thought it was a waffle or something and tried to bite it.

That night, in bed, I began reading it. Reading in French is always harder than speaking it. It's almost as if each word has three dimensions.

J'avais quinze ans. C'était un froid dimanche de Novembre, le premier jour d'automne qui fit songer à l'hiver . . . I moved round and round this sentence, trying translations. 'I was fifteen', or 'I was fifteen years old'. 'It was a cold Sunday in November', or 'It was a cold November Sunday'; 'the first day of autumn', no, 'the first autumn day', no, 'the first day of *this* autumn . . . which made you [or 'he'? or 'one'? or 'everyone'?] dream of [or 'have thoughts about'? or 'remember'?] winter [or 'the winter']'. I wanted to go and ask Mum how she would decide whether 'winter' or 'the winter' sounded best. Did Mum, as a translator, have to be a kind of writer herself, a kind of poet, in order to make a choice instinctively, as if the words came from her and not the original author?

I was comfortable in my bed, with my round window full of city light. I thought everyone but me was asleep and so I said aloud: 'I will now attempt a perfect but fluid translation of this sentence by Alain-Fournier, the Lewis Little Version! "I was fifteen. It was a Sunday in November, very cold. It was the first day of that autumn which made you remember that winter was just around the corner . . ." '

Then a voice said: 'Lewis, are you talking to yourself?'

I looked over the top of the book and realised that Valentina was standing in my room. She must have crept up the stairs, wearing her little jewelled slippers, without my hearing her. She had on a Japanese kimono, black and green and yellow, and her face was oily.

'I'm translating *Le Grand Meaulnes*,' I said. 'I've been working for an hour and I'm still only on page two.'

23

I knew this would make her laugh, and it did. She came and sat on my bed and folded her arms. 'Read to me,' she said.

'Where from?' I asked.

'Anywhere you like.'

'From the beginning?'

'Yes.'

'In English or in French?'

'In your translation.'

'I'll never be a translator,' I said. 'Is that some kind of special oil on your face, Valentina?'

'Yes. It's called Night Repair Cream. It mends me while I sleep.'

I didn't think Valentina looked as if she needed much repairing. Her eyes were really large and gentle and the lines at the corners of them were small, like she might have lain on a feather by mistake. 'How old are you, Valentina?' I asked.

'Forty-one, darling, alas,' she said. 'How old are you?'

'Thirteen. Fourteen on September the sixteenth.'

'Is that the age of François in *Le Grand Meaulnes*? I can't remember.'

'No, he's fifteen. *"J'avais quinze ans."* '

'Off you go, then, from the beginning.'

I lifted myself up in the bed. I noticed that Valentina's night repair cream smelled of wallflowers. In Devon, we grew wallflowers by the back door and, in early summer, the scent of them wafted by you every time you came in or went out.

I turned back to page one of the book. I read: ' "He arrived at our house one Sunday in November 1890. I continue to say 'our house' even though the house isn't ours any more. We left that country since soon fifteen years . . ." '

'Not "soon fifteen years", Lewis.'

'No, right. "We left that country almost fifteen years ago, and we will certainly never go back . . ." '

'Oh yes,' said Valentina with a little sigh, 'I remember that. When you begin a book and you already know in the first line that everything is in the past, this makes you worry so for the character.'

'Why?'

'Because the thing he is writing about will turn out to be the most important thing in his life, you see? Or else why would he write about it? So you know all the rest of his life has been dull compared with that.'

I thought about this for a second, then I said: 'It could be the *worst* thing in his life. He could be saying, "This terrible thing happened to me when I was fifteen and this is what I'm going to tell you about" – like old Oliver Twist in the workhouse.'

'Yes. But not usually. Go on, anyway, darling. You're reading very nicely, Lewis.'

I struggled on, round and in and out of blocks of words, till my mind felt too tired to carry on. While I was reading, Valentina sat very still, listening, as if I were reciting some magical Russian fairy tale. She didn't try to help me or correct my translation again, but just stayed quiet, sometimes nodding and smiling. When I put the book down, she said: 'Would you like to read to me a little each night, Lewis? This way, you will learn very fast.'

I liked the idea of her creeping up my stairs, wearing her wallflower cream, and the story of Meaulnes gradually unfolding in my attic room.

'OK,' I said.

'Good. You prepare a couple of pages for tomorrow and I will come and listen. And now you'd better go to sleep. What I came up to tell you is you may hear some noises on the roof tomorrow. People are coming to do some work up there. So the noise will be the roof repairers and not a murderer, or anything like that. I didn't want you to be afraid.'

'I heard someone today,' I said.

'You heard someone on the roof?'

'No. In the room on the other side of my bathroom, where the door is behind your clothes. Someone whistling.'

25

Valentina looked through to the bathroom, as though she expected to find the person still there. 'Whistling?' she said.

'Yes.'

'Well, I don't know who that can be. That is a junk room. There's no space in it for anyone to whistle.'

The next day, Didier appeared.

A huge hissing truck parked in the street at eight o'clock, just after I'd woken up. I had my head in my astronaut window when it arrived. It was the kind of hydraulic-lift truck firemen use and Didier was put into the cradle of it and transported to the roof. He went inching up about six feet from my window and I waved to him as he passed and he waved back.

I monitored him for most of the morning. He went up and down seventeen times, hauling scaffolding. Then he began to construct a scaffolding cage over the whole roof, with the base of it resting on a ledge below my room. One pole of his cage now cut my view of Paris in half. While he was fixing this pole, I stuck my head out of the window and asked him: 'Comment vous appelez-vous, Monsieur?'

He was very thin and tanned and wore glasses. He said his name was Didier, so I told him mine was Louis. I told him I was the only person living in this attic.

At lunch, Valentina said: 'I hope they've sent sensible people to work on the roof and I hope they don't dawdle, you know.' Valentina's English was so good, she even knew words like 'dawdle'.

'There's only one guy,' I told her.

'One guy? To do the whole roof?'

'Yes. His name's Didier. He's very thin and he wears glasses, which is peculiar.'

'Why's it peculiar?' asked Alice.

I said: 'A roofer should have perfect sight, shouldn't he? If his glasses fell off while he was on the roof, he might not be able to get down, or he could slip and fall. I think I'll go and check on him from time to time, shall I, to make sure every-thing's all right?'

'Well, that's a noble thought, darling,' said Valentina, 'but how are you going to get on to the roof?'

'From the bathroom window.'

'Don't be stupid, Lewis,' said Mum.

'Darling,' said Valentina, helping herself to another piece of veal, 'more people will come to help him. You'll see. They wouldn't send one poor man to do this whole difficult roof.'

But no one else came. Didier constructed a second scaf-folding cage at one corner of the apartment building, which enclosed a complicated staircase made of ladders, and he went up and down this ladder, carrying heavy hods of slates. I knew that he was just the very person Dad needed to help him with his hut.

I liked Didier. I swapped life stories with him. I told him I was Third Year Chess Champion of Beckett Bridges School and he told me he was an existentialist. I couldn't remember exactly what an existentialist was, but Didier looked more like a student of philosophy than a roofer. Sometimes I like people just because I think the way they look is really neat. But I also thought, if you did a scan of Didier's brain, you might see an area of brilliance in it that nobody expected to find.

On his neck was a tattoo of a bird. I didn't know precisely where the jugular vein was, but it looked to me as if Didier's tattoo was near it. So I asked him why he'd got that on his neck and he said it was a tattoo of his name, 'Didier-l'oiseau', or 'Didier-the-Bird'.

'Why "the Bird"?' I asked him.

'Because,' he said, 'there are times in life when you need to fly.'

At lunchtime, he sat on the dusty street, in the shade, eating bread and ham and drinking Coke. When the residents of the building passed him, they might nod or smile, but they never said a word to him.

'No one speaks to Didier,' I told Mum, after a few days.

27

'I expect they do,' Mum said. 'The French are polite on the whole.'

'They don't. I've watched them. No one says anything to him.'

'Except you.'

'Well, I do, but I expect he'd prefer to have conversations with the grown-ups. Will you talk to him, Mum?'

Mum laughed, as if I'd said something outrageous. 'What do you want me to say to him?' she asked.

'You could ask him about his eyesight. You could see if he's got a spare pair of glasses in his shorts.'

She laughed and laughed. I could see her tonsils jiggling up and down. But eventually – humouring me like I was a kid of four – she said that if this was important to me she would talk to him. So, the following day, when I saw him eating his lunch in the street, I persuaded her and Valentina to come down and introduce themselves to him.

As soon as we got outside the door, they both looked embarrassed. I could see them thinking that a famous novelist and her translator shouldn't go down and talk to roofers in the street. And when Didier saw them coming with me towards him, he looked uncomfortable too and blushed and tried to hide his half-eaten sandwich behind his dusty body.

I introduced them nevertheless and they both shook hands with him. I saw him notice Alice's beauty. He probably wished his sandwich would turn into a red rose he could give her. I thought, I must try to keep close track of what everyone's going to say.

Valentina asked him if other men would be coming to help him with the roof, but he kept his eyes on Alice and said he didn't know. Then Mum said in her brilliant, flawless French: 'We ask because this is Valentina Gavril, the well-known writer of Medieval Romances. She has a lot of work to do and it's important she isn't disturbed for too long.'

I could tell this pissed Didier off. It was like that clever bit of his brain thought the whole idea of a Medieval Romance was complete and utter shit. He gave Valentina a mean stare from behind his glasses and said: 'I'm sorry if the roof work disturbs you, Madame. But it must be done. The slates are very old and uneven.'

'Yes, of course,' said Valentina, with one of her sweet smiles, 'I know that.' And then she put her hand on my shoulder and said: 'Lewis is the one who'll be disturbed the most. His room is right under the roof.'

'I know,' said Didier, 'I've seen Louis' room.'

'Oh, you have?' said Valentina. Her smile had gone now and I could tell she was wondering whether I'd invited Didier into my room for a Kit-Kat or something, or made him listen to the phantom whistler.

Alice tried a kind of conversation rescue. 'Lewis is worried,' she said, 'about your glasses.'

'About my glasses?' said Didier.

'Yes. That you could lose them and then—'

'Lose them?'

'Yes, and then . . . not fall, or anything – because I'm sure you're very practised – just feel a bit confused up there.'

'No,' said Didier. 'I don't think so.'

I could feel that the whole encounter was going really badly. I wished I'd never suggested it. And I wished we could now pretend to be on our way to the Parc Monceau, pretend that we'd passed Didier eating his lunch in the street quite by chance. Then I had an idea. I asked Didier if he'd like to see our dog, knowing he'd say yes, so that Valentina and Alice would go away and leave him in peace. So we all trooped back inside the apartment building and I fetched Sergei and brought him down and I could tell Didier liked him and he liked Didier. Sometimes, meetings with animals go better than meetings with novelists.

Later that day, when I told Alice that Didier was known as 'the Bird' and that he was sometimes capable of flight, she said condescendingly that I shouldn't always believe the things the world appeared to say. And when I mentioned to Valentina that he was also an existentialist, she said: 'Darling, either you must have misunderstood or that roofer was teasing you. Nobody uses that term today. It's a completely outmoded philosophy.'

It was like they both wanted to deny that Didier could be anything more than the person who'd come to mend the roof. But I knew better.

Every Thursday afternoon, Valentina went to visit her mother, Mrs Gavrilovich.

She told me that it was on a Thursday in the winter of 1981 that Mr Gavrilovich had died. He had died, said Valentina, in the yard of the *café, bois et charbon*, carrying a sack of coal from the coal bunker to the van. Valentina had glanced out of the window at the back of the café and seen him staggering about, like someone trying to remember the steps of a folk dance. He was still holding the corners of the sack of coal in his hands. Then he tripped over his own feet and sat down on the wet cobbles, 'looking all around him in amazement, Lewis, as if he were seeing the yard for the first time'.

Valentina and Mrs Gavrilovich went running out to him. He apparently leaned back on the sack of coal and swore in Russian, over and over. 'Bad words,' said Valentina, 'words my mother could not tolerate. And in the middle of the swearing, his heart stopped beating.'

I wanted to ask Valentina how Mr Gavrilovich could have been 'in the middle' of swearing when he died. Did one more curse, already lurking in his throat, come out of him after his heart had given up?

I didn't ask. I was afraid Valentina would think me pedantic. And she'd sometimes said that the most extraordinary things could happen to the people of Russia. Anything the human mind could imagine, no matter how strange or grotesque, had at one time or other taken place in Russian history. Which was why she was never shocked or surprised. And this could be one of those strange things: the word or *words*, even, spoken by the dead Mr Gavrilovich on a Thursday afternoon in the winter of 1981.

When Valentina had started to make money from her Medieval Romances, the café was sold. The *charbon* bit of it had already stopped when Mr Gavrilovich died. The remaining coal was just gradually used up by the old range where Valentina and her mother cooked their meals.

Then, when the money began to flood in from America and Germany and Britain and everywhere, Valentina installed Mrs Gavrilovich in a ground-floor apartment in the rue Daru, a short walk from the Russian Orthodox church of Saint Alexandre Nevsky. 'And, you know,' said Valentina, 'Maman believes that God *lives* in that church! She said to me one day, "If you were God and could choose to live anywhere in the world, you'd probably choose Paris!" '

At the moment, though, Mrs Gavrilovich wasn't feeling well. She had an ulcer. She had the blues. The blues were a thing Russians were born with. They lay in their prams, weeping for the greyness of the sky. 'And she is tired of everything, Lewis, and that's a real problem. She telephones her concierge two or three times a day to complain about something or other and it's getting unreasonable. One day, she complained about a thunderstorm and the concierge told her, "Listen, Madame Gavrilovich, if I could create thunder, I'd be something better in life than a concierge, so don't speak to me any more on the subject!" '

Valentina took Sergei and walked down the rue Rembrandt, heading for her mother's apartment. I watched them go. Valentina's shoes were green that day, to match a green silk dress. I decided her smart clothes made Mum look like a hippie by comparison, but I didn't mention this to either of them.

Mum and I took the métro to Jussieu. When you come up at Jussieu station, you arrive under some dark trees with big leaves that clatter in the wind. Mum said these were catalpa trees and that they grew in Africa and so this is what they have always been to me – catalpa trees.

She'd taken me to see the Jardin des Plantes. It was so boiling hot it was as if we were *in* Africa.

We walked along down an avenue of limes, in their big shade, where sparrows bathed in the dust. I could hear frogs calling from the miniature lily ponds. In the flower beds, there were giant artichokes and purple broccoli. Bits of the land had been sculpted and planted to resemble China and Corsica and the high Alps.

We sat down in the middle of China, next to a little waterfall. We didn't speak, but just looked around us.

I thought, I've stepped so far out of my normal life, I may never get back to it. I knew this could happen to people. A perfectly ordinary person – his name could be Paul Berger, say – can arrive somewhere new, like in the Appalachian Mountains, and watch his previous life vanish, as if into a tiny lamp or vial. Paul Berger might keep the lamp or vial in some drawer, but he'd forget about it absolutely. Perhaps, when he was old, he'd discover it there in the drawer and say to himself, 'What's this?' And then he'd give the corroded old vial a shake and remember it contained his former life.

We left China and went into the menagerie section of the park. We stood by a little compound of American bison, their fur all tattered and falling off them. I began thinking about *their* former lives and I said to Alice: 'If you're a bison and you're here, do you think that there's any bit of you that remembers the Great Plains?'

Alice thought about this for a while, then she said: 'More interesting is the question whether a bison who had *never been* to the Great Plains can feel their existence inside him somewhere.'

I agreed that this was more interesting, but I didn't really know how to start to speculate about it. On certain days, in my version of my future, I became a philosopher, but this particular Thursday didn't seem to be one of them. I wondered what Didier would come up with if I put this question about the bison to him.

'When we go back to Devon,' I said, 'I may not be able to fit back into my old life. Too much may have happened to me . . .'

'No,' said Alice, 'it doesn't work like that. When we go back, it'll be as if all of this hardly existed.'

'It won't,' I said.

One of the bison got tired of looking at us and began to lollop towards its shed. I noticed that parked outside the shed, in the muddy straw, was a cocktail trolley. I pointed this out to Mum and she said: 'It's a cocktail trolley, so it is! Well, I suppose things get abandoned in the most unlikely places – things and people, for that matter.'

'Why do you say people?'

'Oh, because it happens . . .'

'You'd never be abandoned.'

'No, I don't think so. But how is one to know?'

'And you wouldn't abandon Dad, would you?'

'Oh, no.'

I glanced up at Alice. Her hair looked very red today, in the sunshine, like the beginnings of a bush fire. I felt glad she didn't yet know what Dad's project was. If you realised that all your loved one could make for you was a hut like a public toilet, you might seriously think of abandoning him there and then.

Now, the other bison meandered towards the shed. They reminded me of the vagrants you saw in England in winter, bundled up in heavy rags and swaying along on worn-out feet. I said to Mum: 'I expect some amazing food is going to be given to them – elephant grass or something.' But no one came to feed them, so we walked on.

'Who's Barthélémy?' I asked suddenly.

Mum looked surprised and was about to say she didn't know anyone called Barthélémy, when she remembered. 'Oh,' she said, 'he's a character in Valentina's book. He's plotting a murder.'

'Who's he going to murder?'

'The husband of his mistress. A duke.'

'How's he going to do the murder?'

'He's the son of an apothecary. He steals poisons from his father's shop and mixes them and experiments with them in secret during the night. He's trying to find a poison that acts fast and leaves no trace.'

I thought this sounded quite good. I asked Mum if I could read some of her translation and she looked at me intently, as though an idea were dawning on her.

'Yes,' she said after a while. 'Why not?' Then she said in a kind of whisper: 'This new book of Valentina's is a thousand times better than any of her others. Much more exciting. A lot more cruel. It's as if it's been written by someone else.'

I liked the idea that there could be some mystery attached to the book. I thought, perhaps our apartment is going to become so full of secrets, it'll get hard to breathe. And one secret that I decided to keep from Mum was Valentina's visits to my room and the work I was going to do with her on *Le Grand Meaulnes*.

The following Sunday afternoon, I was playing Computer Chess in my room when Alice came up and said to me, 'I can't work, Lewis. Let's go out. Let's go now.'

She seemed in a fluster, angry. Her hair was spiky.

I said: 'You know, this computer's making stupid moves, Mum. It captured my knight with its bishop and forgot it needed the bishop to defend its king. It was just greedy for the knight. I moved my queen in and it brought a rook over to defend, but it's going to be too late because—'

'Never mind that,' Alice said. 'Leave it. Let's go.'

We went straight out of the apartment without a word to Valentina. I could hear her talking on the telephone in her study and I was about to suggest to Alice that we wait and tell her where we were going, but Alice had already grabbed her key and was flying down the stairs, so I closed the apartment door and followed her. I knew that when I got back, the stupid Travel Computer could be checkmated in five moves.

It was a peculiar day, still hot, but sunless, with a sky of grey wool. We caught a métro going west. A guy got on and started to play the guitar and sing to us. When he'd finished and was going round with the hat, he said: 'If this experience has been disagreeable to you in any way, please inform me.' But nobody informed him.

We got out at La Défense, the last stop on the line. Someone had recently built an arch here. The Arche de la Défense was the tallest, heaviest arch ever to be built in the history of the world. In front of it was a huge cascade of white steps and a big esplanade, the colour of the grey sky.

We stood around on the steps, looking up at the arch. Mum was scowling. Her beauty vanished a bit when she scowled. The designers of this arch had forgotten to put in a lift to carry people to the top, or so it seemed to me, because they'd added on a little fragile-looking elevator underneath it, like a hoist a trapeze artist might take to get him to his high wire.

I said to Mum I quite liked the trapeze idea, but she wasn't paying me much attention. She was staring out at the esplanade now, which had office buildings and modern sculptures all round it, and when I followed her line of vision I saw that it rested on the word FIAT on the top of a skyscraper. I stayed still by her side and after a moment she said angrily: 'Luckily, we've all outgrown the idea that signs are put up for our entertainment.'

I didn't understand what she meant. There are times when I just don't understand her at all. What I usually do then is let a bit of silence drift by.

After this particular bit of silence had passed, I said: 'What are you cross about, Mum?'

'Valentina,' she snapped.

Her saying this made me realise something: when we'd been in Brittany with Valentina, I'd found her sort of bossy and difficult, but now I didn't; in fact I thought there was something

35

really beautiful about her, something as beautiful and soft as snow. I wanted to walk into this snow, like on a new, fantastic morning, and lie down.

'Why are you angry with Valentina?' I asked.

'Because she treats me unfairly,' said Alice, 'and I simply don't know how long I can go on working like this. She interrupts me all the time. She queries half of what I write. She's always been a self-centred woman and she just doesn't see . . .'

'See what?'

'That I have to be left alone to get on. She thinks she owns me. She doesn't own me!'

'No one owns you, Mum,' I said. But I said this sadly, because the idea that we might have to leave Paris and leave Valentina suddenly seemed really horrible.

I was about to suggest that Mum talk to Valentina and ask her politely not to keep interrupting her, when I heard a voice calling 'Louis! Louis!' and I turned round and saw Didier.

He was zooming towards us on roller blades. He was smiling, as if we were his old friends. He came to a perfectly controlled stop right beside us and shook our hands. And I thought, he didn't have to come up to us at all. There are a lot of people here and he could have pretended that he hadn't seen us, but he didn't.

I think he understood that Alice was feeling miserable, because he turned his attention to her straight away. He didn't seem embarrassed in front of her, like he'd been that day in the street. He pointed out to us the roller-skating slalom run on the right of the esplanade and told us that he and a few friends came here most Sundays 'to show off'. I wanted to see him skate. I reckoned that someone called Didier-the-Bird would have to be a brilliant roller-blader. So I said: 'Will you skate for us, Didier?'

He said sure, in a minute he would, but he wanted to know first what we thought about the arch. Alice began going on about how she knew the architect had conceived it as the western gateway to the city and that it had become part of the 'Great Axis' made by the Arc de Triomphe, the Place de la Concorde, the Place du Carrousel and the Louvre. Then she added that, close to, she didn't really like it. Didier looked pleased. I don't know if it was the bit of history she'd learned or her not liking the arch that pleased him. He asked Alice if we had time to see what was on the other side of it, on the piece of ground 'which had not been in the architect's calculations'.

I knew we had all the time in the world, that Alice wouldn't want to go back to the apartment yet, but she turned and asked me if I thought we had enough time. I nodded and so we walked with Didier through the arch, under the trapeze thing, until we got to a rail on the western edge of the development. 'There,' said Didier.

We found that we were looking down at a cemetery. Didier said nothing. We all three of us stared at the cemetery, which looked as though it had been filled up long ago, because it was chock-a-block with graves. I think this was the first French graveyard I'd seen and I noticed that, instead of having flat slabs put over them, the dead here were put inside proper stone buildings with roofs on and railings round some of them and tiny gardens planted with plastic flowers. It was like looking at the Afterlife Housing Estate. All it lacked were TV facilities.

Then Didier suddenly said: 'My father is buried here.'

Alice said she was sorry, and I immediately thought that Didier seemed too young to have a dead father. I'd worked out that he was no older than about twenty-seven, so his father might only have been fifty or fifty-five. Not many people seemed to die at this age. I made a note to ask Didier whether his father had been a roofer and if the mortality rate among roofers was high.

Didier went on: 'As you can see, it's difficult to get into that graveyard now. There's building work all round it, new roads out to the *périphérique*.'

Alice nodded. It was a bit windy out here above the cemetery and her hair started blowing about wildly. Didier took off his glasses and began polishing them on the hem of his T-shirt. Without them, he looked more like a tennis star or a cyclist than a philosopher. 'So how do you get there?' asked Alice.

'Oh,' said Didier, putting his glasses back on, 'I fly. Didn't Louis tell you I could fly?'

'Yes, he did,' said Alice, 'but I don't necessarily believe everything he says.'

'Would you like a Yop?' asked Didier.

'What?' said Alice.

I told Mum Yop was a yoghurt drink. Students and joggers in the Parc Monceau drank Yop and the litter bins were full of old Yop containers. She said OK, she'd like one. Then she said to Didier, 'Which tomb is your father's?'

He pointed to the far side of the graveyard, where I'd noticed one of the dead people's houses had an angel on the roof. It was the only angel in the whole place. 'There,' he said, 'next to the angel. The small one on the right of it.'

We all looked at Didier's father's tomb. In scale, and in situation, it looked like the garage to the house with the angel. It didn't look as though there was any room for Didier's mother in the garage, and I wondered whether, every time he came here, Didier thought, that fucking angel, overshadowing Papa, and making him seem small, I'm going to knock its wings off one day!

But he didn't seem downhearted. He bought us the Yops and we drank them while we watched the roller-skaters and I could see that Mum's fury was lessening and that she was enjoying herself. I didn't know which thing it was that had cheered her up.

When Didier went off to skate, as soon as he did his first run we could see that he was the best, the niftiest. His slalom technique was perfect and he went faster than all the other skaters.

I said to Mum: 'That could be it, you know.'

'What?' she said.

'Why he's called Didier-the-Bird.'

But her eyes were fixed on Didier and she didn't bother to reply.

When we got back to the flat, it was about six o'clock. Sergei was there alone. There was a furious note on the hall table from Valentina, which said: *Why do you sneak out like thieves? This is not a hotel! Lewis, walk Sergei when you return. V.*

I got Sergei's kite lead. I thought I'd head for the Eiffel Tower and beg it to let me stay in Paris. I'd never begged in French before, to something made of iron, but I didn't see why I shouldn't try.

We set off down the leafy boulevard, which I now knew was the Avenue George V, but we hadn't got very far when Sergei suddenly stopped and wouldn't walk on. I tugged at him, but he just sat down in the street and then he vomited.

He'd chosen a really bum place. We were right in front of the Hôtel George V, almost on its doormat, and when the hotel doorman saw what had happened he started to shriek at me. People arriving in Rolls-Royces and Cadillacs had to step round Sergei and his vomit and I could perfectly well understand that this didn't give them a good first impression of the hotel.

I told the doorman that I was very sorry and I tugged Sergei to a plane tree, where he looked up at me piteously. I stroked his head, like Mum used to stroke mine when I was made of Play Doh and puked in the night.

I'd tried to make Sergei walk towards home, but he refused; he just kept lying down on the pavement. So I had to stagger along with him in my arms. I kept remembering what Valentina had said about Mr Gavrilovich heaving sacks of coal that weighed as much as a child of seven. Sergei must have weighed as much as a child of nine.

Everyone stared at me, a thin boy carrying a gigantic dog, but no one offered to help me and the rue Rembrandt was a long way. I had to keep stopping to rest and I could have done with a raspberry Yop to give me strength.

I was wrecked by the time I got back to the flat. Valentina was on her own in the salon, watering her flower arrangements. When I put Sergei down, he went straight to her and lay down with his head on her feet. She looked at me accusingly and laid aside her little brass watering can. 'What's happened?' she said. 'What have you done to Sergei?'

'I haven't done anything to him,' I said. 'He threw up in front of the Hôtel George V. Practically on the George V's carpet.'

'Oh God!' said Valentina, 'and I lunch there!'

She bent down and lifted up Sergei's head, stroking it, examining the eyes and mouth. 'I'd better get Maurice,' she said, 'if I can get him on a Sunday. Nobody wants to do anything on a Sunday in Paris. And you know I was so upset by what you and Alice did this afternoon. I think at least, when you go out, you might have the courtesy to tell me.'

She seemed very unhappy. I wondered if Mum had told her we were leaving. I wondered how many nights I had left in my room with *Le Grand Meaulnes*.

'I'm sorry, Valentina,' I said.

'You see, aside from anything else, we have so much work to get through, and of course when something worries me like that, I can't work at all . . . and now Sergei is ill . . .'

'I'm really sorry,' was all I could find to say. I stood there uselessly dripping sweat on to the parquet. And I think I must have looked so abject that the sight of me somehow melted away Valentina's anger, because she suddenly came over to me and put both her arms round me and pressed my face into her yellow silk blouse and kissed the top of my head. 'It's not your fault, darling,' she said. She held me like that for a long time, till I almost suffocated in her perfume and my face made a wet patch on her blouse, and I thought, nobody I've ever known is like Valentina; she's come out of a different kind of earth.

Eventually she let me go and went off to telephone Maurice,

the vet. He wasn't in and I heard her leave an angry message on his answering machine. I wondered where a posh Parisian vet might go on Sunday evening and I decided he would go some place where animals were hardly ever seen, like the Hôtel George V.

When I got up to my room, I took off my shirt and poured water all over myself and then won the chess game against the computer in 1.7 minutes. I knew Alice was working downstairs and I wanted to go and ask her whether we were leaving or not, but then I thought it was better not to disturb her.

I began a letter to Hugh. I described my room to him and told him that I'd moved my bed right under the round window, so that I could lie in it and look up at the Paris sky. I put: *If a window is round, you expect to see more interesting things out of it than out of a normal window. The things I can see from my bed are: the sky, which is a kind of orange colour at night, a pole of scaffolding, birds, aeroplanes, stars (sometimes), the moon (sometimes), Didier's legs when he's working on my bit of the roof. If the window had been square, I probably wouldn't have bothered to move my bed underneath it.*

I told him about the Jardin des Plantes and sitting in China and about the bison and the cocktail trolley. I added: *The first thing you see when you come into the Jardin des Plantes from the rue Cuvier is a statue of a lion eating a human foot. The foot isn't attached to anyone. The person to whom the foot was once attached could now be inside the lion.*

I stopped here. Writing to Hugh made me remember the hut. I sat there wishing that Hugh were trying to install a solar heating system or build a motorbike from old spare parts – something that would add to somebody's happiness. Because I knew exactly what was going to happen to the hut: it would remain empty for ever. A desk would be put in it for Alice and a gas heater, even. But Alice would never spend any time there, not even in summer, and so it would be me who would have to pretend to use it, just to make Dad feel better about building it. I'd have to take homework out there on cold spring afternoons and say I liked the peace and quiet of it and the way, when the wind was in the west, it creaked and moved.

My mind started to wander, because thinking about the stupid hut oppressed me. I wondered what we'd have for dinner and whether this would be our last meal. I wondered when Maurice the vet would come. I wondered whether Valentina would ever take me inside the Hôtel George V and what she would wear if she did . . .

I carried on with the letter, but added nothing about the hut. I just put: *I hope you're not lonely, Dad. Please give my love to Grandma Gwyneth and Grandad Bertie when you see them and tell them I really am trying with my French. This guy Didier on the roof is a lonely kind of person. I think he's an only child, like me and like you. He probably lives alone in a room somewhere.*

Must go now. Valentina's called me down for supper.

With love from Lewis xx

Nothing was said at supper about our leaving. We ate salmon with a peculiar sauce that tasted like liquorice and reminded me of being a child. Valentina had put a lot of blue eyeshadow all round her eyes. She and Mum were polite to each other – almost nice, but not quite. Sergei lay under the table, snoring. We didn't talk much and while we ate I could hear the residents of the rue Rembrandt arriving back from their country weekends in their Volvos and Mercedes.

As we were finishing supper, the bell rang and it was Maurice the vet. He was a man with soft, crinkly white hair, and a tanned face, very smartly dressed in a pale suit. We cleared away the supper things and Maurice spread a rug over the dining table and put Sergei on it.

Maurice had long thin fingers, like artists and pianists are supposed to have. With these, he stuck a thermometer into Sergei's bum and I could tell Sergei didn't like this; he kept turning round to try to see what was happening to him. Maurice then started examining Sergei's tummy. I had to help him hold Sergei down on the table, while Valentina watched anxiously, stroking one of Sergei's ears and asking Maurice questions all the time. Maurice talked the fastest French I'd ever heard. It just floated out of his throat like air waves.

I could tell Valentina liked Maurice and I knew it was for him that she'd put on the blue eyeshadow.

When he was leaving, Valentina followed him to the door, and he bent his face down towards her and she kissed him, not quite on his mouth, but just slightly to one side of it, and then again on the other side. She didn't see me watching this kiss, but I was.

When she came back from kissing Maurice, she was blushing and smiling. 'Maurice is so good,' she said. 'He has such a good heart, he even reads my books!' While she said this, she patted her hair and kept on smiling and I thought how amazingly beautiful she looked with her face all pink like it was, as if she'd been out in the snow.

I asked her what Maurice had said about Sergei and she said: 'Oh, he says it's nothing, Lewis. Perhaps it may be the heat. It's nothing to worry about.'

I went to see Mum then, who was working in her room, and I asked her if we were going to leave. She sighed. She leaned back in her chair and grabbed all her fantastic hair and scrunched it up into a kind of ponytail and said: 'I don't think we can. Do you? I'm sorry I got angry. I've told Valentina to leave me in peace a bit more and she says she will.'

I felt so glad we weren't leaving, I gave Mum a hug and she had to let go of the ponytail to hug me back. While she hugged me, I looked down at the work on her desk and I saw she was on page thirty-nine of Valentina's manuscript. The last sentence she'd written was: *The long night passed and, all through it, Isabelle waited for Barthélémy to come to her, but he didn't arrive.*

I went up to my room then and undressed and got into bed. I started struggling with *Le Grand Meaulnes.* I was on *Chapitre VII, Le Gilet de Soie.* But I couldn't get my mind to concentrate on it. What my mind was concentrating on was the kiss that Valentina had given to Maurice the vet. Just as Maurice arrived, Valentina had put on more of her scarlet lipstick, so the mouth that she'd placed near his mouth was very red and shiny, and I kept on wondering whether her lips had been just near enough to Maurice's lips so that, on the way down in the lift, he could taste the lipstick. And if he had been able to taste it, what had it tasted like . . .

I couldn't get my mind off it. I decided that the lipstick would have tasted a bit like the centre of a chocolate, delicious but unreal, as if the chocolate manufacturers had made a mistake and put some perfume into the mix. And I kept thinking that the thing I wanted to do most in the world was to lick all the creamy lipstick off Valentina's lips. I just longed to do this. I'd lick and lick and lick until Valentina's mouth was absolutely bare and then swallow all the sweet lipstick and imagine it inside me, coating everything red. Then I'd get her to put more lipstick on. I'd say to her, really politely, 'Valentina, would you mind just putting on a bit more lipstick?' and she'd say, 'Oh no, darling, not at all. Here we go.' Then her mouth would be scarlet again and she'd lean over me and I'd put my tongue out and start lapping and licking again and move the creamy lipstick round my own lips and over my teeth and then let it slide down my throat.

I touched myself. I felt more sexy than I'd ever felt in my life. I kept rerunning Valentina's kissing of Maurice and then transferred her mouth to mine, and the minute I imagined my first taste of the lipstick it was like the rest of me vanished and all I became was my cock and my hand. I didn't even have to rub myself hard, like I usually did if I wanted to come. I just touched myself lightly for less than a minute and then I had this amazing, colossal orgasm.

Afterwards, I didn't feel guilty or a bit disgusted with myself, but just completely drained and exhausted and happy, and I turned out the light and went straight to sleep.

*

When I woke up, I saw that light was slowly filling my round window and then the birds started their little chirruping noises. My head felt swoony and seemed to fill with the birdsong. I tried to let the birds sing me back to sleep, but my brain wouldn't lie still to be sung to. It had remembered something of importance: Valentina had promised to come up the previous evening and listen to some more of my translation of *Le Grand Meaulnes*, but she hadn't appeared.

My copy of *Meaulnes* had fallen on to the floor. I picked it up and decided I'd do some work on the text right now, so that I'd have some really good stuff to impress her with the following evening.

I went back to *Chapitre VII, Le Gilet de Soie*. I was getting quite fond of the narrator of the story, François, and I thought I would tell Valentina this and say, 'I hope nothing terrible is going to happen to him.' Then I would read her the work I'd done:

Chapitre VII – Chapter Seven, The Silk Waistcoat.

Our room was, as I've told you, a huge attic. Half attic, half room. The adjoining buildings had ordinary windows, but our room had only a skylight.

It was impossible to close the door of our room completely; it scraped on the floorboards. When we went up there in the evenings, holding our hands round our candles against the draughts, we always tried to close it and then we always had to give up.

I went to sleep again for a bit. When I woke, I could hear Didier moving around on the roof and I thought, good, now the real day is going to begin.

At breakfast, Valentina made an announcement: she said we were all going to have a day off. She said she and Alice had been working too hard, that was why she got upset about things so easily, and she said she had been neglecting her friends and everybody, but especially her mother.

'So,' she continued, 'a car is coming at eleven-thirty. Maman will be collected and then we'll all drive out to Les Rosiers, which is a beautiful country restaurant with a swimming pool. You can swim, Lewis. We can walk Sergei in the woods nearby. Maman can snooze on a garden chair. And the food is wonderful.'

The car was a Mercedes E 6000 upholstered in blue leather. The chauffeur wore a blue uniform to match. The air conditioning was so cold, it was like speeding along in a fridge.

Mum and I were introduced to Mrs Gavrilovich. Like Valentina, she was a plump woman with beautiful eyes, but she'd let her hair go grey and rolled the grey hair into a bun on the top of her head. She'd brought a black straw hat with her, to put over the bun the moment we got out of the fridge. She sat in front with the chauffeur and on the journey I counted nineteen hairpins in different parts of the bun.

'Maman has been having trouble with her teeth,' Valentina announced, almost as soon as we left the rue Rembrandt. It was as if she thought this inconvenience had to be explained to us before we went any further. 'But,' she went on, 'we are having some expensive reconstructive work done by an American dentist in rue Chateaubriand. Russians have bad teeth, like the English. The best teeth in the world belong to the inhabitants of Carrara, where there is liquid marble in the water.'

I was sitting between Alice and Valentina in the back of the car, with Sergei draped over all our feet. I could feel Valentina's warm bum snuggled in next to mine.

I said: 'Did Michelangelo have good teeth?'

'Yes,' said Valentina. 'That is well known, darling. Up in the Sistine roof, he sometimes manoeuvred himself around by biting a rope.'

Alice and I both laughed. I thought, if you're a writer, you have to invent things. You have to keep thinking new things up, but what's the difference between the invented thing and the lie? Are the best writers just the niftiest liars? Was Shakespeare simply the most fantastic, brilliant, ace liar of all time? And what about Alain-Fournier? In my intro to *Le Grand*

Meaulnes, it said that Alain-Fournier 'wrote his own life', but I didn't know yet exactly what that meant. Perhaps it meant that Alain-Fournier just wasn't very good at thinking things up?

I began to feel happy in the Mercedes with Valentina's arse pressing against mine. The age I felt myself to be that morning was about eighteen. I longed to reach out my hand and stroke one of Valentina's fat brown arms.

To me, it was as if Valentina had been there in my night, as if she'd actually let me do the things I'd imagined. I knew that any 'normal' woman would probably have felt shocked or disgusted. Girls at school were always telling the older boys they were shocked and disgusted by what they tried to get them to do. But I didn't think of Valentina as a normal woman. She was a crazy, romantic, gigantic Russian who'd told me that nothing on earth surprised her. I'd read in a book I found in Hugh's study that her ancestors had taken their pigs to church; they'd fought German soldiers outside Moscow with toasting forks; they once had an Empress who slept with her grandson. Valentina wouldn't mind what I felt about her. If I told her, she would probably laugh and kiss my nose. She might even let me put my hand on her breasts.

I felt so certain about this that I tucked my arm inside Valentina's. She patted my hand and her bangles jingled. She started to talk to her mother in French, telling her that I was a 'very clever boy' and that together she and I were translating a French text. I looked at Mum, to see if she'd taken this in, but she was looking out of the window and she seemed far away, like she might be thinking about Dad or moonlight or Edinburgh. Mrs Gavrilovich started talking in Russian. This Russian language sounded like the words of a song being spoken.

'What did she say?' I asked Valentina.

Valentina laughed. 'Maman said you are the first English boy she has met in her life. She is sixty-nine. She says this is a strange thought.'

47

I said: 'Tell her I think she's the first Russian woman I've met, apart from you and Raisa Gorbachev. I saw Mrs Gorbachev on a school outing when I was eight.'

Valentina reeled all this off in Russian and Mrs Gavrilovich turned round and smiled at me, and it was only when she smiled that anyone could see the trouble she'd been having with her teeth. Where some of her teeth should have been, there were holes. Then she asked me in French whether I would like to visit her church.

'Did you understand?' Valentina said quickly. 'Maman offered to show you her church. Would you like this? She thinks of it as "hers" and she likes to show people around. N'est-ce pas, Maman? Tu aimes montrer aux gens ta propre église?'

'Oui. Bien sûr.'

The French Mrs Gavrilovich spoke was slow, as if she was still learning it after all this time. I said I'd like to see her church and I asked if we could hear some Russian singing or chanting. The answer to this didn't seem to be simple, because Valentina and her mother had to have a long discussion about it – or else they were talking about something completely different, like the rudeness of Mrs Gavrilovich's concierge. This made me realise that secret language equals power. I thought, when I'm a man – and this was a thing that felt as if it were going to occur quite soon – I'm going to acquire as many secret languages as I can and these will be my prime weapons in life.

I lay under a yellow parasol with my eyes closed.

I counted all the sounds I could hear: one, a fountain cascading water into the swimming pool; two, birds twittering; three, the murmured words of a Russian song; four, a plane on its way to Alaska or Alabama; five, the footsteps of a pool waiter; six, the rattle of drinks on a metal tray; seven, the snoring of Sergei; eight, the clattering of Valentina's bangles; nine, sun cream being squeezed on to Alice's freckled arms; ten, my own breathing.

Lying there, I began to feel amazed at the way the human

ear could tolerate and interpret so much simultaneously. I wondered what the maximum number of sounds was before the brain had to select out, to save its interpretive faculty, and render some of them inaudible. Whenever I asked myself scientific questions, I knew that I could be 99.9 per cent certain that they had been asked before by someone else. Dad once said that only one person in a million contributes anything new to the world. Sometimes, I got ideas about becoming that one.

I'd never been anywhere like Les Rosiers. In fact I hadn't believed in the existence of places like this. I thought they just belonged in the minds of photographers for Sunday colour magazines or car commercials on TV and that, once the pictures had been taken, everything was disassembled and taken back to where it had come from, even the waiters, who were actors really and usually dressed in frayed jeans and old T-shirts from New York.

I tried to work out who owned Les Rosiers, because everything in it was just excessively perfect. Take the swimming pool: in ordinary pools in England there was a whole world of matter that you weren't supposed to see – floating insects and bits of blossom and dust. But here, in this pool, there wasn't one solitary speck of anything in the sparkling crystal-blue water. It was as if someone had poured ten tons of supermarket water, bottle by bottle, on to the little mosaic tiles.

And then there was my sun lounger. The mattress of the lounger had been upholstered in yellow-and-white cotton and tied on to the white wooden struts with white bows. No imprint of any previous body was visible on my lounger; no single drop of sun lotion, no stain of sweat, no watermark of a spilt cocktail. My lounger could have been made that morning, especially for me.

And beside it was a little white table. At the exact centre of the table had been placed a glass bowl, sculpted in the shape of a flower. The bowls had been filled with more impeccable water and white waxy flowers Valentina said were called gardenias had been set floating on the water like tiny boats.

I wanted to ask Valentina who she thought had gone to all this trouble and who for. I knew it hadn't been done for me, Third Year Chess Champion of Beckett Bridges School, wearing dark-blue Adidas swimming trunks. So I guessed it had been done for the kind of person who expected, as of right, to find no trace of a leaf in the swimming pool and who saw so many beautiful things in a single day that his eyes had to be kept amused by floating gardenias. 'Ah,' he would say, 'a floating gardenia, thank goodness.'

I opened my eyes and sat up and looked around. And I saw immediately how faulty my sound-collecting had been: two men had arrived to sit by the pool and I hadn't heard them. They were very tanned and sort of polished-looking, as if they'd put shoe cream on their foreheads as well as on their shoes. I christened them the Gardenia Men. Their teeth glimmered in the sun.

They talked very quietly, with a pile of paperwork on one of the little tables between them. They could have come all the way from the Fiat building at La Défense that Alice had been so rude about. And it was like they knew about this rudeness, because in between reading their balance sheets or their export statistics, or whatever it was they were discussing, they kept glancing up at Alice.

I looked over to her. She was lying with her eyes shut, while all the freckles in the air came clustering towards her and began to fall in silence on her face and arms.

I imagined the Gardenia Men waiting for the moment when they'd inform her what a marvellous company they worked for. They might even go on to refer to their marvellous salaries. In their desperation to get her approval, they would stumble over words, or drop them or spit them out by mistake. As if words were peanuts.

I got up and went to the side of the pool and sat with my legs in the water. The Gardenia Men stared at how white I was and how thin my arms were. It was like those two men had put themselves there to remind me that even if I felt grown-up, I wasn't.

I sat there considering trying to execute a flawless swallow dive, causing the merest ripple, to impress Valentina, but I wasn't that brilliant a diver. I knew my dive would cause gallons of water to bucket out and drench the stones.

I looked up at Valentina and she was watching me. She was smoking one of her yellow Russian cigarettes and talking softly to Alice, whose eyes were still closed. I wanted Valentina to be talking about me.

Then I looked at the others. Mrs Gavrilovich had put on her black straw hat and was eating the fruit out of her drink. I wondered whether fruit was good for an ulcer or not. Sergei lay in the shade of some sculpted hedge and slept. He looked rather elegant stretched out on the grass and I suddenly thought, I expect this is the kind of moment that painters love, when everything is sleepy and still and the people in the picture are dreaming about lunch.

I lowered myself into the pool and swam a few lengths, trying not to splash too much. When I came back to the shallow end the fourth time, I saw Valentina's legs dipping into the water. She'd taken off her cotton robe and was wearing a white-and-gold swimsuit. Now she had only this on, I could see the shape of her whole body and what I thought was that the most beautiful thing in the world would be to be born out of Valentina's vagina and be lifted up on to her stomach and given one of her huge breasts to suck and kept there on her breast with my lips round her milky nipple, sucking and sucking until I passed into oblivion.

I swam up to Valentina's legs and took hold of one of her feet. Her toenails were more convex than mine and painted scarlet. I asked her to come swimming with me.

She said she couldn't swim. I said I didn't believe a person of forty-one had never learned to swim and she said: 'Well, there you are, darling. You see, you're learning surprising things all the time.'

I said I'd teach her how to swim and I thought, now this is going to be fantastic, because she's going to have to lie down on the water and I'm going to have to hold her up with my arms. She called out: 'Alice! Lewis says he's going to teach me to swim!' But Mum wasn't really paying us any attention. She was admiring the embroidery Mrs Gavrilovich had got out and all she did was smile and nod. The Gardenia Men looked from us to her. One of them lit a cigarette.

We began the swimming lesson then and there. Valentina held on to one of my hands and I put my other arm under her stomach and she tried to kick her legs. The weight of her on my puny arm was greater than I'd expected, but it was a beautiful weight, like someone fallen from Michelangelo's famous ceiling.

Valentina wasn't a bit nervous; almost straight away she just started giggling and then I began to giggle and soon we were laughing so much that Valentina began to swallow water and start coughing and so I had to set her down.

'You see, darling?' she said. 'I'm completely hopeless!'

'No, you're not,' I said. 'You just have to trust me more and not hold yourself so rigid. I won't let you go.'

'I'm no good, Lewis,' she said; 'I will never learn.'

'Yes, you will,' I said. 'You can't live and die and not learn to swim.'

'Why not?'

I couldn't think of a reason, really. It wasn't as if she lived in Devon or in a shack by the River Volga. So I said: 'Because swimming is a defiance of gravity. Don't you want to defy gravity, Valentina?'

'Defy gravity?' she said. 'I don't know. Do I want to?'

'Yes,' I said, 'definitely.'

'All right, darling. If you say so. Here we go, then. We'll try again.'

She concentrated harder then. I could tell she was really

trying. She'd tied her blonde hair up into a scrunch on her head, but little wisps of it came loose and trailed in the water. I began to steer her around and around in a circle. I told her she was doing great.

'You know my bum's out of the water, darling,' she said after a circuit or two. 'You don't see the bums of swimmers sticking up out of the water in the Olympics.'

We began giggling again then. Valentina's beautiful laugh echoed all round the pool and through my heart. I made her go on trying to swim because I didn't want to let her go, and then when we stopped laughing I said to her: 'You haven't forgotten about *Le Grand Meaulnes*, have you, Valentina?'

Lunch was served to us on a terrace overlooking a rose garden. Lawn sprinklers fanned water on to the roses all the time. Two tables away sat the Gardenia Men. A yellow umbrella cast its shade over their polished heads.

I made mental notes about everything I ate to put down in my Concorde notebook or to write in a letter to Dad: *First course: 6 prawns arranged around a still-life of titchy vegetables. Yellow-coloured sauce. V says the yellow is saffron, which is made from crocus stamens! Q: Who was the first person on earth to realise you could eat crocus stamens?*

I was really hungry after the swimming. I could have eaten sixteen prawns. Or twenty-six.

The waiters served us some white wine with lunch. A fat white napkin was held round the neck of the bottle to prevent a single drop of wine being spilled on our tablecloth. Mrs Gavrilovich loved this wine; she drank it down as if she had a raging thirst inside her that only it could cure. Her face got red and her big eyes got bright and her conversation drifted into Russian. She seemed to forget that Alice and I couldn't understand a single word. All I could pick up was the name of a person called Grigory. And I could tell, also, that Valentina didn't want to discuss Grigory, whoever he was. She put out a hand and stroked Mrs Gavrilovich's arm and the stroking was telling her gently to shut up.

After lunch, we went back to the pool, which now had three little thin leaves floating on the water, spoiling its complete perfection. The Gardenia Men watched us go and nodded to Alice as she went by, but she ignored them completely. I could have told them that businessmen like them weren't her type.

Mrs Gavrilovich settled herself on a lounger in the shade and put her hat over her face and went to sleep. I stayed in the pool and swam, hoping Valentina would put on her white-and-gold swimsuit, which was drying on the stones, and come and have another swimming lesson, but she didn't.

After a little rest on their loungers, she and Alice took Sergei and went off for a walk. There was this wood not far away which belonged to Les Rosiers and Valentina said that in spring this wood was full of bluebells, which were her favourite flower.

I wasn't invited on the walk. I could tell it was a kind of business walk. So I swam up and down, up and down, feeling a bit pointless because nobody was watching me. I took out the three leaves and arranged them into a triangle on the pool edge. Then I lay on my lounger and started counting sounds again, but there were hardly any; just the pool water sloshing through the filters and its little fountain splattering. The sounds I wanted to hear were Valentina's voice, whispering secret words into my ear, and her laughter, brimming out into the air.

That night, I waited for Valentina, but she didn't come up to my attic. I wanted to go down to her bedroom and fetch her, but I didn't dare.

I translated a page of Meaulnes, Chapitre VIII, L'Aventure. It was becoming more and more clear to me that François's life was going to turn out to have been ruined by the things that happened to him when he was fifteen, because I came across a reference to 'days of sorrow' and then a horrible mention of nothing being left but dust. This made me feel so anxious, I almost felt like giving up the book, but I also realised that I wanted to know what happened, even if it was going to be bad. I was starting to identify with François. His father was a schoolteacher who was stingy about heating. I liked the way he called his mother Millie instead of Maman and I decided that from now on I was going to call my mother Alice – not Mum any more, which sounded childish.

Translating usually exhausted me, but on this night I didn't feel tired at all, so I decided now was the moment to get out on to the roof and explore it. I wanted to find out what or who was in that maid's room next to my bathroom. I thought I'd also try to case the whole roof and make a kind of map of it. I knew there might be skylights in it, above rooms I didn't know about, in Valentina's apartment and in the apartment next door, which belonged to a very thin gay man who often dressed in white and whose name was Moinel. Valentina told me there was someone called Tante Moinel in *Le Grand Meaulnes* and she was the one who helped unravel the mystery.

I knew that getting safely on to the roof wasn't going to be easy, because outside the bathroom window it sloped down almost vertically. Getting on to the bathroom windowsill was simple and I crouched there like a bird, with my feet on the edge of it, smelling the warm night air. About four feet away from me was the first pole of Didier's scaffolding cage. All I had to do was to cross this tiny distance and then I would be safe and could work my way right round the roof, holding on to the cage.

The trouble with this kind of gap is that the psychological distance to be crossed is greater than the actual distance and it's the psychological distance that makes you afraid. I stayed in my bird position and tried to apply mathematics to this, viz: *Actual distance is about four feet. Psychological distance is more like, say, two times my capacity to cross it. Thus (a d = 4) and (psy d = 2 × c). Ergo, I must discover the value of c and multiply it by a factor of n to bring it into equality with (a d = 4). Q: What is the value of c? Principal Q: What is the n factor?*

Working this out took me ages. It was a thing I quite often did – convert interior anxiety to maths, because almost invariably the maths looked clever and then your anxiety looked stupid in comparison and so the maths became like an armour you could put on.

It was my bird stance that eventually gave me the answer. I decided that $n = flight$ *or swoop*. I would have to let my weight fall or 'fly' towards the horizontal pole. The swoop factor would be less if I could set my feet down on the roof itself outside the window, so this would be the first thing to do, climb out and stand with my back to the bathroom dormer.

I went back into my room and put on my trainers. I quite liked the idea of creeping around barefoot on the roof, like a cat burglar, but I could also see that *grip* was a secondary factor in *n*. As I tied my laces in a double bow, I thought, François would have been afraid of this, like me, but Meaulnes would have climbed out straight away without hesitating for a single second.

Then I was back on the ledge. Across the rue Rembrandt, all the attic windows were dark, but I noticed that some of them were open and I imagined that quite a few maids were sleeping there, behind little curtains made of lace. I wondered if they could have seen me masturbating, if they happened to be awake after their long days of ironing and polishing, and whether now they might be watching me fly or fall and then they'd say to each other, 'That English boy, you never know what terrible thing he's going to do next!'

I climbed out and got a footing on the lead outside the window. The slope under my feet was extreme and I remembered now what Didier had said about the slates being old and loose. I stood there, wishing I were taller. Then the cage wouldn't seem so far away. Meaulnes was tall, but François was small and neat, like Millie.

I felt time passing. Time is structured differently for cowards, as if it had ninety-minute hours. I remembered being stuck on the high diving board at a pool in Plymouth when I was ten, with Alice and Hugh staring up at me, waiting for me to dive. Everything felt altered up there, especially time. And the fall had been terrifying. It had been so completely terrifying that I'd never, ever, tried it again.

I let go of the sill behind me. I heard a dog barking. I was breathing so hard I was almost snorting and I thought, what a hopeless noisy burglar I'd make! If you're a villain, you have to breathe quietly. I thought I could tell this to Valentina and she could use it for Barthélémy.

Then I swooped. In mid-swoop, I thought, it isn't maths I need, it's a rope.

My hands reached the pole and held it, but my body was moving so fast, my feet were swept out in front of me and my chest rammed against the pole. I felt a pain come there and I swore loudly, like Mr Gavrilovich swore when he felt himself dying in the coal yard. Partly, I swore at my own stupidity vis-à-vis the fucking rope.

But I was all right. And now, moving along the edge of the roof with the scaffolding to hold on to was easy. I began to feel the thrill of where I was and what I was doing and the pain in my chest lessened. I imagined Valentina down there underneath me. I was pretty sure she'd never been up here. Hardly anybody knows what the world looks like from their own rooftop. But I would map the roof and then I would show her around. I'd say, 'Here we are now above the skylight to Moinel's attic and you will notice how Moinel's maid sleeps with her hands in the prayer position, like a stone person on a tomb.'

I'd worked my way round to the whistler's room now. To get close to its window, I had to climb back up the bit of steep roof underneath it, but I felt braver by this time. I stared in. The window was closed and the room was dark. To see inside, I had to blank out the radiance of the Paris sky with my body. And then I realised I was just staring at a curtain. Whatever went on in this space which Valentina had said was full of junk, someone had put a curtain at the window and drawn it. I stood very still, with my breathing quieter now, and listened, to see if I could hear snoring or sighing or that whistling again. But there was no sound at all.

After listening for some time, I moved backwards very carefully, down to the cage, and then I followed the scaffolding round and up until I was on the flat pinnacle of the roof, where the water tanks and the bulky chimneys and the forest of TV masts made their own kind of landscape. It was brilliant there. I could move confidently around and I could see for miles and miles, right out across the tops of the trees in the park and over the roofs of other apartment blocks to some amazing dome lit with yellow light.

The next day I got a letter from Hugh. Alice got one, too, but she didn't show me hers and Hugh said not to show her mine because it was all about the building of the hut.

I hated reading this letter. I wished it had said: 'Dear Lewis, You will be very relieved to hear that I have abandoned the idea of building the hut', but it didn't. It went on and on about what a brilliant start Dad had made on the hut and how he'd mastered the art of bricklaying in less than a week, thanks to his DIY manual with its clear instructions and step-by-step drawings. It told me he was using a design called 'Flemish Bond' for the ends, corners and junctions and that he preferred this to 'English Bond' because it was 'both more elegant and more difficult to perfect'. Then Dad put: *Once understood, the system of profile boards made level, with strings attached to them to demarcate the lines along which the walls will run, appears so simple and satisfactory that I've come to believe my little construction need have no flaw. On the contrary, I'm determined that it will be a work of art . . .*

I hadn't a clue what a profile board was and I was completely certain that even if the hut seemed like a 'work of art' to Dad, it wouldn't seem like one to Alice. Hugh went on to say he was putting in two windows instead of one, so that Alice would have a view of the house and a view of the sea. But I knew it would be me who would have these views, no matter how hard Hugh worked at his junctions. I'd sit there with my maths homework and from time to time I'd look up and see the house, getting dark on some November afternoon, and then I'd turn and see the sea, cold and English and glittery, and at those moments I would remember Valentina and the smell of her night cream and the taste of her lipstick and all I would long for was to be back in the rue Rembrandt.

Hugh thanked me for my letter. He said he was glad I'd found the bouquinistes and bought *Le Grand Meaulnes*. Then he said: *The book has been criticised, of course, for its melodramatic and sentimental flavour, but I have always found it rather moving. I expect you know that Fournier was 'missing presumed killed' in the First World War in 1914 in the Eparges region. I believe, if he had lived, he would have written other marvellous novels, but that they would all have had his beloved childhood and adolescence at the heart of them.*

One of the things I hated about my father was that, because he was a schoolteacher, he always gave you information about the world long before you asked for it. He introduced most of this information with phrases like 'I expect you know' or 'I'm sure I needn't remind you', to stop you feeling inadequate or too empty of knowledge, but to him historical facts were like breath; if you didn't keep getting your supply of them, you'd start to die. Occasionally, I felt grateful he was like this, but mostly it just totally pissed me off and, for reasons I can't explain, his info about Alain-Fournier irritated me so much I had to put his letter away before I reached the end of it.

Valentina sent me to the market after breakfast. I had to buy some fish called *dorades* from the rue Poncelet, and white onions and tomatoes and cheese in muslin and parsley and green olives. At the end, she said: 'Take Sergei, but don't let him eat sprats out of the gutters.'

It was so hot in the rue Poncelet that after I'd done the shopping I sat down at a café table and ordered a *panaché*, which was a kind of shandy and had become my favourite drink. The tables of the café I chose had been put right in the middle of the market and all the traffic of the market – fat women with baskets that looked like beach bags, kids in push-chairs, wandering musicians, dogs and cats and pigeons – had to squeeze round them.

The café tables were really heavy, like they'd been bolted to the pavement. They reminded me of ships' furniture and so I thought, that's it, the café's a ship and the market is the sea, teeming all round it, carrying in flotsam and birds and the passengers of old ocean liners. And I liked sitting in the ship and drinking the *panaché* and watching it.

I asked for some water for Sergei, who kept trying to snaffle food up from the road – exactly what Valentina had forbidden him to do. When it comes to food, dogs just aren't obedient and that's that. He was even trying to eat the parsley I'd just bought.

The women in that market reminded me of people at a jumble sale. They treated vegetables like they were clothes you had to examine really carefully for stains or holes or the smell of stale deodorant. They sniffed the melons and opened the sheaths of the corn cobs and sorted the beans and rejected almost all the lettuces with a sniff or a snarl. You could tell they were connoisseurs – people with secret knowledge. I imagined that they knew ninety-seven ways of cooking potatoes, that they could take a breathing lobster and turn it into a mousse. Watching them, I couldn't picture myself ever learning to cook. Chess seemed easier. Chess is pure thought, whereas cooking is at the mercy of the natural world. Valentina had told me that mayonnaise could curdle for thirteen different reasons.

My chest ached quite a lot from its encounter in the night with the scaffolding pole. I wanted the *panaché* to take the ache away, but it didn't. I wanted the ache to go because I was plucking up courage to embark on a plan I'd made while I bought the *dorades* and the olives and everything and I thought, if my body hurts, my courage may fail me.

To soothe my mind, I wrote some notes in my Concorde book about the Paris street-cleaning system, which I'd been monitoring since we arrived. I put: *This whole system depends on under-street water points and pieces of fabric laid this way and that at the apex of each street to direct the flow of the water. At first, I didn't understand why so many bits of old carpet had been left lying in the gutters. Now, I see that they are PRIME. Take them away and Paris would become a dirty city, like London.* Then I added: *If you understand what is PRIME, especially when what is prime appears random or accidental, then you are getting somewhere in your understanding of the world. (NB: Last night, a rope was the prime necessity and I didn't see this until it was too late.)*

A gypsy woman came by and tried to persuade everyone at the café to buy some horrible stiff roses wrapped in cellophane, but no one bought one. If the woman with the kitten face had been at the café, I might have got a rose and given it to her out of pity for her and for the flower seller, but she wasn't and I didn't feel pitying that morning, I felt too nervous about my plan. But after a while, when I'd drunk a second *panaché*, I got up and thought, I'm going to do it anyway and I'm going to do it now.

The shop I was heading for was at the top of the rue Poncelet. It sold beauty products like night repair cream and it was the kind of shop I would never normally go into in my life. I'd rehearsed what I was going to say and now all that was left to do was to go into the shop and say it. My heart was beating so hard in my aching chest, I felt as if I'd been in a shipping accident.

I tied Sergei to a litter bin and went in. The shop was ice-cold and it smelled of eucalyptus, as if the air inside it was not only being conditioned but also made ready to cure the colds and sinus blockages of its customers. I breathed it in and the bones in my chest froze with pain.

I was wearing a grey linen sunhat, given to me by my Welsh

Grandma Gwyneth, and I could suddenly see, in the mirrored walls of the shop, that with this on and carrying my pannier of parsley and onions I looked really eccentric and poor, like a peasant boy in some old black-and-white movie about Spanish horse thieves. I also looked about ten years old and I swore I'd never wear this hat again as long as I lived.

Two women assistants, dressed in white overalls, with their hair and make-up perfectly arranged, came towards me and asked if they could help me. So now I said the words I'd rehearsed in French. I told them my mother was ill and that she had sent me to the market to do the family shopping. I showed them the pannier and the half-eaten parsley. 'Voici le shopping,' I said, and they smiled. Then I took a deep breath and told them that my mother had asked me, on my way home, to come into this shop and buy her a lipstick.

They smiled some more. I think they were trying not to laugh. Both of them had pearly teeth, like the residents of Carrara. They took me over to a display counter and began to ask me questions. What *make* of lipstick did my Maman use? Did Maman tell me the *name* of her favourite colour? I could tell they thought I was ten by their use of the word 'Maman'.

I hadn't realised lipsticks had names. The names they had were wild and I really liked them. I wanted to buy them all: *Danse du Feu, Feux d'Artifice, Mardi Gras, Fiesta, Siesta*. They were arranged in a perfect arc, going from pale pink to dark reddish purple. The scarlets were in the middle and so it was here that I focused my attention. I felt so overexcited and nervous, I could have been an actual horse thief. I was looking for the exact colour of Valentina's mouth. As I found it and took it down, my pannier fell over and all the white onions rolled out on to the lino floor. 'This one,' I said. Its name was *Cerise*.

That night, after we'd eaten the *dorades* and I'd gone to bed, I was working on the passage in *Le Grand Meaulnes* where Meaulnes sets out alone in the cart, going to meet François's grandparents at Vierzon, and gets lost and the horse gets lame and the night comes down, when I heard Valentina coming up my stairs.

She had her wallflower cream on and she was wearing flowered silk pyjamas and little jewelled slippers. 'It's hot up here, Lewis,' she said. 'Perhaps we should move you to another room.' I told her I didn't mind it being hot and that I wanted to stay in the attic.

She sat down on my bed and then leaned over and put a heavy box into my hands. It looked like a jewel box, made of pale wood, with its top inlaid with a darker pattern of squares and diamonds. I thought, God, perhaps she's been buying up Cartier instead of working on her book.

'Open it, darling,' she said.

It opened easily from a brass hinge. When I raised the lid, I heard a click and a whirr. It was a musical box. I stared down at its braille-like drum and at the steel fingers, like a tooth comb, that lifted as the drum turned and I found this mechanism really satisfying and clever. I remembered that the music box and the pianola worked on the identical principle of the marked drum turned by wheel cogs. Each line of markings is a bar of notes . . .

'You're not listening to the song, Lewis,' said Valentina.

It was true, I wasn't. I was too preoccupied by the machinery in the box. But now I did. It was a repetitive, sort of sad tune with the tempo of a slow waltz. As it played, Valentina moved her hand in time to the beat, like she was conducting a little orchestra. She smiled all the time. 'You know this old song?' she asked.

'No,' I said.

'Well, I don't know who wrote it, but it's one of the most popular songs in France. Yves Montand used to sing it. So sweetly. We used to play his record of it in the café when I was a child. He sang it less often as he got older, of course, because it's a song about youth and love. It's called *Le Temps des cerises*. You know what that means, darling?'

My heart gave a lurch, as though it had forgotten for a split second that its function was to keep me alive. Underneath my pillow, still wrapped in the shop paper bag, was the lipstick called *Cerise*.

'Cherry . . .' I whispered.

'Yes. Good. Cherry what, though?'

I thought for a moment. My heart began to simmer down and behave normally. 'Cherrytime,' I said.

'Yes, that's it,' said Valentina. ' "Cherrytime". A time which is perfect, you see, full of sunshine and love, and then it's gone.'

I looked up at her. Perhaps my look was a sad one, because she reached out and stroked my face and I stayed very still, not wanting her stroking to stop. After a bit, she said: 'Anyway, darling, I thought you'd like to keep this box. It can sing you to sleep. I bought it one afternoon at a little shop in the Palais Royal. There are two shops there which I love because I'm such a baby at heart: one sells nothing but toys and the other is the shop where I bought this and all it sells are musical boxes. Imagine trying to make a living out of only that!'

I said I couldn't imagine making a living out of anything, except that there were days when I thought I might be a philosopher – just one or two in a year.

'Well,' she said, 'living is hard.'

I was enjoying this conversation. I wanted it to go on all night. But then there was my page of *Meaulnes* to read, and when we'd done this Valentina said she was tired. She put a little kiss on my head, like the ones Alice gave me when she said good night, and she went away down the stairs. I watched her blonde head getting lower and lower until it disappeared.

When she'd gone, I examined the musical box. I sniffed it like the women in the market sniffed the melons, and ran my hands over its surface and polished it a bit with the sheet. Then I put it near the round window and played it over and over and thought about the maids opposite, turning in their beds and hearing it and saying, 'Oh yes, that's "Cherrytime".'

★

Day after day, it was hot. No rain fell on the combed grass of the Parc Monceau, so the sprinklers kept turning and turning there.

When I eventually read the last bit of Hugh's letter, it told me that it had been boiling in Devon too and that Dad had gone for a lone midnight bathe and stood on the beach in the dark and suddenly missed Alice and me. I sent him a card of the Eiffel Tower, setting out what I'd eaten for lunch at Les Rosiers and explaining about Michelangelo's teeth. I didn't like him missing us. I suggested he invite Grandma Gwyneth and Grandad Bertie to stay. At the end, I put: *PS: I have made a new friend, whose name is Babba.*

Babba came from Benin, in Africa. This was a country I'd never heard of until this moment. Babba's skin was so black and smooth, it was like she was made of velvet. She was Valentina's maid. Babba wasn't her real African name, but that's what we called her.

I got to know her by following her around. Sometimes I helped her change the bolster covers. I liked the sight of her velvet arms plumping up cushions and dusting mirrors. She had a slow, sad walk and she spoke French in a sad, slow way.

One day she showed me a photograph of an old woman sitting in the back of a truck. 'My mother,' she said. 'Unfortunately, the truck was stolen.'

'With your mother *in* it?'

Babba laughed. Her laugh was big and silent, like a yawn. 'No, no, Louis. No, no . . .'

We were in the kitchen and I was helping Babba put clean crockery into the cupboards. The apartment was very quiet, with Valentina and Alice working away in their separate rooms. We put the photograph of Babba's mother and the stolen truck on the kitchen table and looked at it. Babba said sadly: 'Four years.'

'Since you saw your mother?'

'Yes. Since I left my village in Benin.'

So then we stood there, thinking about Babba's village, or,

rather, she was thinking about it and I was trying to imagine it. I put a new Renault truck into it and loads of animals – goats and wandering chickens and others. The imaginary houses were small and round and the new truck was blue, like the one in the picture. 'Do you miss it?' I asked.

'Yes,' said Babba. 'But now I have Pozzi.' She got out another photo. It was of a kid, aged about two, not as black as Babba, more lightish brown, wearing a little bobble hat and standing in the snow. He was grinning and by him on the snowy ground was one of his gloves that had fallen off. 'Pozzi,' she said.

It was probably because I told her I thought Pozzi looked great that she began to talk to me about her life – the one she had now in Paris. We both sat down at the kitchen table and I got us some Orangina from the gigantic fridge and Babba described her apartment to me. She said it was out at Nanterre. I knew where this was, beyond the cemetery where Didier's father was buried. There were high-rise buildings there, coloured blue and purple, and that's where Babba and Pozzi lived, in one of those blocks. She said that when you got close to them you could see that the blue and purple was made up of millions of mosaic pieces, but now, bit by bit, the mosaics were falling off.

What Babba had was one room and a kitchen. There were shared bathrooms along the corridors. She said this mournfully and I realised then that in Babba's imaginary village in Benin I'd put no bathrooms at all and I felt really guilty about this, really white and spoilt and guilty.

The main problem with Babba's apartment, she said, was the motorbike. It was a ten-year-old 1000cc Harley Davidson and it had belonged to the previous tenant, and when he vacated the apartment he just left it standing there in the one room where Babba and Pozzi had to live and sleep.

I said: 'Can't you get the council to come and take it away, Babba?'

She shrugged her big shoulders. 'Pozzi,' she said, 'he loves that thing. I have to keep it shiny for him. I say, "Where are you going, Pozzi?" I say, "Where's Pozzi going?" and he says, "Africa. Pozzi's going to Africa!" So that's it, Louis. We got that bike for ever now.'

It may have been because of the bike that Babba liked polishing things. Keeping the chrome good might have given her the habit of making surfaces shine. I liked watching her work on Valentina's parquet floors. She and the electric polisher would go round and round in a series of slow arcs, with Babba swaying as she moved and sometimes singing, with her head bent low, like she was singing to the floor:

Moi, je t'offrirai des perles de pluie,
Venues des pays où il ne pleut pas,
Ne me quitte pas, ne me quitte pas, ne me quitte pas . . .

Then, she'd go down on her velvety hands and knees and rub the parquet with a thick, soft cloth. While she rubbed, she would gaze so intently at the shiny wood, it seemed to me she thought it was a magic pool from which might rise, at any time, a message of hope. I imagined she was asking the floor to bring back the stolen truck to her village in Benin.

Valentina didn't pay Babba that much. She said she knew that Babba didn't have a work permit in France, so she was doing her a favour just by employing her. But she let Babba take stuff from the fridge for her lunch – bits of cold salmon and potato salad and drinks of Orangina. She said to me: 'Don't worry about Babba, Lewis. Women like Babba, they come and they go. One day, she will just leave without telling me.'

Then something happened which I knew might turn out badly for Babba: Valentina slipped on the polished parquet and fell over. It was a Saturday morning and she was wearing silver sandals. I was the one who found her lying on the floor, swearing in several languages, like Mr Gavrilovich in the coal yard.

I ran over to her and knelt down beside her. Sergei was standing there, whining. She looked really white and even her red lips had gone pale. 'Shit!' she said. 'Merde! Porca miseria! Scheisse! Fuck! Help me up, Lewis.'

I tried to help her. I put my arm under hers and round her back and attempted to lever her up, but she couldn't seem to push the top half of her body off the floor. When I tried to move her, she began screaming with pain. I could smell her perfume and her sweat, and then she started talking to me in Russian, as if she were giving me instructions about what to do, but I knew she didn't really realise what she was saying. I wished I could remember a few tips from our First Aid lesson at school, but all I could think about was what you did to a person, mouth to mouth, if they'd stopped breathing, and this wasn't the appropriate moment for that.

Sergei started licking Valentina's feet in their silver shoes, which didn't help. Dogs never know what to do in a crisis. I had to push him away and tell him to fuck off and then I decided that I needed help and so I laid Valentina down as gently as I could and went running to Alice's room.

But Alice wasn't in her room. Her desk was all tidy, with her books and papers in orderly piles, so I knew she'd gone out without telling anyone, which was what she was doing more and more, despite the fuss Valentina had made about this the first time. I had no idea where she went and I'd never asked.

I knew I had to get someone and so I charged up my stairs and opened the bathroom window and began calling to Didier. The job on the roof was so enormous that Didier often worked some part of Saturdays and when I shouted out, 'Didier, aidez-moi!' I prayed he'd still be there. He was there. He came climbing round to me straight away and swung himself in through the window. Didier's body was powdered with slate dust. The bird on his neck looked as though it had gone flying into a grey mist. I hoped all this dust wouldn't stain Valentina's silk dress or fall on to the furniture.

When we got back to the salon, Valentina was crying. Blue eyeshadow was running down her face. I think she thought I'd

68

abandoned her and that she'd just lie there on the floor till nightfall.

I knelt by her again. 'Don't cry, Valentina,' I said. 'Didier's here.' And she gazed up at me with her huge blue eyes.

Didier knelt down, too. Already, I noticed, there was a bit of slate dust on the parquet. It was probably because of the bad old days with the coal that Valentina liked to have everything so totally clean. But right now, she was in too much pain to be aware that her rescuer was covered with grime. And he was very good with her, staying calm and asking her gently what had happened. When her sobs stopped, she said that she thought her arm was broken.

Didier instructed me to fetch cushions. There was no shortage of these in Valentina's apartment. There were embroidered cushions and tapestry cushions, cushions made of satin and cushions with tassels dangling from them, like sporrans. I chose a selection and Didier told me to lay them carefully alongside Valentina's body. He seemed very intent and focused now, like a nurse, and I suddenly thought, I wonder if he once did this before, when his father was hurt?

When we had the cushions all lined up, we slowly, carefully, rolled Valentina on to the cushion bed, so that her weight was off the broken arm. Seeing this, Sergei thought it must be time to go to sleep and so he lay down beside her. Valentina was still trembling with pain and shock and so I fetched a duvet from her room and covered her with this, while Didier went to telephone for an ambulance. I wanted to *be* the duvet, enfolding her.

She asked me to light her one of her Russian cigarettes. So with one hand I helped her to smoke the cigarette, holding it next to her lips and putting it in and out of her beautiful mouth, and with the other I tried to wipe the watercolour sea from her face with one of the Marks and Spencer's hankies Bertie had given me for Christmas.

I wanted to go with her in the ambulance. I thought Didier

and I were the heroes of the hour and that we had to see our mission through, but in the end neither of us went, because Alice came home and took over. I told Alice I wanted to come, but she ignored me. She thanked Didier for coping with the emergency, but she didn't thank me.

When the ambulance had driven away with Valentina and Alice inside, Didier and I sat down on the stairs in the hallway. Moinel came in with his shopping and gave us a nervous smile. When Moinel was out of earshot, I said: 'Did your father fall off a roof, Didier?'

He took off his glasses and polished them on his T-shirt – a thing he often did. Then he said: 'Have you read Zola's *L'Assommoir*? Do you remember how Lantier falls?'

I said I'd never read anything by Zola.

Then Didier went on: 'Well. Lantier is a roofer. His wife comes by with his children and he's so glad to see them, he waves at them, without thinking. He lets go his grip . . .'

'And that's what happened to your father? He let go?'

'Louis,' he said, 'when you are on a roof, you have to pay attention all the time. Especially on certain difficult jobs – a dome, for instance. No matter how good the scaffolding is, you can't take your eyes from what you're doing. And this makes the work very tiring. You know the Salpêtrière Hospital?'

'No.'

'You should go there and see. It has one of the most colossal domes in Paris, on the hospital's Church of Saint Louis – your saint. And it's made of slate.'

'Like this roof?'

'Yes. And everything there is to know about slate, my father knew. It shouldn't have happened. Never, never. It was me who called out to him, showing him what I'd seen in the sky . . .'

'You mean you distracted him? What had you seen?'

'We were putting up the scaffolding. That dome is an octagon. We'd laid scaffolding round seven of the eight sections.

It had been raining earlier and my father kept saying, "Be careful, Didier: the slates are still slippery." And some of them were loose, like they're loose on this building, just barely held, because the pins were broken or rusty . . . But still, it never should have happened that way . . .'

I could tell it was beginning to hurt Didier to tell me this story. He kept fiddling with his shoes and his voice was getting choked-up and faint, and I thought if he got to the bit where his father fell he might collapse or cry or something and I didn't want this to happen, because I knew it was going to embarrass me.

Luckily, he stopped before he got to the bad bit. He just stopped talking and his eyes behind his glasses looked dreamy and far away. I knew he was thinking all about it: the thing he'd seen, and the rain on the grey slate, and the grave like a garage on the housing estate of the dead, but he couldn't go on with the story.

I tried to change the subject by asking him when we were going to start the roller-skating lessons on the esplanade. But he didn't seem to hear this question. He looked hard at me and said: 'Do you have a father, Louis?'

'Yes,' I said. 'His name's Hugh. He's a schoolteacher.'

They had to cut Valentina's silk dress to get her broken arm out of it. Apparently, she said to Alice: 'If they knew what this dress cost!' and the doctor and the nurse both laughed, but Alice didn't. Alice had become very stern with Valentina and that was that.

When they got home, Valentina's right arm was in a sling, lying comfortably between her breasts and her stomach. She was still wearing the mutilated dress which had come from Yves St Laurent and cost 10,760 FF, but she wasn't crying about it; she looked cheerful even, because at the hospital they'd given her something to take away the pain. A nurse once told Alice that the drugs that really take away pain are all heroin-based, so Valentina was having a kind of trip.

Valentina went to bed. Mum helped her get out of the dress and put on a satin nightie. After that she propped her up on millions of pillows and it was only then that I was allowed in to see her. She looked like an empress, lying there on all her pillows and cushions, and when I went into the room she said: 'Here's my brave Lewis. Come, darling, and sit by me.' So I sat on her bed and held her hand. From where I positioned myself, I could see right down the soft valley between her breasts and I had to do some chess moves in my mind to stop myself from laying my head there.

After a while, I started thinking about the way things might change now that Valentina would have to be helped with everything, and when Alice had gone out to the kitchen to get us some supper I said: 'I've got a good idea. I could become your secretary, Valentina. You could dictate stuff to me and I could type it. I'm ace with computers and I've got a word-processor programme on mine at home. What have you got – IBM or Apple Mac or what?'

'Apple, darling. I don't know if it's Mac or not.'

'It's Mac, if it's Apple. What software?'

'I don't know. I don't know these kind of things, Lewis.'

'Well, it doesn't matter. It's all more or less the same in a WP programme. I can familiarise myself with it in two minutes. It's a good idea, isn't it?'

She smiled at me and said: 'Maybe it's better if Alice helps me . . .'

'But then she won't be able to get on with her translation, Valentina. That's stupid. I can't translate your book, but I could help you with typing.'

'Not really, darling. It has to be Alice . . .'

I hated her going on about wanting Alice. I wanted her to want me. 'Let me try,' I said. 'Let's try tomorrow, and if I'm no good you can get someone else.'

'Perhaps I can still type with just my left hand?'

'No, you can't. This system will be much faster, and it's nearly August. We've only got about a month left.'

She sighed at that point. Her sighs were very heavy, like some of the grimy Russian air was still in her lungs. Then she said to me in a whisper: 'You've forgotten one thing, Lewis.'

'No, I haven't,' I said. 'What have I forgotten?'

'I'm writing in French.'

It was true. I had forgotten that. Once again, I'd ignored what was prime. An English boy struggling with *Le Grand Meaulnes* would be a pitiful assistant to a French novelist. I couldn't believe I'd suggested such an idiotic thing. My love for Valentina was turning me into a moron.

I got up and walked around the room, looking at Valentina's things – her hairbrushes and her lamps and her photograph frames and her pots of flowers – and noticing that they were all heavy and expensive. I wanted to hurl one of them at the wall.

After a bit, Valentina said: 'Don't be upset, Lewis. You can help me in other ways.'

'I wanted to be your secretary!' I shouted.

'Never mind about that,' said Valentina, trying to soothe me. 'Now I want to ask you something important. Come here, darling, please.'

I could tell it was going to be something about Alice and it was, so I didn't move, but just stayed looking at all the perfume bottles on Valentina's dressing table and at her mirror, which was draped with beads and chiffon scarves.

Valentina wanted to know why Alice was angry with her. I wasn't interested in this and I didn't want to talk about it, but eventually, with my back turned, I said: 'You shouldn't take any notice of Alice's moods.'

'But what have I done to her?'

'Nothing. She's always a bit like that, wanting to do things on her own. It's just her stubborn Scottish character.'

'But you know I'm very fond of Alice, darling. And if she's going to be so cross all the time, I'm going to be unhappy.'

'Don't be,' I said impatiently. 'She's just *like that*. There's no point in being upset.'

'The thing is . . . I don't know what I've done.'

'You haven't done anything. I told you. It's Alice's way . . .'

'But it never was before. And when she goes out alone, like that, where does she go, Lewis?'

'I don't know. She maybe goes to a café or to the park, or something. She's fond of just sitting and thinking, which is why Dad's building the hut for her.'

'Building a hut?'

I hadn't intended to mention this. I suppose I brought it up to distract Valentina from her questions about Alice and return her to some subject that had more to do with me, but as soon as I said it I regretted it.

'Don't mention it to Alice,' I said. 'I shouldn't have told you. It's meant to be a secret.'

'What kind of hut?'

I'd picked up a silver clothes brush and now I banged this down very hard on the dressing table and two of the perfume bottles fell over. 'I shouldn't have told you!' I said again. 'Forget it. Please forget it and don't ask me about it any more. And don't ask me about Alice!'

I sneaked a glance at Valentina. She looked shocked. She couldn't understand why I felt so strongly about all this. She had no way of knowing that what I dreamed about in my attic room was her.

'Come here, darling,' she said softly.

I felt so moody. I thought, I expect this is what it's like to have a lovers' tiff. I didn't want to go to her just because she spoke to me sweetly now, so I stood angrily by the dressing table, refusing to move.

'Lewis,' she said, 'come here.'

So I righted the perfume bottles and went and sat by her then, and she put her good arm on my knee and said how sensibly I'd behaved in the emergency and what an excellent idea it had been to fetch Didier.

There was a long silence after that. We just sat there, waiting for something to come into our minds to talk about. I started to feel a bit sleepy because I'd had hardly any food that day and had played chess with my Travel Set all afternoon until Alice and Valentina came home. And because I was awake for so much of each night. What I longed to do now was to lie down on the satiny bed and fall asleep with Valentina's arm holding me in.

I closed my eyes. As soon as I'd closed them, Valentina began talking again. I drifted away on the sound of her voice, and when I came to I realised she was telling me about her past. I thought, this could be what real lovers actually do – tell each other about their childhoods.

She told me that her parents, Mr and Mrs Gavrilovich, had come to France with a group of Russian farmers in 1957, on an official visit to a French wine co-operative. The co-operative was in the Luberon region. The Gavrilovichs brought little Valentina with them. She was three. She thought they'd suspected ('or realised in a kind of dream, Lewis') that when they saw the acres of vines growing in the sunshine on the Luberon hills, they wouldn't have the stomach to return to Russia.

So they got on a train for Paris. They just left the Russian group and got on a train. They had almost no money and nowhere to stay, but someone had told Mr Gavrilovich he might find work in the old slaughterhouse at La Villette, and so they went there and he was taken on, and for the first week they slept in a barn where straw was kept and washed themselves in the slaughterhouse yard, very early in the morning, before the trucks of animals started arriving.

It took Mr Gavrilovich four years to make enough money to start the *café, bois et charbon* and only once in his life did he go back to Provence and see the vines on the hills. 'I would have been about your age when we went,' said Valentina. 'We camped in a meadow, in some old tent Papa had stolen or borrowed. It was autumn. I remember cooking mushrooms on a little open fire and I remember the cold dew in the mornings. It hadn't changed, you know, that beautiful landscape. It had hardly changed at all from when we'd first seen it ten years before. And after this, until he died, Papa kept promising we would go to live there and buy land and a house made of stone and grow vines, but we never did.'

'Now, you could. If you wanted to,' I said sleepily.

'Yes,' she said, 'now I could, but it was Papa who wanted that life, not me. You can't live someone else's dreams, Lewis. You have to live your own.'

The next day was Sunday and I wasn't allowed near Valentina's room. She was feeling sick, after all the heroin they'd given her, and her arm was hurting again and she couldn't get up.

Mrs Gavrilovich arrived, dressed in black, with a scarf over her bun and smelling of incense. She brought a bunch of white peonies and her embroidery in a bag. I heard her say to Alice: 'Broken bones are a curse. They make me afraid.'

Alice said it was best for us to go out, to let Mrs Gavrilovich take charge of everything. I thought it was odd that at forty-one a person could still need her mother, and I somehow predicted that when I was forty-one, if I ever got that far, all I would need of Alice and Hugh was just to know that they were alive.

The bedroom door closed on Valentina and Mrs Gavrilovich and I could hear them talking softly in Russian. I said to Alice, 'I expect they could be talking about Provence and the house they never bought, don't you?' but she only shrugged. Either she didn't know the story about Provence, or else she just wasn't interested in it.

She went to the window and looked at the beautiful day outside and said: 'Come on. Let's go out. Get Sergei's lead.'

We walked all the way to the bird market at the Place Louis Lépine, going right down through the Tuileries and past the Louvre and over the Pont au Change to the Île de la Cité. On the way, under the chestnuts of the Tuileries, I said to Alice, 'Do you think Babba will get blamed for what happened?'

Alice shrugged again. 'I expect so,' she said. 'Things that happen to Valentina are never seen as being her own fault.'

'She won't make Babba leave, will she?'

'I don't know.'

Alice didn't seem interested in Babba's fate, any more than she'd been interested in what Valentina and Mrs Gavrilovich had been talking about. I was going to tell her about Pozzi and the Harley Davidson and Babba's village in Benin, but then I thought there was no point, because I understood now that, since we'd come to Paris, Alice was slowly going into some private world, in which these things seemed to be of no importance to her whatsoever. It wasn't just that Valentina had begun to annoy her; something else was preoccupying her mind.

I glanced at her, walking along in the dappled sunlight. She was wearing a skimpy blue dress and some brown beads Hugh had bought her from a craft shop in Exeter. I thought, when a person goes into her own secret world, it isn't a reassuring sign. And then I realised another thing about her, a thing I never would have anticipated: she'd been neglecting me. So this is what I thought about as we walked. I made an imaginary diagram of our two minds, Alice's and mine, and they were like two planets or stars zooming further and further away from each other as time passed and the universe expanded.

When we got to the bird market, Sergei began to tremble, seeing all these hundreds of birds looking out at him and trilling. I don't know whether he was trembling out of curiosity or out of sadness or out of a desire to snaffle up a dozen yellow canaries for his lunch. I stroked his neck to calm him. Some of the birds looked desperate to get out of their cages, sticking their beaks and their eyes through the bars, but the baby parrots were all huddled together in a far corner of their hutch, their green heads in a cluster, like they couldn't bear to see the people going by and wanted to be in darkness. I pointed this out to Alice and we stood and looked at them and Alice said: 'They think *we're* for sale to them and they've decided they don't want to buy.'

We passed mina birds who tried to speak to us in some language we couldn't understand and a flight of Indian sparrows in a wicker barrel and then we came to pairs of budgerigars in very small cages, who had been labelled as being *inséparables*. Some had come from Japan and some from South America. I didn't know who had decided that these ones couldn't be parted from each other or what would happen to them if you did part them.

'Would they die?' I asked Alice.

Mostly they were blue, the colour of her dress, and she smiled at them tenderly, as if they amused her. 'They're just couples,' she said: 'Mr and Mrs.'

'Shall we buy a pair?' I said suddenly.

'Certainly not,' said Alice. 'Whatever for?'

'For Valentina,' I said. 'To cheer her up.' They weren't very expensive. I thought I could use some of my 'book money' that Hugh had given me, because the only book I'd bought was Paul Berger's copy of *Le Grand Meaulnes* and Hugh had seemed to imagine I'd be buying books non-stop all the time, like he did. He couldn't pass a second-hand bookshop without coming out with some bizarre thing like *Letters of an American Slave Trader* or *Sanitation in Roman Britain*, but I was more selective. 'I'll pay,' I said.

'No,' said Alice.

I felt a sliver of fury come into me. Alice sometimes boasted about her obstinacy, but right now it just really pissed me off. I knew Valentina would like the budgerigars. I could imagine her taking them out of their cage and stroking their blue feathers. Russian people weren't afraid to bring birds inside their houses and let them alight on their bodies.

'Please, Mum,' I said, forgetting my promise to imitate François, who never called his mother by anything but her first name.

'No,' she said. 'Absolutely not, Lewis. And now I think we've seen enough caged birds. Let's go to a café for some lunch and then up to La Défense. OK?'

I felt furious, but then our lunch took all my crossness away. It was in one of those big, noisy café-brasseries where pinball machines and *cappuccino* coffee-makers ping and hiss in the background all the time and the conversation is as loud as the sea, and what the atmosphere of this brasserie made me feel was that I was at the centre of the Western world. My reflection in the brasserie glass was aged a cool sixteen.

I drank two *panachés* and then I wanted to sleep. I felt like the green baby parrots, who were tired of all the sale goods that passed their way, so I asked Alice if she'd mind if I didn't come with her to La Défense. I expected her to say she did mind, but all she did was shrug again and say, 'No, it's up to you. Take Sergei home, if you want, but be quiet in the apartment in case Valentina's sleeping.'

When I got back, I left Sergei outside Valentina's room, where he lay down and sniffed her perfume in the tiny gap of air under the door. I stood and listened, but there was nothing to be heard, only the whisper of a few cars on the rue de Lisbonne. I imagined Valentina and Mrs Gavrilovich lying side by side and snoring quietly. I told Sergei not to start whining or whimpering for their love.

Then I went and looked round Alice's room. My sleepiness had gone. I was looking for the manuscript of Valentina's book, and I expected to find a fat pile of pages sitting neatly on her desk but there was no such pile. I began searching in drawers and cupboards, like a burglar. A real burglar could have told from the quality of Alice's underwear that she wasn't rich. Her knickers were all different colours and small and scrunched up, as if they were never ironed, and her bras were made of cotton check. And she didn't have any jewellery, only a few beads and bits of amber. The burglar would have gone away thinking, that's really pitiful: nothing worth nicking.

I couldn't find the manuscript, only a few sheets – pages 39 to 42 – lying under a paperweight by Alice's bed. I could have moused my way into her computer file and printed the whole thing out from page 1, but I wasn't feeling that assertive and, anyway, I didn't want to be here delving around in Alice's things; I wanted to be alone.

I went up to my room. I drew the little curtain across my round window to blank out the light and closed and locked my bedroom door. Then I got into bed with the lipstick *Cerise*. I took all my clothes off and lay in the semidark with my eyes closed and the lipstick caressing my mouth and my tongue.

It tasted of strawberries. Not cherries. It had a texture so fine it was like something chefs might dream of. So then I imagined a line of chefs arriving and presenting Valentina with sugared grapes and lattice baskets of chocolate and redcurrants dipped in cream and she smiled and giggled as she ate them, as some of the sugar dusted her breasts and the cream dripped on to her thighs, and then she sent them all away and said, 'Now I shall have my real feast.' And her 'real feast' was me. She lay on me, with her huge soft weight, and she kissed me again and again and then she put me inside her.

I'd never dared to think about being inside Valentina before. It was like I'd said to myself, if I don't think about *that*, then all my other fantasies will never harm her and never be known by anyone on earth. But it was the lipstick that drove my thoughts there. And then that was what I wanted. I wanted to fuck her. I'd never, ever, imagined fucking anyone before that afternoon, but now I did imagine it and I felt as absolutely crazy with longing as it is possible to feel. Afterwards, when I'd come, I put my hands over my face, which was red and sticky with the lipstick, and cried.

Then I slept for a long time. No one came to disturb me and I supposed that Alice was still out. When I woke up, the sun had moved from our side of the street and I could tell it was getting towards supper time.

I got up and stared at myself in the bathroom mirror. I looked as if I'd stepped out of some really violent movie, bleeding from the face and genitals, punched in the eye, left to die. I wished I was my father, aged forty-six, happy with a hut.

This is undoubtedly what love does to people, I thought: it kills them.

It was difficult to know how to make myself look normal again, but I thought having a bath might help, so I ran a big deep tub of water and soaped and scrubbed the lipstick away and lay submerged in the pink scummy foam like a diver. I wanted to emerge from the water reborn, with no vestige of my longing for Valentina remaining, but I knew this wasn't going to happen and it didn't.

I put on clean clothes. There was lipstick all over my pillow-case, so I yanked it off and threw it into my wardrobe, hoping Babba wouldn't go sniffing around and find it.

When I got downstairs, I found Mrs Gavrilovich in the kitchen, making onion soup. She said in her heavy French: 'Onions. Those I grew in Moscow, Louis. Long ago. In a tin bath, under the skylight.'

Alice hadn't come in. It was half past seven and the country-weekenders of the rue Rembrandt were returning as they always did, but Alice was staying away. I knew that when I saw Valentina – if I was allowed to see her that night – she'd ask me where Alice was, so I made up a convincing story about her meeting a friend from Scotland in the brasserie and going off with her for the rest of the day. I would call her Jean, which had been the name of Alice's friend in Edinburgh. Alice and Jean used to go roller-skating together and one day Jean skated right into a milk float and broke her nose. I would tell Valentina this story, to divert her.

Then Valentina came into the kitchen. She had no make-up on, no lipstick, nothing, and her face looked white, like the faces of heroin users. She was wearing her silk kimono and her hair was a bit flat where she'd been lying on it. She looked terrible really, yet, the moment I saw her, all I wanted to do was to go to her and put my arms round her, or let my hand be a bird, landing on whatever part of her it chose. She peered for a moment at Mrs Gavrilovich's soup, then she came to me and gently stroked my hair that was still wet from my diver's bath.

'Lewis,' she said, 'how are you, my English boy?'

I had my piece of rope now. Getting out on to the roof was a cinch. And I had my private roof kit, which consisted of a torch, a blanket and a Lion bar.

I installed myself on the plateau where the tanks were. The moon was up and smiling.

The blanket was my bed and one of the tanks was my bed head, against which I could lean. If I climbed on to the tank I could see right down to ground level, and this I did that night from time to time, to see if Alice was returning. Not many people walked in the rue Rembrandt at night, because our bit of it led nowhere except to the park. At about one, Moinel came down the street, carrying what looked like a bag of groceries, and I saw him hurry in, as if these groceries embarrassed him. He was dressed from head to toe in white.

I'd told the story about Jean to Valentina, so she wasn't worried about Alice, but after I'd seen Moinel go in I felt a kind of worm of worry slither through me and I was tempted to go down and telephone my father and ask him what I should do if, in the morning, Alice was still missing. But I didn't move from the roof. In Hugh's last letter, he'd told me he went to bed early and slept 'like a child'.

To combat my worm, I began to read pages 39 to 42 of Valentina's book that I'd taken from Alice's room. Neither Barthélémy nor Isabelle seemed to be in this bit of the text. I didn't know what had happened to them.

What I read about was a winter night in the town of Belfort. Belfort was having the ninety-minute hours I'd heard Valentina describe and in these all the people were leaving their homes and moving in ones and twos and groups and families towards the city gate. They were going because a smallpox plague had come to Belfort, '*spreading from house to house on a sneeze or a breath, being carried further and wider in the sewage that streamed along the gutters. A freak wind from the south blew a black dust into the air that swirled like a tornado into the sky and then fell back to settle on the streets . . .'*

I paused here. I thought, this story is meant to be set in the year 1400 or something and probably the first time anyone in the Western world heard the word 'tornado' was when Dorothy's house got blown into the sky in *The Wizard of Oz*, so Valentina's feeling for history is a bit off key in this passage. I made an indentation with my nail in the margin opposite the word 'tornado' and then read on.

I found out why the people were all going to the city gate. They were going because there, on a plinth of stone, stood a statue they believed was blessed with curative powers. It was the statue of a saint called Sainte Estelle de Belfort and the people preferred to put their trust in Sainte Estelle than in the know-nothing doctors. But by going there, and massing together round the statue and refusing to leave, they were gradually turning this place near the city gate into the worst area of contagion in the whole city, *'because, as the people prayed together, the disease was carried from mouth to mouth on the words of prayers, from palm to palm on the strings of rosary beads . . .'*

I began to get a bit caught up in the story at this point, to become one of Valentina's orang-utan readers, blindly following her, with my Lion bar peeled and ready to eat, like a jungle fruit. The Mayor of Belfort, furious at the people's stupidity, had instructed one of the priests, Father H, to go to the city gate near dawn when the people had fallen asleep and remove the statue of Sainte Estelle. He was ordered to hide it in the crypt of his church. He was told, in fact, to barricade it into a niche in the wall with rods of iron and then to close the crypt and lock its gates so that no one could come within breathing distance of the statue. *' "In this way, Father," said the Mayor, "the citizens will be forced to disperse and to seek help from the appropriate sources, namely the good doctors of this town." '*

Then Valentina began to describe the feelings of Father H on being given this order. He wasn't afraid of the anger his action was going to provoke. What really got to him was the thought of imprisoning the statue. He was very fond of this little Sainte Estelle and the idea of barricading her into a wall with iron rods gave him a pain in his heart. He imagined her *'waking from her statue-reverie in the icy crypt with its smell of coal and understood what sorrow she would feel at being rendered useless'*. And so he planned to remove her from the gate as instructed, but then take her home with him to his lodgings, *'where she would still be able to look on human faces and see me, poor penniless priest, go about my daily tasks. And, in order not to embarrass her, he would cover her face with a shawl while he performed his morning ablutions.'*

I didn't like the way Valentina had called her character 'Father H'. When I find this in a book, I always think the writer's been too lazy to think up a proper name. One of my teachers at school once said something about 'universal identification with a letter', but I'd told him I found identification with a letter an impossible task. I was glad Alain-Fournier hadn't called poor old Francois 'F'. That would have ruined the whole thing.

I got up at this point and climbed the tank and scanned the street and listened, but no one was coming down it. I thought, perhaps Alice had just walked out, leaving all her things, and Valentina and I will be alone together from now on. The thought of this was so amazing and odd that I shivered.

I ate my Lion bar and carried on reading. Father H walked towards the statue carrying the wicker pannier in which he normally fetched his bread. Covering his face, he went in among the people huddled asleep round the statue, unscrewed Sainte Estelle's little foot from the plinth, reached up and took hold of her by her waist and put her gently into the pannier. No one woke up. (Luckily.) Father H clutched the bread pannier to his chest and scuttled away.

'Father H hurried through the dark streets, with Sainte Estelle getting heavier and heavier in the pannier, almost as though she were growing as he carried her, becoming as heavy as a child of five, as

heavy as a child of seven, so that by the time he reached his lodgings Father H could barely hold the pannier higher than his knees.

'With one last effort, he hauled the saint up his wooden stairs. He was hurrying so fast he didn't see an old woman lying under the stairs, who woke as he passed and smelled the smell of fear and lay awake listening, knowing without seeing it what Father H had done.

'Father H let himself into his rooms. He looked all around them for a place to hide his terrible burden, but could fine none. The lodgings were meagre. He cursed the Church for allowing him to acquire so little in life. And then, in desperation and misery, he took the saint out of the basket and laid her down in his narrow bed.

'Unhappy Father H! Why did he not leave his room at that moment and go to his church to pray? He did not leave because cold and fear and exhaustion overcame him and so he lay down in the bed beside Estelle. His thoughts were not immodest. He wanted only to sleep. But the old crone under the stairs crept to his door and looked in through the keyhole and saw Father H lying with his arms around the statue. And so she went out to the crowds now waking at the city gate and told them what she had seen.

'The people followed the old woman. There were more than a hundred of them, all in their ragged clothes of despair. With knives they cut off the penis and testicles of Father H. They ignored his terrible screams of agony and the blood that gushed in their faces. With saws and axes, they dismembered him limb from limb and threw the bits and pieces of his body into the icy river.'

The pages ended there. I'd told myself that by the time I'd read this story Alice would have come back, but she hadn't. The air above the roof was still warm, but I began to feel cold and strange at the thought that she might have left me, so I climbed back on to the water tank and sat there with my blanket round my shoulders, like a Mexican peasant in a Western, waiting and watching.

I went to sleep sitting up. Mexican peasants can do this: it's their connectedness to the earth.

It was Didier who woke me. He was beginning his day on

the roof as my far-away church clock struck eight. He said: 'Louis, what are you doing up here?'

I'd fallen sideways in my sleep and lay with my cheek on the galvanised iron tank. I thought, I wonder which country and which century invented the pillow? As I sat up, I knew one half of my face was square and flat.

'I was waiting for Alice,' I said.

'What?' said Didier.

I rubbed my face to try to get it back to its normal shape and then I said: 'Alice never came home. I waited for her . . .'

'Are you sure?'

'She never came in. Did she go up to La Défense yesterday afternoon? Did you see her?'

Didier shook his head. 'No. I wasn't there. I had to go to see my mother. Maybe she came in while you were sleeping?'

I pulled my blanket round me. I wasn't cold, but I just felt in need of something comforting to hold on to. Didier looked a bit worried too. He walked a few paces from me and lit a Gitane and I could see his hand shaking as he held his lighter. Suddenly, I said: 'What exactly is an existentialist, Didier? I've never really understood it.'

'Perhaps we shouldn't discuss this now, Louis,' he said. 'Perhaps you should go and see Alice?'

'Yes, I will,' I said, 'but tell me roughly . . .'

'Well . . .' Didier sighed and then inhaled a lot of smoke and blew it out again. 'The existentialists were concerned with what man makes of himself – in the absence of any God.'

'Existentialists don't believe in God?'

'No. Of course not. They did not believe in God and they did not believe that good and evil have been defined and determined for us by God or any other Superior Being or by any political system. My father explained the logic of this to me when I was quite young. And so, to me, this philosophy is still precious and still relevant to the way I live my life.'

I had to ask Didier to say this again, because some of the

words were difficult. Nobody talked about political systems in *Le Grand Meaulnes*.

When he thought I'd grasped the concept, he said: 'Do you understand? Man acts alone. You, Louis, act alone. You are not compelled by some outside force.'

'Yes, I am,' I said.

'No. You are free, as we all are free . . .'

'No, I'm not. My "outside force" is my parents. I was "compelled" to come to Paris, for instance. I had no say in it.'

'All right, you were compelled to come because you're still a child – more or less. But does anyone force you to feel what you feel about coming to Paris? Do you think what you think and do what you do *in the name of* some group, organisation or belief?'

'In the name of what?'

'Let me put it simply, Louis. No one is the judge of your thoughts and deeds. Only you. You take full responsibility.'

I stared at Didier. I knew I hadn't understood everything he'd said, and this really annoyed me. I promised myself to work harder on my French, to buy some more books from the bouquinistes with Hugh's money – a book by Sartre, for instance.

'Can we talk about it again?' I said. 'Will you explain it to me over and over until I understand it? I want to understand it. Has flying got anything to do with it?'

'Flying?'

'Your name, Didier-l'oiseau. Is that an existentialist name?'

Didier smiled. His hand was still shaking as he took the Gitane out of his thin mouth. 'Yes,' he said, 'in a way. Being alone, unattached, in the air, is the ultimate freedom, isn't it?'

I didn't know how to answer this. I just nodded, like I agreed with Didier, and then I went inside and down to Alice's room. Her door was closed, so I opened it quietly and there was Alice lying in her gigantic bed, sweetly asleep as if nothing had happened.

★

I decided to go missing. I thought, Alice and Valentina can be the ones who worry about *me*.

I took the métro to Jussieu and came up under the green catalpa trees. I went to a café and had a huge breakfast of omelette and chips and coffee, and that feeling of being at the very centre of something came back to me while the noise of the café went on all round me. I asked my waiter if he was an existentialist and he said, 'Non, mon petit. Ca, non,' and smiled, as if I'd cracked a joke. Some students at the next table turned and looked at me strangely, like they couldn't believe what they'd just heard.

I walked through the Jardin des Plantes, where a hundred lawn sprinklers were turning and the frogs were croaking in the artificial rain, then down the Boulevard de l'Hôpital to the Salpêtrière Hospital.

Somehow, because Didier had said it had a church, I hadn't thought it was a real working hospital, but now I could see that it was and it was so enormous it had to mark out routes in different colours on a map to tell you where you were. It had courtyard after courtyard, all identical, and one of these gave on to a little wood or grove, where some of the patients were walking up and down in their dressing gowns. No hospital in England provides a wood for walking up and down in. Not many of them even provide a *lawn*. In England, you just have to get better tramping the linoleum corridors.

An old man came up to me and asked where the door to *Anesthésiologie et Réanimation* was. He didn't say which he wanted, to be anaesthetized or reanimated. Perhaps, when you're really old, you vacillate between wanting one and then the other? I told him I didn't know, that I was a stranger from Devon – 'je suis un étranger, du Devon' – and he walked on, looking up and down and around with his little darting eyes.

I guided myself to the church and stood in front of it, staring up at the dome Didier had worked on. It was so vast, there must have been about a million slates on it, and all these black slates shone like fish scales in the sun. It was hard to imagine men up there, getting scaffolding secure. You just couldn't see how or where they would start. But I tried to picture Didier and his father, looking small from here because they were so high, and then Didier's father being distracted by whatever it was that came out of the sky . . .

What happened next? How far did his father fall? Did Didier fly through the air to try to save him? Did he fall, too, and survive except for something that happened to his eyes which damaged his sight?

I like mysteries. Unfinished knowledge. Most people have to be told everything straight away, get it all explained and wrapped up. But I like trying to work it out for myself, like in a chess game.

There'd been a boy at school who stole things – books, shoes, sweets, fags, T-shirts, tennis rackets, anything that came within his sight when no one was looking – and everyone said, 'Oh, he'll make a mistake and then he'll be caught,' but they didn't *try* to catch him. But I worked out that if he was stealing tennis rackets and shoes he must be selling them somehow, or passing them on to be sold, so I let him steal my football, which was marked with the initials LL. Then I got the local paper every day and looked up when all the weekend car-boot sales were on and cycled to every single one of them until I found my football. And the rest would have been easy. Except I suddenly felt sorry for this fucking stealer. I don't know why. I just couldn't get interested in shopping him. The thing that had interested me was laying my trap.

My neck began to ache, staring up at the dome. But the idea was coming to me that Didier was a kind of hero – probably the most heroic person I'd ever known. I had to blot out of my mind the image of Hugh with his pile of bricks, because if I started to compare my father's hut with this great fantastic dome I knew I'd feel something bad, like embarrassment or sorrow. I decided that the next time I had a talk with Didier I'd ask him whether he thought happiness was as small as a shrimp in a pool.

I went into the church. I didn't know who Saint Louis had been, but he must have appreciated emptiness and space, because this was what there was most of in this building: air that had never been breathed and echoing walls and shafts of light. I sat down on one of the spindly little chairs. I seemed to be the only person there. Except then I heard a kind of rustling and whispering and I realised a Mass was going on behind a huge door in one of the side chapels.

I crept around. The side chapels were all labelled for different categories of worshippers – nurses, parishioners, lunatics, the sick – so that they could each have their own services, and not be upset by the sight of each other or turn the church into a centre of contagion, like the city gate in Belfort. The chapel in which the Mass was going on was the lunatics' one, so I sidled up to the door to see if I could see any mad behaviour, but I couldn't: everyone was sitting still and listening obediently to the priest.

Then a man in a battered old suit came creeping by me. His look was odd, as if he should have been in the lunatics' side chapel. He shuffled round the floor to a stone pedestal where there was an ugly statue of the Virgin Mary, wearing a gold dress. She was almost life-size, like Sainte Estelle in Valentina's novel, and this man climbed on to the pedestal and took her hands in his, like he was Father H about to take her away. He looked into her eyes, which were as bright as polished stones, and started a conversation with her. I hid behind a pillar and listened, but I couldn't hear what he was saying or what she said back. After a while, he took out a hankie and shined up her face a bit and then he left.

It was still only ten o'clock in the morning. I sat down again and wondered how I was going spend my day alone. I decided to make my way to the Luxembourg Gardens and hang round the chess players, seeing if I could learn any new moves. I didn't know how long they'd tolerate me, but I thought, when they're sick of me, I'll go back to the rue Rembrandt. But I didn't plan to go into the apartment: I planned to go up on to the roof using Didier's ladders and get him to show me how to hang slates as perfectly as the ones on the Salpêtrière dome.

It was getting dark when I finally returned to the apartment. I could tell from the faces of Alice and Valentina that they wanted to yell at me, but they didn't because an unknown man was with them and the three of them were sitting in the salon, making charming conversation.

Valentina was wearing a white dress and long silver earrings and the sling for her broken arm was made out of a silk scarf with a field of scarlet poppies on it. There was some writing on it, black and stick-like, which I thought said 'Ypres'. I hadn't known they made women's scarves that commemorated First World War battles, but you never know what the fashion industry is going to think up. Trying to be a fashionable woman must be exhausting. Later, I realised the word on the scarf was 'Yves' and the 'St Laurent' bit was lost to sight.

The man was Grigory Panin. He looked like some crazed American writer of the kind my father read – Kurt Vonnegut or Joseph Heller – with bushy hair and lined cheeks and a jacket of hairy tweed. In fact, he was a crazed Russian writer. Valentina explained that he was here to give interviews about a new book that was coming out in France. She said: 'I have known Grigory for a long, long time, haven't I, Grisha?'

Grigory Panin said: 'I apologise, but my English is sorrowful.'

They talked about Paris, about the price of things, about laser printers, about meat, about the guys in the métro selling yo-yos that unravelled on threads of light. After a while, they all went out to a meal in a restaurant, but I wasn't invited. I thought it might have been because of Grigory's sorrowful English, but Alice said later, 'You weren't invited, Lewis, because you behaved totally irresponsibly, going out on your own like that.' I refrained from saying that I'd spent half the night on the water tanks, waiting for her to come home. Grown-ups have one rule for themselves and another for their children and this has never been fair, since the beginning of time.

They left me a piece of pie and some salad for my supper and I ate this watching TV. The only interesting programme I could find was one about the survivors of the destruction of Caen in 1944. The whole city was virtually demolished and thousands of people died because the British forces stopped for a tea break, when they could have pushed on and taken Caen from the Germans in about half an hour. And during the tea break, the German tanks began to move in on the city.

I'd never really felt bad about being British before, but now I did. I don't know why we're all so fucking besotted by tea; it's lamentable.

They interviewed some French sisters who had lain hidden in Caen half a metre underground for seventeen weeks. The sisters said General Montgomery maybe ordered the tea break because he wanted to save British lives. But they didn't seem to bear the British a grudge, I don't know why. They told a story about how they found some love letters sent to a British infantryman in the place where they were hiding and kept them for forty years until they tracked the infantryman down in Great Yarmouth, by which time, alas, he was too old for love.

Sergei watched this programme with me. He sat there quivering and staring at the screen and I stroked his neck. When the programme told us about the fatal tea break, he let out a whimper of pain. From time to time, he turned round and looked at me longingly and so I fed him little crumbs of my pie. When the pie was finished, we were still both hungry. I thought, I wonder what there was to eat in that cellar in Caen for all those days and days.

At about midnight, while I was working on *Le Grand Meaulnes*, I heard Valentina on my stairs. She came in, still wearing her white dress and her poppy sling and smelling of wine. I said coldly: 'Did you have a nice dinner with Grigory?'

She sat down in her usual place on my bed. Her nose was

shiny but her lipstick was fresh and bright. 'Ah,' she said, 'that poor Grigory. All he talks about is how bad things are in Moscow. You know, there was so much hope there in '89, but the hope has gone. He says some mornings he wishes he had died in the night. Can you imagine how that feels?'

I thought, when I've gone from here, when I find myself back at Beckett Bridges School without ever having touched the most amazing person I've ever met or even tasted her lipstick, I may know how it feels. But all I said was: 'What's his book about?'

'Oh, Russian history, long before the Revolution. I doubt anyone here will read it. I don't think he will get good sales.'

She patted her hair and looked around my room at my clothes all thrown into piles.

'Is Grigory your lover, Valentina?' I said boldly.

She turned and stared at me, speechless for once. I looked away from her and opened my musical box and the tune, *Le Temps des cerises*, began to play softly from my bedside table. Part of me was amazed that I'd asked this question and another part wasn't.

After a while, Valentina said: 'You know, darling, it's none of your business, but then again why shouldn't you know? He was my lover, off and on, for a long time. He has a wife in Moscow, Irina. And Irina is an alcoholic, so, you see, poor Grisha does not have a beautiful life. Far from it. I am very fond of him, but he depresses me. When he is around, I find myself remembering so much that I would really rather forget.'

I looked at Valentina. I thought, Grigory Panin's hands have held her breasts, his tongue has sucked on her red lips . . . 'I see,' I said.

'So there you are, Lewis. One does not go through life without lovers. No one does. You will see.'

'Shall we do some *Meaulnes* now?' I said. 'I'm in the middle of the bit where Meaulnes has returned from his adventure. He's met Yvonne de Galais at this crazy party. He's fallen in love with her, but she says to him, "We're too young, it's no use." '

'Oh yes, all right, darling. Off you go.'

So I began. This bit was near the beginning of *Chapitre XVI, Frantz de Galais*. The musical box went silent because it needed winding. I read: '*During all this dreaming of his, the night had fallen and he had not thought about lighting the torches. The wind blew open the door that communicated with his and whose window overlooked the courtyard. Meaulnes was about to close it, when he saw that there was a glow in this room like the light of a candle. He put his head through the half-open door. Someone was there, someone who must have climbed in through the window and was now walking up and down . . .'*

As I read on, I could tell Valentina was impressed. My translation skills were definitely improving. There were clumsy constructions, things that didn't sound as if a proper writer had written them, but I was well into the book, and the further I went, the easier it was becoming.

I was almost at the end of the piece I'd prepared, when we heard footsteps on my stairs. I stopped reading. I hoped the footsteps didn't belong to Alice. Valentina didn't move and didn't look round when my door opened and Alice came into the room. I put my translation notebook and my copy of *Le Grand Meaulnes* under my bedcover and closed my musical box. Alice stood in the doorway and said: 'What's going on?'

'Nothing,' I said.

Valentina tried to take charge. 'Come and sit down with us, Alice,' she said. 'We were just talking about my poor country, Mother Russia . . .'

But Alice was furious. 'Lewis should be asleep,' she snapped. 'He's been looking exhausted.'

'I'm not sleepy,' I said.

'Maybe not, but your light should be out. Whose idea was this?'

'Alice, Alice,' said Valentina, still trying to soothe her, 'Lewis has been alone all day . . .'

'That was his own choice, Valentina. He must go to sleep now.'

She was wearing a white nightdress Hugh had bought her from Laura Ashley. In the dim light of my room, she looked exactly like an angel in a bad mood.

I knew Valentina would leave then. I wondered whether Grigory was staying in the flat and if she would go down and undress and get into his bed and he would enfold her in his suicidal arms.

She got up. I was afraid that, in front of Alice, she wouldn't give me her good-night kiss, but she did, and I could smell drink and Russian cigarettes and perfume all mingled in that single touch. Then she went away and Alice-the-Angel began her tirade of anger about my disappearance that morning. 'If you do that again, Lewis,' she said, 'I will send you home.'

When Babba came the next day to clean my room, she found the pillowcase in the wardrobe in two minutes flat.

'Louis, what you got here?' she said. 'You been doing voodoo in your bed?'

'Yes,' I said.

She then looked at the sheets and tore them off the bed. 'I better take these home to wash. You don't want Madame to see this or hear what they say at the laundry?'

'Thanks, Babba,' I said. Then I added: 'Perhaps I could buy you something in return, a toy, to give to Pozzi . . .'

She looked suddenly sad. 'Pozzi,' she said, 'he's crying and crying, Louis.'

'Why? What's happened?'

'That man came.'

'What man?'

'The one who had the apartment before Pozzi and me. He took away the motorbike. It's his bike and so he's come and he took it away.'

'Oh no . . .'

'So Pozzi just weepin' and weepin'. Says to me, "Maman, how we get to Africa now?" '

Babba sat down on the sheetless bed and leant her head on her velvet arms. Tears began to run down her cheeks.

'Do you *want* to get to Africa, Babba?' I asked. 'Do you want to leave Paris and go back?'

'I don't know,' she said. 'I got work here, but what else I got? Not mother, not village, not sisters. And no work card. I've applied for my card, but it don't come and don't come. So one day they arrest me anyway and lock me up. They take Pozzi away . . .'

'You must talk to Madame,' I suggested. 'She will sort out your work permit.'

'No. People like me, they won't give me any work card, I feel sure. No skill, no work card.'

'You can polish brilliantly, Babba. That's a skill . . .'

She shook her head and began to dry her tears on her overall. The stupid thing I'd said about the polishing made her laugh her silent yawning laugh. She repeated it: 'You can polish, Babba, hey!' and then we both folded up laughing, despite the sadness of it all.

I helped her put clean sheets on the bed and tidy my room, which had got chaotic somehow without my noticing. We played my musical box while we worked and Babba said she really liked *Le Temps des cerises*. I told her the English word, 'Cherrytime', but she could only pronounce it 'sherrytime'. And so this reminded me of Grandma Gwyneth, who, when you went to stay with her and Grandad, would call from the kitchen at seven o'clock, 'Sherry time, Bertie!' And then he'd stop whatever he was doing and come in and pour her a glass of her favourite sherry, which was called Elegante. I never knew why she couldn't pour it herself. Often, when Bertie handed her the sherry, he'd put a flimsy little kiss on her white head.

When we'd done my room, we went downstairs. I told Babba she had to go into every room in the flat to see whether

Grigory Panin was still lurking around. I waited in the kitchen while she did this with the vacuum cleaner as her camouflage. There were four bedrooms in the apartment and I expected her to find Grigory still asleep in one of them, exhausted after his night of ecstasy with Valentina.

Babba didn't come back for a long time. After waiting and waiting, I tiptoed out of the kitchen and stood in the corridor, listening. I could hear a row going on in Valentina's room and I realised Valentina was blaming Babba for her accident, just as I feared. Babba's voice was louder than usual. I heard her say: 'Madame, I was only doing what you told me – shining the floors.'

When Babba came out, she was shaking her head, as if she didn't understand what she'd just been hearing. I thought, I expect she shook her head like that when that old Renault truck was stolen and again when she realised Pozzi's motorbike was being repossessed.

We went into the kitchen and closed the door. 'What happened?' I said.

'Madame says I broke her arm. She shows me how she type with one hand. I didn't break Madame's arm, never.'

'She didn't sack you, did she?' I asked.

'No. But maybe I leave *her*, Louis. I never did break Madame's arm.'

'I know you didn't. But don't leave, Babba.'

'If anyone would say this at home in Benin, it's like they saying, "You are an evil woman, Babba. You been talkin' to the spirits." And I tell you, if they talk that way to me, I don't stay to hear no more. Or else I punish them. I punish them bad.'

'Would you really? What would you do to them?'

'Perhaps I break their arm!'

'How?'

'You want to hurt someone, you go to your *Manbo* and she makes offerings to the spirits. And then they come to you and ask, "What's to be done, girl?" '

'Does it work? Could they *kill* someone for you?'

'Depends.'

The kitchen door opened at that point and it was Mrs Gavrilovich with a load of groceries in a bag on wheels and she said she wanted us out of there, so that she could make mushroom pancakes for lunch. Since Valentina's accident, Mrs Gavrilovich looked younger and seemed more sprightly, as if the broken arm had been just the thing she'd been waiting for.

'Louis,' she said, 'take Sergei for his walk. He's making bad smells in the salon.'

So I had to leave my conversation with Babba and set off, for what felt like the eightieth time, with Sergei's kite lead. After he'd crapped in the gutter exactly opposite the apartment-house door, he pulled me along at crazy speed towards the Avenue Friedland. I was thinking so much about Babba and her spirits that I didn't attempt to guide him, but just followed him, like a dog is meant to follow its master. It was only after about half an hour that I realised I was lost.

We were at the gate of a little park and Sergei could smell grass and flowers, so he wanted to lure me in there. I wanted to lure myself in, too, and sit down on a bench and try to work out how to get home. I expected some park attendant would come and yell at me, but then I saw that the rules in this park appeared to be different. It was lunchtime and lots of people were camped on the grass, eating sandwiches and salads out of little cartons and drinking Yop. Sergei saw that he'd arrived in paradise, so I let him off the lead and he tore round, pissing against the trees, snapping at pigeons, eating grass and harassing the picnickers. He's a creature who gets away with a lot of bad behaviour because he's so beautiful. I wondered if he was a bit like Valentina in this one respect.

The bench I sat on was near a litter bin and while I tried to retrace our walk in my mind, to lead us home, a tramp came up to the bin and started rummaging in it. He was burned brown by the sun and his thin clothes were black and dusty. He began to eat the remains of people's salads, which had come ready-packed with little plastic spoons and forks. After he'd finished eating, he licked all the spoons and forks clean and stuck them into the waistband of his trousers.

As he lifted up his T-shirt to put them in, I saw that he had a collection of them already there, going right round his body, like a cartridge belt full of plastic cutlery. I tried to work out what he was going to do with them, and decided they must be a currency among homeless people. Grandma Gwyneth had told me that in the war people in England saved everything, because there was so little to buy and you never knew when something was going to come in useful. They saved *string*. So I thought, for a tramp like this, it's as if there's a war going on here and now, in the middle of 1994.

Watching the tramp picking through the lunch cartons made me feel hungry. Imagining going into a café and ordering a *croque-monsieur*, I realised that I had no money, not a centime for food or drink or a métro ticket or a cab or a map. I called Sergei to me and clipped on his lead. I stood up and said 'Chez nous!' to him, thinking, this is the moment for him to demonstrate his fabled knowledge of the city. But he just looked at me blankly with his sweet brown eyes, and when we came out of the park gates he immediately set off in the wrong direction. I yanked him round and I led him towards a bookshop that I remembered passing. Hugh had once said to me, 'In a selfish world, Lewis, booksellers are a category of people who are generally helpful and kind,' so I thought I would go in there and say that I was lost. In French, the words I was going to say sounded pitiful: 'Mon chien et moi, nous sommes perdus . . .' as if we were en route for hell.

The bookshop was large. You had to pass through a kind of turnstile to get into it and this didn't seem to have been designed with dogs in mind. I sidled out again and tied Sergei to a tree. A woman assistant glared at me on my way back in, so I walked past her into the depths of the shop, looking for someone kinder.

Then I saw Grigory Panin.

He was sitting by himself at a table, behind a pile of books. He had a pen in his hand. I hid behind some shelves and watched him. I read in the paper that at Lady Thatcher's book-signing in Harrods people were queuing right round and out of the book department and into Lingerie. But this didn't seem to be happening to Grigory.

One or two people came by the table and stared at him and passed on. One woman picked up a book from the pile and examined it, as if it were an aubergine at a market stall, and put it down again. Grigory looked pale and broken-hearted. He fiddled with his pen. And so I began to feel sorry for him and I went up to the table and spoke to him.

He didn't remember who I was. I had to introduce myself all over again. While he struggled to understand me, I sneaked a look at his book, which was called *La Vie secrète de Catherine la Grande*. And then he smiled at me and said: 'And so you have come to buy a book?'

I explained that I had no money and he said in English, 'Oh dear, catastrophe!'

Then, when he understood that I'd lost my way, he asked one of the shop assistants to fetch a map of Paris. We spread the map out on Grigory's table and the three of us stared at it, trying to work out my route home. Grigory said: 'You have strayed from 8th Arrondissement, Louis.' I thought, I expect his syntax is often devoid of the definite article because everything in Russia has become too complicated to define.

In the end, he walked all the way home with me, giving up on the book-signing. As we left the shop, I looked back and saw that the table was already being cleared of the copies of *La Vie secrète de Catherine la Grande* and restacked with its normal display. Grigory had an odd way of walking, with his head thrown back, as if he were navigating by the sun. I thought this was just a Grigory phenomenon, but suddenly he stopped and looked around him and said: 'Where are we? I forgot to look at streets and signs. I was doing what I do in Moscow, watching sky.'

'Why do you watch the sky, Grigory?' I asked.

He ran his hand through his Vonnegut hair and scratched his scalp. Then he looked at me intently. 'In Russia,' he said, 'to stay sane – to stay *alive* – you must transcend. You understand what I mean?'

My head filled up with the complexity of the world. I thought, I'm way behind with everything. I should be writing stuff down in my Concorde notebook, so that I can remember it, and I'm not, because for two-thirds of the time my mind is choked with thoughts about Valentina.

As we waited to cross the Avenue Friedland, in a brief lull between onslaughts of taxis, I asked Grigory if he thought Valentina was a beautiful woman.

'Yes,' he said. 'Of course.'

'Why "of course"?'

'Well. I love her. Always. Since age of thirty-six when I met her. To me, Valentina is life. Not my life. My life is not life, it is death. But Valentina is *life*. So of course to me she is beautiful.'

We crossed the avenue. I felt the sweet poignancy of the fact that Grigory was leaving Paris in the next two days and going back to his alcoholic wife, Irina, whereas I was staying on in Valentina's apartment for another five or six weeks.

'Have you read her new book?' I asked.

'No,' said Grigory. 'I asked her if I could read this one, but she won't let me, I don't know why. Do you know why, Louis?'

'No,' I said, 'I've no idea.'

We all had dinner that night in a restaurant in the Place de l'Alma. Grigory had chosen it because he wanted to be within sight of the Eiffel Tower, but, as we sat down, Valentina complained he was behaving like a tourist and that he'd be punished with a lousy meal. He laughed a big, furious laugh. 'Lousy meal?' he said and pointed at all the dishes on the menu – sole, halibut, turbot, scallops, chicken, lamb, veal, steak, duck, venison and quail. 'You think this is lousy meal, Miss Gavril?

You have so forgotten your past, you have so forgotten what my existence is, that you really think that?'

'Never mind, Grisha,' Valentina said. 'Forget it. There is your Tower, you see?'

At night, the Tower was gold. Valentina and Alice sat with their backs to it and Grigory and I had it there in our vision whenever we cared to look up. And when the meal came, I agreed with Grigory, I didn't think the food was lousy, but after a bit the evening began to go wrong.

First, some Americans came and sat down next to us. They looked like bankers. One of them was loud and in charge of everything and spoke nutty sort of French to the waiters and bossed the others around, and you could tell that this one, whose name was Gene, worked in Paris and thought he knew everything about France and Europe. At first I didn't mind them: I really like the way Americans have their volume control way up, as if the whole world were far too quiet for them. But then Gene began talking about Britain.

He called it the UK. He went on and on about what a hopeless country it had become, like he was giving a seminar on the decline and fall of everything and everyone in England, like he was saying the whole place was finished and ruined and now just a heap of shit adrift in the Channel. It got far worse than hearing about the British forces' unscheduled tea break at Caen. I'd far rather feel mildly ashamed of my country than stimulated into a pathetic patriotism.

I looked over at Alice, to see if she was getting upset, but she wasn't listening; she seemed to be trying to mediate between Valentina and Grigory, who had never really recovered from Valentina's remark about the 'lousy meal', and now they were arguing in Russian and Valentina's bangles were jingling with fury and Grisha was tugging and tugging at his hair. I was caught between these two zones of agony – the American and Russian, like in the Cold War – and I didn't know what to do or where to put my mind to stop it hurting.

I tried transcending, like Grigory said he did in Moscow, by just staring at the very top of the Eiffel Tower and sending my thoughts to that and then attempting to imagine Monsieur Eiffel in his workshop with all his hundreds and hundreds of fantastic drawings and calculations. But it was difficult to eat and transcend at the same time, and whenever a waiter came to the American table (which one very often did because Gene and the other bankers ordered more and more bottles of wine and water and iced Coke and bread and extra cutlery) he got in the way of my view of the Tower and all my concentration was lost.

Then suddenly Grigory pushed back his chair and stood up. There was a half-full bottle of red wine on the table between him and Valentina and with a sweep of his huge hand he knocked it over and the wine splashed all over the table and on to Valentina's dress and her broken arm in its sling. He yelled at her, one last insult or accusation in Russian, then pushed his way out of the restaurant and strode away up the Avenue Montaigne and out of sight.

Valentina grabbed the Badoit bottle and poured water on to her dress and began rubbing it with a table napkin. 'Damn him!' she said. 'That Grisha just doesn't know how to behave . . .'

Alice got up and went out and I saw her start to run after Grigory. Next to me, the Americans had stopped slagging off England for two seconds and were staring at Valentina, who had begun to cry. A waiter arrived with a clean tablecloth, but Valentina pushed him away. 'Laissez!' she yelled at him.

I felt immobilised in my Cold War zone. I just gaped at everything, like at a bomb landing far away. But then I instructed myself to move and I went round to Valentina's side of the table and put my hand on her shoulder. 'Don't cry,' I said. 'I expect it's only a jealous rage. If I was your lover, I'd get in jealous rages, Valentina.'

Valentina blew her nose on her napkin and smiled at me. 'Would you, Lewis?' she said. 'But with Grisha, it's more than jealousy. He wants my life.'

'What do you mean, he "wants your life"?'

'He would like to have my life here in Paris, so all he ever does is criticise me for it and try to make me feel guilty. He is so envious, I think he could kill me!'

'Do you mean really kill you?'

'Yes, I do. And in some way I understand him. My life is like a ghost haunting his own. He would like to be free of this ghost.'

I stroked Valentina's hair. I noticed that just by her temple there were a few grey strands in among the blonde and I thought she might like to do something about them, so I said, 'There's a bit of grey here, Valentina. Only a tiny bit.'

'I know, darling,' she said. 'I'm getting old.'

'No, you're not. But the next time you go to the hairdressers, you could ask them to dye these bits, couldn't you?'

'Yes. I will. Now, Lewis, you go and get the bill, sweetheart. I want to go home.'

While we waited for the bill, Alice came back and sat down. She said nothing to Valentina and Valentina said nothing to her. The animosity between them was becoming like a cancer or something, growing quietly all the time.

The next day Babba didn't arrive. Usually, she was in the apartment by ten, every day except Saturday and Sunday, but this was a Tuesday and there was no sign of her.

I sat in the kitchen, writing a collection of crazy thoughts in my Concorde notebook, and sort of waiting for Babba. I tried to imagine what Babba was doing or thinking. I wondered if there was a voodoo temple in Paris somewhere, in someone's basement or cellar, and if Babba and Pozzi were on their way to it now with offerings for the spirits, or whether they were just calmly existing at home, doing their washing or making their beds or sitting still and crying for the lost motorbike.

I was drinking Orangina. I could feel this day getting hotter and more stifling than any we'd had. It had got difficult to imagine rain falling ever again. When I thought about winter, it felt like something that had last occurred when I was five.

Valentina came into the kitchen at eleven-thirty. She was beautifully dressed in white and black with her arm in the 'Ypres' scarf and smelling of her favourite scent, *Giorgio*. I knew she was going out, so I said I'd come with her. I loved walking along the street in the slipstream of her perfume.

'All right, darling,' she said, 'but I'm not going far. Later I've got to go to the hospital for an X-ray on my arm, but first I must see Grisha. He's meant to do interviews at RTL and France Info this morning – to talk about his little book – so I must make sure these have gone OK. I will take him to lunch at the Plaza. My poor Grisha! All I can do is buy him meals. I don't know what else is to be done for him.'

'He could just stay on in Paris . . .' I suggested.

'It's not that simple. It never is that simple. And who would care for Irina?'

I closed my Concorde book and got Sergei's lead. I wished Valentina was taking *me* to lunch at the Plaza. Before we left, I went to see Alice, who was working at her word processor. These days, she was either working in her room or out at some unknown destination and I hadn't had a proper conversation with her since we discussed the inseparable canaries.

When I said goodbye to her she turned and looked at me and said, 'Are you all right?' as if she'd suddenly remembered I was part of her life, and yet her look was sort of distracted and far away. And I had an embarrassing moment of my old Elroy longing. If Elroy had been there, ready for action with his beret on, I would have said to him: 'Your mission is to infiltrate Alice's heart.'

The Hôtel de Venise, where Grisha was staying, was nearby. I wished it had been miles away on the other side of Paris, so that Valentina and I could have walked along, side by side, for the whole morning.

When we got there, I saw that it was quite a smart-looking place. It had little trees outside and red awnings over some of the windows. I looked up at these awnings and wondered which room Grigory was in and whether the room and the mini-bar and the guest bathrobes and everything made him feel more suicidal or less.

And it was then that the moment came.

Certain moments in a life are in another tense: they are *going to become*. And only when you get to that other tense do they reveal to you what they were and what they meant, and then you know that one moment is responsible for everything that came afterwards and you think, if only I had understood what was going to happen and prevented it . . .

It was just after Valentina said goodbye. First she leaned down, like she'd so often done before, and put a kiss on my head, and I smelled her perfume and her lipstick and her soft hair with its tiny fingers of grey. And then she went into the revolving door of the Hôtel de Venise, wearing her smart black-and-white dress, and as the door revolved with her in it she turned and waved at me and then she was gone.

And that was the moment: *Valentina goes into the door and the door keeps turning, revolving anticlockwise, and the door is taking her away, but just before it does she remembers me outside on the pavement with Sergei and she turns. She turns and she waves . . .*

That was the moment – before it went into its new tense. But I didn't know it then.

Part Two

The day was so hot and bright, you imagined the roads might melt.

I decided I'd take Sergei to the river, down by the Pont Neuf where people fish and read and lie in the sun. I'd buy us some bread and salami and we could dream the day away where it was cool by the water. I knew from the way he whimpered in his sleep that Sergei had vivid dreams.

Going along the Quai du Louvre, I stopped in front of the bouquiniste who had sold me *Le Grand Meaulnes*. Just like the time before, he was chatting with the other stall holders and I thought, this is how the bouquinistes like to spend their lives, not trying to sell books, but just talking and talking. When he looked up and saw me, he nodded at me, as if he remembered me. I said bonjour to him and then I thought, it wasn't me he remembered, it was Sergei. If you're out with Sergei in a smart city, it's like you're Arthur Miller and Sergei's Marilyn Monroe.

Hugh's letter had made me feel guilty about buying only one book, so I was consciously searching for something, not just drizzling my eye over a row of spines like the tourists do. And I alighted on the title *Crime et châtiment*. I both knew and didn't know what the book was, and then when it was in my hand I decided I had known all along that of course it was *Crime and Punishment* by Dostoevsky.

I told Sergei to sit. It was very seldom that he obeyed me. When he did obey me, he looked embarrassed, as if he'd done something only a stupid puppy would do.

While I looked at the book, he looked at it too, with his tongue lolling out, as if *Crime and Punishment* were a slab of meat. It was an edition dated 1957. It had a battered old cover on it, with a garish drawing of a man coming into a room holding an axe. And as soon as I had it in my hands, I felt a panicky longing to own it. Maybe this had something to do with the axe. I wanted to start reading it straight away.

Warning Sergei not to move, I took the book to the stall holder and began digging out my money. While he searched for an old paper bag, he said: 'It was *Le Grand Meaulnes* last time, wasn't it?'

'Yes,' I said. 'I'm working on an English translation.'

'That's a grand idea. Grand. But it's too sad for my liking, that book.'

'Is it still sad at the end?'

'Yes, mon petit. It's still sad at the end.'

He handed me *Crime and Punishment* wrapped in a bag from Prisunic and I paid him fifty-nine francs. If you're a writer, I thought, you can't ever predict where your work is going to end up or what it will be wrapped in.

In the night, after beginning to read *Crime and Punishment*, I had a dream about Raskolnikov and I woke up sweating. I didn't know whether, in the nightmare, I'd been Raskolnikov or his intended victim, Alëna Ivanovna. For a moment, it seemed to me as if everything in my attic room was yellow and I felt suffocated and sick.

I drank some water, got my torch, then opened my bathroom window and climbed out on to the roof. I thought there might be a night breeze up there, but the air was so hot and heavy, it seemed to weigh my body down.

I climbed past the maid's room, where the curtain was still drawn across the dormer, and out on to the plateau where the tanks were. Part of me was still in my dream of St Petersburg, so for a few minutes the sight of the city below me, with all its sickly orange light, made me feel uneasy. I walked round and round to calm myself, taking deep breaths of the stifling air.

Then I crouched down. I often found this position comforting and I'd noticed that Didier did too. Even on a ledge, he'd sometimes crouch and I thought, that's the bird part of him, waiting to fly.

I began to recall the last conversation I'd had with him, about existentialism. I hadn't told him what Valentina had said about nobody being an existentialist any more, because I didn't want him to feel embarrassed. I guess that sometimes people hang on to things long after everyone else has kicked them into darkness and dust.

We'd been working on slate hanging. As I hammered in my pins, feeling mildly brilliant, like a proper roofer, Didier had said: 'How do you imagine God, Louis?'

I said: 'I don't imagine Him at all.'

He looked pleased about this, like it was a bond between us. Then he said: 'When most people imagine God, they think of him as a kind of artisan, like a toy-maker. They may not realise it, but they do. There God sits in his workshop, making us, his toys.'

I asked Didier if God's place of work was considered to be the Palais Royal toy-shop, and he laughed. He said I was getting to know Paris quite well and might not want to go back to Devon. And I said I was planning never to go back to Devon but to stay in the rue Rembrandt for the rest of time.

He made no comment, just stared at me for a moment, then continued on about God. 'If we imagine God as the toy-maker,' he said, 'then we assume that, with each individual toy, God knows *in advance of its creation* what the essence of that toy is going to be. Certain essential characteristics of that toy are set down before its existence begins. OK?'

I'd told Didier at this point that Hugh, who wants very much to believe in God and is annoyed by all the evidence against His existence, probably thought of himself as 'made' by Him.

'Exactly,' said Didier. 'So it is a crude idea, but you see how it approximates to what people imagine? And what the existentialists are saying is that God is not a toy-maker. There *is* no toy-maker! Therefore the individual has no *prior essence* before he begins his life. He floats out of some primal soup and tries to become something. We become this or that and then we die and that is all. And we can't excuse our failings by saying we were made in such and such a way. Because there was no hand to make us.'

Didier didn't look at me much as he talked, but just concentrated on his slates and I concentrated on mine and I felt glad he was telling me something interesting (even if Valentina would mock it), because I had a sudden scary vision of the void beyond the cage behind me and how falling through the air is one of the things that human beings seriously dread and pray to God – even if they don't believe in God – will never happen.

And then I asked Didier if this was why he called himself 'the Bird' – like he had to *believe* he was a bird – to stop himself being afraid, not just of falling, but of being nothing in a chaotic universe. What he said was: 'I'm always afraid, Louis. Always. All the time.'

Now I began to feel easier in my stomach, crouched there on the roof, and after a while I went to explore what was going on inside the scaffolding cage. I climbed down and inspected the slates I'd helped to hang. I touched them to see if they were stable and they were and I felt suddenly quite proud of them, like I wanted to put my initials on them for posterity: LL. I moved my light along the whole section, to see how much further Didier had got, and I was surprised to find that he'd hardly got any further at all. It was pretty clear to me from this that he hadn't been at work for at least a couple of days.

The last time I'd been on the roof in the middle of the night, I'd enjoyed thinking of Valentina asleep underneath my feet, but on this night I knew she wasn't there. Alice and I had had supper on our own and Alice had said, 'I wonder what's happened to Valentina.' I'd said, 'Yes, I wonder.' But I thought

I knew where she was, I thought I could guess. She was in the Hôtel de Venise. I could imagine the room and the double bed and Valentina's black-and-white dress laid on a chair. I could see Grisha's big hands stroking her bottom and his shaggy head lying on her shoulder. And I thought that the row they'd had with the spilt wine and everything would probably make this night even sweeter for them and in the morning neither of them would want to leave.

I climbed back up to the water tank and sat down, with my back to it. I could feel the great mass of water inside it, waiting.

The next day, I sat in the kitchen, like I'd done the day before, waiting for Babba, and the hands of the kitchen clock went round. I thought, now Grigory and Valentina are ordering room service. A trolley is going to come loaded down with croissants and pains au chocolat and Valentina will stuff them all into herself while Grisha watches her. Under his guest bathrobe, he will be starting to get another erection . . .

Sergei sat with me. He knew we were waiting for something and at every little sound in the apartment he pricked up his ears. In my Concorde notebook, I was making desultory notes for a letter to Hugh. Long ago, he'd said to me: 'Never write thoughtless letters, Lewis. Make notes first of what you want to say.' So far I'd written: *Bought C and Punishment from bouquinistes. Started to read. Brilliant beginning.* Then I stopped.

I couldn't think of anything else I wanted to tell Hugh, because everything else was too difficult to explain and anyway my thoughts weren't centred on this supposed letter, but on Babba dancing in her voodoo cellar and on Valentina fucking Grisha in the Hôtel de Venise. I thought, there is a disparity between what is meant to be in the mind of a thirteen-year-old boy from Devon and what is actually in it.

No one came. The clock hands just kept moving and Sergei and I kept on sitting there with our ears on red alert. Then I thought, perhaps Babba has a telephone number – even in her horrible mosaic building there must be telephones, unlike the village I imagined in Benin, which wasn't connected to the outside world in any way whatsoever.

I went into Valentina's study, to look for her address book. Sergei followed me, wagging his tail, as if I was going to manufacture a strawberry tart out of Valentina's Filofax.

I found a number. The entry in the book, under 'B', said: Babba – voir Mme Sibour. I picked up Valentina's portable phone and dialled. While the number rang, I thought, I hope Babba is known as Babba in her building and not by some fantastic African name with an ancient meaning that she's never told us.

But no one answered.

I sat down at Valentina's desk, in front of her computer screen. I noticed there was dust on the screen and I began to wonder how the apartment would get cleaned if Babba never came back. The only cleaning I'd seen Valentina do was emptying ashtrays.

The computer was a Power Macintosh 7500, a kind of parent to the one I had at home. It was second nature to me to lean forward and switch it on and my hand rested naturally on the mouse and began to move it around. I scrolled through Valentina's file titles and I could tell that she was fond of codifying, because a lot of the titles were just acronyms. One of these was APAL and others were JOPRI and GOH and IRIN and MASP. I was searching for her new novel. I knew the title in English was *For the Love of Isabelle*, but on the first scroll through I couldn't find it. I thought at least the word Isabelle would be there, but it wasn't.

I reminded myself to think in French. None of Valentina's acronyms would relate to English words. As I clicked the mouse, I remembered banging down her silver clothes brush when I realised she wouldn't use me as her secretary and I thought how wise she'd been not to hire me when I couldn't even make sense of her file titles.

The novel was there, of course. It took me about four minutes to find it. It was listed under the acronym POLAMI, which unravelled as *Pour l'amour d'Isabelle* and up on to the screen came page 201 of the text. When I saw it appear, I felt very slightly and stupidly triumphant, like when I'd found my stolen football at the car-boot sale.

I ran the fast-scroll back to the beginning and began to read. With *Crime et châtiment* I had to look words up in the dictionary all the time, but Valentina's prose was quite a bit more simple than Dostoevsky's. She'd learned something from him, though, and this was that novels have to have a good beginning or the bored old orang-utan readers just lay them aside and reach for something to play with or stare up at whatever happens to be passing in the sky.

And her beginning was OK. It described Isabelle's thoughts and feelings the night before her marriage to her fiancé, Pierre, the Duke of Belfort. For some reason, Isabelle is having a calligraphy lesson (as if there used to be medieval evening classes), and as she writes all her beautiful words she keeps glancing round at her wedding dress on a stand in the room, and this wedding dress is made of silver and weighs as much as a suit of chain mail. '*And in Isabelle's heart, too, there was just such a terrible weight. She knew that from the moment when she put on the dress her happy life would be over.*'

Then you see why she feels all this. Pierre comes in and interrupts the calligraphy lesson. And Pierre is gross. He's a duke and an aristocrat, but he looks like a kind of crazy idiot, with mad bloodshot eyes and greasy hair and little tics and twitches that make his face and body jerk around. He tries to kiss Isabelle and when he does this '*through all her body came a chill, like the chill of winter, like the chill of death*'. From this moment, you're on Isabelle's side and I thought, that's one of the important things in a novel – you have to be on someone's side.

The next day, the wedding takes place. You hope, at the last minute, something is going to prevent it, but nothing does prevent it and so there it is, Isabelle with her beautiful handwriting is married to Pierre who is so uncoordinated he can barely write his name. On the wedding night, Pierre is drunk, so at least Isabelle doesn't have to get fucked by him; not yet anyway. He passes out on the bedroom floor and she goes to sleep alone in a carved bed covered with furs.

Meanwhile, down in the old city of Belfort, a certain Barthélémy, handsome son of an apothecary, is working on a potion 'to cure sadness', ordered that day by the calligraphy teacher. The following morning, Barthélémy arrives with the potion at the Duke's residence and sees, at her window, Isabelle, the most beautiful woman he's ever glimpsed in twenty-six years of existence . . .

I read for quite a long time. Not once did I think, I'd rather be looking at the sky. And it wasn't just that I was enjoying Valentina's story. Getting into other people's computer files is quite a sexy thing: like you've started to undress their thoughts.

I closed the POLAMI file only when the narrator started going on about medieval time. Then I decided to surf through the file bank, starting with APAL, which was the first title on the list. The text of APAL was just coming up when I heard the door open behind me. I knew it couldn't be Valentina, who would have come in noisily, so it had to be Alice, and it was.

'What are you doing?' she said.

I turned and looked at her, then straight away looked back at the screen. These days, I was getting cold with Alice; I was giving her a chill of winter, a chill of death. 'Writing a letter,' I said.

'Did Valentina give you permission to use her computer?'

'Yup.'

Then I had a bad shock. I spoke to the mouse in my mind: Get me out of here fast! Because I'd suddenly seen what APAL was I arrowed the Close Box, clicked it and got a blank screen. My heart was pounding. I accessed a new file and wrote at speed: *Dear Dad, Bought Crime et châtiment from the bouquinistes. Brilliant beginning.* I knew that Alice must have noticed me get out of an existing file and into a new one, but she didn't say anything, only came a bit nearer to me, so that I could smell that she was wearing perfume – a thing she hardly ever did. And the perfume reminded me of home, of evenings when Alice and Hugh would go out to dinner and I'd be alone with my homework and my chess and my favourite TV shows.

'OK,' said Alice after a moment in which she read the two pitiful lines of my letter to Hugh but made no comment on them, 'I'm going out for a bit. Is there anything you want?'

'Where are you *going?*' I almost said. '*What is happening in this house?*' But all I did was shake my head.

As soon as I heard the apartment door close on Alice, I put a Save lock on my letter and clicked open APAL.

It was like an essay that hadn't reached its end. And the essay had one prime subject and that subject was Alice. The acronym APAL stood for *A propos d'Alice Little.*

I began reading, translating as I went. It wasn't the kind of essay you whistled right through.

It started by describing Alice's beauty as 'a fatal thing'. It wondered if 'like Daphne she will get so tired of it, she will pray to be turned into a hedge'. It said nothing about Valentina's own fantastic snow-queen beauty – like it didn't recognise she had any – but only kept marvelling at how people in the street and in restaurants and everywhere kept craning their necks to get a glimpse of Alice. It was like a version of my *Exploding Peanut Theory.* It described a cyclist in the rue Saint-Ferdinand falling off his bicycle as Alice turned the corner towards him. He had a bag of apples tied on to his handlebars and the apples all rolled away into the gutter.

And then it said this: 'The first fatality now occurs. The poor handsome roofer appears to have made the (existential!) choice to die of love for Alice Little. And, of course, the dying will be long, will be painful, and in our hearts we will sympathise, but in our heads we will say: "How extremely foolish. What more foolish thing could this young man possibly have done?"'

I was staring moronically at this last paragraph and getting a kind of pain in me, like I'd swallowed a stone, when the telephone on the desk did something of its own accord: it rang. Sometimes, when life feels intense, you forget the function of ordinary things; you can find yourself surprised that the wind moves the trees.

It was Hugh.

I couldn't have a conversation with Hugh in front of the words I'd just read on the computer screen, so I took the portable phone into the salon and sat down in a square of sunlight. As Hugh talked, I realised I was listening for something in the background and that something was the sea.

He asked me how I was and then *where* I was, so I told him I was on my own in the salon with Sergei and *Crime et châtiment*. I didn't tell him what I'd just seen. I didn't tell him that I was alone a lot of the time and that now I knew the reason why. When he asked if Babba was a 'chess friend' I almost said yes because the idea of telling Hugh about the real Babba suddenly wore me out. But I told him nevertheless.

'So,' he said sadly, 'your only friend is the maid?'

'No . . .' I said.

At this point, Grandma Gwyneth came on the line. She said they'd all just been into Sidmouth to buy Bertie a panama hat and that the hat made him look very jaunty and dashing, even at his age. I said, 'How are my chess men?' and Gwyneth said, 'Still black, still white. All lined up, ready and waiting, sweetheart.' And then the subject of the hut came along, as I knew it would.

Hugh got back on the line and said: 'I wish you could see it, Lewis. Bertie's helping me now. We've become bricklaying junkies.'

'Is it tall?' I asked.

'Wait and see.'

'Is it still just a hut, or is it a garden house?'

'Oh, it's more than just a hut. We've ordered the weather vane. And now tell me, how is Mum?'

I felt a silence come. I listened and listened for the sea, but couldn't hear it. Then I stammered on about Alice working very hard. I told Hugh that she was only out of the apartment now because she'd gone to get books she needed from the library.

'Which library?' he asked.

'Oh,' I said, 'the Bibliothèque Nationale.'

'Ah,' he said, 'the BN. Those little green reading lamps!'

I changed the subject to the bison and the philosophical question of a bison's ability to recollect a life it's never lived. Hugh said categorically: 'Bison have no imagination, Lewis.' He didn't want the subject changed. He wanted a rundown on Alice's life. Was she overworking? Why had she written only one letter home? Was Valentina bullying her? Was it hard for her to concentrate in the hot weather?

I reassured Hugh that Alice's room was cool because of the air conditioning and the heavy curtains at the window, like theatre curtains with gold tassels, and that no one was bullying her except me: I had tried to bully her into buying a pair of birds and she had refused, like the sensible woman she was. And then I heard my father laugh and I remembered suddenly that I liked this sound and that when I was a child I'd often thought, if Dad is laughing, then everything's OK and the nuclear bomb won't be dropped on Devon tonight.

Then I said a surprising thing. After I'd said it, I couldn't believe I had. I asked Hugh if he could send Elroy.

I refused to think about Alice.

I closed the APAL file and sat at the desk, waiting for Valentina. But no one came and nothing stirred or changed or happened.

Later, I got through to Madame Sibour. She spoke French as though she had loose false teeth. She said: 'Qui c'est, Babba?'

I tried to explain what she looked like, but my descriptive powers fizzled out and Madame Sibour decided I was a nuisance caller and hung up. Afterwards, I thought, why didn't I mention

Pozzi and the bike? Those were the *prime* identifiers and I never used them.

I called again, but now the phone just rang and rang and rang and I imagined all the residents of the purple building – including Madame Sibour – huddled in the basement, decorating their makeshift voodoo shrines.

It was still only early afternoon, but to me it felt as though it should be time to get ready for supper. I ate three shrimp vol-au-vents from the fridge and drank a litre of Orangina. Then I set out with Sergei for the Hôtel de Venise.

I felt, as I walked, that it was a long time since I'd talked to anyone, so this was what I was going to say to Valentina: 'I don't want to interrupt your days of love, but I'm lonely.' I thought both Valentina and Grisha would understand because they were Russians and would be capable of remembering what loneliness was, even in summer. In Valentina's only recollection of life in Russia, she might have been standing in that prickly maize field all alone.

When we got to the hotel, I hung about on the pavement, watching people going in and coming out, turning like weather-dolls in the revolving door. Then I walked round the building, hoping Valentina would lean out of a window and see me. The thought that she was there somewhere in the hotel and would eventually come out – if I waited long enough – began to console me.

She didn't appear. I sat down on the pavement, with my back to a Volkswagen, and Sergei lay down beside me. I stroked his head. I don't know how much time passed with me sitting, leaning against that car. It was like I dozed or something and then woke up because I saw that the sky was going that deep-blue colour that it goes here just before the night comes, and all the lights in the hotel were suddenly on.

My next thought was that Valentina was probably back at the rue Rembrandt by now, except that she couldn't have come out of the hotel without seeing me, so she had to be inside still and planning to stay another night in Grisha's room, and I thought, I don't want her to stay another night; I want her to sit on my bed and whisper her secret thoughts to me while I curve my foot, under the bedclothes, round the contours of her arse.

I saw that it would be difficult for Sergei to go round in the revolving door, it wasn't the right dimensions for him, so I tied him to one of the little trees outside the hotel and went in.

The desk person was a woman with long fingernails that she started tapping on the desk the moment I spoke to her. I asked her to call up the room of Monsieur Panin and she went away to look up the room number. At my elbow were some smart young blond Australian men in pale suits with tartan luggage. They smelled of men's perfume and their smiles were as wide as coral reefs and I could tell the woman with the fingernails wanted to get back to the desk to deal with them and not with me.

She came back fast. She flashed her own nice smile at the Australians and said to me in English: 'Mr Panin has checked out.'

'Are you sure?' I asked. 'When did he check out?'

She sighed. Sighed and tapped. Then she went to a little computer under the desk and punched something in. I saw her staring at the screen. She came back and said: 'He left yesterday evening.'

I knew this couldn't be right. I looked all around the lobby, like I expected Grisha to be there, so that I could point him out to this nail woman. Then I said: 'Are you saying Mr Panin didn't stay in this hotel last night?' But she ignored me. She'd moved on to the Australians, who were going to be housed in suites with sitting rooms and conference facilities. I moved away from the desk and sat down in an armchair. My eyes kept swivelling round at everyone who passed, hoping to see Grisha or Valentina. I thought, OK, I need some kind of strategy.

I waited till the nail person went away for a moment, then I went up to a man at the desk – young and in a green uniform – and said: 'What room number do you have for Monsieur

Panin?' He went to the computer to check, just like the woman had done, then returned and said: 'We do not have any Monsieur Panin.'

'Yes, you do,' I said. 'Monsieur Grigory Panin from Russia.'

He checked with the computer again. If you work in a hotel, you don't have to hold anything in your brain any more: you just ask the computer. I thought, one day, everybody in the Western world will have brains the size of Brussels sprouts. He came back shaking his head. 'No,' he said. 'No Monsieur Panin.'

'When did he leave, please?' I asked. The young man shrugged and at that moment the Nail returned and saw me still there. She scowled at me, but I didn't let the scowl affect me. 'This is extremely important,' I said. 'I have to talk to Mr Panin and I know he's here. It may be possible that he's registered under the name of Gavril.'

The Nail tapped again at the computer. She and the young green man stared at it and shook their heads. 'No,' said the Nail. 'No Gavril.'

'OK,' I said. 'What room *was* Monsieur Panin in? Please could you call that room. This is very urgent.'

Tap, tap, went her hands. The colour of her nails was scarlet. 'Number 257,' she said at last, 'and there is a new guest in that room.'

'Could you call it anyway?'

'No,' she said. 'I cannot call it. Monsieur Panin got a taxi to the airport at three-thirty yesterday afternoon.'

Alice was in when I got home. She was lying on the Louis XVI couch, listening to a Francis Cabrel song. In the soft lamplight, I noticed that the freckles on her face had become more dense, as though she'd spent all day out in a cornfield. I thought, she's maybe going to break Hugh's heart and Didier's and even scores of others' – but not mine.

I gave Sergei his supper and then came and sat beside Alice.

I waited for the CD to end, then I said: 'I want you to listen to me, Alice. Something's happened to Valentina.'

Alice turned her head lazily towards me and looked at me with her clever eyes. 'What do you mean?' she said.

I told her I didn't know yet exactly what had occurred. I said: 'I have a theory.' Alice was about to get up. She was going to put the music on again, but I stopped her. Then I said: 'I think Grigory Panin captured her and made her go back to Russia with him.'

Alice threw back her thorny head. She was going to roar with laughter, but I put my hand over her mouth.

'Don't!' I said. 'Don't laugh.'

She looked at me tenderly, like I was her baby again. She touched my hand. 'Lewis,' she said. 'You worry about everything too much. You imagine things. Remember the German fighter pilot you thought was living in the cellar?'

'I'm not imagining this. I went to the hotel where I last saw Valentina. She was going to have lunch with Grigory yesterday. That's all she told me. Grigory left for Moscow yesterday at three-thirty.'

'So? Valentina went on somewhere else. Perhaps she has a lover?'

'Grisha is her lover.'

Alice got up then. I didn't try to stop her. She went to one of the tall windows and looked out, turning her head this way and that, as though she were expecting Valentina to come walking along the street in the next minute.

I told her this wasn't going to happen. I said: 'You can stand there all night and she won't come.'

Alice looked round at me. 'Why are you so sure?' she asked.

'Because,' I said, 'something has happened to her. Just as I've told you.'

Alice took me out to supper. She chose a Vietnamese restaurant with black tablecloths where the air smelled of ginger and the beer was served with limes. She let me drink the lime-scented beer. It was like she'd forgotten I was thirteen and me.

Then she began talking about the Vietnam war. She said: 'That was the moment when language changed.'

In the bright pencil lights above our table, Alice's hair looked tangled. A Vietnamese hummingbird might have liked it for a nest. 'What do you mean, "language changed"?' I said.

'I think it dates from then. When the Americans came back from the war, their sentences were mined with expletives: fucking this and fucking that. If you're in a war you don't understand, no doubt you begin to swear at everything because swearing is an expression of inarticulate rage. And then that way of speaking just passed into common usage – first there, in the States, then in Britain.'

I said I imagined people had always sworn, especially in Scotland, but Alice said, 'Yes, but not like they do now. These days it's as if swearing is the skeleton of the language, the thing that holds it together.'

I was eating chicken pieces with green chillies and some kind of nuts and my nose felt as if it was on fire. I said: 'It means the rage went on when the war ended, does it?'

'Yes. Of course the rage went on. We're not just in a war we don't understand. We're in a *life* we don't understand.'

I was silent for a few seconds. Then I said: 'Yes. I suppose we are.'

In the night, I went down to Valentina's bedroom and got into her bed. The sheets were silky and cool and the pillow smelled of the wallflower night cream. I lay in the dark and waited.

After a little while, Valentina came in and undressed silently and the light from the street fell on to her blonde hair and on to her fat arse as she pulled down her cream satin knickers. My penis was erect and I whispered to her: 'You'll soon understand, Valentina, that I will always be ready and waiting.'

She slithered into the bed and took me into her arms. I attached my mouth to one of her big rosy nipples and sucked like a babe and a little moisture came out of her breast and trickled down my throat. Then I rolled over on to her and she put me inside her and said: 'Now, darling, let's see if you can do this like a grown-up,' and no sooner had she said that than I lost consciousness and felt my body fly to heaven.

When I woke, everything was just as it had been when I went to bed, except for the damp in my sheets and the beginnings of morning light at my round window. For a moment, I thought I really had gone down to Valentina's room and that she really had come back and got into bed with me. Then my next thought was: she's there now. If I go down now, at four o'clock, she will be there, she will have come back.

Her bedroom door was closed. I knocked on it softly, thinking it was a shame to wake her when she must be tired from wherever she'd been, but continuing to knock all the same. There was no answer, so I went in.

The room was empty. On the bed was the big pile of cushions that lay there in the daytime and with which she'd propped herself up when she got back from the hospital.

I didn't go to the bed, but just stood staring at the cushions. An old-fashioned silver clock on the mantelpiece ticked away another fragment of time. I calculated that it was now forty-one hours since Valentina had been in the apartment. Forty-one hours and at supper Alice had refused to talk about it, absolutely refused. She said I was whirling off into fantasy. She reminded me that my imaginary German fighter pilot had supposedly slept wrapped in his parachute, and lived on grass. I reminded her that I was seven then, or even six, when I believed all that, but she said, 'It makes no difference. You've always had a nervous imagination. Perhaps you'll become a writer.'

The curtains in Valentina's room hadn't been drawn. I sat down on a little chair and watched all the furniture creep out of the darkness, as though something or someone were displacing it by magic. I put Valentina on the hill of Montmartre, still wearing her black-and-white dress and her 'Ypres' scarf, and tried to displace her with the power of my will. Step by step, I brought her nearer to me. Down she came, down the winding streets as the cafés opened and people began going to work, down through flurries of pigeons, down through light and shadow, walking on her high heels right across Paris and back into my life.

At breakfast I told Alice I thought we should go to the police and report a missing person. She said she didn't think Valentina would want us to do that yet; it would be embarrassing for her when she came home.

Just as she said this, the telephone rang and I ran to it, thinking I was going to hear Valentina's voice, but when I picked it up there was no one there. I kept saying 'Hello, hello', like a moron: 'Hello, hello, hello . . .' There was something at the other end, a not-quite-silence, as if a voice were trying to make itself heard from deep underneath the sea.

When ten o'clock came, I waited for Babba. I thought, if Babba comes to work, then everything may be all right. But she didn't come. So I said to Sergei: 'Right, I've had enough of waiting. Now we're going to begin the search.'

I told Alice I would be out most of the day. She smiled and said: 'When you come in, Valentina will be here. We'll make dinner for you.'

Before leaving, I checked the roof and discovered that Didier was back. 'Where were you?' I asked.

'Oh,' he said, 'ill. I had a summer flu.'

I stared at him. He didn't look pale. He looked as if he'd been lying in a boat on the lake in the Bois de Boulogne with Alice Little.

'How are you, Louis?' he said.

'I'm reading *Crime et châtiment*,' I said. 'I think Raskolnikov's a kind of existentialist, isn't he?'

'Yes,' said Didier. 'Of course. He takes absolute responsibility for what he does.'

'Is it easier for an existentialist to commit a crime – or do something bad – than for other people?'

Didier put his glasses back on. 'No,' he said. 'It's harder. Because he cannot pass on his guilt. He must endure it all alone.'

I looked hard at Didier. 'Why does Raskolnikov put the money he finds under a stone?' I said.

Didier smiled. 'Do you want me to tell you,' he asked, 'or do you want to find out for yourself?'

I said I'd find out for myself. I was going to explain about the stealer at school and how I enjoyed tracking him, but all I said was: 'I like mysteries. I like solving things. And I'm good at it.'

I knew that the only person I knew who really cared about Valentina – apart from me – was Mrs Gavrilovich. So this was where I went first, to her apartment in the rue Daru.

When the concierge opened the street door, she smelled of drink and her eyes were wet, as if the drink had been making her cry, but she let me in without any fuss because she recognised Sergei and began crooning over him and stroking his head. I thought, now I'm Arthur Miller again.

The flat was on the ground floor, so that Mrs Gavrilovich would never have to walk up any stairs, and on every windowsill were pots of red geraniums. As soon as she saw me, she put a watering can into my hands. 'Louis,' she said, 'you have answered my prayers. Water the flowers.'

There was a fusty smell in the apartment, strongest in Mrs Gavrilovich's bedroom, where there was a little altar set up in front of an icon in a heavy silver frame. Red candles were burning there and a prayer book with an ivory cover lay on an embroidered shawl. Plastic flowers had been arranged in a red glass vase and near to this was a photograph of Mr Gavrilovich. The face of the icon was sad and thin, with a halo like a cymbal banged against the head.

I did all the watering and then I sat down with Mrs Gavrilovich at a table covered with hand-embroidered lace. She poured me a glass of home-made lemonade and offered me some little dry cakes that smelled of some peculiar spice. She seemed to have all these things prepared, as if she'd been expecting me.

I waited. The lemonade was very cold and sweet and the cakes were full of caraway seed. Mrs Gavrilovich nibbled a cake carefully, nursing her broken teeth. I prayed she was going to tell me she knew where Valentina was, but all she said was: 'This heat, I think it's going to kill me, Louis. I never remember any summer in Paris quite like this.'

'Yes,' I said. 'It never seems to rain.'

'No. Never rains any more. God has forgotten the flowers. But when I first came to Paris, it rained like the devil all through the summer, day after day. You ask Valentina. She remembers that long time of rain.'

I put down the cake I was eating and looked up at Mrs Gavrilovich. 'I can't ask Valentina,' I said. 'She hasn't been home for two days.'

Sergei had found a butterfly on the windowsill. Now I saw him catch it in his mouth and eat it, wings and all. Mrs Gavrilovich saw this too and looked shocked. Perhaps she'd never seen the stuff Sergei could gobble up from the Paris gutters? I was about to smack him for eating the butterfly when Mrs Gavrilovich said: 'Where is Valentina, Louis?'

I explained about the visit to Grigory Panin's hotel. I had to repeat everything twice because she found my accent difficult to understand.

Eventually, she said: 'You know he is mad, that poor Grigory, mad with suffering. A man who is mad with suffering is capable of anything.'

We sat there opposite each other, not speaking for a moment, imagining the kind of things a mad suffering man might do. Sergei noticed the stillness in the room and looked at us anxiously while the butterfly began its journey through his intestines.

Then Mrs Gavrilovich got up. 'I am going to telephone Moscow,' she said. She put on her glasses to search for Grigory's number.

While she searched, I noticed that her room was untidy, with newspapers lying about and her embroidery silks strewn over the arms of the chairs and candle grease on the surfaces of tables.

Mrs Gavrilovich found Grigory's number and began dialling. I didn't know exactly what the time was in Moscow, but I wondered if it was the hour when Grisha's wife Irina started her drinking for the day.

It was Irina Mrs Gavrilovich was speaking to. I thought I could be sure of this because she spoke gently, like she was talking to a child, and with Grisha she probably would have been angry. I sat still and listened to the Russian language. If I closed my eyes, it was Valentina I could hear, talking Russian in the Mercedes on the way to Les Rosiers.

When Mrs Gavrilovich put the phone down, she said: 'Well, Valentina isn't in Moscow, not as far as we can tell. That was Grisha's wife, Irina. She says Grisha returned, like he planned, on the evening flight. She says what he wanted to talk about were the roast quail he had eaten for lunch at the Plaza.'

I was about to say that if Grisha had taken Valentina to Moscow, he wouldn't have brought her home to Irina, he would have booked her into a hotel, but I didn't. I just kept quiet while Mrs Gavrilovich began to search for something in her untidy room, looking behind cushions and in half-open drawers, as if she suddenly thought Valentina had become tiny and might be found under a pile of embroidery silks. Sergei and I watched her and waited, Sergei licking his mouth after his gourmet meal of the butterfly. The thing Mrs Gavrilovich was searching for was a blue shawl, and when she found it she put it over her head and said she was going to church. It was time for a Vigil.

She invited me to come with her. She said that in church we would think about what to do. She told me that when she lived in the slaughterhouse at La Villette, she used to make pilgrimages to the Nevsky church whenever she could afford the métro ticket; it was her place of refuge and from it she got the courage to start the *café, bois et charbon*. Then she said: 'Perhaps, when the Vigil is over, Valentina will be home,' and I thought, we all keep saying or thinking this: that when a certain amount of time has passed, Valentina will materialise out of the stifling air. But she doesn't materialise. The minutes keep passing. They turn into hours. And where Valentina should be, there's only my invisible longing for her, silent in empty space.

On the way to the church, which was only about two minutes from the apartment, Mrs Gavrilovich whispered to me that there were 'some people' who came to this church who were 'bad' and that when she saw these bad people she had to close her eyes because she couldn't bear to look at them.

'Why are they "bad"?' I asked.

'Louis,' she said, 'they are the worst.'

'What have they done?'

'They destroy lives, that's all I know.'

'How?' I asked, but Mrs Gavrilovich didn't want to talk about this any more. She just wrapped the blue shawl more firmly round her head. And we were in the courtyard of the church now, so she signalled to me to be quiet and leant on my shoulder as we walked up the steps. Way above us was a mosaic of Jesus reading a book he seemed quite bored with and I thought, if it had been *Crime and Punishment* he would have been more engrossed.

Inside the church, it was cool. On the floor was an old red carpet, burned in places and stained with candle wax, and up in the air was a yellow bowl of light, where the sun came in through the sides of the glassy dome. A few people walked around, looking at the saints and martyrs on the pillars and walls and lighting candles and talking to each other. There were no pews, only a line of chairs arranged around the edges of the carpet, and on these chairs the people had put carrier bags and shopping baskets and pieces of knitting, like they were planning to have a jumble sale there during the service. When you looked up at the dome, what you saw was a swathe of netting, like a hammock, strung across it, to catch the flaking paint and plaster that was floating down from the figure of God on high.

Mrs Gavrilovich went down on one of her rickety knees and touched the red carpet. She whispered to me that the carpet was a piece of Russian earth, right there in the middle of Paris. She didn't seem to notice that this earth had been burned in places. Then she headed for a cabinet made of glass, with a border of flowers, and she laid her head on this, so that her mouth came close to the mouth of the icon inside. The glass was smeary where it had been kissed by dozens of people believing they were kissing Jesus, and I thought, this isn't a very hygienic church.

I looked around for the people who destroyed lives. I wondered if Mrs Gavrilovich had drug dealers in mind, or what? More and more Russians had come in now, with their bags from Prisunic and cheap briefcases and pushchairs and parcels, but they seemed too old or too busy to be criminals. One thing I did notice about them, though: they all looked quite poor. You could tell they weren't French, from the 8th Arrondissement. You could imagine them having dental problems they couldn't afford to fix. They wore clothes like the stuff you see hanging on chrome rails in street markets – shiny trousers with flares; dresses that remind you of tablecloths. I thought, when they kiss Jesus, they ask him to let them win on the loterie nationale.

Mrs Gavrilovich seemed to have forgotten about me. She was intent on examining things – old flags and ribbons and medals and candle sconces and particular pieces of the wall. When the priest and his helpers came through from the *sanctuaire*, she was staring at a picture of St George, probably making sure that it and everything else was just as it had always and always been. As some chanting began, I saw her reach out and touch St George's leg.

I sat down on one of the chairs, next to a string bag full of potatoes. I could smell the earth on them and I suddenly thought, what if Valentina is dead and buried in the ground?

When it came to the time for communion, big hunks of white bread were handed round in a basket and I wondered whether, in the old days, or during the war or something, people came to church to be fed. But now, some of the congregation, including Mrs Gavrilovich, found this bread a bit indigestible; she just nibbled a crumb or two and put the rest in her handbag. In Devon, you never saw people put the body of Christ into their handbags. And the priest had his eye on her. He was small and his chanting voice was weak, but his eyes were piercing, and when he took off his jewelled crown he looked straight at Mrs Gavrilovich accusingly and she closed her bag with a snap. And she wouldn't look at him. Her eyes were shut tight, either from guilt at hiding the bread or because she'd just seen one of the 'life destroyers' come into the church.

People entered all the time. Some of them came in and looked around and went out again, as if they were sampling the church and found this one too dilapidated and peculiar for their liking. From my chair, which was under a picture of Jesus walking on the water in the moonlight, I kept watch on everybody and on the number of flakes of plaster that fell out of the dome on to the netting. Twenty-nine flakes fell. The beautiful singing may have disturbed the air in the roof.

Among the faces that I watched, I half expected Valentina's to appear suddenly, as if she'd been in the church all along, as if she'd been hiding there for two days. But there was no sign of her. At one point, I turned round to the thin Jesus stepping over the moonlit waves and talked to him. I told him I quite liked this picture, then I asked him not to let Valentina die.

The Vigil lasted a long time. If a world-wide survey was conducted, Russians might turn out to be the most patient people on earth. At the end of it, Mrs Gavrilovich stood with some other women in a huddle, talking Russian, and while she talked they shook their heads. I thought, I expect they all knew Valentina when she was young and dressed in clothes bought at street markets; I expect they admired her blonde hair that never darkened.

When we got back to the apartment, Mrs Gavrilovich had a tot of vodka. Then she said she had to rest. I wanted to ask her more about the bad people and about what we were going to do, but she said she was too tired to talk; she said when I got old I would know what this kind of tiredness felt like.

I hovered by the door, while Sergei wagged his tail. Mrs Gavrilovich started taking the hairpins out of her bun and her grey hair came down in coils. I said: 'Shall I go to the police and report a missing person?'

The snakes of hair made her look younger but sadder. I imagined her running across the coal yard the day Mr Gavrilovich had his heart attack and died. His name had been Anton.

She didn't answer me, but began mumbling in Russian.

'Tell me what to do,' I said.

But she was confused now. It was like she was half asleep already, and without replying she went into her room with the red candle and closed the door.

I called our own number. I expected Alice to answer, but what came floating up was Valentina's recorded voice telling me she couldn't come to the telephone right now. The voice told me to leave a message. I wanted to say, 'Valentina, come back to me, please,' but what I said was: 'Mum, this is Lewis. I'm going to look for Babba.'

Sergei and I got on the métro at George V. In this station was a brilliant busker, who suspended a piece of black cloth across the handrails and started doing a puppet show there and then between George V and the Étoile. His puppet was a skull. The skull talked to us and told us how lonely it was.

The skull got off at Porte Maillot. I felt bad about not giving it anything, but all I'd eaten that day was Mrs Gavrilovich's caraway cake, so I had to keep the bit of money I had. Nobody in the world knows how hungry I can get.

Sergei went to sleep in the hot train and I noticed suddenly that he was starting to smell a bit, as if he needed a shampoo, and I remembered that Valentina took him to a dog parlour off the Avenue Matignon, where he'd once fallen in love with a poodle called Manon. 'And you know, Lewis,' Valentina had said, 'when dogs fall in love, they are not well behaved like you and me; they are very vulgar indeed.' I liked this idea of Sergei fucking a poodle at a dog hairdressers', with all the owners and beauticians looking on. Everyone was shocked, apparently, except Valentina, who just laughed and said: 'Well, it's lucky they don't care about privacy.' She knew Sergei wasn't a monk: he was a star and he had to get laid sometimes. If he'd been a person, he would have fucked somebody or other every night and snorted cocaine and been driven round in a stretch limo with an inbuilt cocktail cabinet. So you could say in a way that he was *less* vulgar than a human being, not more.

We got out at La Défense. To get to Babba's building, you had to cross a walkway hung across the new road works, then come down into Nanterre, which didn't feel like part of Paris, but like some other city, where football was played in the street and where the trees were small. There were a lot of open spaces, where nothing seemed to exist, not even a closed market or a car park, like the space was mined, and only a few pigeons came there (too light to trigger the mines with their skinny red feet) and walked around on the asphalt, waiting for a breeze.

On one of these spaces, something had been put: it was an enormous snake. Children played round it. Part of its body was under the ground and part above. It was made of brown and white mosaic pieces that glistened in the sun and its head reared up about five foot out of the earth.

I stood and gaped at it, with Sergei growling, and the kids climbed along the snake's back and into its mouth. Some of these kids were black and I looked at them carefully, in case one of them turned out to be Pozzi, but it's hard to recognise a child you've only seen once in a photograph taken in winter.

Part of me was searching for the little glove dropped in the snow.

We went on, getting nearer to the building. There were no cafés here, or boulangeries or dry cleaners or anything, just some old garages sprayed with graffiti and chain-link fencing keeping you off some dusty grass. You could have been in Idaho or Birmingham or somewhere. There was loud rap coming from a garage mechanic's cassette player and, further off, a police siren screaming. And it was autumn here; that was another odd thing. In Paris proper, it was high summer, but here the leaves were yellow and falling, I don't know why.

The building was in a group of seven, mosaicked green and beige and purple and blue. Whoever designed the flats had probably designed the snake, using the leftover bits of ceramic. Both the snake and the buildings looked as if they had been designed in a dream. You could imagine the architect waking up from the dream and starting to scribble with purple chalks. Tears of pride and joy began to fall on to his scribblings and so he'd thought, this is how the windows will look, like teardrops! But now, like Babba had said, there were rusty rivets holding the tears to the wall, holding bits of the wall to itself. Some of the tears were smashed and these ones looked more like tooth cavities. I thought, I bet the residents hope this architect is crying with shame.

When you got close up to the building, you could hear a lot of noise coming from it – music and shouting and some kind of machinery whining. I hoped it was all ordinary noise and had nothing to do with voodoo. A door was open on the ground floor, so we went in and found ourselves in a kind of launderette that was full of scalding air. An old woman in an overall sat on a plastic chair staring at the tumbling clothes, as if the washing was an old movie she couldn't take her eyes off. I was about to ask her if she knew Babba, when she looked up and saw Sergei and yelled at me that dogs weren't allowed in the laundry. I put my hands up, like someone being arrested, and said, OK, I'd take Sergei out but please could she tell me where to find Babba.

She reminded me of the concierge in Mrs Gavrilovich's block, with her wet face and her hair all greasy and stuck to her head. 'Babba?' she said. 'Babba qui?'

I explained carefully that Babba was the woman from Benin who lived with her son Pozzi in the apartment where the motorbike had been. 'Oh,' she said, 'you mean Violette?'

'Yes,' I said quickly. 'Where is Violette?'

'Seventh floor,' she said. 'Now take your dog out of here.'

We had to walk out of the building and in at another door to find the stairs. On the concrete pathway there was a disgusting splurge of vomit we had to step round. Sergei doesn't always know the difference between fresh and recycled food.

Near the second door there were two lifts, gaping open, but they looked broken somehow, and dark like coffins, so we started going up the stairs.

I forgot to count the floors and there were no numbers or signs anywhere. I imagined guys coming home stoned and trying to get into the wrong apartment. Then I realised that each floor was painted a different colour; this was another marvel thought up by the architect at four in the morning. He expected the residents would identify with their colour and take pride in being green or yellow. The first line of a song out of my childhood flashed into my mind. *It's not easy being green.* I didn't know who sang this or when. To some youths smoking on the stairs, I said: 'What colour is seven?'

They started giggling. Some of them had shaved heads and some had blond dreadlocks. I'd been told at school that you could turn your hair into dreads just by washing it regularly in Badedas. I stood by the wall, out of breath and foreign and pale. With a single movement of their tattooed arms, the Badedas guys could have lifted me up and thrown me down the stairwell.

'What's your dog's name?' one of them asked.

I held tightly to Sergei's lead. 'Michel,' I said.

136

They fell around, laughing. Then they began calling
'Michel . . . Michel . . .' and Sergei looked at them haughtily.
We were on floor orange. It could have been five or six, I
hadn't a clue, but I tugged Sergei on up the next flight. The
youths called after me: 'Where do you come from, kid? Are
you German? Heil Hitler!'

I thought they were going to follow me, but they didn't. It
had never occurred to me that anyone would want to steal
Sergei, but now it did. I just told myself to keep going, even
though my ribs were aching and my legs felt weak. I wished I
hadn't come here. I wanted to call out to Babba, wherever she
was hiding; I wanted her to put her velvet arms round me.

The next floor was red, so we set off down this red corridor.
It seemed to go round in a circle, on and on, dark and blank.
I heard a sound like a dentist's drill coming from behind one
of the doors, so I stopped and listened. The sound came and
went. Then I noticed a name on a card that was taped to the
door: *Arletti, Jean-Christophe, Chirugien Dentiste*. I wondered if
I was on a kind of trade floor, with doctors and solicitors and
private detectives behind all the doors, but then I saw that the
dentist's apartment also had a number, 729. The numbers were
so minute, you could hardly read them, but with the 7 coming
first I figured I must be on the seventh floor, so I rang the
dentist's bell.

A nurse opened the door. She was black and wore a bright
white uniform. I wondered if she might be a relation of Babba's.
'Excuse me,' I said. 'I'm looking for Violette.'

'Not this apartment. This is the apartment of Doctor Arletti,'
she said.

'Can you tell me where I can find Violette?'

'Violette who?'

'Babba . . .' I stammered.

The nurse turned back into the room and said something to
the dentist. Sergei gave an involuntary whine, as if he was
getting impatient and wanted to be back in the sunshine, in
the Paris that he knew. I felt a bit the same. It would have

been so easy to find the coffin lifts and drop down and walk away through the yellow leaves.

The nurse came back and said she didn't know the person 'Violette Babba' and nor did Doctor Arletti. I thought, I expect you're afraid of dentists, Babba, and have never been near one in your life. I expect you would scream if a man tried to put his fingers into your mouth.

We found her door by going along and reading every name. Hers was apartment 741. On a piece of pink card was written: *Babbala, Mlle Violette.* Before I rang the bell, I wiped my face with my sleeve.

I had to ring three times before anyone answered. Then I heard slow footsteps and I knew they belonged to Babba because of the slowness. When she saw me, she said: 'Mon Dieu! Que fais-tu ici?'

She was dressed in a sleeveless T-shirt and a thin flowery skirt and her feet were bare. Her flat smelled of sweat and disinfectant and it was shadowy from lack of light from the teardrop windows. As I walked into it, she said again: 'Louis, what are you doing here?'

Sergei was barking and jumping up, so I let go his lead and Babba had to give him some attention, while I looked quickly round the room. I was scanning it for voodoo offerings – a wax doll, a skull, a dead chicken – but there was hardly anything in the room at all, only a double mattress on the floor and an old leather chair with its stuffing coming out and a table spread with oilcloth and on the walls a poster advertising the Tour de France. Lying on the mattress, with nothing covering him, was Pozzi.

Babba closed the door, holding Sergei by the collar. She stared at me crossly. 'Louis,' she said, 'how you find your way here? What you want?'

I didn't say anything, I was so out of breath and scared. One of the things I was thinking was, how did they get that huge motorbike up to Floor 7?

Pozzi woke up and began grizzling. Babba let go of Sergei and gathered Pozzi into her arms, from where he stared at me through his tears. I felt as though I would like to cry, too, and only the resolution to act like François Seurel, who never blubbed, not even when things started to get sad, kept me from giving in. I sat down on the leather chair and stared up at Babba.

'Something's happened, Babba,' I said.

'What's happened? What "something"?'

'Something bad. Why haven't you been to work? Why haven't you been to the rue Rembrandt?'

'You know why,' said Babba.

'No, I don't. You just didn't come . . .'

'I telephoned Madame.'

'When?'

'When Pozzi get ill. And Madame say, "No, you stay home, Babba, and take care of him." '

'When? When did Pozzi get ill? When did you telephone?'

'I don't know what day. Monday.'

'And you spoke to Madame?'

'Yes. Now, what's this thing happened? Louis? What's this thing?'

I looked over at the mattress. In the space where Pozzi had been lying was a damp patch on the nylon sheet. Next to this dampness lay a man doll dressed as a soldier that reminded me of Elroy.

'Madame's disappeared,' I said.

They all three stared at me when I said this: Babba, Pozzi and Sergei. Nobody whined or spoke or cried. They just looked at me and I looked at them. Then Sergei turned in a circle and lay down on Pozzi's bed. He seemed to know that we might be there a long time. After a moment, Babba said: 'Louis, you want some Orangina?'

She had a little kitchen next to the room with the bed, the kind of kitchen where there is just space enough for one person to move around. The cooker had only two rings, but the fridge was huge, like the kind of fridge you see in old American movies. Babba got out the Orangina bottle and poured some into a plastic mug and gave it to me and I drank and drank, like people drink in desert commercials for beer, when they're parched dry.

Then I sat down with Babba and told her about Grisha and the black-and-white dress Valentina had been wearing when she went into the Hôtel de Venise. I said: 'She waved at me from the revolving door and she hasn't been seen since.'

Babba looked around and around the room, as if she were lost and trying to orientate herself. Pozzi quietened down and went to sleep in her lap.

When Babba had scanned the room for about the third time, I said hesitantly: 'You didn't do anything, did you, Babba?'

'What you mean, Louis – do anything?'

'I mean, you didn't ask the spirits . . . to do anything?'

She looked at me gravely and shook her head. 'Never,' she said. 'I never would hurt Madame.'

I had to believe her. I couldn't go on pestering her and it was true that Pozzi seemed a bit ill, sort of listless and snotty. I wondered if he'd got ill because he missed the motorbike. People can fall sick for the oddest reasons. I read in a paper about a woman who had died of heartbreak over the loss of her pet rat. Neighbours were reported as saying: 'From that moment, Elsie was never the same woman.'

After a few minutes, in which we were just quiet, listening to the weird sounds of the building, one of which was a tambourine being bashed, I asked Babba if she was ever going to come back to the rue Rembrandt. She stroked Pozzi's head and said she would come, but she didn't know when. She couldn't leave Pozzi yet; his temperature was still too high. I said: 'You could bring Pozzi with you. We could put him to sleep in one of the spare rooms.'

'No,' said Babba. 'Madame told me, "You can't bring your child to work. A child would disturb me." '

'Madame isn't there,' I reminded her.

Babba shook her head sadly. 'You sure she didn't go to Russia, Louis?'

'No. I'm not *sure*. I'm going to find out. I'm going to speak to Grigory Panin. Then, after that, we'll have to go to the police.'

At the mention of the word 'police', Babba looked anxious. 'Police,' she said, 'they don't care 'bout anyone. All they care is about papers and permits.'

So then I realised a bad thing: when the police were told about Valentina, they might start questioning everyone; and their 'everyone' would include Babba and they would discover she was an illegal immigrant and send her back to Benin. Her life would be ruined. She would have to go and live in her village, where there were no launderettes and even the old trucks were stolen, and all her dreams of making a life in Paris would be at an end. And I would be responsible.

I changed the subject. I asked her why she didn't call herself by her real name, Violette.

She smiled and shifted Pozzi on her knee. 'Yes,' she said, 'I call myself Violette. I am Violette. It is only the Parisians who invented the word "Babba", from my father's name, Babbala.'

On the way home in the métro, I remembered what Alice had said in the morning – that Valentina would be there in the apartment when I got back and that she and Alice would make me a meal. So now I started to imagine this: Valentina standing in the kitchen, surrounded by shiny vegetables – peppers and aubergines – and bits of garlic and bottles of olive oil, singing softly to herself as she chopped and stirred, as if this intermission of her absence had never happened.

Then, when I got out at George V and started to walk up the rue Washington, I thought, why have I suddenly got this stupid surge of hope? I keep getting it. I'm as deluded as Hugh, who hopes his hut will turn out like a summerhouse, when he knows in his heart that, brick by brick, he's building a toilet.

And then it came to me why, in *Crime and Punishment*,

Raskolnikov takes all the watches and jewellery that he's stolen and puts them under the stone. He could sell them to make his pitiful life better, but he doesn't, he leaves them under the stone. He leaves them there because he's the exact opposite of me: he no longer hopes for anything; he knows he's doomed.

Coming into the rue Rembrandt, I bumped into Moinel, who was turning in from the rue de Courcelles. He was wearing white, as usual, and his hair looked the colour of a clementine. He gave me a kind of half-smile and said in English: 'How are you enjoying Paris?'

Sergei looked up at Moinel and barked. Moinel's hairdresser could have said to him: 'Let's go for the tone of an Irish Setter rather than a tangerine,' but he hadn't, unfortunately, and I think it was Moinel's hair that Sergei was barking at.

I said I was enjoying Paris.

Moinel smiled again. It was the kind of smile that looks as if it's causing the smiler a minute amount of pain. 'I expect Mademoiselle Gavril is spoiling you,' he said. 'I hear she's very generous.'

His English sounded really good, as if he'd learnt it at Oxford or somewhere. This good English of his made me like him and feel less worried about his peculiar hair. I pulled Sergei towards me and stopped in the street, not far from our apartment door. Moinel stopped too, when I turned to him.

'Did you hear what's happened?' I said.

'What has happened?'

'Something frightening. You're Monsieur Moinel, aren't you?'

'Yes. That's me. Everybody just calls me Moinel.'

I looked up at Valentina's apartment. I saw that the windows of the salon were wide open and I gazed at them for a second, wondering if I was going to see a puff of Russian cigarette smoke come through them into the hot evening air.

'It's Valentina,' I said. 'Mademoiselle Gavril. She's vanished.'

'Vanished?' said Moinel.

'Yes.'

'Are you serious? I know the English like to joke about everything.'

'Yes, I'm serious.'

'Well, if it's true, it's quite ingenious, you know. She devised it herself, surely? Didn't she? She's playing a game. She's acting out one of her medieval stories!'

I stared at Moinel. Smiling as he was, I noticed how beautiful his eyes were, very wide and grey. 'Why would she do that?' I said. 'She's meant to be working really hard on her new book. That's why we're here, so that my mother can do the English translation straight away.'

'Publicity, chéri! I know writers. I know stars of all kinds. "Famous writer missing". "World-wide search for famous writer". What better advertisement for a new book than that? The publishers will adore it. Perfect for her genre of fiction. And, of course, in a few days she will turn up safe and well. How long has she been gone?'

'Nearly three days.'

'Voilà! It's not long. She's probably hiding out down in Monte Carlo. You'll see.'

I was about to say to Moinel that I thought if Valentina had been going to do a stunt like that she would have told me first, but then I remembered that it was only in my imagination that she confided in me, not in reality. So I couldn't find anything to say and just gaped at Moinel like a *dorade*. He resumed his progress towards the apartment door. He walked with tiny little steps, as though he were wearing a skirt too tight for his thighs.

Inside the building, he went straight to the lift and, although I normally walked up the stairs, I hung around, so that I could say something more to him before we went into our separate flats. I didn't really know what it was that I wanted to say, so when the lift came we just got in and rode up in total silence. Then, at the top floor, I stammered: 'If she doesn't come back . . . will you help me find her?'

Moinel's grey eyes didn't even flicker. 'Bien sûr,' he said. 'I love a mystery. Count on me.'

Valentina wasn't in the kitchen chopping vegetables. The apartment was cool and silent and I thought at first that no one was there, but then I found Alice by herself in the salon, reading a letter from Hugh.

I sat down opposite her. I thought, the time has come for her to stop pretending that nothing unusual is happening. But I couldn't talk to her yet; I was so hungry, I felt dazed, so all I said to her was: 'Please can I eat something? I'm dying.'

She came over to me and put a kiss on my head. It was a long time since she'd done this. She said she'd made a lamb casserole with haricot beans, which was a meal she used to make in Devon and serve with a huge dish of mashed potato.

I couldn't talk while I ate the casserole and potato. I just had to eat and eat and Alice watched me with a smile on her face, waiting for the moment when I'd eaten enough to behave like a civilised person again. When I looked up from my plate, I said: 'Valentina said she never, ever, wanted to be hungry again. Do you think she's hungry wherever she is?'

Alice began rolling a cigarette. I looked at the freckles on her thin, elegant hands. After she'd lit the cigarette, she said: 'I talked to Mrs Gavrilovich. She'd spoken to Grigory Panin and he'd sworn to her that Valentina wasn't with him in Moscow. She wants me to go to the police tomorrow.'

All I said was, 'Yes.' What I was thinking was, now it's really final. We're not going to pretend any more that we just have to go out somewhere and by the time we're back Valentina will have turned up.

And so this is what we talked about for the rest of the evening – about which commissariat we had to go to and what we were going to say to the police when we got there. The subject of the spell Alice was casting over Didier never got mentioned. It was like part of me wanted to mention it and another part wanted to hide it inside a huge airship of silence, where it would float around, sealed in, for ever.

The next day, I went back to working on Valentina's computer. I'd been thinking, if the detective Porphiry Petrovich in *Crime and Punishment* had had computer files and not just pawn tickets at hand, he would have looked there for clues to the mystery. And I'd decided he'd be my role model from now on: I'd follow every single trail and never give up until Valentina was found.

I could tell at once that the alphabetised menu of files was different. I can remember lists of things in a photographic kind of way and I saw immediately that the APAL file, which had been at the top of the menu, was no longer there. I scrolled down, searching for it, knowing as I did this that it's impossible to de-alphabetise a file menu; the computer just overrides you. The file had been wiped.

Alice, I thought, I've never, as long as I've been alive, really known what was in your mind. Hugh doesn't know either. He thinks you'll be happy in a garden hut. But I know that you're hardly ever happy anywhere, in any season.

And then I remembered something: when we took our bird kite out to the cliffs and took turns to fly it and watched it fluttering miles above us, a look would come into Alice's face. A look we hardly ever saw. It was as if this grey-and-white paper bird was the one and only thing in Alice Little's existence she could truly admire.

For about ten minutes I sat staring at the place in the file where APAL should have been. I reminded myself of Elroy, stuck in one position, with his eyes locked on to a near or distant object, unable to move them. What I was thinking was, our household in Devon will never be the same now, no matter what happens.

Eventually, I jolted myself back into the here and now. Porphiry Petrovich doesn't get slowed down thinking about his future and his past.

I opened files at random. The most interesting one I opened was MASP. There were no clues in it, but I really liked it.

MASP was the acronym for *Un mas de Provence*. The file was a kind of diary. It described a journey Valentina had made down to Provence in 1992. She wrote that her quest was to find the field where she and her parents had camped long ago when they still ran the café. I remembered her telling me about this camping trip when I lay by her on the bed the night she came back from hospital after she'd broken her arm. She told me they found mushrooms in the fields and cooked them over an open fire. She said it had been a cold September and that there was always dew on the tent in the early mornings.

Now, on this journey, Valentina was driving a Mercedes and staying at a five-star hotel called the Château d'Arly. She found the field and stood in it and it was more or less as it had been when the Gavrilovichs had pitched their old tent in it, except that then it had been sown with grass and now it was planted with carrots. This field made her feel incredibly sad. She thought about her father's life and how, in the war, in 1941, when he was a soldier in one of General Zhukov's Far Eastern Divisions, the cold had been so terrible, the men had to hack into the earth with picks to dig up carrots and swede and saw ice from the rivers to stay alive. She wished her father could be alive now, installed here, in the place of his dreams.

She went to an estate agent and asked to see some stone farmhouses, known as *mas*. She was shown one overlooking a stream, with its own water wheel. She thought that Anton Gavrilovich would have found this one perfect. So she asked the estate agent to leave her alone in it for half an hour.

He drove off and Valentina wandered on her own through the fantastic house. She imagined old Anton in each of the rooms: sitting in a rocking chair by the living-room fire, sleeping in a high bed listening to the turning of the water wheel, reading comic strips on the mahogany toilet, eating his favourite meal of roast guinea fowl in the kitchen. When she found that the owners had installed a jacuzzi in one of the bathrooms, she remembered an accusation of his about the Americans, who in 1942 had single-handedly supplied the Red Army with weapons and food and clothing: 14.5 million pairs of boots alone were sent to the Russians and a quarter of a million tons of canned meat. But Mr Gavrilovich used to say the Yanks had bought victory with Russian blood and paid in spam. There's no French word for spam, so she just put spam. She had tried to turn on the jacuzzi, but no water came.

When she went out into the garden, she strung an imaginary hammock between two plum trees and laid old Anton in it. She stood by, rocking him gently. He told her that he'd never grumbled about the coal-heaving in the *café-charbon*, because it was a million times better than working and starving on the collective farm, where food could be confiscated or requisitioned without warning; where the firewood was rationed and there was no coal to burn. 'At least,' he used to say to her, 'we are safe, Valya, and in the winters the café is warm.'

When the estate agent returned, Valentina gave him back the keys to the beautiful house with the jacuzzi and the water wheel and got into her Mercedes and drove away. She could have afforded the house five times over, but the person who wanted it was no longer alive. She had to pull into a lay-by and cry. She had nothing to wipe her eyes with except the car duster.

On the way to the commissariat, I asked Alice: 'When you're grown-up, is there always something to regret?'

'I don't know what you mean,' she said.

'Like something that hasn't turned out the way you thought it would?'

'Almost nothing turns out the way you think it will,' she said.

The commissariat had tall windows with grilles over them and a polished wooden floor, worn down by people's feet. On the reception desk an electric fan turned, moving the warm air around. Only when you were right next to it did it make you feel cool.

Quite a few people were there, waiting. One was a woman dressed completely in pink, with pink ankle socks and pink high-heeled shoes and a pink beret on her head. She was smoking and blowing the smoke towards the fan.

Behind the desk, a young officer, with a gun on his hip, saw the waiting people one by one and wrote things down in a ledger. Alice said the officer's rank was *brigadier* and the ledger was known as *La main courante*. A corner of Alice's brain is full of knowledge you might never need in your entire lifetime.

When our turn came to talk to the *brigadier*, he began a new page of *La main courante* and wrote everything down very slowly. He looked as if he was learning to write. From time to time, his eye couldn't help glancing over at the pink woman. When Alice said we'd come to report a missing person, he said: 'Missing how?'

'Just missing, disappeared,' said Alice, and I knew she thought 'Missing how?' was a stupid question.

'Right,' he said with a sigh; 'but missing from where?'

Alice ran her hands through her thorny hair. I could tell she was getting impatient already. She said slowly: 'Mademoiselle Gavril was last seen going into a hotel, the Hôtel de Venise, by my son here, at lunch time last Tuesday.'

I nodded. The *brigadier* stared hard at me, with the kind of cross, stupid stare a teacher gives you when he knows you've been smoking in the school toilets. He wrote down 'Venise'. Then he asked us if we were related to Valentina. When we said we weren't, he said: 'Why didn't a member of the family come?'

Alice explained about Mrs Gavrilovich being old and afraid.

'Afraid of what?' he asked.

'Of the police,' said Alice.

The *brigadier's* pen paused before it let him write this down. Then he said: 'Could Madame Gavrilovich, or anyone in the family, gain material advantage by the death of Mademoiselle Gavril?'

'Yes,' said Alice.

'Very well,' he said; 'then we will have to put in hand an RIF.'

'What's an RIF?' asked Alice.

'Une recherche dans l'intérêt des familles.'

Then he moved on to questions about Valentina, such as her approximate height and the colour of her hair. He asked us whether she was in the habit of going missing. 'What do you mean?' said Alice. He said, well, people disappeared all the time – young people mostly; they went missing for a week or two weeks, then turned up somewhere. This pattern was part of modern life. And it was pointless for the police to search for people like this; they did search, of course, because this was their duty, but they also knew that in ninety-nine per cent of cases it was a waste of time and resources.

Behind us, the pink woman started coughing and so the *brigadier*'s attention went away from us and on to her. And I heard Alice start to get angry. She said she'd already given Valentina's age: she was a forty-one-year-old writer, not a young unemployed drifter. She was not 'in the habit of going missing'. On the contrary. She was in the middle of a book, which had a deadline, and her disappearance was therefore absolutely unexpected and out of character.

The *brigadier* looked at Alice, unmoved. He seemed to be one of the few people on earth on whom Alice's beauty had no effect. All he said was, 'Well, it will be put in hand. We will make a report to the Neuvième Cabinet de Délégation Judiciare.'

'What's that?' asked Alice.

'It is where information on missing persons is centralised. If you wish to have a photograph given to them, you will have to provide us with one.'

'What will the Neuvième Cabinet do?'

'They will open a dossier on this Mademoiselle . . . Gavril.

They will make enquiries in the place of last sighting. They will check with the register of motor-vehicle accidents and with the Paris hospital morgues . . .'

When I heard the word 'morgue', it did an odd thing to me. I felt suddenly detached from the whole scene, as if I'd gone behind a wall of opaque glass and everything else – the *brigadier*, the fan, the desk, Alice, the pink woman, the sound of the telephones – existed on the other side of it. I knew I could still talk, but my own voice would sound as if it was behind the glass wall too.

I held on to Alice's arm while she said something else, I don't know what, to the *brigadier*, and then he said we could go now. I felt Alice take my hand and we walked out of the commissariat into the street. I gripped her hand so hard it must have hurt her and then, as we strolled on, hand in hand, the glass panel slowly faded and the world came back.

To console us after our ordeal at the commissariat, we went to Fouquet's and ordered ice creams and *sirop à la menthe*, and sat in the sun, watching the people and the traffic and the movement of the trees.

After a while of just sitting, I said to Alice that I supposed they didn't have anyone of the calibre of Porphiry Petrovich at that commissariat, or at the Neuvième Cabinet de Délégation Judiciare, and she laughed. I said: 'You can laugh if you want to, but if they're not going to send anyone I'm going to do the detective work myself.'

I thought I'd begin by talking to Didier.

I had two reasons for this: one was that you can see things from a roof that no one else notices and the other was that Didier's face and Raskolnikov's face had become almost identical in my mind. Part of me was thinking, if he's planning to steal Alice away from her former life, he might want everybody round her to disappear. Including me.

Instead of climbing out of my bathroom window, I went up to the roof using Didier's ladders. There were nine ladders in all, roped to the scaffolding cage. At night, he removed the bottom two ladders, so that no one could use them to get up on to the building. He said that, to him, getting to the ground after he'd stowed the ladders was as easy as blowing his nose, but most people would find it hard.

At first, I thought he wasn't on the roof, but then I found him asleep in the shade by the water tanks. He was in the exact spot where I'd looked up at the smiling moon.

I crept over to him, without waking him. He was in such a stupor of sleep that a dribble of saliva had run down his chin and made a tiny stain on the lead. I didn't move, but just stared at him. I thought, the similarities between him and Raskolnikov are quite striking: he's lying curled up, like Raskolnikov lies huddled in his truckle bed; he's been ill; he looks as if he hasn't shaved; he's definitely getting thinner . . .

He woke up while I stood there watching him. I wondered whether Alice had seen him like this, asleep beside her.

When he saw me, he looked startled and scrabbled to his feet. He brushed the dust off his body. 'How are things going, Louis?' he said.

'Why were you asleep?' I asked.

'I told you,' he said, 'I've been ill. It's left me a bit tired.' Then he picked up his can of Coke from the roof and drank some down. He offered me the can, but I refused it. 'Well,' he said again, as if everything was perfectly OK and normal and fine, 'what's the news?'

I walked a few paces away from him, then I looked straight at him and said: 'Valentina's disappeared. Didn't you know?'

'Yes,' he said. 'Your mother told me.'

I let a bit of silence go by. Then I said: 'We went to the police this morning.'

'The police?'

'Yes. We reported a missing person. I expect they'll be sending an inspector round.'

Didier nodded. He didn't look afraid or anything. He asked me if I'd like to help him hang a few slates. His friendliness towards me hadn't diminished one bit and I knew that trying to dislike him or even hate him was going to be really hard. It was going to be hard mainly because I'd seen the Salpêtrière dome. I'd felt the hugeness of it and the puniness of people compared with it. There was a part of me which refused to despise someone who had restored something as vast and fantastic as that.

I wasn't totally in the mood for slate hanging. It was burning hot up there on the roof. The thing I most wanted to be doing in all the world was swimming at the Les Rosiers pool with Valentina in her white-and-gold swimsuit. But once I started on the slates, I began to enjoy it and to take pride in getting each of my slates perfectly positioned and squared up before I drove in the pin. It was as though I imagined that if I kept working with Didier, I was practising for some kind of future.

'So,' said Didier after a while, 'where has Valentina gone, do you think?'

'She could have been murdered.'

There was a moment's pause before Didier said: 'Why would anyone murder her?'

Without looking up from my work, I said: 'Because they wanted her out of the way.'

He tapped in a slate pin. His straight, shiny hair was getting a bit long and flopping over his glasses. 'For what reason?' he asked.

'Any number of reasons. Like she was getting in the way of what someone wanted to do. Don't you think that's possible?'

He shrugged. 'I suppose so, yes,' he said. 'That is always a possibility in any disappearance. But I'm sure this isn't a question of murder, Louis. I think that's just in your mind, isn't it?'

'No,' I said. 'I don't think it's just in my mind. On Tuesday morning at about twelve, she went out. I walked with her to a hotel where she was meeting Grigory, this Russian writer she knew. And she hasn't been seen since. So anything could have happened – including a murder.'

'But perhaps not. Perhaps she will come back?'

'That's what Alice keeps saying. But I know she won't. I know I have to track her down. And I *will*. I'm going to be the one to find her.'

I felt choked as I said this. I heard my voice begin to go odd. I didn't want Didier to notice, so I pretended to cough. I looked down at the hammer in my hands.

'How are you going to set about it?' said Didier.

I didn't reply for a moment, then I said: 'I'm making a plan.'

I saw Didier stop work and look tenderly at me. It was the sort of look I sometimes got from Hugh.

'Better to let the police make a plan, isn't it?' he said.

Alice said to me that evening: 'I had a call from Bianquis, Valentina's French publishers, today. They want to know when the book's going to be finished.'

'What did you say to them?' I asked.

Alice was sitting on the Louis XVI sofa, where Valentina normally sat. I didn't like her sitting there and I'd been willing her to move, but she didn't move. Alice's own will is so strong, it can outmanoeuvre everybody else's.

'I stalled,' she said. 'I said Valentina's mother was ill and she was concentrating on that at the moment.'

Then she told me something interesting. She said that on our first day in the rue Rembrandt, Valentina had admitted to her what pressure she was under all the time from Bianquis, to produce the next book and then the next and the next, like she was a writing factory. And she'd said she knew this couldn't go on. It was wearing her out and she wanted it to end.

'That couldn't be it, could it?' I said. 'She couldn't just have decided to abandon the book and go to Australia or something . . . ?'

'It's possible. She'd been very tetchy about the book. It didn't seem to me that she was enjoying writing it. She wanted it to be finished and done with.'

'But what about us?'

'What about us?'

'She wouldn't have left us without a word.'

Alice sighed. 'In Valentina's equation,' she said, 'we're nothing. I do my job. You amuse her and you look after Sergei. She tolerates us in this apartment. But we're of no importance to her. She leads a smart, international life and she makes a lot of money. These are the only things that count: nothing else. We're like her servants – like Babba.'

'No, we're not!' I blurted out. And what I wanted to describe were the things that had happened in my attic – the translation sessions and the present of the musical box – to show Alice that Valentina cared about me and my future and gave me things that were precious to her. But then I decided not to. These were secret matters and I didn't want Alice's cool mind dissecting them and reducing them to ruins.

'That day when we went out without telling her, Valentina was upset,' I said. 'That means she cares about us.'

'Not necessarily. It means she needed us and was irritated when she discovered we weren't there. Again, it's the reaction of the employer towards the servant.'

'It's more than that!' I said. I was getting upset now and I felt almost like I might cry. I swallowed and tried to calm myself down. 'And anyway,' I said, 'you've got Babba wrong. Her name isn't Babba. That's just a stupid name invented by people here. Her name's Violette and from now on we should call her Violette, which is her proper African name!'

Alice sat completely still on the Louis XVI sofa. She didn't move a muscle. Then she said: 'Violette isn't African, Lewis. It's French.'

I got up and walked out then and went straight to my room and lay down. My heart was beating like a bongo drum. I thought, Alice is too much for me. I hope Didier takes her away, up into the sky.

When I went to Valentina's computer the next day, I found Mrs Gavrilovich in the study.

'Louis, help me,' she said. 'Your eyes are better than mine. I have a feeling we could learn something from what is in this room. So we should go through all the documents we can find. I'm searching for Valentina's passport, but I can't see it.'

I didn't say I'd accessed the computer files and that I'd found a piece about Anton and the stone house in Provence. I just said I would help search. I began on the desk where the computer stood and Mrs Gavrilovich started going through the drawers of a bureau, where I'd seen Valentina writing cards and signing cheques. There were also three filing cabinets in the room and about a mile of shelves.

After a bit, I wished I'd taken the bureau and given Mrs Gavrilovich the desk, because more interesting things turned up in the bureau. There was a bag of champagne corks with dates written on them, each date apparently corresponding to the publication of one of Valentina's books. There was a leather lizard stuffed with dry beans, a packet of Polish joss sticks, some broken amber beads, a town plan of Beijing, a bottle of Ambre Solaire, an old photo of nurses and prams in the Luxembourg Gardens, a collection of theatre programmes, a bottle of scarlet nail polish, a magnifying glass with a pearl handle, seven boxes of old Christmas cards, a Russian history book, a paper knife stamped Made in Iceland and bank statements for five different bank accounts. I put the leather lizard on top of the computer, where he gazed out at the room, while I worked through the desk drawers.

All I found in these were stacks of envelopes and typing paper, staples and paperclips and rubber bands and scissors. There were files of press cuttings and a stash of manuals showing Valentina how to programme her telephone memory, set up her video recorder and mend her vacuum cleaner, should it ever break down. I was going through these when I heard Mrs Gavrilovich say: 'Louis, here's something,' and when I turned I saw that she was reading Valentina's Filofax diary.

'Hospital,' said Mrs Gavrilovich. 'On Tuesday, after lunch with Grisha, Valentina had an appointment at the hospital.'

I put down the instruction manuals and we both stared at the diary entry: *Déjeuner G. Hôpital 16h 10.*

'Unfortunately,' said Mrs Gavrilovich, 'we don't know which department . . .'

'X-ray,' I said.

Mrs Gavrilovich took off her glasses and rubbed her eyes with her stubby fingers. Then she found the hospital number and dialled it. She had to wait to be connected to the X-ray department. I saw the leather lizard watching me. I felt really stupid that I'd forgotten all about Valentina's hospital appointment. Porphiry Petrovich would never have had such a fatal memory lapse.

Mrs Gavrilovich had a short conversation with the receptionist at X-ray, talking slowly in her heavy French. 'This person says,' she said, 'that she didn't personally check Valentina in when she arrived, but saw her in the waiting area. She remembers admiring her dress.'

I thought, that's right: nobody who'd seen Valentina in that beautiful black-and-white dress would ever forget it. And I saw her again, clear as light: *she goes into the revolving door of the hotel and she turns and she waves . . .*

I tried to blank the image out. I said: 'I guess this tells us that Valentina definitely left Grisha when he got into the taxi at three-thirty, or before,' but as I was saying this I was getting a new thought. 'Suppose,' I said, 'that the taxi which left the hotel wasn't going to the airport? Suppose the taxi was taking Valentina and Grisha to the hospital and then later, after the hospital appointment, Grisha somehow persuaded Valentina to go back to Russia with him?'

Mrs Gavrilovich stared at me and the lizard stared at us both. The *brigadier* had told Alice that all evening flights to Moscow on that day would be checked for Passenger Gavril, but I knew and Mrs Gavrilovich knew that this was more or less a waste of time; if Valentina had wanted to disappear, she wouldn't have travelled under her own name.

We talked about all this for a while, then drifted back to our search of the bureau and the desk. In the last drawer of the bureau, Mrs Gavrilovich found a photograph album. As she hauled it out, she said: 'Come, Louis, now I will show you when we were younger.' She laid it on the bureau and I stood by her as she began turning the pages.

It was 'the time of the café', she said. Twenty years ago, before Anton died. And there was Anton, looking handsome, with thick dark hair and a walrus moustache, smiling by the bar, smiling sitting on his coal cart, smiling in a garden, wearing his best clothes, smiling with his arm round a beautiful blonde girl. 'Valya,' said Mrs Gavrilovich.

The girl was Valentina. She was wearing a white embroidered blouse. Her hair was long and piled up on the top of her head. She'd lain her head on her father's shoulder. I thought, it's not surprising that I'm in love with someone so fantastically gorgeous.

We spent a long time going through the album. I saw the coal yard where Anton had died and the little dog, Semion, he'd owned at the time. There were photographs of a New Year's Eve party in the café, where everyone looked drunk and Valentina was kissing a man wearing a wastepaper basket on his head. 'Alexis,' said Mrs Gavrilovich. 'Valya's husband, long ago. Crazy, he was. You can see it, no? Completely crazy.'

'What kind of crazy?' I asked.

'Just crazy, Louis. Valentina came to me about one year after the wedding and said, "Matushka, last night Alexis tried to burn down the flat." So she left him and came back to live with us over the café.'

'What happened to Alexis?'

'I don't know. Valya divorced him long ago. Perhaps he's still living, still crazy somewhere, still poor. Who knows?'

By the last page of the album, Valentina was fatter and Anton's hair was going grey. Mrs Gavrilovich had lost one of her front teeth and the terrier, Semion, had a white muzzle. The café, which was called the Café des Russes, had acquired an awning and the old horse and cart used for the coal deliveries had been replaced by a second-hand Citroën pick-up truck. There was only one other photo of Alexis. In it, he was lying on the ground in the snow, looking up at the sky.

Tucked loosely into the back of the album were two pictures of a young woman, sitting at a desk. I recognised the desk: it was the one I was going through right now. There was a different, smaller computer on it, but it was definitely Valentina's desk. 'Who's this?' I asked.

Mrs Gavrilovich glanced at the photos and then looked away. She shook her head. 'Aach,' she said. 'That girl! Put them away.'

'What girl?'

'Trouble, that one. Nothing but trouble for Valya. Put her away.'

I took the pictures over to the desk and laid them face down in a drawer. I thought, I'll do as she says now, but I'm not going to forget about them.

That evening, a rainstorm came. I stood at my round window and looked out of it for ages, remembering rain. There were a few people in the windows opposite, staring out too, like you'd stare if war had broken out, or if the street had caught fire.

When the storm was over, the air smelled odd, like damp wool. I felt lonely. I thought, the days are just passing. What if September comes and we have to go back to England and Valentina still hasn't been found?

I picked up *Le Grand Meaulnes*, which had fallen under my bed. It was getting dusty under there. It was a long time since I'd read a word of it; I'd been diverted by *Crime and Punishment*. But now I thought, I want to see how François is holding up. I knew what he'd called his 'days of sorrow' could be coming soon and I wanted to see what he did to get through them.

He was on a quest to find someone. It wasn't really his quest, but Meaulnes', whose only single waking and sleeping dream was to get back to the 'lost domain' where he'd glimpsed Yvonne de Galais and made friends with her brother, Frantz.

François has never met either of these people. The only evidence he has that they exist is this silk waistcoat Meaulnes brings back with him after his adventure. But this is all Francois thinks about, too – helping Meaulnes to find them. He never says, 'Listen, Augustin, perhaps you dreamt up this fantastic château and the dazzling Yvonne and the fancy-dress party and Frantz's fiancée who never arrives; perhaps you fell asleep in the cart when you got lost and had the most brilliant dream of your life?' He just makes all that the centre of *his* existence and then his first real 'day of sorrow' arrives.

Meaulnes announces suddenly that he's leaving Sainte-Agathe, because he's heard Yvonne is living in Paris. He just deserts François and Millie and Monsieur Seurel and everyone and goes off with hardly a word. François watches his carriage disappear at the turn of the road, then he says: 'For the first time in months, I found myself alone before the prospect of a long Thursday afternoon, feeling as though my adolescence had been borne away in that old-fashioned carriage for ever.'

The thing that made me feel worst about the departure of Meaulnes was that Millie was embarrassed in front of the superior Madame Meaulnes, who came to collect him. It had been Millie's washday and all the damp sheets and towels were draped around the classrooms to dry, which made the schoolhouse seem like some old stinky laundry, and so she was ashamed. Millie is a tragic character. She makes new hats out of bits and pieces sewn on to old ones; she cooks on the school stove to save fuel.

The rain had stopped, but the wet wool smell seemed to linger in my room and merged in my mind with the smell of Millie's laundry. I was thinking about the power a book can exert over my psyche, when I suddenly asked myself a question. I may even have asked it out loud. The question was: 'Why, when every other book in Valentina's study is on a shelf or in a pile on her desk, was that one Russian book hidden in a bureau drawer?'

I sat up and looked at my clock. It was just after midnight.

In the maids' rooms opposite, some lights were still burning. I crept down to Valentina's study. Sergei still slept on his tatami mat in her bedroom, just as though she were snoring there in the enormous bed. Dogs' memories are meant to be good, but Sergei's sometimes seemed a bit flawed.

I took the book out of the bureau drawer and went back up my stairs with it. The cover had no picture, only a lot of Russian writing in red and black. In my search with Mrs Gavrilovich I hadn't paid it any attention, but now I saw that it was interleaved with yellow Post-It notes, about twenty of them, going right through the book. As well as these, there were pencil writings in the margins – all in Valentina's handwriting. They said, for example, *voir Pierre, voir Isabelle, utilise ceci à prop. de B, idée possible pour Belfort (ville)?, quels étaient les poisons?, voir Père H . . .*

I could guess immediately from this what she was doing. It was completely transparent: she was snitching ideas from this old Russian history to use for *Pour l'amour d'Isabelle!* I remembered what Alice had told me about the pressure on Valentina from Bianquis and I thought, this is how she's getting through the new novel – she's stealing stuff from a Russian source that nobody will ever unearth.

I turned back to the red-and-black jacket. The author was called Григорий Панин. I thought, I bet Григорий Панин, whoever he may be, lives in some horrible little apartment, worse than Violette's, where the electricity comes on for only a few hours a day. He's probably never earned any proper money in his entire life and would die of shock if he knew what Valentina had spent on her 'Ypres' scarf.

I went to sleep dreaming about the scarf. I was counting the number of poppies on it and the number came to ten and then to thirty-one and then to fifty-three and then to a hundred and seventy-five.

In the morning, it was as if the rain had never been. The rue Rembrandt was dusty and dry again and the sky was bright.

Alice told me there was a parcel for me, from Hugh. 'What's he sent you, then?' she asked.

I said: 'I can't tell you. It's to do with his project,' and took the package up to my room.

Hugh had wrapped Elroy in a piece of kitchen roll. When I took him out, I saw that his Royal Marines uniform, which had got dirty over the years, had been washed and ironed. The feel of his plastic body in my hands evoked for me all the hundreds of missions I'd sent him on and, to my horrible shame, I found I was quite affected by this. I threw him on my bed and thought, God, I'm a retard.

Included with him was a letter from Hugh, which went:

Dear Lewis,

Just a quick bulletin from the Home Front.

Bertie and I have had a go at mending Elroy. (We're getting so skilled at building things, we believe we can fix anything now!) His body won't be quite as mobile as it was, but at least he's in one piece! We hope you approve.

Drove Bertie and Gwyneth into Portsmouth yesterday, for shopping and tea. Your Gran spent a fortune on a splendid new outfit for Cousin Minnie's wedding next month (you and Mum will be back in time for this; a rather glitzy affair in London), then we found a wonderful Danish tea room with a garden at the back, serving excellent pastries. All in all, a very enjoyable outing.

Trust all continues fine chez Valentina. I miss you both and have started to count the days till you return.

With love from Dad

I made my bed and buried Elroy in it, so that Alice wouldn't find him. I put all the packing stuff and Hugh's letter in the wastepaper basket.

I heard footsteps on my stairs then. Footsteps on those stairs were always Valentina's in my mind.

Alice's head appeared and she said: 'I just had a phone call from the commissariat. An Inspecteur Carmody. He wants to see us straight away.'

'Why? Has something happened?'

'He wouldn't say. He wants us to go there now.'

I sat down on the top step. Alice sat three steps lower. All I knew was that if I was going to be told that Valentina was dead, I wouldn't be able to bear it. I'd start screaming or howling like a wolf, or throwing chairs around, or biting the wall. I just wouldn't be able to get through the next moments of my life.

'How did he sound?' I said. 'Did he sound as if he had bad news.'

'He sounded ordinary . . .'

'What do you mean, "ordinary"?'

'Calm. Polite. He just said he wanted to talk to us.'

'About Valentina?'

'I assume. Shall we go now and get it over with?'

I didn't want to 'go now'. I felt as if I wanted to sit rooted to this step for the rest of time.

I said quickly: 'If anything terrible had happened to her, he wouldn't have wanted *me* to go, would he? He'd have tried to protect me, because I'm thirteen. He'd just have asked to see you on your own, wouldn't he?'

'Yes, probably.'

'Definitely, he would. Then you would be able to tell me later, when I was at home, when I was sitting down, or something . . .'

'Perhaps.'

'No, it's certain. Are you sure he asked to see us both?'

'Yes. "You and your son", he said.'

'Then it's OK. I know it's OK . . .'

The walk to the commissariat took only about four minutes. Part of me wanted to get there right away and another part didn't want to get there at all, ever. We didn't talk on the way, but just walked hand in hand, like we used to do when I was small. It was Saturday and some of the residents of the rue Rembrandt had their chauffeurs there, polishing their cars, and

I wished I was a chauffeur with nothing to worry about except a Mercedes.

There was a different *brigadier* on the desk, older-looking, with better handwriting. He asked us to wait. I wondered if there was ever a moment in this commissariat when there was no one waiting and the *brigadiers* could all lounge around and talk about football.

We waited quite a long time. I thought I was going to get that feeling of being behind a glass panel again, but I didn't. I just had a pain in my chest that felt like a tumour. Grandma Gwyneth told me that shock and terror can give people cancer. It makes their immune systems forgetful.

A woman police person came to get us. She wore trousers like the men and carried a gun in a holster on her hip and the *brigadier* addressed her as Denise. She had black hair in a ponytail. As we followed her up a flight of echoey stairs, I thought, I hope Denise will hold me when I start to hurl the chairs around.

We were shown into Carmody's office. The room was small, on the sunny side of the building, with a venetian blind drawn down. Inspecteur Carmody didn't look like a policeman; he looked more like a flamenco dancer. He had large brown eyes that glittered in a tanned face. He wore a white shirt and a smart little blue waistcoat, undone all the way down because of the heat. 'Sit down,' he said.

We waited. I wanted Alice to say something, but she didn't. Carmody had a piece of paper in front of him with typed notes on it. He picked up a pen and rolled it in his brown hands.

'She isn't dead, is she?' I blurted out.

Carmody looked at me kindly. 'I hope not,' he said. 'We don't know where she is or what has happened, but we have realised now *who* she is and so we are treating this as a possible kidnap. This is why I wanted to talk to you.'

So, he didn't know anything. He wasn't about to describe finding Valentina's black-and-white dress on a piece of wasteland or floating in the river. Nothing was going to become final – at least, not yet. I began to breathe deeply again and after a minute I felt my tumour get small again, as if the air I was taking in was making it melt away.

We bought hot dogs and sat in the Parc Monceau near the kids' roundabout. The children all had big smiles on their faces, as if this carousel ride were the most brilliant thing that had ever happened to them. Alice said: 'Sometimes I wish you were a child again,' and I said: 'I *am* a child for about two point three minutes in every twenty-four hours. But on certain days I'm seventeen, as I expect you've noticed.'

Alice smiled. Then we started to discuss our meeting with Inspecteur Carmody. He told us that the likelihood of a kidnap having occurred was, in his opinion, high. The motive would be money. Everyone knew that Valentina Gavril was rich. If she had been kidnapped, he would expect a ransom demand to arrive within the next few days, sent either to Valentina's publishers, Bianquis, or to Mrs Gavrilovich, or possibly even to us at the flat. He said the case had been assigned to him and he would be talking to everybody who had had anything to do with Valentina in the last year.

He watched us closely all the time he was speaking, as if, in the back of his mind, lay the idea that we might be guilty in some way, and then asked us to state exactly what we were doing in Paris and how long we intended to stay.

Alice remained calm. She smiled at Carmody and I watched him to see if her beauty was going to affect him and I saw immediately that it did. He leaned forward as she began speaking and rested his chin on his hands. He wrote nothing down.

Alice told him about Valentina's new novel and the need to translate it quickly. She said the period of time we intended to stay was a further four weeks and then we would go home to Devon. Carmody interrupted her and said: 'Would you go home in four weeks even if the translation isn't finished?'

'Yes,' said Alice. 'Lewis has to return to school.'

Carmody said: 'So if you can go home in four weeks, you don't really need to be here in Paris at all to do this work. Is that right? Mademoiselle Gavril could send you her text, or fax it to you, and you could work on it in England. Is that the position?'

'Yes,' said Alice, still staying calm, 'but Mademoiselle Gavril likes to have her translator there, with her, when a deadline is approaching. She did it before, when she employed an American translator. She – I don't know her name – lived for a while in the apartment, working on the book, just as I'm doing.'

'How long have you been her translator?'

'This is my second book of hers. I started working with her in 1992.'

'And this arrangement was going all right?'

'Yes.'

'You get on well with Mademoiselle Gavril?'

'Yes, I do.'

'Does she pay you fairly?'

'She doesn't pay me. The English publishers pay me.'

'Pay you well?'

'Yes.'

'Good. And your son. Why is he here? Does he speak French?'

'Yes.'

Carmody turned to me. 'Tell me why you are here,' he said.

I opened my mouth. I didn't know what words were going to come out of it, if any, or in what language. 'Pour apprendre . . .' I said.

'Pour apprendre le français?'

'Oui. Pour apprendre beaucoup de choses.'

Carmody smiled kindly. 'Quelles choses?' he said.

I thought, I can't tell him what I've learned – that women's lipsticks have names, that the bouquinistes aren't really interested in selling books, that Russians eat real bread in church, that there are eight different strains of broccoli growing

165

in the Jardin des Plantes, that Paris roofs are complicated, that cheap cafés once sold coal, that Yves Montand used to be Valentina's favourite singer and that I had become her favourite lover in my mind . . .

'Tout est différent ici,' I said. 'J'ai appris cela.'

He nodded. He seemed to be satisfied with that. He was a man who could look very severe one moment and gentle the next.

He asked Alice a lot of questions about Valentina's routine and the answers to these he wrote down. He wanted to know if she had any enemies and I was afraid Alice was going to mention the 'killing' of the American translator, but she didn't. She said Valentina had no enemies as far as she knew.

Then he asked who came to the apartment and who worked there and I knew that what Alice said next might alter Violette's life for ever, but I couldn't change it or stop it from happening. At least Alice called her Babba, and I knew that as Babba she was difficult to find.

We were there for about an hour, then Carmody said we could go. He said he didn't want this story coming out in the press and that we should mention nothing to anyone. He said we should phone his personal number if anything happened that worried us, or if any information of any kind came our way. He gave Alice a card with his name on it: Inspecteur Francis Carmody. The only person who never got mentioned in the entire interview was Hugh. It was as if it had never occurred to Carmody that Hugh might exist.

I thought I'd have nightmares about the things that were happening, but I didn't. I had a velvety kind of sleep, quite soothing and still, and I woke up feeling hungry again. But when I went down to get some breakfast, I realised there was hardly any food left in the fridge.

I woke Alice up and told her everything was disintegrating round us, without Valentina and without Violette. 'Without who?' said Alice, but I ignored this. I pointed out to her that there was a smell under the sink and that we'd run out of tins of dog food and the oranges Valentina kept in a glass bowl were going grey.

Alice made coffee and sent me out to buy croissants in the rue Sainte-Honoré, and while we ate this breakfast she announced what we would do that day: we would go to the Sunday market near the Bastille and buy the kind of provisions we'd never eat at home. Then we'd bring them home and clean the apartment from top to bottom and cook ourselves a crazy meal and watch TV. Just occasionally, the plans that Alice makes are reasonably good.

The market was in the Boulevard Richard Lenoir. Alice told me this was where Inspecteur Maigret supposedly lived. I said: 'Well, it's a shame he isn't real and still living here. He'd be useful now.'

I liked the market. I wished we'd been there in the very early morning, before anybody got there, when it was setting up, when the vans came in and all the fish and flowers and cheeses and cooking pots were unloaded on to the stalls. You guessed that some stuff had come from far away because the stall holders looked really tired, with grey circles under their eyes; they could have driven all night from Brittany or somewhere to sell red mullet or pine nuts or helium balloons.

One stall had nothing on it but tiny little turtles, made of flimsy brass, inside walnut shells. The limbs of these turtles palpitated all the time, to make it seem as if they were alive, and a whole cluster of people gathered round to watch them. Things which look alive but aren't sometimes interest the human mind more than things which look alive and are. Waxworks, for instance. The sellers of the turtles were a Japanese couple. They kept calling out: 'No batteries in these turtles! No batteries anywhere!' I don't know where they'd driven from, but they'd had to bring their two babies with them, and these Japanese babies were fast asleep in a double pushchair, with their round faces nodding towards each other like sunflowers in a breeze. Some of the people took their eyes off the turtles to watch the babies instead.

We walked a long way before we bought anything at all, because Alice wanted to see everything before she decided what we were going to get. During this long walk, it was my job to restrain Sergei from eating everything in sight, even old cabbage leaves and squashed grapes. Then we stopped at a fantastic caravan selling fish and Alice got squid, mussels and prawns. She'd decided she was going to cook a gigantic paella. She bought a bunch of coriander the size of a bouquet of flowers, a rope of garlic, peppers, tomatoes and onions, a yellow-looking chicken with its feet still on, a twist of saffron in a muslin bag, a sack of rice and 250 grams of cashew nuts. I said: 'This paella's going to feed about ten people, Alice.'

We were wandering back with the pannier full of all this food, with our heads in the kind of trance you can go into in a market, when we came face to face with Didier. He looked as if he were in a trance, too, not really paying attention to things, but when he saw us he seemed shocked almost and just stopped dead in his tracks.

He wasn't alone. There was a girl of about twenty-two hanging on to his arm and they both had shopping bags filled with stuff from the market. I thought, it's like they're a young married couple doing the Sunday grocery shopping. I was about to say to Alice, 'I thought Didier lived by himself,' but there was no time to say anything because there we were, right near to him.

He stared at us and we stared at him. It was like we were German infantry and they were French Resistance fighters and we'd met by accident in a lonely wood, and now Didier thought we were going to kill them.

The girl's name was Angélique. Didier introduced her in an embarrassed way, as though he thought Angélique was a stupid name. We both shook her hand and she nodded at us, but said nothing. She had a big pale face, with no make-up on it. She wore an ugly dress with a pattern of violets all over it. She said: 'Vous venez d'Angleterre?'

She annoyed me somehow. It was the way she clung to Didier. I didn't like the thought of someone trying to cling on to Didier-the-Bird. And I could tell she infuriated Alice. When Alice is irritated or angry, a kind of electric current seems to fizz out of her and her arms go pink. She ignored Angélique's question about where we came from and said to Didier: 'What have you been buying, then?'

Didier didn't even look down at his carrier bag; he just gazed at Alice, his eyes pleading, Don't shoot me, let me live . . . 'Oh,' he said, 'provisions. You know . . .'

Alice then told him about our paella. She said, 'It's a shame. If you had been there on the roof, we could have invited you,' and smiled her most devastating Alice Little smile, and then she took my arm and swept us on without saying anything more. Angélique had begun a sentence about Sergei, saying she thought he was a beautiful dog, but we didn't wait to hear the end of it. We just rudely said goodbye and went past them and straight away Alice said to me that she was thirsty and we had to find a café and have a drink. In the café, she ordered a *demi* and drank it down fast. As she drank, I could see that electric sparks were still exploding on her skin.

I said nothing. Sentences came and went in my mind, but I didn't utter them. I turned away from Alice and focused on some hippies at the next table who were trying to pay for a cup of tea with a credit card.

The first sound we heard when we got back to the apartment was the vacuum cleaner. I thought, either it's Violette or . . .

But it was Mrs Gavrilovich. She had an old scarf tied round her head and she told us she was vacuuming because she couldn't stand the silence.

When we'd put all the food away, we sat down with her in the salon. The vacuum cleaner stood near the door, like a sentry on guard. It was a German make of cleaner, with the most powerful kind of motor you could buy. Violette once said to me: 'You could suck up the Sahara desert with that machine, Louis.'

Mrs Gavrilovich told us that Inspecteur Carmody had been to see her. He'd called and requested that she went down to the commissariat, but she told him bluntly that if he couldn't be bothered to make the journey to her flat he shouldn't be in charge of the investigation. 'Carmody,' she said. 'What kind of name is that? He looks like a Georgian. I don't trust him one bit.'

He'd said he had to verify the 'interêt de la famille', and when she'd asked him what this meant he'd demanded to know if she would profit financially from Valentina's death. 'I ask you!' she said. 'What does he mean? How do I know what is in Valya's will? I said: "The thing I've profited from, Inspecteur, is my daughter's life." '

He'd asked her for a photograph of Valentina. She said this had broken her heart to give away a picture and to imagine that this beloved picture might be put on to posters in police stations, with the word *disparue* written across it. She couldn't believe these terrible things were happening to her.

I went on with the vacuuming, while Alice started preparing the paella and Mrs Gavrilovich fed Sergei and brushed his coat. She, too, had noticed that he'd begun to smell a bit and I asked her if I should take him to the grooming parlour. She said: 'I don't think he would be welcome back there. He behaved very badly last time,' and we had a laugh about this, then and there, in the middle of vacuuming and sorrow. Mrs Gavrilovich took the scarf off her head and used it to mop her laughter away.

I decided to fetch the Russian book. I wanted to see if Mrs Gavrilovich knew who Григорий Панин was. I'd worked out two possibilities: (1) that he was dead by now, so he'd never know that Valentina was snaffling his ideas, or (2) that he was absolutely not dead, but had found out his work was being plundered and was so furious that he'd kidnapped Valentina, to teach her a lesson.

Mrs Gavrilovich put her glasses on when I handed her the book. 'What do you want to know, Louis?' she said.

'Who the author is and what the title means.'

'Grisha,' she said. 'It's Grisha's book,' and she traced the Russian characters with her finger: G-r-i-g-o-r-y P-a-n-i-n.

'*La Vie secrète de Catherine la Grande?*'

'Yes. *Tainaya Zhizn Ekateriny Velikoi.*'

I stared at her. I was remembering the conversation I'd had with Grigory on the way back from the book-signing, when he'd told me that Valentina hadn't let him see any of her new novel, and now I understood why – and why Valentina kept saying that hardly anybody in France would read Grisha's 'little' book.

But was Grisha lying? Had he somehow got access to Valentina's text and seen exactly what she was trying to do? Grisha's career as a writer was probably the only hopeful thing in his life. To discover that Valentina was just taking and using whatever she liked from the only book of his that had been translated outside Russia could have driven Grisha into a fury so great he could have lured her – on some research pretext? – to a deserted horrible place in the *banlieue* and strangled her. He was a strong man. He could have dug a deep hole and buried her. Then he could have gone to a public toilet and washed the dirt off his hands and shoes, found a taxi and caught his plane for Moscow. It could still be several days or even weeks before her body was found . . .

'What's the matter, Louis?' Mrs Gavrilovich asked. And I realised she was watching my face and that my mouth had been hanging goofily open while I tried to work all this out.

'Nothing,' I said.

Then I remembered the hospital appointment. If Valentina really had kept her appointment, which could have lasted till, say, four-thirty, Grisha would barely have had time to do all this strangling and grave-digging *and* catch an early-evening plane back to Russia.

'When you rang the hospital,' I said to Mrs Gavrilovich,

'were they absolutely one hundred per cent certain that Valentina arrived for her appointment?'

'Yes. That woman said she saw her.'

'And her appointment was at ten past four. Do you think Grisha was with her?'

'Why would Grisha be with her, Louis?'

'To keep her company . . .'

'Well, she didn't say. They wouldn't remember if someone was with her necessarily. In hospitals, they don't remember anything. She admired Valya's dress, that's all.'

'Did you tell Carmody about her hospital appointment?'

'That Carmody! I told him nothing. He wanted to see my passport. He treated me like someone illegal. I told him, "Inspector, I and my husband were working in France, in that stinking abattoir at La Villette, before you were born!" '

'Perhaps we should tell him about the hospital. The hospital is the last place where Valentina was seen.'

'OK. Well, we'll tell him that. He can go down there and deport a few nurses and doctors . . .'

I didn't show Mrs Gavrilovich all the notes and markings in Grisha's book. I decided the next important thing to be done was to read the book in the French edition, and find out exactly how much stuff Valentina had taken from it.

The apartment began to smell of steaming mussels and garlic. Quite often when I was hungry these days, I got this image in my mind of the battle for Caen and hundreds of people living under floorboards or in cold cellars, with nothing to eat.

We invited Mrs Gavrilovich to share the paella. She said we were good people. She said, 'The English are cold, but good.' Alice poured us all some white wine and we sat in the salon, waiting for the paella to be ready and watching the light at the windows deepen to blue. Alice reminded Mrs Gavrilovich briskly that she wasn't English at all.

Just as we were going to start the paella, the doorbell rang. We all had the same thought: we believed it was Carmody.

Neither of the women moved, so I got up and answered the door. It wasn't Carmody; it was Moinel. He said: 'Louis, can I talk to you?'

We went out on to the landing. Moinel was wearing a seersucker shirt and baggy trousers made of sailcloth. His tangerine hair looked mussed, as though he'd just got out of bed. 'Is she back?' he whispered.

I didn't know why we had to whisper, but I assumed there was a reason, so I said quietly: 'No, she isn't.'

Then he put a hand into one of the pockets of his sailcloth trousers and he brought out a thin gold chain. He let it rest on the palm of his hand. 'I found this,' he whispered. 'I was walking home last evening, about eight o'clock, and I stopped by the scaffolding on the corner of the building, to get my key out. I looked down and I saw this chain on the pavement, almost under one of the scaffolding poles, almost hidden, and I wondered if it might be hers, if it might be a clue . . .'

I recognised the chain. It was Alice's. It had been a Christmas or birthday present to her from Hugh. I took it from Moinel's palm and said calmly: 'I think it belongs to my mother, Moinel.'

'Ah,' he said. 'Oh well. Good. Then I'm glad I found it.'

Moinel went into his apartment and closed the door, but I didn't move. I put Alice's gold chain into my pocket and thought, I'll let her search for it; I'll let her search and search and never find it.

The following day, Babba turned up. I was standing on the balcony and I saw her coming slowly along the street. I waved to her, but she didn't see me. Babba always walked along looking at the ground – unlike Grisha who looked at the sky. Perhaps only a few nationalities of people are able to stand their surroundings well enough to take them in as they pass by?

I ran in to Alice and reminded her to call Babba Violette, and not Babba any more. She looked at me and said: 'You're becoming bloody bossy, you know, Lewis.'

The first thing Violette said was: 'Is Madame back?' I said no. I told her then that we'd been to see Carmody and that Alice had to give him her name and she shook her head, like she was exasperated with everything in the world.

Then I sat down at the kitchen table and said: 'If you can help find Madame, if Carmody knows you can help, then he won't be concerned about your work permit.'

Violette opened her bag and took out a purple tissue and blew her nose. She was still shaking her head, side-to-side, side-to-side. 'How can I find Madame?' she said.

I didn't mention the word 'spirits'. What I said was: 'There are a lot of things Carmody doesn't know. If we can give him useful information . . .'

''Bout what, Louis?'

'About . . . I don't know. About *why* someone would have done her harm . . .'

Violette began putting on her overall. She looked down at the kitchen floor, which hadn't been swept for days. Then she mumbled: 'Maybe it was that American girl?'

'The translator? The one who stayed here?'

'Yeh.'

'Were you here then?'

'No. My friend worked here. Lisette-Marie. She got me this job.'

Violette was going to begin her cleaning, but I stopped her. I saw suddenly that there could be a line to follow here. Valentina used to boast about the 'killing' of this person and no doubt it's impossible to 'kill' someone without consequences, even if they aren't actually dead.

'Who was the American girl?' I asked. 'What was her name?'

'I don't remember. All I know is Lisette-Marie told me this girl was ill. Then she went away.'

I fetched the two snaps that had fallen out of the photo album. I laid them in front of Violette and she looked at them, with a sad and sullen expression on her face. The girl had straight mousy hair. You would have described her as 'ordinary'.

'I think this may have been her,' I said. 'Have you ever seen her here?'

'No.'

'Will you show these to Lisette-Marie? Ask her to tell you if this is her and about what happened?'

'She doesn't know what happened. Just some trouble, that's all she know.'

'She might know what *kind* of trouble. If she was working right here in the apartment . . .'

'She said to me she didn't know. Because I asked her, I said, "If Madame Gavril is causing trouble, I don't want to work there." And she said, no, it was just that American girl, always screaming. But once she went away, everything was nice and quiet.'

'Screaming? Why?'

'No one knows, Louis. Only Madame.'

'Please try to find out more, Violette. Please take the pictures and talk to Lisette-Marie. Get her name and the exact date of when she was here. Will you? It might turn out to be important. Then we can tell Carmody—'

Violette was shaking her head again. She thought Alice and I had betrayed her, which we had. She left the photographs lying on the table. She wasn't really interested in them. She went to a cupboard and got out a broom and began sweeping the kitchen floor. Quite often, she sang while she swept, '*Ne me quitte pas, ne me quitte pas*', but today she was silent.

As Violette was finishing off cleaning the flat and preparing to leave, Alice came and found us and said she was going out.

'Where are you going?' I asked.

'To the Bibliothèque Nationale,' she said. 'I need to check some references.'

She smiled at Violette, but Violette turned her face away. Alice was wearing her blue dress and her amber beads. Her dark glasses were stuck on her head, in amongst her hair. I knew she wasn't going to the library.

I went as far as the apartment door with her. As she left, I touched the gold chain in my pocket, safely hidden from Alice's sight. I watched her hurry away down the stairs. The idea of following her was lapping at my mind like an icy tide.

I came back into the kitchen and made Violette put the two photographs of the American girl into her bag. As her rubbery hands snapped the bag shut, I thought, I may never see Violette again. She may have to leave us and leave her flat in the purple building and disappear into the crowd. So I said pleadingly: 'Carmody doesn't know your name. Only Babba. That's all he knows. No real name and no address. And if he asks, I'll say we don't know any of it.'

Violette nodded. 'OK, Louis,' she said.

I didn't follow Alice. I climbed up on to the roof. Exactly as I expected, Didier wasn't there. Some of his tools were lying around, so he'd been working that morning, but now, of course, he'd gone. He was hovering above Paris: a bird on a string, waiting for Alice Little to wind him in.

I sat down on the burning lead. I thought, where is it they go?

What I longed for was for Valentina to come and sit down in the sun beside me, so that I could talk about Didier and Alice with her. And she'd make it seem like something insignificant and ordinary. She'd put her arm round me and say: 'Nobody goes through life without lovers, Lewis. You'll see this for yourself very soon.' She would laugh. She would stroke my eyebrow with her finger, and I would lay my head against her breast.

I took Sergei for a walk in the Tuileries, where it was cool under the chestnuts. I sat down at the Pomone café and drank two *panachés* and the shadows of the trees on the gravel began to seem fantastic. No one yelled at me to get my dog out of the park.

When we walked on, I came across a brilliant bronze statue

of a woman sitting with her elbow on her knee. Her thighs were big, like Valentina's, but her breasts were small and pointy, like lemons. I walked all round her, looking at different bits of her bronze body. One of her legs disappeared into the plinth underneath her. The name of the sculptor was Aristide Maillol.

We were on our way to the grooming parlour. Even in the fresh air, the smell of Sergei had begun to waft towards my nostrils and I told him: 'We're going there right now and that's that.'

It was called 'Chiens etcetera' and it was up above an art gallery off the Avenue Matignon. It must have been the smartest animal-grooming parlour in the whole Western world. When you went in, there was a din of all the hairdryers blow-drying the four-legged clients and the clients barking and whining in the hot air.

I pretended Valentina had made an appointment. I thought she might have an account there and that everyone would know Sergei, and I was right about both things. As soon as they saw him, they produced an orange-flavoured chocolate drop for him and started stroking his head. 'Sergei . . .' they cooed, 'le méchant . . . !'

We had to wait for about ten minutes, till a bath-booth became available. I sat on a pink couch and Sergei stood on the white tiled floor, looking at everything and wagging his tail. I hoped he wouldn't do anything embarrassing. No white poodles came by. I don't know whether he remembered what had happened the last time or not.

Then a girl in a pink overall and wearing pink surgical gloves arrived to take him away for his shampoo. She gave me a scowl. At 'Chiens etcetera', they knew what I was: I was Valentina's slave.

Sergei looked like a star again. His tail billowed. He smelled of lemonade. In the street, the heads of the smartly coiffed people turned as he trotted along with his high step, like a prancing chestnut pony. I swear he knew he was beautiful.

On the way home, I began to think, if Alice is back, perhaps I'll give her the gold chain after all and confront her and then the air we breathe will get sweet again, like the Devon air.

But I could see her yelling at me and I didn't want this. She'd say I shouldn't believe, at the age I was, that I had a right to know everything. She'd say the world was far more complicated than I was capable of imagining. She didn't know how complicated my world already was.

I thought, what would François have done if Millie had taken the pony and trap and said she was going to Vierzon, say, and then he'd found out she'd been in the back room of the bakery in Sainte-Agathe? He would never have said: 'Millie, you're betraying us.' He would have just lain in his attic, listening to the wind, trying to figure out why. And eventually, he would have discovered why.

But Millie is a really different character from Alice. François always seems to know more or less what Millie is going to do and feel, but with Alice no one ever knows. When I was at infant school and she'd come and collect me in the old green Citroën 2CV she had, I'd never know where she'd be. I got used to not knowing. Sometimes, she'd be there talking with the other parents at the school gates, but on other days not.

Once, I found her sitting on the top of the slide. When she saw me, she slid down it towards me. In summer, she'd occasionally park the Citroën way down the lane and stand on the car seats, with her head and shoulders sticking out of the rolled-back roof, waving. Or else she'd be walking in the field behind the playground, or lying on a hay bale, smoking a cigarette. One day, she arrived in her bikini with just a towel round her and her hair soaking wet. She said she'd been swimming in the sea for three hours. I don't know what had happened to her clothes.

Another time, she didn't arrive at all; she just forgot about me and the head teacher had to ring her up and remind her. My best friend called Carl used to say to me: 'Is your mother really your mother, or is she someone else?'

She was mine. She got tired of me sometimes. I'd see her lose concentration while I was speaking to her and I'd know she was wishing she was somewhere else – in an Edinburgh late-night bar, or diving for pearls in the Indian Ocean. But, even though I looked nothing like her, I knew I belonged to her. She had a smell about her that was like mine; we neither of us could stand Lloyd Webber show tunes; we were both good at languages. Oh and Hugh told me he'd seen me being born, the bit of Play Doh that I was. He said my head had been as pointy as an elf's and Alice had laid my pointy head on her shoulder and cried with joy.

She wasn't in the apartment. And as soon as we went in, I knew something had happened there. The furniture in the salon had been moved around. There was a ton of ash and soot in the fire grate and the room smelled of this soot and of something else strange that I couldn't recognise.

I stood on the first bit of the parquet, listening and waiting. Then I called out: 'Alice? Alice? Qui est là?'

Sergei could smell the soot. His body began quivering. I held tightly to his lead and walked to Alice's room. Usually she left the french windows open, but now they were closed and when I looked over to her desk I got a real shock: her computer had gone. And it was clear that every bit of her room had been searched. One of her cupboard doors was open and all her clothes inside it were in jumbled heaps. I called her name again. Sergei began to whine, but no other sound came.

I went from room to room then, searching and calling. I knew what the goal of the burglars would have been: Valentina's jewellery. She had a safe somewhere in the apartment, but she'd never shown me where it was and I'd never found it. Keeping Sergei close to me, I went first to her study and then into her bedroom. The idea that men had come in and gone through Valentina's clothes and stolen her precious possessions was really bad.

Both rooms were a mess. Her dressing-table drawers had

been taken out and emptied and put back in the wrong order, so that they wouldn't shut properly. Some of her dresses lay on the bed and all her hundreds of pairs of different-coloured shoes had been heaped into a pile.

There was the smell of her perfume and I saw that one of her scent bottles had fallen over. The little TV she sometimes used to watch at night was still there on a chest of drawers, but in the study all the computer hardware had gone. And the desk and the bureau, where Mrs Gavrilovich and I knew every item, had been stripped of everything. Even the champagne corks had been taken and the street map of Beijing.

I sat down in her desk chair and unhooked the lead from Sergei's collar. He sat close to me, waiting to see what I was going to do. Then suddenly, I remembered my own room and got up and ran hurtling up my stairs.

My bed had been moved. There was a space between it and the round window. They'd been through my books and my chess set and the things on my night table. My Kermit alarm clock was upside down. But I was glad to find that Elroy was still there. He was lying on the bed, gazing up at the attic ceiling. He looked dazed, as if a tiny drop of chloroform had been splashed on to his face. The burglars had known he was of no use or value.

Sergei had followed me upstairs. I sat down on my bed, holding Elroy, and Sergei sat on the floor, twitching his blow-dried tail and watching me to see what bright ideas I was going to get. His breath smelt of dogs' toothpaste. After a few moments, I said to him: 'We have to call Carmody.'

We went back downstairs. I knew it would be better if Alice spoke to Carmody, because she'd be able to explain what had happened more precisely, but I didn't know when she was planning to come home; it could be hours before she did, and I didn't want to sit here alone, breathing the vandalised air. And Carmody had said: 'If anything occurs or if anything worries you, don't hesitate to call.' A burglary was definitely an occurrence.

I'd copied his number, from the card he'd given Alice, into my Concorde book. Carmody answered straight away, after half a ring, as though his hand had been poised above the receiver, waiting for my call.

'Oui?' he said.

I said it was Louis calling. I began to explain that there'd been a burglary in the apartment, but I'd hardly got started before I heard Carmody laugh.

'We are the "burglars", Louis,' he said.

'What do you mean?'

'We obtained the correct authorisation to search Mademoiselle Gavril's apartment. Her mother, Madame Gavrilovich, oversaw the operation and we assumed she had remembered to warn you and your mother. We have simply taken away the computers and some related material for investigation. It will be returned in due time, but we think it might yield some clues.'

'Oh,' I said. 'Are you sure it was you?'

Carmody laughed again. 'Yes. Quite sure. I think we left everything tidy.'

'No, you didn't,' I said. 'You moved the furniture around and you left Valentina's shoes in a pile and you made soot come down the chimney . . .'

'Oh, please accept my apologies.'

It pissed me off a bit that Carmody was mocking me. I said crossly: 'How's my mother going to work without her computer?'

'Don't worry,' said Carmody. 'Her computer will be returned tomorrow.'

There was a silence then. I wanted to ask Carmody what the peculiar smell was in the apartment, but at that moment I thought, it might be some kind of chemical dust used in fingerprinting. If they'd dusted the vacuum cleaner and the polisher, they could have found perfect prints of Violette's hands.

'I'm sorry you were frightened,' said Carmody after a while. 'Are you alone? Is that it?'

'Yes,' I said. 'I'm alone, except for Sergei.'

'Who is Sergei?'

'He's a dog.'

'Ah.' Then Carmody cleared his throat and said: 'Louis, where is your father?'

Alice came in at six forty-five. She'd been out for almost seven hours. She said she'd been reading in the Luxembourg Gardens. She told me she'd discovered they kept bees there, in little hives with pagoda-shaped roofs. She said she'd lost all count of time.

She found me in Valentina's room, going through her shoes and putting them all back, in pairs, into her wardrobe. Some of the shoes had a faint smell to them, of Valentina's scented feet. Some silver ones, in particular, and before Alice got in I'd lain on the rug in Valentina's bedroom with one silver shoe held to my nose and had an orgasm without touching myself, just by pressing against the carpet. I imagined her naked foot, with its scarlet toenails pushed into my crotch, rubbing me slowly. 'Come on, darling,' she whispered, 'come on.'

Alice helped me tidy the rest of the flat. She didn't know what I'd been doing on the floor of Valentina's room and I didn't know what she and Didier had done, out in their private sky. We cleaned in silence, not even talking about Carmody's untidiness.

When Alice knew her computer had been taken, she just said: 'Well, they won't find anything in it – only Valentina's novel, as far as I've got with it.'

'What else is on the hard disk?' I asked.

'Nothing,' she said. 'Absolute blank zero. Whatever was on there has been wiped.'

I watched her. Her nose and cheeks looked red from sitting in the sun. I thought, perhaps they made love in that park that's built on a mound of slaughterhouse bones?

When we sat down in the salon, I said: 'Everything's getting frightening, isn't it?'

She sat on the Louis XVI sofa again. It was like she was trying to make the apartment hers. She put her freckled arms up behind her head and looked at me. 'Do you want to go home?' she asked. 'Do you think that would be best?'

'No,' I said.

'Perhaps I should talk to your father and see if he thinks you should go back to England?'

I knew that when Alice referred to Hugh as 'your father', she'd put him into some far-away compartment of her heart, like he was a stranger in the street. I said: 'I'm not going back till they find Valentina.'

'I think Hugh may want me to send you back.'

'Then don't tell him what's happened.'

'We have to tell him.'

'No, we don't. Not yet. Carmody told us to tell no one. We don't have to tell him till it's over.'

We neither of us knew what I meant by 'over'. I stood by one of the windows, looking at Alice, watching her brain cells struggle with all the alternative meanings of this word.

'In September, you'll have to go back,' she said.

'So will you.'

'Not necessarily. I may have to stay and finish the work. It depends on whether the book can be finished or not.'

This didn't seem fair to me: Hugh and I starting our school terms and Alice staying on in Paris alone with her lover. I said: 'You can't do that. Think of Dad.'

'I do think of him,' she said. 'But Dad's very happy on his own. Can't you sense it in his letters?'

I said I thought he was only happy now because he was working on his project and because he had Bertie and Gwyneth with him. I said he was having a kind of second childhood, but in the autumn he'd have to be grown-up again and then he'd want us to go home. I expected Alice to say this was a stupid notion, but she didn't: she laughed loudly and brightly, like people laugh at old sitcom reruns on TV. Her laugh was like a bell, echoing all through the empty flat, trying to summon other laughter that wasn't there.

A wind began to sigh in the evening. In the streets, you could hear the café awnings rattling. On the pavement of the rue Rembrandt, I saw some yellow leaves flying along, like the ones I'd noticed at Nanterre, and when I went up to my room I felt more than ever like François, lying in his attic alone after Meaulnes has left, listening to the wind in the plane trees, except this was a warm wind and the wind at Sainte-Agathe always seemed to be cold.

At about one o'clock, I got up to pee. I didn't put on the light, but stood in my bathroom peeing by the reflected street light, and gradually, in the semidark, I became aware of a noise I'd never heard before: the door behind the clothes rail – the door to the locked room – was rattling.

I didn't flush the lavatory, but stood still, almost without breathing, and listened. It was as if the catch was loose in its metal socket, letting the door move very slightly, as the wind from the open window caught it. As I crossed the bathroom and moved aside the rail of Valentina's coats and dresses, I suddenly knew what I was going to discover: the lock had been forced by Carmody's men. And when I turned the handle of the door, it opened.

The attic was a junk room, just as Valentina had said. A lot of the junk must have come from the Gavrilovichs' café, long ago. There was a red-and-white awning, folded up. There was a huge Wurlitzer jukebox, an old billboard advertising Dubonnet, stacks of dusty bentwood chairs, an oven. But there was also a bed. The bed was against the wall, under the window, across which the curtains were still drawn. It looked tidy and ready for use, with a faded yellow bedcover thrown over it and a bedside table near it with a lamp and an ashtray. In the ashtray, there was a single cigarette butt, with a tipped end.

And there was a kind of pathway through the junk that led

directly from the door to the bed. You could imagine the occupant of the room moving things around, so that he or she didn't have to step over the oven in the middle of the night. I didn't blame them. I'd never shared a room with an oven. I thought, that's one way to measure whether someone is poor or not – if they have to share their room with a kitchen appliance.

I crossed to the bed and sat on it and looked at everything. There were stacks of boxes round the walls and when I got up to examine them I saw that Carmody's guys had only ripped open a few of these and then given up. They contained a mountain of Valentina's books. On the covers were garish pictures of damsels wearing tall hats and knights in armour on white horses flying through dark forests in the moonlight. You could just hear the *brigadiers* from the commissariat sneering and saying: 'Nothing here, Inspecteur. Only what appear to be medieval romances.'

And then they would have moved on, past a café umbrella stuck into a stone, a pile of red and blue curtains, two medieval-looking typewriters, a wire plant holder, a toolkit and a roll of carpet, to the Wurlitzer, where the titles of old songs, typed and numbered, were still faintly readable: *Chanson d'amour, La Bohême, A Whiter Shade of Pale, Que c'est triste Venise, Milord.* I stood by it, selecting numbers. But the records were gone and I didn't recognise any of the titles. I needed Valentina to tell me what they sounded like and which ones were her favourites in the old days of the Café des Russes.

I liked the Wurlitzer. I wouldn't have minded sharing a room with it. The body of it was a candy-pink kind of colour and you could tell it weighed about a ton. Hugh once said technological progress could be measured in weight alone. He said by the time I had children of my own, a CD player might weigh less than a daffodil.

I was wondering whether the Wurlitzer could ever be made to work again and where all the records had gone, when I noticed that on its pink body, on the left-hand side, there was a tiny little dial and a lever. I knelt down and tried to turn the lever. I thought that if they'd put this door on the Wurlitzer, the records might be inside. But the lever wouldn't move. Then I saw why. The dial was a combination lock. Valentina had turned the jukebox into a safe.

There was a tiny dusting of white powder, like talcum powder, on the floor directly underneath the lock. I assumed from this that Carmody had found it and dusted it for prints. What I couldn't tell was whether he'd worked out the combination and looked inside, where the plunder of Valentina's visits to Cartier must lie.

I began to spin the dial, trying combinations at random. In certain movies, safe-breakers can crack number codes just by putting their ears to the lock, as if the lock were a human voice whispering to them, but it's never explained to you how this works. The only kind of movies that I like are ones where you understand exactly how everything works. If I were a scriptwriter, I'd spend a lot of time on research into the material world.

When the safe didn't open and didn't open, I started to wonder how much Valentina's jewellery was worth. It had to be a lot. I thought I would say to Carmody that if a ransom demand came, all we had to do was blow the safe and hand over the jewellery. And then, when Valentina was back again, sitting at her dressing table while I brushed her hair and she put on her lipstick, she would say to me: 'I think I shall wear the sapphire-and-diamond earrings tonight, darling,' and I'd tell her they were no longer there. I'd say: 'We bought your life with them. You'd be in your grave now if it hadn't been for Cartier.'

I had a dream that Valentina *was* in her grave, but still alive, trying to breathe in the tiny bit of air between her nose and the coffin lid. I was digging in heavy, wet clay, digging with my hands trying to reach her. As I dug, I called out: 'It's OK,

Valentina! It's Lewis. I'm going to get you out!' But I kept on and on digging down and down and found nothing.

I woke up to the sound of hammering. I thought I was in my dream and the hammering was Valentina in her box under the earth, but then I realised it was morning and what I could hear was Didier on the roof.

It was quite early. I got dressed and climbed out of my bathroom window and I noticed that the wind had dropped and the trees in the street were still.

Didier was wearing a black T-shirt with an African mask printed on it. It didn't look faded like his other clothes, but brand-new, as if he might have bought it at the Richard Lenoir market. I thought, if Violette gets sent back to Benin, this is the kind of job she'll have to get – working in a T-shirt factory. I imagined her walking to work through miles and miles of dust.

I asked Didier why he hadn't been on the roof the day before. I watched him closely while he answered. He didn't take his eyes off the slate he was hanging. 'I was ill again,' he said. 'This flu keeps returning when I'm not expecting it.'

I didn't say: 'I know that's a lie. I know you're having a love affair with Alice.' Instead, I told him my dream about Valentina in her coffin, and when I described her hammering on the lid he took off his glasses and wiped some sweat from his face. 'What are the police doing about it?' he asked.

'There was a raid,' I said.

'A raid?'

'Yes. They searched the apartment and took lots of things away. Everybody's under suspicion, including me and Alice. And you.'

When I said this, he put his glasses back on again and shook his head. I could tell he didn't believe a word I was saying. The clever bit of Didier's mind could see right through me. It could see far more of me than my mind could see of him.

And he didn't want me there, asking him questions. He seemed serious today, sort of sad or depressed or something.

His bird tattoo looked as if it was breathing its last breaths as the pulse in his neck vein ticked. I thought, perhaps it's all over with Alice. It was Angélique who came along and destroyed it . . .

'Who's Angélique?' I said.

'Who do you think, Louis?' asked Didier, without looking at me.

'I don't know. Your new girlfriend?'

'My wife.'

I'd known this the moment I'd seen Angélique, but it shocked me then and it still shocked me. I should have been pleased that Didier-the-Bird wasn't all alone and free to snatch my mother away from her former life and break my father's heart, but somehow all I felt was disappointment.

I couldn't think of anything to say. I just hung about there, saying nothing, and Didier ignored me and worked on.

After about five minutes had passed, I said: 'I didn't think existentialists had ordinary things like wives.'

Didier still didn't look at me. 'Well,' he said, 'now you know that they do.'

Carmody arrived. He came with some lowly *agent* with acne, who'd been given the task of carrying in Alice's computer. Carmody looked like a man who never carried things. He had lazy eyes and the beginnings of a fat belly. While the spotty *agent* set up the computer on Alice's desk, Carmody sat in the salon, leaning back on the Louis XVI sofa, like a dinner guest. It was weird the way everyone kept putting themselves in the very place where Valentina should have been.

The *agent* left and Alice made coffee for Carmody. I watched him watching her as she came in from the kitchen and set the coffee down. Then he took out a notebook and said he had some good news for us.

'You've found Valentina?' I blurted out.

He turned to me and smiled. 'Perhaps . . .' he said.

'What do you mean – "perhaps"?'

Carmody took a sip of the too-hot coffee. He flipped through the pages of his book. 'We think,' he said, 'there is a strong possibility that she's in Moscow. Aeroflot confirm there was a last-minute passenger booked into the flight taken by Monsieur Panin. She was travelling under the name "Marya Narishkin", but the description of her – blonde, quite large, aged about forty – shows she could have been Mademoiselle Gavril. We have asked the Moscow police to trace this person, but they tell us they are so far unlucky. We have also discovered that Monsieur Panin is not at his home. His wife believes he is in Kiev. If he turns up there, we will be informed.'

Carmody looked delighted and proud of this information. He seemed to expect Alice and me to applaud him, but all we did was just look at him in silence.

'It's still strange,' said Alice. 'Don't you think, if Valentina had been planning to leave for Russia, she would have told us?'

'Perhaps it was not planned,' suggested Carmody. 'Perhaps she was coerced into it – by some means that we do not yet know – by Monsieur Panin, at the last minute?'

Alice shrugged. 'Knowing her as I do, I don't think she would be "coerced" into anything, Inspecteur.'

'With all respect, you may not know the nature of her relationship with Monsieur Panin . . .'

I got up. 'What time was the flight to Moscow?' I asked.

'17.40,' said Carmody.

'Then it's not possible that she was on it!' I said. 'She's not in Moscow or Kiev or anywhere in Russia!'

'We believe she is. The question of *why* she's there we haven't yet understood. No doubt there is a very important reason – which would be unknown to you.'

'No,' I said. 'She's not in Russia. I *know* she's not! At ten past four, she was at the hospital, in the rue de Vaugirard, for her X-ray appointment. She wouldn't have had time to get to the airport for a flight that left at 17.40.'

'Not so,' said Carmody. 'We spoke to her radiologist, Dr Bouchain. She didn't arrive for her appointment at the hospital.'

'Yes, she did!' I was screaming at Carmody now. I thought I might start to cry. He was the man in charge of finding Valentina and now he was wandering off on a completely stupid trail. 'Mrs Gavrilovich rang the hospital,' I said. 'She rang it while I was with her. The receptionist said she saw Valentina. She admired her dress . . .'

'Well, she was not checked in. There was a cross against her name.'

'The receptionist said she *saw* her. Who else in that hospital would have a dress she'd bother to admire?'

Carmody smiled. 'I don't know, Louis. But she must have been mistaken. There is a cross against the name. The receptionist was quite clear about their procedure: a cross indicates that the patient has not turned up for the appointment. In any event, Dr Bouchain never saw Mademoiselle Gavril at the hospital on that afternoon.'

I felt a kind of sob come into my chest, so I walked over to the window and put my hand over my mouth, so that the sob wouldn't escape. Suddenly I saw what was *prime* in the whole question of the hospital visit. If the receptionist had said 'black-and-white dress', this would have been absolute proof that Valentina had been there. But she hadn't said that. She hadn't described the dress; I'd just reimagined the black-and-white dress in my mind. The *prime* proof was missing.

I kept staring out of the window. An ambulance siren went screaming along the rue de Lisbonne.

'Does this mean,' I heard Alice say, 'that you're going to stop searching for Valentina in France?'

'No. Of course not,' said Carmody. 'When someone is missing, we go on searching until they are found – dead or alive. But we have no leads in France, absolutely none, whereas—'

I turned and faced Carmody. 'She's not dead!' I shouted. 'But she could be dead soon, if you don't hurry up and find her!'

'Why do you say that?' said Carmody.

'Because it's obvious! Someone's taken her. They want to get hold of her jewellery and her money. She's probably being kept in some horrible place. She could even be buried alive . . .'

'If she had been kidnapped, I would have expected some ransom demand to come by now. But there is complete silence. It's possible that such a demand may come, but as yet there is nothing to lead us towards a kidnap, except, as you say, Louis, the general motive of money.'

Carmody turned back to Alice. I could tell he thought my fury was amusing. He cleared his throat. 'However,' he said, 'the trail to Russia is beginning to emerge. Among the possessions we took from the bureau in Mademoiselle Gavril's study, we found two love letters, hidden inside a street map of Beijing. They are from Monsieur Panin, dating from earlier this year.'

Carmody leafed through his notebook again, then went on: 'One of the letters talks of suicide and the other includes the following sentence: *What I would like to do is drag you back here with me, so that you could see the misery that is my life.*'

Carmody rested his notebook on his knee and looked at us both in turn. He made an expansive gesture with his hands. 'Do you not feel,' he said, 'that this may at least be a pointer to what has happened?'

Sergei came into the salon at that moment, still smelling of lemonade and wagging his billowing tail. I made him sit by me and concentrated on stroking him, so that I didn't have to answer Carmody's question. I felt really confused and wretched, like my brain was being trussed up with wool. Inside the wool tangle somewhere was the thought that Grisha hadn't struck me as an evil man.

I wanted an ally.

Alice wouldn't do. Half her mind was elsewhere. I wanted somebody with an analytical brain, a kind of pedantic genius, like Porphiry Petrovich.

191

I was sitting alone in the salon, wondering if I actually knew such a person, when I heard a sound at the apartment door. It was Violette. I knew it was her because she always turned the key to the left to start with and then had to turn it the other way three times for the door to open. She never seemed to remember which way that lock turned. She wouldn't have been much good at chess.

As soon as she saw me, she started whispering. 'Come in the kitchen, Louis,' she said. 'I can tell you something.'

I followed her in. She put her bag down on the kitchen table, took out the two photographs I'd given her and handed them to me. 'I saw Lisette-Marie,' she said in her whispering voice. 'This American girl was called Gail. Gail O'Hara. Lisette says she was very bad to Madame. Very bad.'

'Bad how?'

'What is "bad", Louis? Cruel.'

'What did she do?'

'I don't know. But Lisette-Marie says, all the time she was here, Madame was unhappy. This girl used to shout. Lisette-Marie could often hear this shouting and insulting. And Madame was often crying.'

I looked at the two pictures. Gail O'Hara looked a bit neglected. Her hair was rather stringy and her fingers were stumpy, as if she chewed her nails. I looked up at Violette and said: 'Madame once told Alice she'd "killed" this girl, Violette. Does Lisette-Marie know what happened to her?'

'What you mean, "killed her"?'

'I don't know what I mean.'

Violette shook her head and made a gesture over her chest a bit like the sign of the cross. Then she sighed one of her sad sighs. 'All I know is she went into the hospital. Lisette had to pack a bag and Madame said she was taking this to Gail in the hospital. She was sick for a long time. And she never came back here. Lisette-Marie was told to pack all her things into a new suitcase Madame bought and this suitcase was put into a taxi. But I don't think she died, Louis. I think she just went home to the United States. That's what Lisette was told: "Mademoiselle O'Hara has gone back to her home." '

'Did Lisette-Marie see her after she went into the hospital?'

'No. I don't think so.'

'So she could have died?'

'No. If she had died, I think the police would have come.'

'Are you sure they didn't come?'

'They didn't come.'

'How do you know?'

'Lisette would have seen them.'

The Orangina supply had been replenished, so I poured us out two glasses. My brain was going into a kind of cash-register mode, trying to add things up.

I went on: 'Maybe they came when Lisette-Marie wasn't there?'

Violette shrugged. She had a shrug more expressive than anyone else's I'd ever seen. What it expressed was Violette's relationship with the world. It was like the world was the night sky and Violette couldn't say if the stars were pieces of rock or whether God had sprinkled the dark with luminous muesli.

I gave up nagging her at the point of her shrug and told her about Carmody's search. I didn't look at her while I described how thorough the police had been, even prodding about in the chimney and going through Valentina's shoes. I expected her to seem frightened, knowing the next thing Carmody might do was start questioning everybody in the building, but she didn't. And then, quite suddenly, she stood up and her face broke into a smile. She said: 'Never mind those untidy police; I can tell you some other news, Louis.'

'Can you? What other news?'

'Today is a good day. My work permit came through!'

'Hey!' I said. 'That's brilliant. That's fantastic!'

'Oui, c'est fantastique!'

And Violette began a little dance round the kitchen table, with her hands in fists, gyrating and her bum sticking out and swaying. 'C'est fantastique, c'est fantastique!' she kept on saying

193

and I joined in: 'C'est fantastique, c'est fantastique!' and tried
to dance with her. Sergei stood at the kitchen door, barking at
us, like we were two loons, and then Violette started singing
what could have been a voodoo chant or a wedding song or a
prayer or just a rhyme people sang in Benin when something
good happened to them, like the return of a stolen truck:

'Heh-heh, neh-neh, ciel, livrez-moi
Des beaux poissons et la main du Roi!'

I had to follow the Grisha trail. I knew more than Carmody
because I'd seen the Post-It notes in Grisha's book.

The next thing I had to do was to buy the French edition
of the book and make notes about what was in it. After that,
I had to get access to Alice's English translation and compare
the two. Then I'd know how much or how little Valentina had
pinched from Grisha. What I still wouldn't know was whether
Grisha knew about it or not.

I was thinking, I hope Valentina is in Russia. I hope we'll
get a call from her today saying she's coming back at the
weekend. Then we can all go out to the airport to meet her –
Alice and me and Mrs Gavrilovich and Sergei – and I'll be
able to stand where the passengers come out, knowing that
within minutes I'm going to see her . . .

On my way out of the door with Sergei, en route for
the bookshop, I heard the telephone ring. Alice wasn't in the
apartment, so I ran back and picked up the receiver. Every
time the telephone rang, I expected Valentina's kidnapper to
be on the other end of the line. I imagined his voice, muffled
by a balaclava. I imagined the phone booth he was in, outside
some horrible factory, or in a village miles away in the mountains. I would say to him: 'We'll pay whatever you're asking.'

It wasn't him. It was a woman from Bianquis, Valentina's
publishers, and her name was Dominique. 'C'est Dominique
Monod,' she said. 'Est-ce que Valentina est là?'

She sounded completely calm and normal, so I knew she
didn't know a thing. I thought for a moment, then I told

Dominique that Valentina was away in Russia and we weren't certain when she'd be back. To get this lie out, I had to hold on to the arm of the hard chair by the telephone table. I had a feeling that this news would upset Dominique and it did. She began shouting at me. 'In Russia? What on earth is she doing in Russia when she has a book to finish? Has she forgotten there's a deadline?'

'I don't know,' I said weakly.

'Who am I talking to?' asked Dominique crossly.

I said I was the son of Valentina's English translator. This didn't impress her. It was like translators were way down in her hierarchy of important people and the sons of translators were even further down, like the things Sergei found in the gutter.

'Well,' she said, 'do you have a contact number for Valentina? I suppose she has a telephone in Russia?'

'No,' I said.

'Yes, she must have a number.'

'No, there isn't any number.'

She started talking in English then. She thought I hadn't understood what she was saying, that I was an English moron who spent his life throwing beer cans at Eric Cantona.

'We think she's in Kiev,' I said. 'Why don't you try all the hotels in Kiev?'

'O, mon Dieu!' she said and hung up. I imagined she had long hard nails, like the receptionist in the hotel. She would slit open her post with these nails and slit the throats of her authors who missed their deadlines.

It was a beautiful day. Not as stiflingly hot as it had been, but just sunny and blue with all the traffic gleaming and the plane trees heavy and still. I walked down the Champs-Élysées, past guys trying to sell things to the tourists in the shadows of doorways. One of the things being hawked here were little rubber acrobats, smaller than a human hand. You threw them at the wall and they somersaulted backwards down the wall a few times and then fell off. You were meant to marvel at their agility and their ability to hold on to the wall before they fell, and the first time I saw them, I did marvel. Now, they looked a bit stupid, somehow, like I'd already outgrown them without ever buying one.

I found a pile of Grisha's book, *La Vie secrète de Catherine la Grande*, in the librairie of Virgin Megastore. I thought, if Grisha were in Paris, he'd probably come in here every day, to see whether the pile had diminished. On the back of the book was a photograph of Grisha, looking wild, as if he'd just woken up from a hectic dream. The price of the book had been printed over his left hand.

I was in the queue, waiting to pay, when I heard a soft voice say: 'Louis.'

Moinel was standing behind me. He was smartly dressed in a pale-blue suit, with his hair combed flat, and he held a pile of books. I felt quite glad that he'd spoken to me.

'Moinel,' I said. 'Comment allez-vous?'

He smiled and answered me in his perfect English with the Radio 3 accent. 'OK,' he said. 'But tell me what's happening in your apartment. Has Valentina come home?'

'No,' I said, whispering, so that no one else could hear, 'and there was a police search. They've taken masses of things away. It's getting quite frightening.'

I hung around while Moinel paid for his books. He spent 1161 francs and wrote out a cheque in very small writing. Then he invited me to come and have a coffee with him and tell him what was going on.

We walked into the sunshine and I untied Sergei from his bollard and Moinel held my elbow as we crossed the Champs-Élysées to a café on the other side called the Deauville. The waiters there wore rugby shirts and held their trays athletically high. They knew Moinel and shook his hand and I heard him order coffee and pastries and we sat down at a table just behind the glass, where the noise from the boulevard receded. I felt glad he'd ordered the pastries.

He told me to tell him everything that had happened, so I

ignored Carmody's instructions not to say anything to anyone. It was a relief to be able to talk in English and be precise and be understood. I described Carmody's Russia theory and my own forthcoming research into Valentina's snitching of ideas.

'Are we talking about plagiarism?' asked Moinel.

'Yes,' I said, remembering this word from one of Hugh's unasked-for lectures. 'That's it. Plagiarism.'

He said this was a serious matter, that Grigory was bound to feel really angry if he knew about it, and that Carmody's belief that Valentina was in Russia could turn out to be right.

I said: 'It could. But the thing I keep going back to is: what happened at the hospital? Was Valentina there or not? If she was never there, why did they tell Mrs Gavrilovich she was?'

'I know that hospital very well,' said Moinel. 'I go there all the time.'

'Do you? Why do you go there all the time?'

'Oh, check-ups and tests. Just routine. But I can find out their exact procedure for checking in patients. As far as I can remember, they put a tick when you arrive for your appointment, then when you go through to see the doctor, they make another mark, but I don't know what this is.'

The pastries were incredible, sugary and light, with a syrupy apricot, like the yolk of an egg, in the middle. Moinel gestured for me to eat them all and I saw one of the sporty waiters smile. While I was munching, Moinel went on: 'What we have to do is to go there and find out which receptionist was on the desk at around four o'clock that afternoon and talk to her. We take a picture of Valentina: that way she will be able to tell us if it was her she saw, or someone else. You can describe her dress. Then, to be absolutely certain, we have to try to get a look at the register.'

'Yes. But suppose Carmody finds out what we're doing?'

'He won't unless someone tells him. Who would tell him?'

'No one. Shall we go now? Why don't we just go now, straight away?' I said.

'No,' said Moinel, 'I have a business appointment now. What about tomorrow morning at ten-thirty?'

'OK,' I said.

'I'll meet you in this café at ten. I'll order some more pastries for you.'

'So we won't tell anyone, not even Alice?'

'Better not. It may lead nowhere.'

We sat on, drinking the good coffee. I asked Moinel where he'd learnt his brilliant English and he said he'd spent four years living in Pimlico. He said he had a share in an antique shop that sold nothing but garden statues. He said that in the 1980s, the minds of thousands of people in England had turned towards garden statues and then, slowly and sadly, turned away again when the recession came, and the shop had failed.

I said: 'What happened to all the leftover statues?' I imagined them in a yard somewhere, waiting for people's minds to turn back towards them, lions and urns and nymphs without arms, but Moinel said they were all sold off at auction to pay the shop's debts. He said: 'That was a bad moment. Like losing a group of friends.'

The bill came and Moinel paid it. I looked at him in admiration. I thought, I've found my ally. I'd never imagined my ally having tangerine hair.

When I got back, I began Grisha's book. The résumé on the back told me that Catherine's last lover, Plato Zubov, was forty years younger than she was. I thought, I want to get to that bit. I want to see whether Valentina uses this idea of the boy-lover in her novel.

But it was impossible to match the page numbers of the French text with the Russian. I couldn't identify where Valentina's margin notes fitted it, so I just had to begin collecting the kinds of things I thought she might use and write my own margin notes against these. My main margin note was *P?* for Plagiarism.

The first thing I collected was that Catherine la Grande had beautiful handwriting, as a result of getting calligraphy lessons. The *P* I put in the margin had no question mark against it.

It became obvious after a few pages that Catherine la Grande had had the kind of unexpected life writers could be tempted to steal things from. She was born in Germany and named 'Fike', but then she was taken away from her family and everything she knew and loved and sent on a long journey to the freezing cold Russian court. She was supposed to become the bride of Archduke Peter, the grandson of Peter the Great and the chosen successor to the Tsar. Nobody seemed to care what Fike thought and felt about this. An old Russian proverb in those days went: 'A chicken is not a bird, nor is a woman human.' They put her into a cold room under a bell tower and gave her lessons day and night on how to behave. They wouldn't let her write letters home to her mother.

Archduke Peter, her intended husband, was a puny wreck. He had what Grisha described as 'a very poor mental endowment'. He couldn't sit still, but fidgeted all the time. His teacher, Stehlin, had to walk up and down the room with him while he gave him lessons.

As a child, he'd had smallpox, so his skin was a mess. He refused to take baths or even wash his face. His favourite pastime was playing with his toy soldiers. He kept pet animals and birds and tortured them. On the night before her wedding to this disgusting Peter, Catherine looked at her wedding dress on its stand, made of spun silver and weighing as much as a suit of armour, and 'felt a chill of winter, a chill of death'. Against this sentence I put a gigantic *P*, underlined three times.

I went to see Mrs Gavrilovich. She said she was glad I'd come; she'd just been sitting in her apartment, staring at the wall. She served me cold tea and some hard biscuits like macaroons.

I refrained from telling her she should have remembered to warn us about Carmody's search. When we'd settled down with the tea and Sergei was crunching his share of the macaroons, I said: 'Carmody is convinced Valentina is in Russia with Grigory. Do you think he's right?'

She looked at me intently with her once-beautiful eyes. 'Louis,' she said, 'you are a boy. It's too soon for you to learn everything in the world.'

I said I didn't want to learn everything in the world; I just wanted to know whether, in her opinion, Carmody's theory had an ounce of sense in it.

She leant back in her armchair and gazed intently first at one bit of the room and then at another, as if she were trying to locate where God had got to in it. Then she sighed. 'Grigory Panin is a very unhappy man,' she said. 'And now, I believe, he sees what his life would be if he had married Valentina — and this makes him very bitter.'

'Did he ask Valentina to marry him once?'

'She refused him. She didn't want to be married. She wanted her freedom.'

'Does she love him?'

'Yes. A little.'

'Enough to go back with him to Moscow?'

'No. She has a good life now. She never knew Moscow. We were farmers, miles from the city, near Gorodnya, south of St Petersburg. Valentina was three when we left Russia. Why would she do that — exchange her good life for a bad one? If she is in Russia, then Grigory threatened her with something very serious. What that serious thing could be, I don't know, Louis. I rack my brain. But I'm an old woman and my brain is slow . . .'

I took a sip of tea and said: 'Could it have something to do with Valentina's new book? Has Grigory seen a copy of the book?'

'I don't think so. Nobody has seen that book — only Alice.'

An image flashed into my mind then, like a photograph. It was the view I'd had that night from our restaurant table, with the Eiffel Tower gold and vast to the right of me. In the photograph Grigory had his back to me; he was walking away, in his fury, up the Avenue Montaigne and just coming into the frame, running to catch him up, was Alice.

I must have looked like a zombie suddenly, staring at this imaginary photograph, because Mrs Gavrilovich said: 'What is it, Louis? What are you thinking now? Look at Sergei! I've given him four macaroons and he's asking for more.'

'No more!' I said to Sergei. Then I asked: 'What is Kiev like?'

'Kiev? Once a beautiful city. The frescos at Kievo-Pecherskaya, I remember, and Kotsiubinsky Park. I suppose a lot of it was pulled down, but not all, and I was told some new cafés were opening now on the river. It may have lost all its heart since the accident at Chernobyl, I don't know. The climate in summer is very good.'

'Can you imagine Valentina living there?'

'No. I can't imagine Valentina living anywhere but Paris.'

Then Mrs Gavrilovich got up and shuffled into her bedroom where the shrine with the candles was. She seemed to have forgotten about the geranium-watering today. She came back with the photograph of the white-haired man that I'd seen and which I knew from the album was Anton Gavrilovich, and she gave it to me. 'I've been talking to Anton,' she said. 'You see what a kind face he has? And he loved Valentina so much. I believe he is somehow protecting her. Between them, Anton and God are keeping her safe: this is what I must believe.'

It was stuffy in Mrs Gavrilovich's apartment. When I came out, I decided to take Sergei for a walk along the river, where you could sometimes feel a breeze blowing in from the north.

We sat down on the Pont des Arts and listened to a saxophonist playing some old bluesy number from a distant era. In the streets of Paris, you can hear music from every century and every time. In London, all you get is rap and rock and the lousy buskers on the Tube. Hugh once said that England is a country slowly losing its hearing.

Sergei didn't listen to the saxophone player. He watched the green water and barked at the gulls. But I closed my eyes and imagined myself in some dark-brown cellar that smelt of smoke and sweat, dancing with Valentina.

I stood very upright, holding her close to me, and after a while she laid her blonde head on my shoulder. We hardly moved our feet at all, just swayed around to the music, and I could feel all her body – her breasts and her stomach and her thighs – pressing against me. She sang a few phrases now and then, so softly you could hardly hear her voice. Her warm breath tickled my neck and the smell of her perfume mingled with the smell of smoke and aniseed. And the music just went on.

Then I did a peculiar thing: I tried to replace my image of Valentina with the image of the sixteen-year-old sister of my friend Carl at Beckett Bridges School. Her name was Ingrid. I'd had a wet dream about her the night after I'd found my football at the car-boot sale. She had long dark hair and she wore her school shirt buttoned up at the top and she called me 'Lew'. Half the boys in the sixth form were in love with her.

So now I held Ingrid and wrapped her arms around me in the brown cellar and her hair made a kind of curtain round my face. She smelled of Timotei shampoo and her breasts were small.

For a while, I quite enjoyed dancing with Ingrid, but then she vanished of her own accord. She just slowly slipped away from me until I was alone, and so I waited, holding out my arms, for Valentina to come back. And when she was there again, I laid my head on her shoulder and thought, OK, she's back now and she's holding me and I can go to sleep . . .

Sergei woke me by licking my hand. The saxophonist had moved on and where he'd been a group of bongo drummers were setting up. They were women bongo drummers – white women with shaved hair and earrings, wearing tattered shorts and sandals. I stared at them and one of them stared brazenly back. They reminded me of the people I'd met on Violette's stairs, who'd asked me Sergei's name. So I got up and, keeping Sergei close to me, walked over the bridge and on.

I tried to imagine what a Kiev hotel would be like and how thorough the search for Grisha would be. I wondered whether, right now, Valentina was walking through Kotsiubinsky Park in search of a telephone connected to the outside world.

I wanted to ask Alice whether she'd given any pages of Valentina's book to Grigory, but I didn't. I just let this question, along with all the others, stay in a limbo of silence.

I called up Hugh, just to tell him I was fine. Grandma Gwyneth answered. She told me there was a threat of water rationing in England. 'Water rationing, I *ask* you!' she said. 'This is the wettest country in Europe and they can't get through a fine summer without cutting off the water. What are we coming to, Lewis?' I said I didn't know what we were coming to and I privately thought, I may never go back to England. Never.

When Hugh came on the line, I thanked him for mending Elroy. He said it did him good to hear my voice. He was starting to miss us really badly and only the building of the hut (which he now referred to as 'the summerhouse') kept him from feeling miserable. I made myself enquire after the hut. He cleared his throat and said: 'Well, Lewis, I think you're going to be surprised. I couldn't have made it what it is without Bertie's help, but together we're building something really rather beautiful.'

I couldn't believe he'd used the word 'beautiful'; he was normally quite precise with language. I said: 'Do you mean beautiful, or just OK?'

'I think it's going to be beautiful,' he said, 'but of course I'm biased. You can ask Grandma.'

Then he wanted to know what I'd been doing, so I told him about some of the things I'd seen: the mosaic building at Nanterre, the dog-grooming parlour, the Vigil at the Nevsky church, the woman drummers on the Pont des Arts. I didn't say I'd spent an hour inside a commissariat. I said I'd done a dance in the kitchen with Babba to celebrate the arrival of her work permit and that I was still enjoying *Crime et châtiment*. All this came out in one breath, like I had to say it and get it over with, and Hugh noticed this and was silent for a moment before he said: 'Is everything OK, Lewis?'

'Yes, it's good,' I said. 'I feel I live here now.'

'You know you can come home any time you want?'

'Yeah.'

'You're not lonely, are you?'

'No.'

'Only I was a bit surprised, when you asked me to send Elroy . . .'

'I just suddenly wanted him, that's all. I mean, only for about fifteen minutes. I had a kind of regression, but it's passed.'

Then he said: 'How's Valentina?'

I didn't let myself pause or hesitate for a single beat. 'She's fine,' I answered. 'The book's coming on really well, but it may not be finished by September. Mum may have to stay on . . .'

Hugh sounded suddenly irritated. 'Oh no,' he said. 'I don't think Valentina can expect that. You must both come back on the third. You have to be back for your birthday. Eh? Alice can finish the translation here. We can put in a fax, if necessary. Let me talk to her.'

'She's out,' I lied.

'OK. But tell her she must stick to the arrangements and Valentina must honour them. It was the summer holidays she agreed to, nothing more.'

I was glad when Hugh handed me over to Bertie. His voice was loud and burbling, like a highland stream, and he told me that the day-to-day routine of building with Hugh, then sitting in the garden in the evening drinking gin and tonic, had taken years off him. 'Years!' he chuckled. 'When you come home, you won't recognise me, Lewis!'

'Maybe you should stay,' I said.

'Stay? You mean stay in Devon with you lot?'

'Yes.'

'Oh no. Couldn't do that. You can't have me and Grandma hanging around in the house.'

'We could. Why not?'

'No, no. Lovely thought. Not suitable, old chap. Lovely thought, all the same.'

When I put the phone down, I thought, that's what ought to happen. Gwyneth and Bertie ought to come and live in Devon with Hugh. Then if Alice and I never go back, he won't be lonely.

I sat on the hard telephone chair, thinking about this. A surge of worry for Hugh – and for Bertie and Gwyneth – went through me. I pictured their washing flapping on the clothes line: Gwyneth's bulgy knickers like bloomers, Bertie's frayed old vests, Hugh's shorts made from cut-off jeans, his towelling socks. I thought, they could be in a tragedy and not know it yet.

Without noticing it, I'd started doodling on the little pad Valentina kept by the telephone. Among twirls and circles, I'd written the name Gail O'Hara and suddenly I forgot about the household in Devon and focused on this. Seeing the name written down, I realised that the computer file labelled GOH in Valentina's Apple must hold a mass of information about Gail O'Hara – far more than I could ever get from Violette's friend Lisette-Marie.

Carmody hadn't returned Valentina's computer. Presumably, he and his men were going through the stuff in it, so if there was any link between Gail O'Hara and what had happened to Valentina he'd suss it out. But I also thought, if I had access to the file, I could do it faster; I'd know what was important and what wasn't, and if there were any gaps Lisette-Marie might be able to fill them in.

I called Carmody's number. Last time, he'd had his hand poised over the telephone, but now there was no answer from his office. I dialled renseignements to get the number of the commissariat and rang this and asked for Carmody. After waiting for about five minutes, the receptionist told me Carmody wasn't in the building. I left my name and number and a message asking him to call. 'Louis qui?' asked the receptionist. 'Louis Little,' I said, 'Little comme Petit.'

Then I went into Valentina's room and stood at the door, looking at the bed and the dressing table and the cupboards that were tidy again and filled up with coloured shoes. I was wondering whether Valentina had kept back-up disks for all her computer files and whether these had been hidden somewhere the police hadn't searched. I hadn't found any disks in her desk and Mrs Gavrilovich hadn't found any in the bureau, as far as I knew. I thought there had to be a back-up disk of Valentina's novel and there might be others with this one, if I only knew where to look.

Being in this room always made me feel sexy. I remembered lying on the bed with Valentina the evening she got back from the hospital and going in and out of a beautiful sleep while she told me about Anton's dreams of a house in the Luberon hills. In a drawer somewhere would be the satin nightdress she'd been wearing then, washed and ironed and put away by Violette.

I closed the door of the bedroom and began going through the drawers. I was half looking for the computer disks and half for the nightdress. I found the nightdress and took it out and held it up, letting it unfold. I laid it against my cheek. It was silk, not satin, slinky as a glove. And despite the washing it smelled faintly of Valentina, as if her body had just stepped out of it. I wanted to lie on the bed and take my clothes off and lay the nightdress over me and drench it with all my pent-up love, but I was afraid Alice might come in and find me, so I folded it up again and took it to my room, where I hid it under my pillow with Alice's gold chain.

When I got back down, Alice was in the salon, smoking one of her thin little cigarettes. 'What have you been doing?' she asked.

★

In the night, I fucked Valentina's pink silk nightdress about four times. It was like having a snake in bed with me – the snake out of the garden of Eden. As I finally drifted off to sleep, as the birds started singing, I thought, I'm like a drug addict, I can't control my cravings; I'll die from longing or from a surfeit of pleasure, one or the other. I wanted to ask someone – a doctor, say – whether these feelings were normal for a boy who would be fourteen in three weeks' time.

And then in the morning, when I got up to go and meet Moinel at the Deauville, I felt so exhausted I could hardly move my legs or lean down to wash my face. And what I kept thinking was, perhaps I'm harming Valentina by fucking her in my mind? Perhaps if I stopped myself doing this, she'd come back? Perhaps it's all my dirty thoughts that have put her in danger?

I went out without seeing Alice, who was having a bath. I left her a note asking her to walk Sergei, but I didn't say where I was going or when I'd be back. I knew that one of the things that would happen that morning was that Hugh would telephone her, but I said nothing about this either. I was sure that Alice wouldn't mention Valentina's disappearance to him; she wanted to keep all her secrets silent and safe. As I went down the stairs, I said softly in Alice's Scottish voice: 'Two can be as secretive as one, bonny lady.'

Moinel was already at the Deauville when I got there, at the table we'd occupied before. The moment I sat down, two apricot pastries were put in front of me with a foaming cup of coffee. I thought, Moinel's really thin but he understands about hunger better than most people.

He was drinking orange juice and he smiled as I ate. I had the feeling that because I felt so famished all the time my table manners were becoming disgusting. Crumbs from the pastries snowed my thighs.

On my way to the café, I'd remembered that I should have telephoned Carmody again, to tell him about the GOH file. I looked up from the food and asked Moinel: 'Did you ever meet the translator that Valentina had before Alice? The American who stayed in her flat?'

Moinel made a face like he'd just been stung by a bee or by a horrible word. He put a hand up to his cheek. 'Don't *talk* about that one!' he said.

'Why? What was wrong with her?'

'Gail. That was her name. In my darkroom, I sometimes heard her through the wall. She was like a gale!'

'What did you hear?'

'Shrieking. Insults. She was crazy. She didn't know what she was saying. My theory was she was a junkie.'

I was so impressed at Moinel knowing the word 'junkie', like Valentina knowing the word 'dawdle', that my mind didn't immediately recognise the seriousness of what he'd said. 'Where is your darkroom?' I asked.

'In the attic. I knocked two attic rooms into one. It's a work of art, my darkroom, the envy of my friends!'

'Are you a photographer now?'

'I'm lots of things. One of the things I do is photograph furniture – for magazines like *Connoisseur* and for sale catalogues.'

I told Moinel that my room was in Valentina's attic and that the room with the Wurlitzer must be next to his darkroom. Then I thought, why was Gail screaming in the attic? What were she and Valentina doing up there?

'Do you think Gail slept in the attic?' I asked.

'I presume she did sometimes. That was when I used to hear her, when I was in my darkroom.'

I was silent for a moment, giving my mind to the idea that Valentina had once chosen a drug addict as a translator. 'How do you know Gail was a junkie?' I asked.

Moinel shrugged. 'I don't,' he said. 'It's malicious of me to suggest it. But she looked ill a lot of the time and she behaved like a crazy person, so I infer it.'

I began to clean up the pastry crumbs with my paper napkin. 'Is it easy to get drugs in Paris?' I asked.

'I don't really know. I suppose in any big city it's easy, if you know who to go to.'

Moinel called over one of the athletic waiters then and paid the bill. He kept his money not in a wallet, but in a little gold clip in the shape of an M. I saw that he was a neat, fastidious man and the only wild thing about him was the colour of his hair. Moinel was about forty-five and underneath the tangerine, I supposed, its natural colour was grey.

We got a taxi to the hospital. I'd hardly been in any taxis and I liked the way this one was driven really fast. On the way I saw a sign on a garage window saying 'Voitures blindés à louer'. I knew what a *voiture blindée* was from the TV programme about Caen: it was a tank. I thought how brilliant it would be to ride to Valentina's rescue in a tank, just bulldozing my way smash bang through every obstacle.

They knew Moinel at the hospital reception desk. The minute they saw him come in, the two receptionists smiled and said, 'Bonjour, Moinel. Ça va? Oui?'

He explained that we had to go to *Radiologie* and they gave us directions in the way that people do when they know their way round a place and you don't – exactly the way we gave directions to parents at Beckett Bridges School – not stopping to see if you're following their instructions or not.

We set off down a corridor. I hadn't often been inside a hospital. I asked Moinel if he didn't think it was spooky to think how many varieties of illness people could suffer from. He smiled and said a hospital was like an illness department store, with designer-illnesses and infinite choice. Then he said: 'You see how English my sense of humour became in Pimlico?'

When we got to *Radiologie* we found a waiting area with a few chairs and plants arranged around a square of green carpet. There were two doors, both closed, leading off from it.

We went up to the desk. I felt more afraid, suddenly, than I'd felt in Carmody's office. I wanted to hold on to Moinel's arm. It was as if I expected there to be mines under the carpet. But Moinel was calm. He sauntered. When our turn came to talk to the receptionist, he said politely that we wanted to clarify a small clerical detail. 'On Tuesday, 7th August,' said Moinel, 'a Mademoiselle Valentina Gavril had an X-ray appointment with Dr Bouchain. Were you the receptionist who checked her in?'

The receptionist was young, with short fair hair and a freckled face. She wore an earring in one ear.

'I don't know,' she said. 'I check in hundreds of people every week.'

Moinel took out the photo of Valentina we'd brought with us and showed it to the girl. In the picture, Valentina's blonde hair was tied with a red ribbon.

'This is Mademoiselle Gavril,' said Moinel. 'Do you remember her?'

The receptionist looked hard at the picture and said: 'No. I've never seen her.'

'So,' said Moinel, 'it wasn't you who told Madame Gavrilovich on the telephone that you had admired Mademoiselle Gavril's dress?'

'I'm sorry. I don't know what you're referring to.'

Moinel kept cool and calm. 'What we need to know is whether she kept that appointment or not,' he said. 'That's all.'

'Are you members of the family?' asked the receptionist.

'No,' said Moinel. 'We are friends. But the information is extremely important.'

Unlike the women at Main Reception, this person didn't know Moinel. She didn't smile at him or ask him how he was doing. And now, all she said was: 'This is confidential information. I can't give out any information of this kind, I'm afraid.'

'Just let me stress,' continued Moinel, 'that we wouldn't ask this for trivial reasons. We understand your code of confidentiality, but this is, as I say, a very urgent matter.'

'I'm sorry,' she said. 'I have no authority. I can't help you.'

'What authority do you need?'

'Permission from a doctor, or—'

'Fine,' said Moinel. 'Fine. Let's go, Louis.'

We walked out of the waiting area and along the corridor a little way. I noticed we'd come to what looked like the day room of a geriatric ward, with men and women on zimmer frames standing completely still, like garden forks stuck into the earth.

'Wait here,' said Moinel in a whisper. 'I'm going to find some "authority".' And he danced off towards an elevator, leaving me with all the old tottering people, who, one by one, looked up from their zimmers and stared at me.

I sat down on a plastic chair and folded my arms. I did some chess moves in my mind to stop myself staring back. I was playing Black, and White had just captured my only remaining rook, so it was looking difficult. We could exchange queens, but I was too much material behind to go into an endgame. I just got a bright idea – knight to bishop seven, check – when I saw that an old man was slowly zimmering his way towards me. He was smiling, and when he got near to me he stopped and fumbled in his trouser pocket for a handkerchief, and then he began waving the handkerchief, like people used to wave things at departing ocean liners.

White's king was just coming out of the corner and I could feel the game begin to turn round, but the old man was right by me now, so I had to look up at him. His smile was turning into a weepy kind of laugh and a tear started to roll down his cheek. 'Henri . . .' he babbled. 'Henri . . .'

I shook my head. 'Non,' I said. 'Louis. Je suis Louis.'

'Ce n'est pas Henri?'

'Non, Monsieur. Je m'appelle Louis.'

'Je croyais que c'était Henri. Mon petit-fils.'

'Non. Je suis desolé . . .'

'Oh non, je vois maintenant . . .'

With great pains, he executed a three-point turn with his zimmer and slowly walked back to the place where he'd been standing. He dropped the handkerchief he'd been waving, but he didn't notice. Other old people clustered round him, consoling him. No one picked up the handkerchief.

I got up and went out into the corridor. I couldn't focus on my chess game any more. I hoped the day would never come when Bertie mistook some other boy for me and waved at him in a hospital day room. I thought, you must know life has got really bad when you can't recognise the people you love any more.

I still felt a bit weak from my night of passion, so I slumped down in the corridor, waiting for Moinel to come back. I knew I'd have to wait quite a long time. Alice had told me that when she arrived here with Valentina, no doctor was to be found for twenty minutes. In English hospitals, you could wait all night lying on a trolley before any doctor came to see you. You could probably die on the trolley and no one would notice.

Moinel returned after ten minutes. It was like he had special privileges with the staff of this hospital. A woman doctor was with him, and when they got level with me Moinel stopped and the doctor went on into the waiting area of *Radiologie*. 'OK?' Moinel said.

I told him about the grandfather with the hankie. He said: 'The villain of the story is the boy, Henri, who never comes to visit.'

The woman doctor had a heart-shaped face. Ingrid had told Carl that this was what girls longed for – to have heart-shaped faces. Around the heart was a lot of straight, shiny black hair and you could imagine all the highly tuned brain circuitry underneath it.

She came back to us quite quickly. She shook my hand and she led us to a different waiting area further down the corridor. We sat down on some comfortable chairs and she said: 'There may or may not have been some confusion. It looks, on the register, as if Mademoiselle Gavril's name has first been ticked and then the tick has been crossed, like this.' She got out a piece of paper and drew a cross and showed it to us. The lines of her cross were curled at the bottom; it looked almost like a little running man, but without a head.

'But if there was a tick,' she said, 'which is what is put when a patient arrives, it was put there in error. The cross firmly indicates that Mademoiselle Gavril did not keep her appointment.'

'OK . . .' said Moinel.

'I suggest you leave the photograph with the receptionist,' said the doctor. 'She may not recognise her, but can show it to her colleagues. There's no law of confidentiality preventing them from remembering a face.'

We nodded. I got out the photo again. It looked as if it had been taken at a fancy-dress party. I looked at it while Moinel and the doctor talked. The doctor's voice had a crack in it which, if I had been ill, I knew I would have found soothing. While I gazed at the ribbons in Valentina's hair, the doctor held Moinel's fingers in hers and asked him how he was and he said: 'Perfectly all right, darling. Thank goodness. When I'm not, you'll be the first to know.'

Then the doctor had to rush away. Doctors are always in transit, never staying. They drink tea standing up. Moinel smoothed his hair and we walked back to the *Radiologie* reception area.

A different receptionist was sitting at the desk. She looked up and stared at us as we came in. She had a pale face that looked as if it had never seen the sun.

I let Moinel be in charge. He took the photo of Valentina and leant across the desk and showed it to this new woman. 'Excuse me,' he said, 'for taking up your time, but I want to leave this photograph with you. I need to know if you, or any of your colleagues, have ever seen this person in the waiting area here. We believe she was here on Tuesday last, the seventh—'

'No,' said the receptionist. 'I've never seen her.'

'Fine. Please ask your colleagues if they saw anyone like this. Her arm was in a cast and we think she would have been wearing a black-and-white dress . . .'

I could tell the receptionist didn't want to take the photo, but then she snatched it out of Moinel's hand and put it face down on her desk. Reluctantly, she scribbled down Moinel's telephone number, then she suddenly looked at him and said: 'Etes-vous police?'

Moinel smiled. 'No,' he said. 'Do we look like flics?'

Something nagged me as we walked back down the long corridors to the exit, but I didn't know what it was. I thought it might swim into my mind during our taxi ride back to the rue Rembrandt, but nothing came, only a mild sadness at the loss of the photograph. I kept wondering where Valentina had bought the red ribbon and who had taken the picture.

When I came in, Violette was there. She'd decided to wash down all the cupboards in the kitchen and she was standing on the worktops, so what you most noticed about her were her legs, which weren't thin like her arms, but big and strong. Under her overall, she was wearing an orange skirt. She said: 'I want all these cupboards looking good for when Madame comes home.'

I helped her with this task. The cupboards looked clean, but when you began to wash them you discovered they were dirty. While we worked, Violette told me that since getting the news about her work permit she was making an effort to resume Pozzi's toilet-training. She said everything changed when you knew you had a future.

When the kitchen was done, I got Violette to help me search Valentina's room for the back-up disks I thought might be in the apartment somewhere, if Carmody hadn't taken them. I knew they could be in the safe, but it was still worth looking for them, because we had Alice's computer back now and, if I found them, I could run the GOH file through that. I said to Violette: 'If we find that file, we'll know the whole story of Gail O'Hara,' and Violette shook her head and replied: 'The whole story might be too terrible for us to bear, Louis.'

We went through Valentina's bedroom wardrobes, all six of

them, shelf by shelf and drawer by drawer. We found thirteen musical boxes, some as small as a matchbox, and some quite large and inlaid with mother-of-pearl. Each one was on a different shelf, among different pieces of clothing, and each one played a different song – *La Mer, Les Feuilles mortes, La Vie en rose, Je ne regrette rien, Sur ma vie* . . . The smallest one played *La Marseillaise* so quietly, it sounded like it was a little marching song for mice.

Violette loved the musical boxes. She stroked the mother-of-pearl with her velvety hands. We set them in a line along the carpet, and opened all their lids at once. Then we moved down the line on our elbows and knees with our bums in the air, listening. Violette's bum stuck up much higher than mine. I said it was possible to imagine you were moving down a corridor where pianists were practising in tiny rooms, like Alice had told me she'd done at school. Her friend Jean had been a better pianist than Alice. Jean could play one and a half Mozart piano sonatas and Alice could only play one. She would hear this half-sonata stealing through the sound-proofed wall and weep with fury.

We didn't find any disks. A sea of underwear frothed round us on the floor and spilled over the line of musical boxes. Some of the bras looked too small to contain Valentina's tits and could have belonged to another part of her life, when she was thinner. I wondered if she'd bought all the stuff herself or whether her lovers, like Grisha, had gone round department stores picking out knickers and camisoles and suspender belts and carrying them back to her in miniature carrier bags. And then I thought, if she's alive, if I ever see her again, I'm going to get her a present. It won't be underwear. It will be something she's never seen before. And she will turn to me and say: 'Oh, darling, I thought there was nothing new in the world, but I was wrong!'

Alice found us sitting in this surf of knickers, playing the *Marseillaise*. She said: 'Lewis, what on earth are you doing?'

'Searching,' I said. 'Did Carmody call?'

Violette lowered her head and closed the musical box lid. I

could tell she was in awe of Alice, as if Alice were a parakeet from a forest in Benin, who might suddenly fly at her and start pecking her face.

'What are you searching for?' said Alice.

'Did he call?' I said.

'No. No one called. Only Hugh. You're making a terrible mess of this room. Why?'

I felt like saying: 'If you were my chosen ally, I'd tell you everything, but you're no good as an ally because of your guilty secret.' But I didn't say this. There was a bit of me that was afraid to be pecked by the parakeet, too. All I said was: 'I need to find Valentina's back-up disks. To follow a hunch I have . . .'

'I expect the police took them,' said Alice.

I shrugged. 'I don't think so,' I said. 'They weren't in the desk or in the bureau; that's the stuff they took.'

'Well,' said Alice, 'I need to talk to you, Lewis. I think we should go out.'

We took the métro to Jussieu. I thought the catalpa trees might be turning yellow by now, but they were just the same, green and clattery in the shallow breeze.

Alice didn't say much on the journey, but when we came into the Jardin des Plantes and passed under the statue of the lion eating the human foot she took my hand and said: 'I had a long conversation with Hugh this morning. He's worried about you. He thinks I should send you home.'

'Why?' I asked.

'He said he's been worried ever since you asked him to send Elroy.'

I pulled my hand away. There are times in a life when you imagine lowering your parents' heads into a rock pool and holding them there until their bodies go still.

I ignored everything Alice had said and walked past some lettuces and tomatoes towards the largest of the hothouses. Alice called after me, but I didn't turn round. I just went on into the hothouse and began looking at the rainforest plants, as if I were on my own. The heat in there was damp and smelled of earth and almost all the trees and cacti in it were vast and I felt my habitual admiration – of the kind that I felt for the Eiffel Tower – for enormous things. I should have been born a beetle.

By one of the ponds, there were some tiny turtles on a stone. They were so immobile, I thought they were made of plastic or something. Then they began slipping and sliding into the pool and swam down into the murk of it and out of sight. I thought, one of the thousand things human beings find difficult is staying absolutely still.

I saw Alice lurking on the other side of the pool. For once, she was looking at me anxiously, almost tenderly, but I didn't want to speak to her, so we each went round the hothouse alone, until we met up behind the waterfall and Alice said: 'Did you see the turtles?'

'Of course I saw them,' I answered.

We couldn't stay in there all day, it was too hot. There was sweat on my T-shirt and I began to feel thirsty. I walked out, knowing Alice would follow, and went to a little stall selling junk food and bought a can of Coke. Alice came up and offered to pay for it, but I said I'd already paid. Then, when I'd drunk half of it down, gulping like a frog, I announced: 'I'm staying till Valentina's found. Dad can't make me go home and nor can you.'

'No one's "making you" do anything,' said Alice calmly. 'Hugh just gets the impression you're not happy here. Is that right?'

I told Alice this was an absolutely stupid idiotic question. Of course I wasn't 'happy' when, at any time, we could get a call from Carmody telling us that Valentina's body had been found in a forest or dumped in a lime quarry. How could anyone be 'happy' under circumstances like these?

Alice gave me one of her scrutinising looks. You could tell her brain was whirling with questions, and to forestall the one that was going to come out of her mouth next I said: 'I want to know something. Did you show Grigory Panin Valentina's manuscript?'

There was a silence, during which Alice blinked. She hadn't expected me to come up with a question of my own.

'No,' she said.

'Did he ask you to show it to him?'

'No. He asked me to tell him what it was about, that's all.'

'And did you tell him?'

'Yes.'

'In detail?'

'No. There wasn't really time. Just the thrust of the story, as far as I've got . . .'

'And how did he react?'

Alice shrugged. 'He wanted to clarify a few things. He seemed interested in it, more so than I would have expected. Why do you want to know all this, Lewis? It was you we were talking about . . .'

We began to walk on. We were going in the direction of the menagerie, where we'd first seen the bison and the cocktail trolley. I said that I didn't want to talk about me, that I had no remembrance of the me Alice was referring to, it had existed so far back in time. Then I added: 'If you send me back to Devon before I find Valentina, she stands no chance of ever coming back.'

'The police will find her,' said Alice gently.

'No, they won't,' I said. 'They don't have enough facts. They don't know what's important and what's useless. But I know. And one thing I think is, she could only be in Russia with Grigory *if* Grigory has seen her new book, so I hope you're not lying to me about that.'

Alice shook back her thorn-tree hair. She said she was surprised how I spoke to her these days, so rudely. We were in the *allée* of limes now and in this lovely shade I wanted to whisper that I was only rude because I knew she'd started lying to me. I felt cool and deadly, as if, without the least effort, I could dance along here, like a kick-boxer, laying waste everyone who got in my way.

I ran on a little way. My legs and feet felt light and I called back: 'I don't mean to be rude to you. I just want to get at the answers, that's all.'

It was then that we came upon the bear. I don't know why we'd never seen him before; he must have been lurking in his tunnel under the ground, ignoring the sunlight and the world. But he was there now, in his pit, twenty feet below us, a yellowy-brown bear with his long nose always pointing towards the people above him, trying to smell them and work out what creatures they were. The young kids called to him and held their arms over the wire. They thought he was something they could take home with them and put into their beds on winter nights to keep them warm.

Alice and I hung over the pit and stared. There was almost nothing in the pit except a pathetic tree-sculpture the bear was meant to feel happy about climbing, but you could tell he didn't feel happy about anything; he wanted to be out of this awful place and back on a Canadian mountainside, munching bees. His world was empty of everything except the smell of people and this smell confused him and kept him wandering round and round the pit, with his nose lifted into the air.

The bear made me feel ridiculously sad. I actually felt like holding on to Alice and weeping. Some of my sadness was for the bear and all the rest was for me. After enduring this choking feeling of misery for several minutes, I said: 'I don't know why this had to happen!'

'I know,' said Alice.

She didn't 'know', of course. She couldn't have begun to imagine. If I'd told her one half of what I felt about Valentina, she would have just thought my brain was overheating, like it did when I was a child and imagined the German paratrooper alive in our cellar.

I didn't want to stay in the Jardin des Plantes after seeing the bear. I wanted to be back in the flat, so that I could call

Carmody and continue my search for the disks. Alice suggested we go to a café and have a meal, but for once I didn't feel hungry. I said to Alice: 'We can't just act normally, you know, going to cafés and things, when Valentina could be dead.'

'Lewis,' said Alice firmly, 'don't be such a prig.'

Then we travelled all the way home in total absolute silence. As usual, men on the métro stared at Alice, but instead of keeping watch over her I turned my face to the window and let the sooty tunnels and the bright stations alternate in front of my eyes.

The flat was tidy when we got in, with all Valentina's underwear and the musical boxes put away. Violette had also polished the parquet and the floors were gleaming and slippery again, like in the days before Valentina's broken arm. I didn't know whether Violette was getting paid any more or if she was working for nothing until the day when Madame walked back into the apartment and I ran towards her and put my arms round her.

There was a message on the answering machine. It was from Dominique Monod at the publishers, Bianquis, inviting Alice to supper that evening 'to discuss the situation vis-à-vis Mademoiselle Gavril'. It said a car would call for her at seven-thirty. I said to Alice I thought it sounded more like a summons than a charming invitation to dinner, but all Alice said was: 'At least she's sending a car.'

I wasn't invited, needless to say, so Alice gave me some money and told me to go to Prisunic and get some food. In the old days of our life in Devon I never had to get my own meals, but now everything was altering all the time.

I took Sergei with me and tied him up outside Prisunic, where he started barking at the bird whistler, and as I went into the store I heard the bird whistler bark back.

Alice hadn't told me what food to get. Valentina would have devised some delicious concoction for me, using ingredients you never imagined putting together, like, say, petits pois and anchovies. But now I just walked along the shelves, staring at tins of vegetables and packets of meat and cartons of yoghurt and felt my brain go numb. I wished I were Sergei and could make do with a tin of dog meat. The idea of cooking anything without Valentina's step-by-step instructions felt much too difficult.

In the end, I just got two litre-bottles of Orangina, a packet of crisps, some bread and some ham. I knew this was pitiful and that, when the time for supper came, I'd wish I'd bought Mexican chicken wings and oyster mushrooms and sour cream or something, but I just didn't understand the *science* of cooking, and that was that. I couldn't see what the connection was between a raw leek, say, and leek soup. I couldn't envisage what it was that the leek had to undergo.

On the way home, I approached the bird whistler. I said: 'Show me what you do,' and he took out of his mouth a tiny little plastic gizmo, the shape of a half-moon, and coloured pink to match his tongue. 'Sifflet du chasseur,' he said, 'pour imiter la perdrix, la caille, le merle, la grive et le cri du lapin.' I'd never noticed rabbits had a cry. But I didn't mention this to the whistle-seller; I bought one of his whistles instead, with the rest of the supper money given to me by Alice, and all the way home, with the whistle pressed against my tongue and the roof of my mouth, pretended to be a bird. I don't know what kind of bird I was pretending to be.

When I got back, I put my food away. Already, it looked hopeless and unappetising and even the bread was hard. I began wondering if Moinel was a good cook and whether, once Alice had left, I could invite myself to supper next door. Then, thinking about Moinel, I began to reconstruct our visit to the hospital and I knew, suddenly, what had been nagging at my mind on our way back from there: the second receptionist we'd approached had asked us a question without using a definite article – exactly the mistake that Grisha made all the time. She'd said: 'Etes-vous police?' And it was this phrase that had stayed in my mind, hidden just under the surface of consciousness. But my French simply wasn't perfect enough to know, for certain, whether it constituted a linguistic error or not.

I went to ask Alice, but the door of her room was locked. When I knocked on it, Alice called out to me that she was sleeping. She told me to go away. I got the suspicion that, just as I had moments of wanting to drown my parents, so Alice had moments of wanting to drown me. But I needed an answer to my question now, so I said, 'Just tell me, if you wanted to ask someone, in French, if they were from the police, how would you phrase the question?'

There was a silence, into which I knew Alice was fitting a sigh. Then she said: 'You'd either say: "Etes-vous de la police?" or "Etes-vous des policiers?" '

'Could you never, ever, say: "Etes-vous police?" '

'You could say it but it wouldn't be correct.'

'So no French person would ever make this mistake?'

'I doubt it. Now please go and play chess or something, Lewis. I'm feeling really tired.'

I went up to my room and opened my Concorde notebook. Sometimes I can write something down that I didn't know I knew and I hoped this would happen now – that I'd suddenly see the significance of there being a Russian receptionist at the very desk where Valentina had or had not checked in for her X-ray appointment. I knew it had to be important, but I couldn't see why. All I wrote was: *Second receptionist was (probably) Russian. Her behaviour was rude. She didn't want to take the photo of V. Why?*

I picked up Elroy absent-mindedly and we both stared vacantly out at the room. After about ten minutes had passed, something dawned on me. Perhaps this Russian receptionist hadn't wanted to take the photograph of Valentina *because she'd recognised her!* She'd recognised her because Valentina *had* reported for her appointment on that Tuesday afternoon. The Russian receptionist had been the one to check her in. And then Valentina had disappeared. She had disappeared *from the hospital.* The Russian receptionist had been involved in the disappearance.

In this way, when the time came for her to be called in to Dr Bouchain's consulting room, she was no longer there. At this point, a different receptionist was at the desk. In the crucial ten or fifteen minutes between Valentina arriving and being called to go in to see the doctor, the shift at the desk changed, and so the new (non-Russian) receptionist looked around and called and told Dr Bouchain that Valentina had never arrived.

I scribbled down this hypothesis. I thought, if I'm right, everything will hinge on the lack of a definite article. But the question remained: if Valentina had been abducted from the hospital, who had taken her and how? Had she been called to the phone? Had someone come in posing as a doctor? Who, apart from Dr Bouchain, knew she had an appointment with the X-ray department that afternoon? Was Dr Bouchain himself involved? Was the Russian receptionist definitely the one who had led her away? And what happened next? Assuming she left the hospital, where was she taken and how?

My brain felt a bit exhausted, as if I were in the middle of a difficult chess game. I hesitated between two actions – calling Carmody or going straight to the hospital, myself, now. I just sat where I was, hesitating, mainly because, for some reason I couldn't actually express, I felt frightened by both things.

Didier had explained to me that when an existentialist is faced with two choices and can't decide between them, and so does nothing, he is still making a choice: *he is choosing not to choose.* He said: 'But we can't take refuge in a non-decision, Louis. A non-decision is a decision of a kind. We have to take responsibility for whatever comes from it.'

I didn't want to make a non-decision. In one of my reports, the head teacher Mr Quaid had written: *Lewis is a person of resolution.* So I decided to call Carmody. It was still only mid-afternoon and I was fairly sure he'd be in his office. Calling him frightened me less than going to the hospital. It was like

I knew that if I went to the hospital I'd see something I'd rather not see.

Carmody wasn't in his office. I was told he was 'out of Paris' for twenty-four hours. I wanted to say that he'd said we could call him any time, day or night, and he'd be there, but I didn't. Perhaps he hadn't said this at all, only somehow made me believe it because I wanted to believe that someone was watching over us?

Now, I had to go to the hospital. I tried to dream up a third option, but there wasn't one and that was that.

I took Sergei with me. I was in the habit of talking to him quite a lot. He didn't show much sign of listening to me. All he did was just trot along, ignoring me, flicking his tail in the sunshine, but I found talking to him consoling, nevertheless. In a survey done in California, it was revealed that ninety-one per cent of female dog owners talked to their pets 'about intimate matters'. It didn't say what the men talked about. The surveyors just probably assumed that men never talked to dogs, which isn't true. Bertie used to have a West Highland Terrier called Sally and he often talked to her. Once, I heard him say: 'Sally, that wife of mine sometimes drives me absolutely potty.'

We took the métro to a station called Convention. Some of the names of Paris stations are weird. My favourite is Mairie des Lilas. I imagined coming up there into the arms of a woman in a lilac tree.

Convention wasn't far from the hospital and as I walked along the rue de Vaugirard, getting nearer to it, I felt myself long to turn round and go back to the apartment. If I hadn't had Sergei with me I might have turned back, but I kept going and when I arrived at Main Reception I recognised the girls who had been so nice to Moinel and my courage improved.

But then they weren't nice to me. They told me I couldn't bring Sergei inside. They were furious that I'd thought of it, as if dogs were radioactive or something. I had to take him out and tie him to a railing and this made me uneasy. I could just imagine some deranged patient walking out and seeing Sergei and stealing him then and there. 'Reste!' I told him. 'Ne bouge pas!'

When I got to *Radiologie*, the Russian receptionist was at the desk. I hid in the corridor, planning what to say. Then I moved towards her, and when she saw me she looked startled, like I was a radioactive dog. And seeing her get startled like this made me feel suddenly sure that she knew something about Valentina and that my hypothesis had been set out along the right lines.

I asked her if she'd shown Valentina's photograph to her colleagues and she nodded and said: 'Oh yes. Nobody in this department has seen that woman.'

'What about Dr Bouchain? He knows her, doesn't he?'

'Yes, of course. I do not include Dr Bouchain.'

'Is Dr Bouchain certain he didn't see her on that day?'

'I cannot tell you this.'

'Can I talk to Dr Bouchain, please?'

'You have appointment?'

I thought, there she goes again: no article. And this was a stupid question. She knew perfectly well I didn't have an appointment.

'Yes,' I said. 'I have an appointment.'

This confused her just for a second, as I hoped it would. 'Your name?' she said.

'Petit,' I replied. 'Louis Petit.'

My heart was jumping about inside my skinny T-shirt. One of several differences between Porphiry Petrovich and me was that Porphiry Petrovich was never afraid.

The Russian receptionist pretended to scan the appointments list. Just then, one of the doors opened and a doctor appeared, holding some X-rays clipped to a line. I dived towards him, as fast as I tried to dive towards the line in a rugby game. *Lewis is a person of resolution.*

'Dr Bouchain?' I asked.

Over my boring supper, I reconstructed my two and a half

minutes with Bouchain. I was trying to see if there was some-thing in it that was important, but which I hadn't seen.

There didn't seem to be anything.

He was a friendly man. He wore small glasses that looked as if their frames were made of gold. He asked me to come into his consulting room. He confirmed to me that he had X-rayed Valentina's arm when she was brought into the hospital on the day she fell down and that she had fractured it in two places. Then he said: 'I was booked to see her about ten days ago, but she missed the appointment. I hope the arm is healing correctly. She isn't in any pain, is she?'

'I don't know . . .' I stammered. 'We think she's in Russia, possibly in Kiev, but we're not sure . . .'

'What has happened?' he asked, looking at me kindly.

'We don't know. We only know she isn't at home. Did Inspecteur Carmody call you?'

'Yes. He asked me if I saw her on that day – last Tuesday – and I told him that I never saw her.'

Then I said: 'Can you be absolutely certain that Valentina never arrived at the hospital?'

'Well,' said Bouchain, 'she never arrived in my consulting room. I came out, into the reception area, and she was not there. We had her paged, but she never turned up.'

'One of your receptionists told Valentina's mother, Mrs Gav-rilovich, that she'd seen her . . .'

'I have a lot of patients. She thinks now that she must have muddled her with someone else.'

'Could there ever have been a tick against her name on the appointments list?'

'Your Inspecteur asked me that. No, I don't think so. A tick indicates that the patient has arrived. When the patient is seen by me or one of the other radiologists, the name is barred with a highlighter pen, but if the patient doesn't keep the appoint-ment, a cross is put against the name. This procedure never alters and there should be no confusions at all.'

I left then. I was very polite and apologetic to Dr Bouchain and thanked him for giving me his precious time, et cetera, et cetera. Hearing this polite voice of mine, I thought, when I'm old, I'm going to sound exactly like Grandad Bertie.

Dr Bouchain shook my hand. On my way out, the Russian receptionist stared at me and when I looked back from the corridor she was still staring, like she was a marksperson keeping me in her sights. So I dodged down and began to run and I ran very fast through all the long corridors till I came to the main entrance and went out to Sergei, who was safe and sound, just as I'd left him, and we began the journey home.

Now, we were both eating bread and ham in the kitchen. Alice had put on her one smart dress for her dinner with Dominique. Her one smart dress was made of a thin creasy kind of velvet and it had a tiny slit in one of the seams that she hadn't noticed was there. But she looked beautiful, I had to admit. The dress was dark green and her fiery hair fell on to the green like the colours of the fall in New England I'd once seen in a calendar picture.

Round her neck was a rope of false pearls that didn't look false, and before she left I took these pearls in my hand for a moment. It was difficult to feel angry with Alice when she looked really beautiful, and I wanted to say I was sorry, but somehow no words of apology would come out of me. Alice patted my hair. 'Enjoy your supper,' she said. She didn't know that all I had was ham and crisps.

After supper, Sergei and I watched TV. There was a programme about the Women of Europe. One of these women was a brilliant intelligent mayor of a German city and another was a Spanish garment worker. These two people were the same age, forty-four, but the Spanish garment worker earned one fifteenth of the salary of the mayor. There were no English women mentioned in the programme, as if England wasn't really part of Europe.

The woman I liked best was a dairy farmer in the Auvergne.

If I'd had to choose any of them for a mother, I would have chosen her.

She was about forty. She got up at four in the morning to milk her cows and lived in a white house by a row of poplars. Her name was Arlette. She ate lonely dinners of bread and soup with her dog, Michou. She had huge bright eyes, like Valentina's, and her hair was as wild as hay. You could be sure that old Michou was a dog who knew a lot of 'intimate matters', and when Sergei saw him he went nearer the TV set and barked at him.

Alice told me she might be home late. I said: 'Fine. It doesn't matter. I'll go to bed.'

When the programme about the Women of Europe ended, I took Sergei for a walk round the block, just as far as the Avenue Friedland, and we both looked for a second at the Arc de Triomphe on its mound of light, with all the traffic swirling round it. And I thought, this is where my existence is now: I've chosen Paris.

I went to sleep reading *Crime et châtiment*. I read the bit where Mrs Marmeladov, who's dying of tuberculosis, goes crazy and starts making her children dance in the street for money and I thought it was just about the saddest passage I'd ever read in any book ever.

When I woke up, I knew before I opened my eyes that something was odd in my room. I'd heard a noise and it was this noise that had woken me. And then I noticed that it was much darker than normal in the room – almost pitch dark, which it never was because of the light from the street coming through my round window.

I thought something had happened to the sky. I was still half in a dream about the blood coming out of Mrs Marmeladov's mouth, and I thought, there's blood in the sky now, making everything go black. Then I sat up.

There was a face at my window.

I stayed absolutely still, with my breaths coming out as

whimpers. My right hand slowly curved itself around the body of Elroy, who was lying near my thighs on the bed. I didn't look back up at the window. All I knew was that the face had something wrapped around it and the only bit of it you could see were the eyes.

I got up and ran. I was out of my door and down the stairs and yelling for Alice in less than ten seconds. Then I was in her room switching on the light and screaming at her to wake up. But she wasn't there. I stared at her bed, with its blue-and-gold bedcover. I just couldn't believe she wasn't in it. 'Alice!' I kept shrieking, '*Alice! ALICE!*'

But I knew I should keep moving. I knew the next thing that was going to happen was that whoever was at my window was going to come into the flat. He would come in through my bathroom window and he would follow me down here and kill me . . .

I heard Sergei begin to bark then. I tore out of Alice's bedroom and skidded across the parquet of the salon and into Valentina's room. As I went, I flicked on every light and all the time part of me was listening for footsteps coming down my stairs. I fell over on to Sergei, then scrambled to my feet and got a hold of his collar and together we went slithering over the parquet as fast as I could make him go. As we went, I yelled in French: 'Don't come down! I've got a dangerous dog here! I've got a very dangerous dog!'

Then we were out of the flat and on the landing. All I was wearing was my underpants. I knew that at any moment I might piss in them.

I found Moinel's doorbell and, still holding on to Elroy and holding on to Sergei, I held my fist against it and heard it buzz. I began knocking with my head against the door and calling out to Moinel.

Nothing happened. I imagined Moinel far away in some other part of the city, drinking in a bar, listening to jazz, and my calling to him turned into a kind of prayer:

'S'il vous plaît, Moinel, soyez là. Aidez-moi. Moinel, aidez-moi . . .'

Then I heard him on the other side of the door. 'Qui est là?' he whispered.

'Moinel! C'est Louis. Aidez-moi . . .'

His door had a security chain on it. Above the chain, I saw Moinel's tangerine head appear and I let out a sob of relief. When he opened the door, I stumbled towards him and he held me up, just stopping me from falling. He thought I was wounded or ill, so he began to look me over and ask me questions, but all I said was: 'Close the door, Moinel. Close the door!'

He closed it. I sat down on a hard couch in Moinel's little hallway. I'd let go of Sergei now that we were safely inside, but I was still clutching Elroy. The breaths coming out of me weren't just breaths, but half sobs, like the breaths Mrs Marmeladov has to breathe when she goes begging on the street.

Moinel crouched down by me and stroked my hand. He was wearing a navy-blue-and-white kimono. 'OK . . .' he said in his reassuring English. 'It's OK, Louis. Take your time. Breathe. That's it. Are you hurt? Breathe. Take your time . . .'

'A face . . .' I said. And I raised my hand feebly, pointing up.

'OK. Take your time. A face. Where?'

'Someone . . .'

'In the apartment?'

'At my window.'

'Has anyone hurt you?'

'No.'

'But you saw a face at your window?'

'Looking in . . . Wrapped in a scarf or something. He was going to kill me, Moinel!'

Moinel stood up. He said: 'OK, you're safe now. You're safe now. I'm going to get you something warm to put on. Wait there. Hold on to Sergei — he's nice and warm.'

I did as he said. I put my arm round Sergei and made him come close to me and then I started sobbing like a kid into his furry neck. Then I felt something soft on my shoulders. Moinel was wrapping me gently in a duvet, then helping me up and we walked together into his salon, which was painted brilliant staring white with big white sofas in front of a marble fireplace.

He sat me down on one of the sofas. I was aware of an ache in my hand and I knew this came from gripping Elroy so hard. Then Moinel handed me a glass of something and told me to drink. I didn't know what it was. It was like all my senses were muddled and would never again get sorted out. I let go of Elroy and laid him on my lap. Then I drank and felt the liquid go down into me and warm me and I kept drinking till I reached the bottom of the glass.

Moinel took the glass from me and pulled the duvet round me, till every part of my body was covered. I knew I was behaving like a boy of five, but I couldn't help it and I didn't care.

The night kept on being strange.

The police came. Not Carmody, but two others, in uniform. I supposed they were *agents* or *brigadiers*. They asked me to describe the face I'd seen, but all I could say was: 'I didn't see it. Only the eyes.'

'How were the eyes?' they asked.

'I don't know,' I said.

I'd locked myself out of the apartment – I had had no time to think about keys – so I couldn't let the *brigadiers* in. They said they would go down and wake up the concierge.

When they came back, they said they'd searched the apartment and cased the roof and there was no one there. One of them told me that the time was three o'clock.

They said they'd patrol the street and keep watch. And all I wanted to do then was lie down and go to sleep, but I remembered Alice, so Moinel wrote her a note and pinned it to our apartment door. And while we waited for Alice to come in, I let myself lie down on the white sofa and close my eyes. Moinel stayed in the room. I could feel him there, just out of sight. He put some Mozart on his CD player and played it very quietly and then I heard him moving about and opened my eyes. I saw him put down a bowl of water for Sergei. I thought, he's doing everything right, in the right order, and keeping so calm and contained, it's as if he knew this was all going to happen and planned exactly what he had to do . . .

Then I slept for a little while. The next thing I remember was that Alice was there. She smelled of smoke. She and Moinel were trying between them to lift me up, but I knew what they were going to do, they were going to take me back to my room, and I didn't want to go there. I just wanted to stay here, with the Mozart on the CD. So I fought them. And then I heard Moinel say: 'Leave him. He can sleep there. He'll be fine.'

Then it was morning. It was light and cool in Moinel's airy white room and I could hear the pigeons in the street. I knew that somewhere quite near, both Moinel and Alice would still be sleeping.

When I remembered the face at my window, it was like a part of my brain got suddenly dark. I lay very still, looking at the ceiling. I felt grateful that the room was white.

Moinel made us a breakfast of pink grapefruit and hot brioches and coffee. The coffeepot was silver and the grapefruit halves were put into cut-glass dishes and the brioches were folded inside the blue-and-white napkin. It looked like a painting of a breakfast and I didn't want to mess it up by eating it. I just sat at the table, watching Alice and watching Moinel, trying to keep this peculiar darkness from seeping across my mind.

'Eat, Louis,' said Moinel.

'Yes, eat,' said Alice. 'Come on.'

'I'm not hungry,' I said.

When we left Moinel's and the door closed on us in Valentina's apartment, I couldn't move. I sat in the salon, staring at the dust in the squares of sunlight on the floor. It was like I didn't really see the whole room, but only the bits of it that the sun lit up.

Alice went off to have a bath. She was still wearing her velvet dress that smelled of smoke. She stayed in the bathroom for a long time and I knew she was lying there, dreaming about Didier. But now, since I'd seen the face at my window, I no longer wanted to be told about it. I wanted her to keep absolutely silent and closed like a clam.

Later, someone called Inspecteur Villeneuve arrived and began to ask me questions about the face. I was still sitting in the salon, not moving, and Violette had gone round and round me with the floor polisher, watching me with her sad brown eyes.

Inspecteur Villeneuve wasn't a bit like Carmody, but tall and pale with a long nose that sniffed the air as he talked. I told him I'd prefer to talk to Carmody, but he didn't hear this. He probably didn't hear it because I didn't even say it, only thought I said it.

Alice sat by me. She smelled of soap now and she'd changed into jeans and a white shirt. She took my hand and held it in hers and though I wanted to remove it I didn't have the strength. 'Try to remember . . .' she kept saying.

All I said was that the face was wrapped up. I said it could have been wrapped in a bandage or in a dishcloth, like you might wrap a head that was severed. And Alice and Villeneuve stared at me, as if I'd said something wrong or embarrassing. After a moment, I said: 'I can't help it if this upsets you.'

Then Villeneuve disappeared. Alice said he was going to question everyone in the building, but I knew he was on the roof, looking for footprints in the slate dust and fingerprints on the glass. I said to Alice: 'I'm going to throw up now.'

She ran and got a bowl. All that seemed to be inside me was a bit of pale-green slime. Then Violette came and knelt by me and gave me a little sip of Orangina to drink through a straw, and what I thought then was, I wish I were Pozzi,

233

learning toilet etiquette, small and safe in Violette's skinny arms.

Violette and Alice put me to bed in the room I once thought had been Grisha's. It had apricot-coloured curtains and a bed head made of gold wood. They fetched everything out of my attic – all my clothes and my musical box and my Concorde notebook and my lipstick and my books – and stowed these away in drawers and cupboards without comment, without saying a single word. The only things they didn't find were Alice's gold chain and Valentina's silk nightdress under my pillow.

I wanted Alice to go away and Violette to sing to me:

Moi, je t'offrirai des perles de pluie,
Venues des pays où il ne pleut pas,
Ne me quitte pas, ne me quitte pas, ne me quitte pas . . .

But it was Alice who stayed and Violette who went, and all she did was sit there in silence.

Then I heard the telephone ring and she went away and I noticed that the apricot curtains had been drawn, like it was night time, so I thought, well, OK, if it's a sort of night, then I'll go to sleep. I tried to call Violette back, but she didn't hear me.

I went straight into a dream about Hugh. I was helping him with his hut, buttering bricks with cement and handing them to him, but this hut had got so large, it filled up every inch of ground that had once been the garden. It was like Hampton Court, with bell towers and arches and vaulted ceilings and square windows that let in the sound of the sea. He worked like someone in a cartoon, in a sort of speeded-up way, slamming brick after brick in place, so that I couldn't prepare them fast enough for him and he began to get angry. 'It's not my fault,' I said. 'I'm not really there.'

*

When I woke up, I was drenched in sweat and the bedclothes over me felt as heavy as mud.

The light in the room had altered and I thought it might be dusk and I remembered Valentina saying, on our first night in Paris: 'Now you see the evening begin to come down. The evening is a bird covering us with its wings,' and I thought, well, now this bird is going to land on me, on this bed of mud.

Then I felt something settle on my head. I knew it was a bird of some kind, but I'd forgotten the names of every single bird in the universe.

'Louis?' a voice said.

I stared up. The thing I saw wasn't a bird, but Mrs Gavrilovich's mouth, full of broken teeth. She was trying to talk to me, but I couldn't hear her very well. She put something into my hand and I saw that it was a spoon. I was sitting up now, but I didn't know how this change in my position had occurred. In front of me was a bowl of soup. It was a deep dark red, the colour of wine.

Mrs Gavrilovich took the spoon from me and began to feed me tiny sips of the red soup, but I knew if she went on with this I'd throw up again, so I asked her to take the soup away. I found my thoughts had wandered to an imaginary Kiev and to Grisha walking around in some park full of chess players, with his head tipped back, looking at the sky. 'Has Grisha been found?' I asked, but no one answered and then I saw that Mrs Gavrilovich and the bowl of soup and the spoon had gone and I was alone and the night had come.

With the night came something else. I saw a shape at the end of a long tunnel like a railway tunnel – very cold and dark, with water dripping from the curved walls – and the shape got gradually larger, as if I were a slow train in the tunnel, inching towards it.

The nearer I got to the shape, the more it filled up the mouth of the tunnel. I thought it would get out of the way and that I'd emerge into the sunlight in a landscape of rocks and grass and tall trees with grey roots clinging to a railway cutting, but all it did was move on the spot, like something dancing. I stopped and stood watching it and I began to feel that it had come there for me and that whatever I did – even if I retreated back down the icy tunnel – it would follow me and fold itself around me. So I went forward, step by step, holding on to the tunnel wall, and then an old familiar scent came wafting towards me: it was Valentina's wallflower night repair cream.

I tried to speak, but by that time I was *in* the shape and it was in me, moulding itself round me like heavy air. It didn't hurt me or push me, but just gradually enfolded me, and, despite the beautiful scent of the wallflower cream, being enfolded like this made me start to shiver; instead of being soft and warm, as Valentina's body would have been, it was soft and *cool*, and then I began to understand that the shape was Valentina's ghost.

When I woke again, I was crying and my top lip was covered with snot, just like it'd been when I was a kid and made of Play Doh. I heard someone say: 'It's OK, Lewis. It's going to be OK.' And what I said was: 'No, it isn't.' Then more covers were put on top of me and I entered a soundless, dreamless state.

What I remember next is surfacing back into consciousness and hearing church bells and deciding the day of the week was Sunday. I didn't know what had happened to Saturday. Where it should have been, there was only a black hole in my mind.

I sat up and looked round this new room of mine. On the bedside table lay Grisha's book, *La Vie secrète de Catherine la Grande*, and my next thought was, I've got way behind with my investigation into Valentina's plagiarism and I should focus on that now, so that we can either pursue or eliminate the Grisha Theory, but when I went to pick the book up my arm felt weak and I had to put it down again. So I just lay there, waiting. The thing I seemed to be waiting for was for someone to bring me a bowl of red soup.

Later, Alice gave me a bath. My body stank like cheese; I

could smell it the minute I pushed back my bedcovers. She washed my cheesy hair and scrubbed my back and I just sat in the water, obeying her instructions. She said: 'You've been quite ill. Moinel thinks it may have been shock.'

And it was then that I remembered the face at the window and said: 'It's only a matter of time before that person comes back.'

Alice poured water over my head. The feel of the hot water running down my spine made me shiver. She said: 'I don't think he will come back. The police are keeping watch now.'

'Keeping watch where?'

'In the street.'

'It won't be enough. He'll get on to the roof by some other route.'

'Well,' said Alice, 'you're safe now. The door to the attic stairs has been locked. You needn't go up to that attic ever again.'

I asked Alice to print me out a copy of Valentina's novel and she brought it in to me almost straight away. People who are ill have to be obeyed. Then she made up my bed with clean sheets and I lay there, propped up with cushions, like Valentina when she broke her arm, reading Alice's translation of *Pour l'amour d'Isabelle*. Outside, the church bells kept ringing and ringing.

I thought the book was quite exciting and good in a weird kind of way. It wasn't exactly *Crime et châtiment*, but for something supposed to be a medieval romance it was almost brilliant. The portrait it painted of Isabelle's husband, Pierre, the Duc de Belfort, was really frightening and strange. Valentina had made him a total retard. He had a set of toy soldiers made of lead and this was what he liked to do all day, play with his lead soldiers and imagine battles for them. The room where he kept them – set out on two huge tables – was furnished with muskets and kegs of gunpowder and military helmets. His moments of retardation were a good deal more frequent than mine with Elroy.

When Pierre wasn't playing with his soldiers and setting up executions for the poor toy generals who had lost his wars, he was torturing live things, like pet rabbits and mice. He kept alive a snake, called Serpentine, uniquely for the pleasure of torturing it. Part of the torture included suffocating it by sticking it up his rectum. And this was the only way he could get any sexual pleasure – with his snake, Serpentine. I thought, God, did Valentina make this up or does it come out of Grisha's text?

Whenever Pierre tried to make love to Isabelle, it was a hopeless failure and he just fell asleep before he'd hardly started. Not that Isabelle minded. She didn't want him near her. She'd been forced into the marriage by her ambitious mother, but now she despised Pierre. She sat in her room under the bell tower, doing her calligraphy lessons and praying that Pierre would die. She became the mistress of the apothecary's handsome son, Barthélémy, and told him how she wanted Pierre dead and he started to talk to her about finding a clever poison 'that would leave no trace'.

I was still hoping that Valentina was going to include something about a woman, like Catherine la Grande, who had a lover forty years younger and that that lover would turn out to be thirteen years old, when I got to the passage about the smallpox plague coming to Belfort. Isabelle, who was immune to smallpox, having had it as a child, persuaded Pierre – who was mortally afraid of the plague – to join the throng of people who were praying to their favourite saint, Sainte Estelle, at the city gate. She didn't tell him that, because so many people were gathered here, this place had become the most infected part of the city, and he was too stupid to realise this. It was here that I found the bit I'd already read, about Father H being sent to remove Sainte Estelle and being dismembered by the people, and now I saw how it fitted in. Pierre was the man who cut off Father H's testicles. He took them back to the palace and fed them to Serpentine for supper.

I was so engrossed in this story that I didn't want to stop, but Violette came in with a meal on a tray and said to me: 'You better eat something, Louis. If you don't eat now you won't get well, and if you don't get well we're never going to find Madame.' So I put the book aside and Violette stayed with me while I ate a sliver of chicken and a few grains of white rice.

Then, after a while, I realised Violette shouldn't be here. It was Sunday and she never worked in the apartment on a Sunday, so I said: 'Why are you here, Violette?'

She didn't reply. She got up and closed the door of the room and then she came and sat down closer to the bed and whispered to me: 'I made a *vèvè* last night, Louis. We asked Ogou Feray to come.'

'What's a *vèvè*, Violette?' I said.

'A pattern. You make it on the floor with rice or grains or flour and through the *vèvè* the spirits come . . .'

'Is Ogou Feray a spirit?'

'Yes. We say, at home, he lives in the calabash tree. His colour is red, so we made the *vèvè* with red beans. And one of his days is Saturday, so we had to get him to come last night.'

'What did you ask him to do?'

'Ogou Feray is the one who fights against all bad conditions – including bad illness. When he comes, he makes you swear, I tell you! You curse and yell when Ogou Feray comes into you.' Violette laughed. 'But I got used to him,' she added. 'I've been asking him to help with my bad conditions for a long time now. I think he got those Social Security people to give me a work permit, you see?'

'What did you ask him to do this time?'

'Make you well. And now you're sitting up, eating a bit of chicken!'

'Is this why you came today, to see if I was better?'

'No. Since you were ill, I come here every day.'

I tried to finish the chicken, but I couldn't. I didn't know where my famous raging hunger had got to. If Valentina had been there and invited me to lunch at the Plaza, I would have had to refuse. I told Violette I was sorry about not eating the food and she said: 'Tomorrow, you will,' as if this was something that Ogou Feray had informed her.

Then she took my tray away and told me never to tell anyone about the spirits; this was a secret between me and her and could never be revealed. As she was going out of the door, I said: 'Violette, could you ask Ogou Feray to do something about Valentina?'

She shook her head. 'Ogou Feray might not be the one to ask. You have to choose which spirit you want – this one for a love charm, that one to protect your home, this one for a good harvest, that one to bring you money – and how do I know what's happening to Madame?'

'Ask Ogou anyway. If she's been taken, she may be held somewhere very cold or dirty or horrible . . .'

'Or else there is some spell on her. Then I have to talk to Gédé, to get it removed. But Gédé is the spirit of death and he makes me afraid.'

Alice came to see me. All we talked about at first was the pathetic bit of chicken I'd eaten. Then she handed me something she'd been holding in her lap. It was Elroy. His beret was missing, but I didn't mention this. I just took him and laid him on one of my cushions, face down. The cushion was gold and he looked a bit as if he were slithering up a hill of sand towards an enemy position below. When a real enemy had come, he'd been completely useless.

Alice sat there, looking at me. In the street, I could hear two people having a conversation about the price of flowers. And then Alice said: 'Hugh called yesterday and I had to tell him that you were ill. I didn't tell him what had happened, but he's not stupid, he senses that something is odd here . . .'

'I'm not going back to England.'

'I think you may have to go, Lewis. Bertie and Gwyneth are leaving the house at the weekend and it's only a fortnight or so before your term begins. Dad wants me to send you home no later than next Sunday.'

'And you agreed?'

'I said I would talk to you . . .'

'Well, you've talked to me. I'm not going. We have to find Valentina.'

Alice took my hand and stroked it with hers. I didn't look at her, but at Elroy scaling his dune. Sometimes I envied Elroy his indifference towards everything in the world.

'You're very fond of Valentina, aren't you?' said Alice.

I still didn't look at her. What I said was: 'Is Carmody back?'

'Answer my question,' said Alice.

'Answer mine,' I said.

So we just stayed silent, like people do when they're trying to work out how to get their way, and the conversation in the street went on and on, clear as a bird: peonies so much, lilies x or y, geraniums bla bla bla, cheaper at Fleurs Monceau than in the rue Ponthieu, cheaper still at the *marché aux fleurs* . . . if one didn't mind the walk, or if one included the price of the taxi . . .

Alice caved in first. She said: 'Carmody's back. He came round and I took him up to your room. He's now talked to everyone in the building.'

I didn't want us to go into silence again, so I kept asking questions. Did Carmody have any news of Grisha? Had Alice told him to examine the GOH file? What did Dominique want?

When I mentioned Dominique, Alice turned her head away and looked out of the window. 'She doesn't know anything,' she said. 'She's in the dark.'

I stared at her. I thought, I've lost my feeling for when Alice is telling the truth and when she's lying, but I knew it was pointless to pester her; she wouldn't tell me anything more.

I returned to the subject of the GOH file. Alice said it contained a list of expenses and that was all.

'What kind of expenses?'

'I don't know.'

'Aren't they identified?'

'I suppose not.'

'If they're identified, they could prove to be important because they could tell us what happened to that translator, Gail, and this could be connected—'

'Stop!' said Alice. 'Now look at me, Lewis. This has got to end. You've got to stop taking responsibility for everything and believing you can fix it. Nothing is your fault and nothing can be solved by you, however much you want to solve it.'

'Wrong,' I said. 'I *am* solving it. I'm getting close. That's why that face came to my window. They're trying to frighten me.'

'Carmody said there was no trace of anyone having been on the roof.'

'You mean you don't believe I saw a face?'

'I believe you saw something and it frightened you.'

'It wasn't "something". It was a man's face!'

'All right. Then the reasons for going home become greater, don't they? If you're actually in danger because of what you've found out, the only sensible thing is to go back to England. If we told Hugh what had really happened, I'm sure he'd insist on you being sent back.'

'He might insist on *you* being sent back.'

'No, I don't think so. He'd realise I had to stay until something's resolved. And there are other things, which you don't know about . . .'

Alice got up and walked to the window and stood with her back to me, looking out. And I knew that when she turned round towards me again, she was going to reveal everything that was happening in her secret life. The moment had come for her confession. She was going to talk to me man-to-man. But I had to stop her. I just couldn't take her man-to-man stuff right now, because I knew it could turn out to be far more serious and shocking than I'd imagined and alter my life and Hugh's and everyone's for ever and this wasn't the moment when I could endure it.

So what I did was begin babbling about some of the things I'd discovered: Gail O'Hara's possible connection to the drug world; the confusion about Valentina's hospital visit; my realisation that the second receptionist had been Russian . . .

Alice turned and gaped at me. She didn't know until this moment how hard I'd been working on the case.

'Don't give in to Dad,' I said. 'Please. Be on my side, not his. All I need is a bit more time and I'll find her.'

I could see her hesitating, weighing everything up. In arguments at home between her and Hugh, it was Alice who usually won. Then, finally, she shrugged. 'OK,' she said, 'but you know you have to be home in time for the school term. Right? There's no argument whatsoever about that. So all you've got is two weeks.'

I'd done so much sleeping that, when the night came, I didn't feel sleepy. I wanted to carry on reading Valentina's novel, but instead I made myself go on with Grisha's French text.

The further I read the more frequently I wrote a huge *P* in the margin. I also translated and copied out the following passages from Grisha's book:

1. *Archduke Peter was preoccupied by his collection of military toys. He owned 126 soldiers, made of lead, wax and wood. He set up mock military battles on two large tables in a special room in his apartments and moved the soldiers around by means of ingenious mechanical devices.*

2. *Archduke Peter was extremely superstitious about water and in consequence refused to wash his body. He once said that he feared the bath more than the fortress.*

3. *Peter received very severe treatment at the hands of his tutor, Governor Brummer. He was often beaten and deprived of meals. Tales were told of his being forced to kneel naked on a harsh surface of dry*

peas. And it was widely assumed that it was these punishments which led him, in his turn, to punish. His victims were his inferiors: his servants, his grooms and his pet animals, which included a snake . . .

4. On his wedding night, the Archduke – unwashed, as he always was – came into Catherine's chamber and demanded to watch while his bride was undressed and made ready for him. By the time she had lain down in the great fortress of a bed, her new husband was asleep. In nine years, Archduke Peter never once succeeded in achieving sexual intercourse with his wife and when he died at the hands of her lover, Orlov, some wondered why the murder had been necessary.

Virtually everything, supposedly original, that Valentina had written so far about Pierre was based on the Archduke Peter in Grisha's book. She hadn't even bothered to change his name. I was leaning towards the Grigory kidnapping theory more and more when I found this and I numbered it 5:

The story of the Varvarsky Virgin is indeed strange. In the autumn of that year, Moscow, never at this moment in its history a clean city, was visited by a terrible plague. It was a plague of smallpox, not uncommon at the time and deeply feared by the people, who chose on this occasion not to put their trust in the doctors of the city, but to flee to the city wall, where they congregated at the feet of a statue of the Virgin Mary at the Varvarsky gate. They spent their waking and sleeping lives there, praying and beseeching the Virgin to save them from the pox.

The city fathers soon understood, however, that by gathering there all together, the people had turned the Varvarsky gate into a terrible centre of contagion. They went to the crowd and asked them to disperse, but no one was willing to move.

In desperation, under cover of night, Father Ambrosius, Bishop of Moscow, had the Varvarsky Virgin removed. At dawn, when the people woke and found the Virgin gone and word went around that Father Ambrosius was responsible, they rose up in a great bloodthirsty mass. They pursued Father Ambrosius into the fortress of the Kremlin, where he'd taken refuge. He was discovered hiding in a crypt and he was savagely killed and dismembered and his limbs thrown into the river.

The night was slowly passing as I read all this. The Volvos and Mercs of the weekenders were back in the rue Rembrandt, their fantastic engines gently cooling; the maids in their high rooms were sighing in their narrow beds, wishing Monday morning wasn't going to come.

And I was thinking, that's it, it's almost conclusive proof: if Grisha knows what is in Valentina's book, then she's in Russia and all the hospital stuff is a blind trail. She never went to the hospital, because she was on a plane.

But as I put the book down I thought, perhaps, after all, Grisha wouldn't kill Valentina. What he'd do is make her live *his* life, with him, in Moscow or Kiev or wherever he decided, in some old concrete block of flats with broken windows and dangerous electric wiring. He'd make her see how half the population of the world had to live; everything she saw and touched and ate would irritate her: the plastic chairs in the living room, the grey toilet paper, the slices of pink sausage served up for her dinner . . .

And then there'd be his bed. It would be just a mattress on the green lino floor. The blankets would be thin and scorched-looking; the sheets would have patterns of marigolds on them. And every night or night and morning Grisha would fuck Valentina and the ugly marigolds would get tangled around their bodies and part of Grisha's pleasure would come from knowing how much Valentina was hating every minute of her life. He'd stroke her hair, which would be going more grey by now. He'd say: 'Valya, I am never going to let you go.'

On Monday, I got up and walked with Alice to the Parc Monceau. My legs felt like sticks of cooked asparagus.

On the way, we heard Didier at work on the roof, but neither of us looked up.

In the park, we sat on a bench and watched a wedding party having their photos taken. It was a double wedding and both the brides were fat and smiling and both the bridegrooms were serious and small. One of the mothers-in-law parked herself on our bench and pulled her straw hat over her eyes and went to sleep. Alice said: 'Well, you're looking a bit better, Lewis.'

I didn't feel like talking. I just watched the wedding people and the stupid photographer with his huge camera on a tripod, diving in and out of his black head-cover, like photographers of long ago. He reminded me of my dream of the tunnel and this made me shiver. Alice was carrying a soft little blue cardigan and she put this round my shoulders. With this on and my wimpy-feeling legs and my eyes that kept watering in the sun, I felt like a girl.

My hands were cold and I put them into my pockets, and in my right-hand pocket I found my sifflet du chasseur. Without letting Alice see, I put it into my mouth and began my lark-practice. I saw Alice turn and stare at me in amazement. This is probably why people can make a living out of selling bird whistles – because everyone on earth has a secret longing to amaze.

'How are you doing that?' said Alice.

I just shrugged, pretending I was able to sound like a lark unassisted.

The mother-in-law woke up and looked at me. The thing about the cry of the lark is that it sounds like two little stones being crushed together in your hand. This could be the unlikely reason why it has a world-wide effect on the human heart.

'Mon Dieu,' said the mother-in-law. But I don't know if she was admiring my skill or if her heart was breaking.

I didn't want to talk to anyone, in any language, so I got up, leaving the cardigan behind on the bench, and walked to the children's carousel and watched the smart little babies being whirled around in miniature cars and miniature fire engines and miniature spaceships. One kid was whirling and trying to eat a toffee apple at the same time, and when I arrived the toffee apple flew off its stick and landed on the gravel at my feet. From then on, although her body kept moving forwards, her eyes remained fixed on the lost apple. She didn't cry or anything, but just kept staring round and back at the apple, like she wanted her head to fall off and be with the apple in the dust.

Moinel called in to see me. He'd bought me a little bunch of anemones, wrapped in yellow paper. He told me he'd been photographing an English Carolinian mortuary chair for an international periodical.

When Alice left the room, I told him about Valentina's plagiarism and showed him the passages I'd noted down in my Concorde book. I said: 'I've begun to believe she's in Kiev.'

Moinel took out some tiny little glasses and put them on. I knew he was one of those people who was older than he wanted to be. After a while, he looked up and said: 'I suppose she thought Grigory's book would never be published outside Russia?'

'Yes, I guess so.'

'And *her* books never appear *in Russia*. She thought no one would ever make a connection – provided Grisha never saw her text. Except she knew his book was out in France.'

'Yes.'

'So why did she go on with the plagiarism, once she knew that?'

I picked up the anemones. They didn't really have any scent, but I liked them. They looked like a little clutch of people all having a bad-hair day. I said: 'I think she went on with it because she was running out of ideas. Alice said this was her worst fear – to run out of stories.'

Moinel nodded, as if he knew exactly what this might feel like. Then he took off his glasses and said gravely: 'Despite all this, I don't think Valentina is in Russia, Louis. I think we may have got close to something at the hospital. You know, I believe that last receptionist was Russian . . .'

I then told Moinel about my return visit, based on the same conclusion, and my meeting with Dr Bouchain and Moinel said: 'To have taken Valentina from the hospital would have been easy – provided the register was safely amended to make everyone believe she never arrived. If you have a hospital appointment and someone calls your name, you follow that person, whoever it may be. You believe, automatically, that the person is going to take you to an X-ray room or a consulting room or whatever. You don't question anything. I believe she went to the hospital that afternoon and checked in at *Radiologie*, and someone was waiting for her there and called her away before Dr Bouchain was ready to see her. And now, because you and I made our enquiry and you went back there again on your own, whoever took her believes they're in danger of being discovered. This is why they tried to frighten you.'

I nodded. In their separate lonely spaces, Moinel's brain and mine had arrived at identical theories. If it hadn't been for Grisha's book, I would have been certain we were close to uncovering the truth.

Then Moinel sighed. He looked at me sternly. 'You must listen to me now, Louis,' he said. 'I believe that you must stop all your enquiries. You must cease them absolutely. OK? Are you listening to me? You must tell everything you know to Inspecteur Carmody and leave the rest to him. Will you promise me you will do this?'

'No,' I said. 'Why should I stop when we could be getting close? Don't you care about Valentina?'

He sighed again. He put his glasses away. 'We all care. But anything we can do can be done better by the police . . .'

'That's not true. The police are too visible.'

'*You* are visible now. They know who you are and that puts you in danger. Who knows what that man on the roof was trying to do.'

'You're as bad as Alice,' I said. 'She wants to send me home.'

'Well, perhaps that isn't such a terrible idea? Perhaps you should try to forget about Valentina and—'

'Forget about Valentina?'

'I don't mean "forget". I know this can't be forgotten. I only mean I think you should leave it to someone else now.'

'No,' I said. 'I can't do that.'

Then I laid the anemones aside. I felt tired suddenly and I had nothing more to say to Moinel. I closed my eyes, pretending to sleep, and after a moment I heard him tiptoe out. Then I summoned Valentina's face to my mind and laid my cheek against hers, which was smooth and cool. Something touched my neck and it was one of her long dangling earrings, made of silver.

'Don't worry,' I said to her, 'I am Porphiry Petrovich: I am François Seurel: I never give up.'

Part Three

Things happen in ways you never expect. When I was a child, my imaginary German in the cellar suddenly left a turd down there. The turd was small but it was real and had a human smell.

And the next thing happened like this: a note came, addressed to me. It had been posted in Paris, in the 9th Arrondissement, and it was written in English on squared paper, like we used for maths at school, torn out of a spiral notebook. It said: *Lewis, Meaulnes can tell you where to meet Valentine. You work it out by Thursday. You are safe if you do not go to the police.*

We were in the kitchen at the time, Alice and Violette and I, and Alice said to me: 'Who's your letter from?'

I said it was private. I wanted to add: 'You're not the only one with a secret life, Alice.' But I didn't. I went straight up to my room. I still couldn't think of this guest room, where I'd once imagined Grisha making love to Valentina, as mine, but Alice referred to it this way. 'My room' would always be the attic with the round window. That room would contain part of me in it for ever.

I sat down at the little bureau and spread the note out in front of me. It was written in biro and the writing was large and loopy, a bit childish. There was no date or other word on it. I wished I was Sherlock Holmes and had a magnifying glass in my pocket with which to examine it.

Then I picked up my copy of *Le Grand Meaulnes*. It was a long time since I'd read it. I'd been too preoccupied by Grisha's text and Valentina's novel. And I couldn't remember what was happening, except that Meaulnes had left Sainte-Agathe for ever. He was in Paris, searching for Yvonne de Galais.

I held the book in my hands. It had only 177 pages and somewhere in them lay the answer to where Valentina was. I thought, whoever sent me this note already knows something about me: he's set me a puzzle and he knows I'll solve it, because that's what I'm good at, solving puzzles. And this *proves* that he (or she) is the person holding Valentina. He's given me proof of his credentials by revealing what he knows about me.

I thought this was neat. I almost admired him, whoever he was – just as long as Valentina was safe. 'OK,' I said to him in my mind, 'I'll play your game.'

I knew I should start reading straight away, but I was almost afraid to begin. Because it depended on my accurate translation from French, this puzzle just might prove too difficult for me. Suppose I just couldn't work anything out from the *Meaulnes* text? The kidnapper didn't seem to have thought about this. Suppose the clue was so obscure that I missed it and Thursday came and I just didn't know what to do or where to go?

The chapter I was on was called *Je trahis* . . . and I remembered now that, as soon as Meaulnes has left, François takes up with his old friends again and tells them everything he was meant to be keeping secret. Then he knows he's betrayed Meaulnes and feels bad.

I finished this chapter and began the next, in which François gets a letter from Meaulnes in Paris. The letter says: *Dear François, Today, as soon as I arrived in Paris, I went to the house. But there was nothing to be seen. No one was there. No one will ever be there* . . .

My heart was beating faster at the realisation that I could already be near the clue. The clue would have to be in Paris, not at Sainte-Agathe, which is an invented place miles away in the middle of France somewhere. The letter went on: *The house Frantz told us about is small, two-storey. Mademoiselle de Galais' room must be on the first floor. These windows are hidden by trees, but from the pavement one can see them clearly. All the curtains are drawn and one would have to be mad to hope that one day, between these curtains at last drawn back, the face of Yvonne would appear . . .*

Alice appeared in my room. She startled me and I felt irritated at being interrupted. She sat down on my bed without asking for any kind of permission.

'That was Mrs Gavrilovich on the telephone,' she said.

'Yeah?'

'Carmody called her. They've found the person travelling under the name of Marya Narishkin, and it's not Valentina.'

I only nodded. Part of me wanted to show off, to say that I already knew, because of the note, that Valentina wasn't in Russia, but I didn't say this. I thought, I wonder whether Alice and I will ever again be like we used to be before we came to Paris.

I wanted her to leave then, but she didn't. She sat very still on my bed, staring at me, but I could tell just by the look on her face that it wasn't really me she was staring at, but into her own mind, packed with its lies and secrets. And I knew for certain that the moment had come when she was going to tell me about Didier. Parents think they can time everything to suit themselves: they just don't see what they might be burdening you with. As Alice opened her mouth, I said: 'Don't!'

I thought she'd understood by now that I didn't want to hear any words coming out of her lips on this particular subject, but she hadn't. She blundered on: 'Listen, Lewis, you'll realise, when you're older, that things happen sometimes . . . things you never intended . . . and they seem terribly, obsessively important at the time . . . but they don't necessarily last and they don't necessarily disturb the way one's life is going to——'

'I don't want to hear about it, Alice,' I said icily. 'Don't confide in me. I'm your son and I don't want you to say anything more.'

She looked really surprised. I guess when people are about to make a confession, they're too preoccupied with what they're going to say to take into consideration the state of mind of the confessee.

'Lewis,' said Alice. 'All I want to do is explain . . .'

'Don't explain,' I said. 'I'm not listening. I'm just bricking up my ears!'

I'd enfolded my head with my arms and shut my eyes. I thought, if she says another word, I am going to start screaming.

I had supper in Moinel's apartment. He invited Alice as well but Alice said she was having dinner with Dominique. I thought, that's a good alibi she's found – these supposed meetings with the editor from Bianquis.

Moinel was a brilliant cook and this was the first proper meal I'd eaten for about four days. I was so hungry, I couldn't talk for a while. We had roasted goat's cheese with olives and then pasta with tomatoes and clams. Moinel's dining table was made of a slab of glass, attached in some invisible way to a sawn-off stone Corinthian column. He said he'd bought it in London.

I showed him the note when we were halfway through the clams.

He stared at it for a minute and then put down his fork and said: 'Valentine is the clue.'

'Why? They mean Valentina, don't they?'

'No. They mean Valentine in the story. Don't you remember who Valentine is?'

'There isn't anyone called Valentine.'

'Yes, there is. You haven't got to the end, have you?'

'No . . .'

Moinel got up. He passed a bowl of salad towards me and I began helping myself distractedly to red and green leaves.

Moinel returned with a battered copy of *Le Grand Meaulnes* and began leafing through it. I chewed on the leaves, waiting. Then he found Chapter XIV, called *Le Secret*. It was very near the end of the book. He didn't take the time to explain to me everything that happened between Meaulnes' first letter from

Paris and this chapter, but told me only that François finds an exercise book in his attic, in which Meaulnes has written an account of his time in Paris, spent searching for Yvonne de Galais. Then he began to read: '. . . *On the quay I met the girl who, like me, had been waiting in front of the closed house last June and who told me about it.*

'*I spoke to her . . . It is night already and there is no one about. The gas street lamp is reflected on the wet pavement. Suddenly, she moves nearer and asks me to take her and her sister to a theatre, tonight. For the first time, I notice she is in mourning . . .*

'. . . *At the theatre: The two girls, my friend whose name is Valentine Blondeau and her sister, arrive wearing cheap scarves.*

'*Valentine sits in front of me. Every little while she turns uneasily, as if trying to make me out. All I know is that to be near her makes me feel almost happy, and each time I respond with a smile . . .*'

'Who is she?' I asked.

'Can't you work it out?' said Moinel. 'Remember when Meaulnes first finds the party going on at the lost domain and then the party breaks up because Frantz de Galais' fiancée never arrives?'

'It's her? Valentine is the fiancée who never arrives?'

'Yes. Meaulnes finds her waiting there, in front of the house once occupied by Yvonne. They've both gone there in search of their lost past, but they don't know each other.'

'But what can we work out from that? Where was the house where they waited?'

'As far as I can remember, we're never told. But I'm sure that what happens is that Valentine arranges a second meeting with Meaulnes, after the visit to the theatre. All we need to remind ourselves is where this meeting took place and on which day and we have decoded your note.'

I gave up on the salad. Moinel was scanning the text, which he held very close to his face. Then he read:

'. . . *They wouldn't let me see them to their door or even tell me where they live. But I followed them as long as I could. I know they live in a little street not far from Notre-Dame. The number, I don't know. I think they must be dressmakers or milliners . . .'*

'Moinel . . .'

'Wait. Listen. We're getting to it. *"Unbeknown to her sister, Valentine gave me a rendezvous for tomorrow, Thursday"* – Thursday, you see, Louis! – *"at four, in front of the same theatre. 'If I'm not there,' she said, 'come back Friday at the same time, and Saturday and so on . . .' " '*

Moinel looked up. 'There you are,' he said, 'I think that's it: Thursday at four o'clock. Or Friday – and so on. You would have worked it out for yourself if you'd got to the end and they must have counted on this. They're the most literary kidnappers in the Western world – if kidnappers they are. But of course you won't go; you *mustn't* go! It's far too dangerous. You must give the note to Carmody.'

'Go where?' I almost screamed. 'It doesn't say which theatre!'

'No,' said Moinel, his voice staying quiet and calm. 'But we're told Valentine lives in a street "not far from Notre-Dame". The theatre would have to be the one nearest to Notre-Dame; that's what I'd guess if I were your Porphiry Petrovich. Don't you think? It must be the Théâtre de la Ville or the Théâtre du Châtelet. We'll look at the map, but I'd put my money on the Théâtre de la Ville, which is very slightly further to the east.'

I wanted to give Moinel a hug. Once he'd led me to it, the coding seemed so simple and obvious. And all I could think about now was that only three days separated me from the moment when I would see Valentina again.

But then Moinel started trying to make me swear that I wouldn't go to the rendezvous. He said: 'You're thirteen. Do you want to die?'

I knew nothing in the world was going to stop me, but I didn't say this. 'I could die if I go to the police,' I said. 'Look what the note says.'

'OK,' he said, 'don't go to Carmody – not yet. Do nothing.

Hide the note and keep it safe, but you must swear *on your life* that you won't try to meet these people, Louis.'

I pointed out to Moinel that it hadn't been worth his while decoding the note for me if he was going to stop me acting on it. He replied that, like me, he enjoyed unravelling things, but that if I couldn't see what danger I was now in I was acting like a moron.

I thought, the time has come to lie. There's no other option. I said: 'All right. I won't go, Moinel, but in return you have to swear to me that you won't tell Alice about the note. If Alice knows about this, I'll be sent home, definitely. So if you don't swear to this, I'll break my promise to you.'

'Sure,' said Moinel. 'It's a done deal.'

We were loading our supper things into Moinel's dishwasher when we came to this agreement. As he bent down, I could see that the roots of his tangerine hair were completely white. I thought, later, when I do break my promise to him, the thing that may really get to me will be my remembrance of this white hair.

As the day got nearer, I started to feel afraid. I was afraid because I'd realised that the sender of the note was probably the person whose head had appeared at my window. Instead of seeing Valentina on Thursday, I was going to see that face again, wrapped in its rags.

I tried not to think about this, but I knew that the things you try not to think about just take an alternative route into your mind via your dreams. So I gave Elroy a task. He used to have this task when I was about nine: I put him on dream-guard. I attached him to the gold bed head with a bit of string and he hung down, like a paratrooper, with his arms outstretched above my pillow, staring at the night.

What I tried to concentrate on was my plan. I thought Moinel might hang around secretly on Thursday afternoon, to make sure I wasn't going anywhere. But I knew how to get round this: I'd cover myself by seeming to be with Alice. If I left with Alice, at, say, two-thirty, he'd think I was safe with her. Under these circumstances, he wouldn't follow me. Then, all I had to do was to get from wherever I was with Alice to the meeting place by four o'clock.

The other thing that preoccupied my mind was the question of what I was going to take with me. I thought a weapon of some kind might be useful, just in case things got really terrifying, so I said to Violette: 'If you were planning to defend your life, or someone else's life, with something from the kitchen drawer, what would you take?' I was hoping she might say a corkscrew or a garlic press or something and explain to me some brilliant voodoo method of using a harmless culinary utensil as a lethal weapon, but she didn't; she said: 'I'd take a knife, stupid!'

So, when Violette had gone home, I chose a small knife, made by the firm of Sabatier, that Valentina used to use for chopping white onions. I sharpened it up and wrapped it in some kitchen paper. Even wrapped, the knife was small enough to go into one of my trouser pockets.

Then I remembered my promise to myself – that if ever I saw Valentina alive again, I'd take her a present. I looked through all my things, as if I expected to find some marvel there that I didn't know I possessed. But my things seemed sort of stupid and worn. What I really wanted to give her was something extraordinary, that she'd never seen before in her life.

On Wednesday morning, Hugh called when I was alone in the apartment.

He asked me how I was after my illness and I said I was fine. He didn't sound that concerned or interested because he started on immediately about the hut. He said it was finished! He sounded like he'd just completed the Forth Bridge. He said: 'All that's left is to paint the interior and this is why I'm ringing, to ask you what colour you think Mum would like it to be.'

I was completely silent. I couldn't think of any colours. All

I could think of was that moment, in my room, when Alice had taken a breath and started to tell me about 'things you never intended . . . things that don't necessarily last . . .'

'Are you there, Lewis?' asked Hugh.

'White,' I said. 'Paint it white.'

'Isn't white dull? Isn't it cold? What about magnolia?'

'Yes, or magnolia. Magnolia's good.'

'Or do you think she'd like a brighter colour, like terracotta or red, even?'

'I don't know, Dad,' I said.

There was a pause and I heard Hugh say something to Bertie or Gwyneth. 'Bertie's suggesting green,' he said. 'He says green is the most restful colour for the eye.'

'Yeh,' I said. 'Green's OK.'

'But I can't remember if Mum likes it, can you?'

I thought of her dark-green velvet dress, the one she'd worn the night the face came to my window, the night she'd come home at three in the morning, and I said: 'Dark green, she likes. I know.'

'What about one wall dark green, then, and the other three magnolia, or the other three terracotta?'

I gave up on this conversation. I said: 'You decide.'

Then Grandma Gwyneth came on the line and said: 'We're so excited here, darling! This hut really is a masterpiece. We're dying for you to see it. I never thought Bertie and Hugh could pull off something like this, but they have, bless them. And we think Alice is going to love it – absolutely perfect, in summer, for her work.' Then she said, in a whisper: 'But Hugh's missing you so, Lewis. He's counting the days now. Couldn't you come back at the weekend and then Alice can follow on? I'm sure your air ticket could be changed. They say there's only going to be another week of this wonderful weather . . .'

'I can't, Grandma,' I said.

'Why not, sweetheart? Think of the lovely swims you can

go for. The sea's never been so warm in twenty years, apparently . . .'

I told her my last days in Paris were going to be very important, that there were friends I'd promised to see and thousands of things to do that I hadn't done yet. I hoped she wasn't going to ask me what things or what friends, and she didn't. She just changed her tack, because really and truly, even though she was fussy, she was a sweet and lovely woman.

When I hung up, I remembered that Alice had told me Bertie and Gwyneth had been about to go home to their flat in Salisbury, but there they still were, babbling about master-pieces and green paint. So then I thought, I really hope Hugh has invited them to live there, for always. I hope they've agreed and put their flat up for sale.

Part of me wondered if I would ever return to the rue Rembrandt after my meeting with the writer of the *Meaulnes* note.

This gave me the idea that I wanted to say a sort of goodbye to Didier, so on Wednesday afternoon I climbed out on to the roof and stood in the shade of the water tanks, looking all around for him. Alice was back in the apartment, so I thought he would be there, but at first I couldn't see him.

He appeared by me silently, as if he'd been two metres away all the time and I hadn't spotted him. He had a sad smile on his face.

'Didier,' I said. 'You're a philosopher . . .'

'Not really. That's too grand a word.'

'Yes, you are. Sort of. And I've been meaning to ask you something.'

His eyes flickered behind his glasses. He could tell I was in this serious kind of mood and he was worried about what I was going to say. 'Ask me what?' he said.

'Well,' I said, 'my father once said to me – when we were meandering about by the sea – that I should think of my life as a rock pool and my quota of happiness as a tiny little shrimp in the pool and then I wouldn't be disappointed. Do you think he was right?'

Didier crouched down into his bird stance. The bird on his neck was shiny with sweat. He let a bit of time pass before he answered. Then he said: 'There was a period in my life when I might have said that. I wasn't optimistic. But now, no. I would say he was wrong. What do you think, Louis?'

'I don't know yet,' I said. 'I haven't lived long enough. That's why I wanted to ask you.'

We were quiet. The heat from the roof shimmered all around us. Then Didier suddenly said: 'I was very happy until my father died. Then angry and miserable for a long time. When something seems random and almost without cause it always strikes us, I think, as particularly unfair. And then we truly suffer. But we get over it in time.'

'Are you talking about that day on the Salpêtrière dome?'

'Yes.'

'You never told me. You were going to tell me and then you didn't. What was it that came out of the sky?'

Didier didn't pause. He just went straight on. 'An air balloon,' he said. 'You know these things? It had been raining, but now the sky was clearing and I saw it a long way off, a striped balloon coming towards us. And I pointed it out to my father, because I knew he'd always wanted to do that – go up in a hot-air balloon.'

'And then?'

'Well, he looked at it. That's all. He took his eye off the scaffolding, just for a split second, to look at the balloon.'

Didier stood up. He took out a cigarette and lit it. I knew he wouldn't say anything more and wouldn't expect me to say anything. We just hung around, saying nothing.

And then I looked at him, alone up here on this enormous roof and thought, he's marooned. He could choose to stay in his life with Angélique or he could choose to abandon her and go off with Alice. But right now, he can't decide. He's choosing not to choose.

'Goodbye, Didier,' I said after a while. 'I guess I have to go now.'

When Thursday morning came, I said to Alice: 'In all the time we've been here, I've never been inside the cathedral of Notre-Dame.'

She was working in her room. I thought, if she knew, as she will one day, that Valentina has stolen half her ideas from Grigory Panin's *Secret Life of Catherine the Great*, she would go completely and absolutely insane.

'Haven't you?' she said mechanically, without paying me any attention. Then she turned back to her computer and told me that only thirteen more pages of Valentina's text remained to be translated; after she'd done these, she'd have nothing more to work on.

'What have you been telling that person from Bianquis? Where does she think Valentina is?'

Alice still didn't look at me as she spoke. 'Oh, in Kiev,' she said. 'Just as you suggested to her.'

I sat down on Alice's gigantic blue-and-gold bed. I imagined Hugh and Bertie at work inside the hut, sloshing on green paint with furry paint-rollers. I thought, that kind of childish happiness is always doomed.

'Can we go this afternoon?' I asked.

'Go where?'

'To Notre-Dame. Say, at about half past two?'

She looked at me then. It was like she was really surprised that I wanted to go on an outing with her when it had seemed to both of us that the time of our Paris outings was long past.

'Yes,' she said. 'Why not? We could have lunch in a café near by. Would you like that?'

'Sure,' I said. 'That'd be good.'

We agreed to leave in an hour's time.

I went to my room and made my final preparations. I was very near to confiding in Violette and asking her to ask the spirits to protect me, but I knew this would be too dangerous. I had to think and act, from now on, with a cool, clear head.

I changed into the trousers that had the kitchen knife in their side pocket. Into the hip pocket, I put all the money I had – about four hundred francs – and my bird whistler. Then I put on a denim jacket I hadn't worn for days in the stifling hot weather, and in the pockets of this I hid my Concorde notebook and my copy of *Le Grand Meaulnes*. At the last moment, as I heard Alice coming towards my room, I untied Elroy from the bed head and stuffed him, string and all, into the waistband of my trousers, hidden by the jacket.

We left Sergei behind. Alice said they didn't allow dogs into cathedrals. As we went out of the apartment I saw him standing in the salon, in a square of sunlight, staring expectantly at us, and I thought, if I never see him again, at least I'll be able to say later on: I once knew a really fantastic, ace, brilliant dog.

I thought Alice was going to nag me to take my jacket off in the boiling heat, but she didn't, and while she was buying a new métro carnet I was able to transfer Elroy to one of the eight pockets that jacket had. All Alice was wearing was a black sleeveless T-shirt with *Save the Rainforests* written on it and a flimsy skirt the colour of rice. Her sunglasses nested in her hair and she carried an old canvas bag slung over her freckled shoulder. As we walked along, the faces of the men turned towards her like sunflowers turn towards the sun.

At Châtelet station, where we got off, I saw a guy standing and waving at the train. I'd seen him before. His face and clothes were both a kind of grey-brown, like he'd had his clothes made from different bits of his own hair and skin, and what he did all day was breathe the fug of the métro station and wave at the trains. Sometimes people waved back. Not often, though. I thought, maybe, long ago, he arranged to meet someone here and that person never arrived, and so now this is where he lives his life, just in case they turn up before the end of the century.

When we came out into the air, we walked right past the Théâtre de la Ville and over the Pont au Change. I looked at the theatre as we went by, to see which door I'd have to use when I went in. The play that was on was *Le Misanthrope* by Molière and quite a few people were going in and out to book tickets and I began to wish I was one of those ticket-bookers and not me. That's what cowardly people do all the time, when they're approaching some frightening thing: they wish they were sparrows or news vendors or dead.

The street where we had lunch was called the rue de la Colombe. Alice smiled and said: 'We're in Dove Street.'

I wasn't a bit hungry, so I ordered a Badoit and a salad and just pushed everything in the salad round and round on my plate. Alice ate an omelette and drank three glasses of white wine and started talking about the winter. She said she just couldn't imagine it ever coming, and I said: 'It won't. This is the last season of our lives.'

We went into the cathedral of Notre-Dame at 3.05. I kept checking the time without Alice noticing.

It seemed cooler in the cathedral than in any place I'd been for months and months, and I really liked the coolness of it and its darkness and the way human voices – even all the squeaky voices of the tourists – sounded tiny because of the massive weight of air between them and the vaulted roof.

Now I had to lose Alice.

I told her we might as well separate, so that we could each look at the things we wanted to see, and without waiting for an answer or a comment I wandered away from her and she didn't call me back. I thought, suppose this is the last time I ever lay eyes on her?

I walked very slowly on and on, creeping past the huge stone columns, into the transept, where a bunch of Italian kids were milling around, all wearing little coloured rucksacks. They looked kind of spaced out, as if their eyes just couldn't get accustomed to the saintly darkness, as if, in this empty place, they were getting weak from lack of ice cream.

Then I found myself in one of the side chapels, and it was called – just completely by chance – the Chapelle Saint Louis, so I stood in it for a long time, looking at a tomb, which had Cardinal de Noailles written on it, and listening to time passing. A cold little bit of daylight fell on to the tomb. I didn't know who Cardinal de Noailles was, but I spoke to him in my mind and to Saint Louis. I said: 'OK, guys, it's a quarter to four and I'm going to go now.'

I moved. It took me a while to be able to make myself move. Then I kept on moving slowly past four or five other chapels, round to the north door, keeping a watch out for Alice. Once I was back in the sunlight in the rue du Cloître, I knew I was exactly five minutes from my rendezvous.

I suppose I should have felt guilty about what was going to happen soon to Alice. She was going to start walking round and round and round the cathedral, in and out of chapels, behind the choir screen, between the lines of chairs, searching for me, knowing I was there somewhere and not finding me. And then she'd get worried and maybe ask people to help her look.

But it would be all right. Later, she'd find the note I'd written on a paper table napkin in the restaurant. I'd stuffed it into her canvas bag, next to her purse, while she was in the toilet. It said: *Following important lead to V. Tell no one where we were today. Will telephone. Love, Lewis.*

The theatre had four separate glass entrance doors, of which two were open.

I stood just inside one of them, looking in and looking out by turns. Under my arm, with the title visible, I carried Paul Berger's copy of *Le Grand Meaulnes*. I thought, this is the riskiest thing I've ever done in my life.

I felt a bit faint. The floor of the theatre foyer was made of marble or some slippery kind of stone slabs, and every time I took a step I seemed to slide around on it, like I was on ice. What I longed to do was to sit down.

When my watch said 4.20, I decided no one was coming and I felt relieved at first, thinking, well, I can just go home now and take Sergei for a walk, and then frantic, knowing that my last hope of seeing Valentina again was disappearing as every minute passed.

I slithered over to the stairs, which had open treads made of wood, and sat down on one of them. I put the book next to me on the step and stared at the sunlit afternoon outside. In a mechanical kind of way, I began to count the number of vacant taxis that went by.

Then I heard someone coming down the wooden steps behind me and, just as I was about to turn round, a man's foot appeared right next to me. It trod on my book. I tried to move my head, but the man was crouching above me on the next step and he had his hand on the back of my neck, forcing my head forward.

I could still just see his foot, in a scuffed brown shoe, resting on *Meaulnes*, then the foot moved to one side and a voice said in French: 'Pick up your book.'

I reached out with my left hand. I saw that the shoe had left a mark on the white cover of the book. 'Don't turn round,' whispered the voice.

When I'd gathered up the book, I felt the man's arm go round my neck and his hand tap my shoulder, as if he was pretending to be my old friend.

'So,' he said, 'I'm very glad to meet you, Lewis. Will you stand up now, please? Don't turn to look at me. That's it. We are buddies, OK? And I have a car outside, so let's just walk towards the door . . .'

I didn't say anything. The next moment, we were outside, with the hot sun and the people and the traffic. I was wondering what kind of car these kidnappers had, when a Citroën drew up in front of me and the man's hand pressed down on my head, and I was shoved into the back seat.

The man got in beside me and I felt the car pull out and away, very fast. I was looking to see who was driving the car, when I felt something pressed against my nose and mouth and all I had time to think was: I don't know what this is, but whatever it is it smells bad, like the end of the world . . .

When I woke up, I knew I was in England.

I could hear someone moving about and I was certain that someone was Hugh, going downstairs to put on the kettle to make a cup of tea.

I lay and listened. My head was aching. I had no recollection of any plane journey or any arrival or any words spoken by anyone.

My body was itching. I began to scratch my arms and it was then that I realised I was lying under a blanket and not under my duvet, as I'd thought. And so I knew I wasn't at home in England at all, but somewhere else that I couldn't recognise.

I lay as still as I could, because it hurt my head to move it. Then, very slowly and carefully, in case thinking was going to damage my brain inside my hurting head, I put together everything I could remember: making my way out of the cool of the cathedral towards the rendezvous, waiting for someone to arrive in the foyer of the theatre, seeing a foot coming down on my copy of *Meaulnes*, being led out to the car. But after I got into the car, there was nothing. My brain circuitry kept searching and finding a blank, a black hole.

I felt my arms and legs, to see what I was wearing. All I had on was a T-shirt and some underpants. I knew the loss of my trousers and my jacket was important, but I couldn't remember why.

I floated into another dream. In it, I was on a ship in a rough sea and I was feeling terribly sick. Valentina had laid my head in her lap and was stroking my eyebrow with her finger.

I woke up, puking. I couldn't see what or where I was puking into, but it wasn't a toilet, and when I'd stopped, the puke just stayed near me, stinking. So I started to call out. 'Help me!' I called. 'Someone come! I've been sick!'

269

It was so dark where I was, I couldn't make out where the walls were or the door, or anything. I thought, it must be night.

Being sick seemed to have exhausted me and I wanted to lie down again under the blanket, but I made myself keep calling. Then my elbow touched something and I realised that just to the left of me was a wall. It felt cold, as if it had been built hundreds of years ago and no light had ever fallen on to it. I knelt up, with my face turned away from the puke, and began banging on the wall with both my fists. And I changed my calling into French: 'Aidez-moi! Quelqu'un! Je suis malade! J'ai vomi! Aidez-moi!'

No one came. My head was hurting so much, I had to lean it against the wall. And I think that's how I must have stayed for quite a bit of time, kneeling there, with my head pressed to the cold wall. Then, just as I was about to float back to sleep, kneeling up like that, I heard a sound coming from the other side of the wall, right where my ear was. I waited and it came again – a knocking, like a human hand knocking on a door.

It went on. When it paused, I knocked back, then I called softly: 'Qui est là?'

The next thing I heard were footsteps and they were coming towards me. Then a door was opened and a bright light, like a searchlight, shone on to me. It was so blinding, it gave my whole body a shock, like it'd been thrown into freezing water. I closed my eyes and tried to blot out the light with my right hand.

I felt someone come into the place where I was. I realised quite quickly that it was two people. Then a voice said in French: 'O merde! Il a dégueulé partout . . .'

One of the people came behind me and took my arms away from the wall and my hand away from my eyes, and I fell backwards on to someone's chest. It was a man's chest and the man smelt strongly of cigarettes. He pushed me up and wrenched my hands together and snapped something metal on my wrists.

A piece of cloth was put over my face and tied round my head. At least it helped to blot out the blinding light. Then I was pushed over and fell back on to the mattress where I'd been lying. The blanket was snatched away.

I kept still, just lying how I'd fallen. I thought, I've often wondered how handcuffs feel and now I know: they hurt your wrist bones.

I knew there were at least two men in the place. It could have been three. One of them went away and then came back in again. All the time, I could see the light shining on to me through the blindfold.

The men started to move round me. They were swearing as they moved, but I didn't know at first what they were doing. I thought, they could be about to kill me.

Then I smelled disinfectant and I knew they were trying to clean up the puke on the floor. Some cold water splashed on to my legs and I realised that, for the first time in ages and ages, I was shivering. I thought, wherever I am must be underground for the temperature in here to be so low. 'J'ai froid,' I said, but the men didn't hear me. They were moving a mop or a brush or something over the ground. It sounded as if the ground was made of brick or stone – some hard surface, which the mop scraped on. Gradually, the smell of puke began to go and was just replaced with the horrible disinfectant smell.

I heard one of them go out again, probably with the mop and pail, and so I said to whoever remained, 'Where am I?'

'Tais-toi,' someone said, then in broken English: 'You quiet. You shut. Or we hurt you. Compris?'

'J'ai froid,' I said again, and then I felt the man smelling of smoke come near me.

'You shut!' he yelled. 'Nothing! You say nothing, English boy!'

Then the men and the light went away. The men went first, then the light, and a door was closed and locked. Before the men left they removed the handcuffs, and slowly I reached up and pulled down the blindfold. I blinked. My eyes kept seeing round circles of light, floating on the darkness, paler and paler ghosts of the one that had been there.

The feeling of wanting to sleep had gone. I was preoccupied by the cold and, now, by a new thing, a sudden thirst that was so acute, it was as if I had no moisture left in my body.

I lay down, with my knees curled up to my stomach. I was on a mattress, but the mattress had no cover or sheet or anything and I could feel underneath me the little tufts of twine or whatever it is they put in the pockets of mattresses. I thought, I wonder if this mattress was made in another country, by women working for hardly any wages, like that garment worker in Spain on the TV programme about the Women of Europe? And asking myself this question reminded me that what I needed to acquire now was information about where I was.

I didn't stand up. I just got on to my knees and like this – like I'd gone up and down the line of Valentina's musical boxes, with Violette, that time when we were searching her room – I started to move around, off the mattress and on to the floor, which was hard and gritty, using one hand to keep guiding me along the wall and then stopping and feeling in front of me for objects in the room.

I hadn't gone far when my head nudged against another wall. Just before it did, my right hand located an iron pipe, coming out of the wall about six inches above the ground and turning and running almost to the corner, but not quite. I went back, to where the pipe began, and then moved forward again, keeping my hand on the pipe, which felt wider than normal heating or water pipes usually were, till it reached the place where it ended or broke off. I felt all around the broken end. It hadn't been capped off; it was just a hollow length of pipe, old and heavy, made of lead or iron, not copper, sticking out into the room. And I knew that one of two things might be attached to the other end of it – water or gas. I hoped it was water.

I knelt crouched by the pipe for a long time. Outside the room, some distance away, the men were talking. I thought I could hear at least three voices, but I couldn't make out what they were saying. I wanted to call out to them, to bring back the blanket, to bring water, but they'd warned me not to speak and I didn't have any idea what they might do if I disobeyed them. I thought, cold and thirst could turn out to be *nothing*; cold and thirst could be a state of luxury compared with what they might do . . .

I decided to go on with my investigation of the room. As I crawled around, I made a mental note of the probable distance I was covering. I calculated that my mattress was placed against the wall about a metre from where the pipe began. The length of the pipe was less than a metre, so the distance between my mattress and the back wall was less than two metres. I expected the back wall to run for only a few feet, as if the room was going to be a small rectangle, like a cell. But it wasn't. The back wall carried on for at least three metres, or possibly more.

There was nothing near it or on it at ground level, but my knees touched something soft as I came to the corner and it felt to me like hay. I began to pick it up in handfuls. Even holding it close to my eyes, I couldn't see what it was, but it smelled like hay and I thought that if there was enough of it I could burrow down in it and get warm. But there wasn't much – no more than an armful – so I let it go and carried on round the corner, along the third wall.

I was getting tired. I was less cold now, because I'd been moving around, but my thirst was really bad. An image of Violette's black arms holding the fat Orangina bottle and pouring it out into two glasses came into my mind, drenching it with longing. I let myself fall to the floor and rest.

I lay there for a long time. It was like I dreamed that I was asleep. When I sat up, I hit my head on something hard. I reached up to feel what it was and I realised it was a table. It was made of wood, like a table you might put in a kitchen. Slowly, I got to my feet, holding on to the table, and I felt all over the surface of it, just in case the kidnappers had kindly left me a glass of water. They hadn't, and my thirst went on, but then my hand touched something solid and I knew straight away what it was: it was my copy of *Le Grand Meaulnes*. I picked it up and pressed it to my face. I thought, if only they would give me some light in here, I could read to the end of it and find out whether Meaulnes is ever reunited with Yvonne de Galais or not.

I found other things on the table – my things. There was no kitchen knife and no wallet and no Concorde notebook. The men had been through my pockets and taken everything that could be useful to them or give them information. But they had put the rest of my stuff in a little pile on the table: a handkerchief that had once belonged to Hugh, a used métro ticket, one of Sergei's dog biscuits, the sifflet du chasseur and Elroy. And then on a wooden chair, drawn up to the table, I found my clothes. My trousers and denim jacket were there, but every pocket was empty and my shoes seemed to be missing.

I put on the jacket. Then I picked up everything else and stowed the things in two pockets, including my book. Before I tucked Elroy away, I spoke to him, which was a thing I hadn't done for years. I said: 'War zone now entered.'

The jacket comforted me. I knew that this was what happened to people taken out of their lives and put into prisons or cellars or bombed-out buildings: they got attached to the tiniest thing, like a beetle or an empty tin or a pellet of fluff. And already, within an hour of finding myself in this place, I'd started to behave like one of them, almost crying with joy at recovering some of my clothes. I was sure that if anyone planned on torturing me I'd tell them whatever it was they wanted to know in five minutes.

I wished I knew what time it was – day or night. My Kermit alarm clock, with its luminous green hands and numbers, would have been a useful possession. When I was a child, I used to talk to the Kermit frog on the dial. I used to say, 'Seven-thirty, Albuquerque,' and Kermit used to reply, 'Seven-thirty, Albuquerque!' in his ace American accent. At that time I thought the word 'Albuquerque' was the most brilliant word in the English language.

With my jacket on and everything safe in the pockets, I continued my casing of the edge of the room. By my measurements, it was about four metres long by three metres wide. The door was wooden and had no handle on the inside. A metal plate had been screwed over the place where the handle had been. Underneath the door there was a tiny gap of air, about a centimetre high, but no light came in through the gap, so it was difficult to imagine where the door led. I still had the feeling that the room was underground, except that the hay could indicate that an animal had once been kept in it and you probably wouldn't keep any animal in a cellar, in total darkness. And I still hoped that when the day came, a bit of light would get in somehow, from somewhere.

When I got back round to my mattress, I lay down on it. I knew it was old because it had a kind of mushroom smell about it. I thought, if I was going to kidnap someone, I'd at least provide them with a pillow. Then I got Elroy out and rubbed his balding head with my finger and thumb and went to sleep.

There *was* light in the room. It didn't come from under the door or from a window; it came from above. The shape of the morsel of light was oblong and thin.

I lay on my side and stared about me. The table and the chair were just visible and there was some other object, under the table, that I hadn't seen before. As far as I could tell, there was nothing else anywhere in the room.

I got up. I didn't feel cold any more. I walked to the middle of the room and stared up at the sliver of light. It was grey-white and flat and no wider than a Mars bar. It was the sky.

As time passed, it got whiter. It cast a little replica of itself on the floor at my feet. Quite soon, it was enough to see everything by.

I was in an attic. The roof was quite shallow, made of wooden rafters, with wood batons laid over them and slates fixed to the batons. The covering of slates was solid except in this one place, where one slate had slipped free of its pin and moved, leaving this minute opening of sky. There was a window in the attic – not round, but small and square and boarded up from the outside, with no single gap or chink anywhere in the boarding.

But I knew that the bit of light in the roof was going to make a difference to my life in this place and I also thought, the kidnappers probably haven't noticed it; they think it's pitch black in here, and what I have to do is to guard the light and keep it secret from them.

First, I counted the number of slates from the top of the wall above my bed to the slate that had moved. I counted them twice, to be sure, and the number was eleven. Then, as quietly as I could, I moved the table to the middle of the room, exactly underneath the eleventh slate. The ceiling wasn't very high, so I thought I might be able to reach it just by standing on the table, but I wasn't tall enough. I fetched the chair and put this on top of the table and stood on that. Now, my head came up almost to the roof. I slipped my hand through the gap and felt the air touch my fingers. I could hear a solitary bird singing, quite far away. And I could hear another sound, that was like a small boat moving through water.

Next, I moved the slate. I could make the gap wider by a few centimetres, or close it off completely. With the gap closed, the thick darkness returned and I thought, counting the slates is no good, because when the gap of light isn't there I can't see them. I'd understood what was prime – my ability to locate the slipped slate – but not *how* to achieve it.

I made the gap of light as wide as possible and looked round the room. The object that had been under the table was a bucket with a lid and I supposed this was meant to be my toilet. I considered placing this toilet exactly under the slate, but I knew it would get moved from time to time by the kidnappers and I had to measure with something that never moved.

Then I remembered Elroy's string. All I needed to do was run the string along the floor, out from my mattress to where the light's reflection fell on to the floor, and tie a knot in it at the exact place. I noticed now that the floor was made of dusty tiles. The only area where they weren't dusty was where I'd thrown up and the men had swabbed around with their bucket and mop. A tiny bit of colour was coming into things now and I could see that in the swabbed area the tiles looked brown.

I was about to climb down and fetch the vital string, when I heard, close to my mattress wall, the little knocking I'd heard before, like that of the knuckles of a hand, on the other side of the wall. I stood completely still on my chair and listened. This was the only noise in the building. I assumed, from the flat light, that it was still early and that the kidnappers or guards, or whoever they were, were still asleep.

Leaving the gap in the slates open, I climbed down and crossed to my mattress. I pressed my ear to the wall and I heard the knocking come again. Gently, I knocked in answer. I thought, if I'd learned Morse properly when Hugh wanted to teach it to me, I could send a message. But you often don't know, in a life, what's going to be useful and what's going to turn out to be a complete waste of time.

'Qui est là?' I said. 'Qui est là?'

There was a reply. But it was so quiet and tiny, it sounded like it was a beetle trying to speak.

'Plus fort!' I said. 'Parlez plus fort!'

Nothing came, so I resumed knocking. I knocked in sequences, one-two-three, one-two-three. And then I heard, as if from far, far away, a voice saying my name, my English name, Lewis. And I knew it was Valentina.

★

We tried to have a conversation through the wall. It was difficult for me to speak, because a crazed feeling of joy was spreading through my heart. I put both my hands against the wall, as if that was going to bring Valentina nearer to me.

The wall was thick, like it was made of blocks of stone. Our voices seemed to go into the stone and stay there. 'Why?' Valentina kept saying. 'Why?'

'Why did they take me?'

'Why you, Lewis?'

I was going to try to describe the way I'd pieced together the trail that led to the hospital, but I knew she'd only hear half of what I was saying, so I just said: 'I don't know. I don't know. Are you all right, Valentina? Have you got a blanket?'

'What, darling?'

'Are you all right? Have they hurt you?'

'I can't hear, Lewis . . .'

'Did anyone hurt you?'

'Hurt me?'

'Yes.'

'Oh no. They don't hurt me. They just exasperate me. They think they're big-time villains. They've read some crime novels, I expect. Alexis thinks they're going to get away with this, but he's wrong.'

I was about to ask who Alexis was, when I heard shouting. It came from underneath us and I heard a door open, so I left the wall and climbed as quickly as I could on to the table and then on to the chair and moved the loose slate back into position, so that the little block of light went from the room. Then I replaced the table and chair by the wall, where they'd been. The moment I did this, I realised I hadn't had time to measure the distance from my bed to the slate. I'd just have to work patiently in the dark till I located it again.

I returned to my mattress and lay with my head close to the wall. I could still hear the men's voices. Sometimes they spoke in French and sometimes in Russian. They sounded now as if they were arguing and cursing. I imagined Valentina lying very still on her mattress and listening to them too. I thought, her body is probably no further than half a metre away from mine.

How I imagined Valentina was exactly as I'd last seen her, looking smart, wearing her black-and-white dress and her 'Ypres' scarf, and smelling of her *Giorgio* perfume, going into the revolving door of the Hôtel de Venise. But three weeks had passed. They might have taken away her expensive clothes. They might have given her some old, horrible dressing gown to wear. They would have pulled off her rings and her bracelet and sold them. Nobody would have thought about letting her wash her hair . . .

The voices quietened down and then a door banged and there was silence. Then I heard Valentina knock on my wall again and I gave an answering knock. In the pitch dark, her voice, when it next came, sounded nearer than before.

'Lewis,' she said. 'What's happening outside? Where's Alice?'

'In the apartment. Alice is safe and your mother is safe and Sergei is safe.'

'Thank God. Pauvre Maman . . . What about the money?'

'Money?'

'Yes. What's happening about the money?'

'What money?'

'The ten million francs. Are they going to pay it?'

'Who?'

'Can you hear me, darling?'

'Hardly . . .'

'Money, Lewis. Ransom money. Can you hear? Are Bianquis going to pay it?'

I lay very still. I was about to say that no ransom demand had come, but then I suddenly realised that perhaps it had. It *had* and no one had told me! I'd thought I was way ahead of Carmody and Alice in my detective work, but all the time Alice was going to her meetings with the editor from Bianquis and what they were discussing was a ransom demand I knew nothing about. I thought, that's why Alice wanted to tell me about her and Didier: she was getting too full up with lies and she had to make room for others.

'I don't know . . .' I said.

'Speak louder, darling. I can't hear.'

I thought, I mustn't invent anything. I must stay close to what I know, as far as I can. I said: 'Alice had some meetings with Dominique Monod. That's all I know. And the police have been told . . .'

'The police?'

'Yes.'

There was a moment's silence, then Valentina said: 'I warned Alexis . . .'

'What?'

'I told him that the police would be involved by now. He's such a baby. He doesn't know how the world works.'

When the kidnappers came into my room again, they were wearing masks. They were the kind of cheap plastic masks you could buy in toy-shops anywhere and the ones these kidnappers had chosen were monkey faces. It made them look really stupid. If I'd been a kidnapper, I would have chosen something evil like a skull.

They didn't blindfold me or handcuff my wrists, because they knew they couldn't be recognised through these monkey masks.

One of them gave me a tray. On the tray was a slice of baguette and a tin mug of coffee. The other one crouched there with the light, watching me. Then he suddenly laughed. It was a high, tittering laugh, like you could imagine a real monkey might have. 'Le grand Meaulnes!' he giggled. 'English translator!'

I said nothing. I wanted to ask him to bring my blanket back, but I didn't. I thought if I said anything or asked for anything, he might jump forward and snatch the bread and coffee away.

They went out and I heard them go next door, into the

room where Valentina was. I put my ear to the wall and listened. The moment the men entered Valentina's cell I heard a furious burst of Russian coming from her lips.

It was the guy with the tittering laugh who answered her. His voice was high like the laugh and he yelled at her, also in Russian, and both of them were just yelling and not listening to the other. Then Valentina screamed and I heard something fall on to the floor of her room. I wanted to call out to her, but I put my hand in front of my mouth. She was really yelling now, repeating a phrase that sounded like '*yob tvoyu mat! yob tvoyu mat!*' and the man was laughing, just as he'd laughed at me. Then I heard Valentina's door being slammed and locked and the men went away.

I knocked on the wall. 'Valentina . . .' I said.

'Son of a bitch!' she said. 'How could he have done this?'

'Done what?'

'To capture you . . . how could they do such a stupid, terrible thing? I told Alexis he was slime . . .'

'What was the noise? Did something fall?'

'He threw the hot coffee over me.'

'He threw the coffee?'

'Yes. Exactly like a child, you see? I curse him. I curse the day I met him!'

I waited for a moment, then I asked: 'Who's Alexis?'

'Alexis?'

'Yes.'

There was a long silence. I reached out in the dark for my own coffee, not just to drink it, but to see how hot it was, to see how much I would have burned . . .

'Alexis was my husband,' said Valentina.

I remembered it all then: the young man in the photo album, the man with the wastepaper basket on his head, the man lying with his arms outstretched in the snow. I heard Mrs Gavrilovich say: 'He was crazy, Louis. Just crazy.'

I ate the bread and drank the coffee. I thought, I shouldn't be eating and drinking when Valentina has been burned by the scalding coffee, but I can't help myself.

After that, I needed to pee, so I crept over to my bucket toilet and took off the lid. Inside the bucket were some sheets of newspaper, torn up. They were to wipe my bum with, like people in England had to do during the war. Grandma Gwyneth once said to me: 'The secret was to scrunch the paper up, Lewis. You scrunched it up several times and this made it almost soft.'

I put the paper in a pile under the table. I thought, I must know exactly where everything is located, so that I can get to it in the dark.

In my whole life, I'd never peed into a bucket. In hospital, they made you piss into a sort of papier-mâché jar. But I knew that in certain prisons in Britain that was what the men still had to do – use a bucket as a toilet in their cells – like this was meant to be part of their punishment. But a prison inmate said in a newspaper interview I'd read that the thing he hated most, worse than the shit pails, was the boredom of every single day.

And it occurred to me now, now that we'd been given our breakfast, that I'd been expecting something to happen today, like I was anticipating that Valentina and I would be put into a car and taken somewhere, out in the air. But *nothing was going to happen*. That was the reality of our situation. Absolutely nil zero was going to happen. We'd just be left here, in these cold, dark rooms, for hour upon hour and day after day. There would be no variation whatsoever. We were hostages. We were in medieval time.

I thought one of the men would come and collect my breakfast tray, but he didn't. After about an hour had passed, I moved the table and chair to where I thought the loose slate was and began to feel around to find it. It wasn't so cold in the room any more and I thought, what may come through when I move the slate is sunlight.

Valentina had been silent for a while. I'd knocked gently on the wall, but no answering knock had come from her side. I wondered if she was asleep or whether she was lying there thinking, and, if so, what she was thinking about. In all the time that she'd been here with nothing to do, she might have been finishing her novel in her mind.

I tried to work out how much ten million francs was. I calculated it at about £1,200,000. And then I wondered: will Alexis ask for money for *my* life? Will Hugh and Alice have to sell the house in Devon and the car and everything they own? Suppose he asks them for a million pounds? What happens if a ransom just can't be paid?

It took me quite a long time to locate the loose slate. Before moving it, I stayed still, listening, in case the monkeys were coming back, but there was no sound of them. I didn't know whether they stayed in this place all the time, or whether, in the daytime, they just left us locked up and went back to their apartments and got on with normal life. I tried to remember what else Mrs Gavrilovich had told me about Alexis. I wondered what had happened to the wastepaper basket he'd once put on his head and whereabouts the snow had been falling when he lay in it.

When I moved the slate, just as I thought, a shaft of sunlight came in and seemed to light up my whole room. I felt so pleased and delighted, it was like the sunlight was a fucking crock of gold. I put my face up into the light and felt the warmth of it. I thought, I must never, never, let the kidnappers discover this.

Listening all the time for the return of the monkeys, I got Elroy's string and, fixing one of his arms to a tear in the edging of the mattress, ran the string out along the floor and knotted it where the light fell. I knew reflected sunlight can move; it can go in a kind of spooky arc around the walls, but at this time in the morning it would always be more or less exactly here.

Now that I could see the room better, I realised that it was incredibly dirty. The walls were rough-plastered and had once been whitewashed, but now the paint was flaky and there were stains and cracks and dirt everywhere. Some of this dirt was suspicious kind of dirt: it was dark brown. I wondered if the room where Valentina was being held was as dirty as this and whether she could see it.

I got down from my chair and began casing the room again, searching every inch of it, like people search every inch of ground in a murder hunt. Under the hay, I found some mouse droppings and the idea that there was a mouse in here with me was bad. And I didn't want there to be spiders, either. I found one, quite small, and killed it with my tin mug. I don't know what it had been living on. You never know with them; it's like they can live on dust.

I could hear a bird on the roof. I thought, if I get crazy with loneliness, I could talk to birds with my sifflet du chasseur. And it was thinking about this that made me realise that, if I could disturb a second slate, it might be possible to make a hole in the roof large enough to stick my head through. Then I'd not only be able to look at the sky, but also try to fathom out where this place was and whether we were still in Paris or out in the *banlieue*, or way off in the country somewhere, with fields and poplar trees round us, like on that woman's farm in the Auvergne.

So this is what I tried to do next, work on the slates adjacent to the loose one, trying to feel where each pin went in and loosen the slate around the pin. I worked from above and below. Anyone flying over this house could have seen my hand sticking out through the hole. But I couldn't get any other slate to move. I needed some kind of levering instrument, to prise the pins out from the batons.

I gave up for the time being and returned to my inch-by-inch reconnaissance. When I arrived at the sawn-off pipe, it suddenly had a new significance: where it turned and went into the wall, it had to arrive on the other side – in Valentina's room.

I knocked on the wall and she answered. 'Lewis,' she said, 'I promise you, you will get out of here, darling. I shall make Alexis release you.'

I didn't know whether she could 'make' Alexis do things or not. I thought, people in captivity probably only have one kind of power over their captors and that's a sort of moral power. Even in their darkest hours, when they're being beaten or tortured, they still have it. But it's invisible, it's just in people's minds.

'Listen,' I said. 'Can you hear this?'

I got my tin mug and began drumming on my end of the pipe. The song I was privately drumming was *Le Temps des cerises*.

'Yes,' said Valentina.

'Does this pipe come into your room?'

'Does it come into the room?'

'Yes.'

'Yes. It comes into the room.'

'Where does it go? Does it go to a tank?'

'It doesn't go anywhere.'

'What? Speak louder, Valentina.'

'The pipe doesn't go anywhere. It just sticks out of the wall and stops.'

'It stops?'

'Yes.'

'Is the end open?'

'No. It's been capped.'

We both heard it then, the sound of someone returning. Underneath us, there were some noisy stairs that sounded as if they were made of wood.

I scuttled over to the table and chair and moved the slate, shutting off the sunlight. Replacing the table by the wall always made a noise, as it scraped on the tile floor. I put the chair back and began winding in Elroy's string. As I was doing this, my door was unlocked.

The light shone in, as usual. There were two kidnappers and their masks were on. I was hauled to my feet and I felt the handcuffs going on. Then I was tugged several feet and slammed against the back wall. I thought, I hope they're not as rough as this with Valentina.

'Stand up!' said the monkey who smelled of cigarettes. 'Stand up, English boy!'

I saw him move away from me, just a couple of paces. I thought, now's the moment when something really bad is going to happen. I held on to the wall.

'Stand up!' one of them shouted again. I wanted to say that I *was* standing up. Were they blind, or what? But I kept quiet.

They began photographing me. I heard the click and buzz of a Polaroid camera. When I was little, Hugh went through a passion for Polaroid photography. There I am in my Baby Bouncer, dangling from a doorway; there I am on the lawn, on a plastic tricycle; there I am in my playpen, staring through the bars . . .

They took three pictures. Hugh told me that the reason he gave up Polaroid photography was because the film is too expensive. All the pictures he took faded in time to pale green.

I thought the kidnappers were going to go away without taking off the handcuffs, but they seemed to remember them at the last minute. They were really rough with me, pushing me around. As they were going out, I said: 'Je voudrais de l'eau, s'il vous plaît.'

'Yes,' said one of them, 'water. OK.'

And then I imagined one of their photographs of me arriving in Alice's post and her staring at it and knowing, finally, that things couldn't go on and that now she'd have to send for Hugh.

All morning, I could hear the monkeys hanging around in the house, quite near us, talking. I knew that if I put the chair in the right position, I'd be able to read by the tiny gap of light, but I made a rule for myself: I'd only open the hole in the roof when I was pretty sure they were downstairs or out of the place altogether.

I sat on my mattress, thinking. No one had taken away my breakfast tray or emptied my bucket and the water I'd asked for never came. I'd never been in a situation in my life before where I longed so badly for something as simple as water. I thought, millions of people could be dying of thirst at this moment, in countries like Violette's that I never even used to know the name of. I'd *known* about these millions out there somewhere. But, before, I'd never been one of them. At home, day or night, I could go into the kitchen and open the fridge and take out more or less whatever I wanted. Hugh and Alice always made sure there was a supply of Coke in there, just for me.

I remembered Hugh reading me a fairy tale when I was about seven, about a guy who's thrown out of his land for stealing some king's daughter. The story didn't say how he'd stolen her, only that he had, like you might steal a cabbage or a pumpkin from someone's field. But the punishment is she turns into a stone.

And then a wise fisherman or someone comes to the man, who's about to be driven out into a desert with no possessions at all, and says to him: 'Pick up the stone and take it with you and the stone will become whatever you want it to become.' I couldn't remember all the things the stone became. It never became the princess again, or a night-club hostess. This story was written long ago, when writers and readers had innocent minds. But the bit I remembered now was where the guy had put the stone into his mouth and it had become water.

There were thousands of questions I wanted to ask Valentina and I tried to list these in my mind, to make me forget about my thirst. After the water, the thing I longed for most was to *see* Valentina. I knew she'd probably look quite bad and that she wouldn't smell like she used to smell, of perfume or wall-flowers, but that wouldn't stop me feeling the way I did about her. I'd still want to touch her and lie down with my head on her breasts.

When I'd listed most of my questions and time was still

going so slowly and the monkeys were still talking down below us somewhere, I imagined the moment when Valentina and I, instead of being separated by a wall, would have to share this cell and share our every waking and sleeping moment and spend our nights together on my mattress.

I went to sleep and had a dream about Hugh. He was lurking there, on the edge of some dark place, biding his time.

What woke me was Valentina knocking on the wall. I might have been asleep for five minutes or five hours, I couldn't tell. I listened. The house was quiet.

'Lewis,' said Valentina, 'how are you, darling?'

'OK,' I said. 'I was dreaming.'

'You know you must walk?'

'What?'

'You mustn't just lie down, Lewis, or you will get very weak. You must walk round and round your room, to exercise.'

I didn't feel like exercising. I felt like lying completely still until someone brought me two litre-bottles of Orangina.

'I'm thirsty,' I said.

'They didn't give you water?'

'No.'

'I will tell Alexis. They must bring it to you. Now we are going to walk. Where shall we walk to?'

'In our minds?'

'Yes. Shall we walk to Switzerland?'

'OK.'

She said I had to walk round my room twenty times, then knock on the wall, and she would do the same. Then we'd do another twenty and so on. She told me to imagine all the things I was going to see on my walk: cows with bells round their necks, *edelweiss* flowers, groves of larch, people chopping wood for the winter, the high mountains covered with snow. 'Off you go,' she said.

I preferred to walk in daylight, so I moved the chair and table first and found the slate and let the sun in. The sun had moved and was hotter. It fell on to the floor in a slightly different place.

Then I began my journey round Switzerland. I tried to imagine grass under my feet and the smell of the high pastures. The sky was blue, but there were quite a few clouds floating on by. I was walking along one side of a valley. At the end of my journey, there was going to be a freezing spring running down through a gully of stones.

Some time in the course of the day, the monkeys brought me a meal and a bottle of water. Before I could eat anything, I had to drink almost all the water.

The meal had been cooked by someone: it was a sort of stew with bits of meat and vegetables in it. I wondered which of the men had cooked it or whether one of them had a wife, who had stood at a stove wearing a flowered overall like Violette's, cooking this stuff to keep us alive. I thought that being married to any one of these monkeys might be terrible. Because I knew what they were now and who, and what I learned was really seriously frightening.

I'd said to Valentina: 'Why are they doing this? Are they pill-heads or something?'

'They're all on heroin, darling,' she said in a matter-of-fact way. 'I know two of the others, Todorsky and Shukov; they're users and dealers. They were in prison for a while and now they're out. That's why they need a big amount of money. A heroin habit is very expensive.'

'How do you know them?' I asked.

Valentina let a long silence go by before she replied. Then she said: 'I used them once.'

'You were on heroin?'

'No. Never. I just did a bit of cocaine and so on, you know. It was at a very unhappy time.'

'Unhappy time?'

'Yes. When I had that American translator living with me.'

'The one you killed?'

'I didn't really kill her, darling. I just assisted her.'

'Assisted her how? What to do?'

'I knew these people – Alexis and his friend Leo Todorsky. I paid them and I said, "You give her what she wants, as much as she wants . . ." '

'Of heroin?'

'Yes. Of course. Why help someone to live, if they are killing you?'

'Killing you?'

'Yes. Why help them if they are just ruining your life? Better to let them go.'

'How was she "ruining your life"?'

'Oh, you know, the way a person can.'

'What?'

'I was her plaything. She despised me. She knew my background, my poor education. She tried to alter things in my books, without my knowing. She kept forgetting the one thing I was good at was languages. She once smuggled a lover up to that junk room in the attic. She made me suffer – too much, you know . . .'

'I thought she went back to the States.'

'She did.'

'So she didn't really die?'

'She did die. She died a month after she left me.'

I was silent. Now I knew about the end of Gail O'Hara's life. I wondered what still remained on the files I'd never found. I couldn't remember now what Lisette-Marie had told Violette about the two women screaming. Had it been Gail who had done all the screaming, or Valentina, or both of them? I just couldn't bring Violette's words back into my mind.

My next thought was, well, it doesn't matter now. I can forget all that now. But I immediately understood that I shouldn't forget it. I shouldn't forget it because the fact that Valentina *knew* her kidnappers, not just Alexis, and they knew that she knew them and could just give them up to the police the minute they released her was the most sinister realisation of the whole business. It was *prime*! With me, they used their stupid monkey masks because they wanted to conceal from me who they were, so that I'd never recognise them. This meant that when they'd got their ransom money, they could let me go. But how could they ever dare to let Valentina go? They couldn't! It was absolutely naïve and stupid to think that they would. Even if they stopped operating in Paris and went back to Russia, or something, she could still guide the police straight to them and the whole kidnap would have been in vain. So they weren't planning on letting her go. That was the truth of it. The moment they got their money, they would kill her.

I lay in the dark, holding on to the plastic bottle they'd given me, taking small sips from the water that remained in it. I was waiting for the men to go further away, so that I could talk to Valentina, but all the while a voice in my head said: 'You have to save her. There's only you who can do it. You have to think of a way.'

I talked to her through the night. I knew it was night because the slit in my roof gradually faded and got dark.

We'd walked about five miles across Switzerland and Valentina said she was tired and that her broken arm still hurt from time to time and this was one of those times. She told me that on her walk she'd seen an avalanche, way up above her on the snow line.

When I asked her whether she thought Alexis and his friends would kill her when they'd collected their money, she said in a sort of laughing voice: 'No, darling. That isn't part of the plan.'

I asked her why, but all she kept saying was she just didn't think Alexis would let her be killed. Only after a long time had gone by and I'd watched the moon come sliding up into the tiny gap above me did she say: 'You know the reason they will definitely release me, Lewis?'

'Tell me.'

'Because Alexis is a poet.'

She was talking very quietly and I could hardly hear her. I kept having to say 'What?' She told me Alexis was the first poet she'd ever met and this was why she'd fallen in love with him and agreed to marry him. She wanted to live in what she called 'the world of the poet'; she thought life would be different there. It was through Alexis that she'd first got the idea of becoming a writer herself.

I said: 'Just because he's a poet doesn't mean he couldn't kill you or let you be killed.'

'Yes, it does,' she said. 'You don't know Alexis. How could he write about anything after that? And his poetry is the only thing left in his life – the only thing.'

As we talked, the moon crept away from the gap in the slates and the room started to go dark again. I thought, the moon often travels across the sky faster than you think; it's never in medieval time, but always hurrying along in the here-and-now of absolute night.

Alexis had brought me a blanket. I knew it was him because he referred to me again as 'le grand Meaulnes' and laughed his high-pitched laugh. I was tempted to tell him that I wasn't Augustin Meaulnes, I was François Seurel, listening for voices on his attic stairs, with his schoolteacher father and the mother he called by her first name. But I didn't want to antagonise Alexis. I didn't want him to snatch the blanket away. He was wearing his monkey mask when he came in with the blanket, but I could see his silhouette in the bright light. He looked very thin and his hair was long, right to his shoulders. And he breathed differently from the others, like there was something in his lungs or something eddying on the air that kept making him gasp.

When he'd gone, I said to Valentina: 'Tell me more about Alexis. What kind of poetry does he write?'

'What kind of poetry? Well, you know, it's quite good. Or it used to be. Depressing, but not bad, you know?'

'Can you remember any?'

'Remember any?'

'Yes.'

'No. When something is so depressing, it doesn't stay in my mind.'

'Not even one?'

'There was one he wrote about my father. The title was *Ugolny Sklad.* That means "coal bunker" or "coal store". He said in the poem that my father's heart was becoming hard and black and brittle, like the coal, because the burden of the coal was too great, too great . . . and that poem was right . . .'

The blanket Alexis had given me was less prickly than the one I'd vomited over. It was sort of softened by wear. I pulled it round me, right up to my face, and I remembered Valentina saying, on that first evening in the Place des Ternes, that she never wanted to be cold or hungry ever again, nor have to live in a horrible little room smelling of coal. I lay in silence for a few minutes. I thought, she said this because she had a premonition that this was where she was going to die, but now she's refusing to believe in the seriousness of what's happening.

After a while, I said: 'Why does Alexis have that strange laugh?'

'What, darling? Speak louder.'

'Why does he have that peculiar laugh? Does he put it on?'

'I don't know. It's got more strange as time has gone by. I think it's not a laugh any more, but a cry.'

'A cry?'

'Yes. Like an animal cry – a rabbit or a rat or something.'

'What's he crying about?'

'His life. What else?'

After the breakfast of coffee and bread, I had to have my first shit into the bucket. I didn't dare sit on the bucket, in case it fell over. I thought, if you know you're going to have to live with your shit, right next to it, in the very room where you are, you try your best to keep it inside you.

The bits of paper I scrunched up were from a newspaper

called *France Dimanche*. It was like a tabloid newspaper at home, full of photographs of celebrities. I wiped my bum with about ten famous people.

I was glad there was a lid to the bucket. I couldn't remember whether the shit buckets in British prisons had lids or not. But even with the lid I didn't like it being there, so when the monkeys next came in I asked them to empty it.

It was the cigarette monkey who laughed this time. He said in French that nobody would empty my bucket for me; I had to do it myself.

'Where?' I said.

'Vasily will show you later on.'

Valentina had told me that the cigarette monkey was called Shukov. As well as burning his brain out with heroin, he smoked about sixty fags a day. He'd once owned a small press, called *Editions d'hiver*, that he ran from a room above a glove factory in Charenton-le-Pont. When the press had folded, he'd joined Leo Todorsky to make money from drug dealing. She said: 'It's a natural occupation for Russians, Lewis. It's the first thing they turn to when other things fail. More than fifty per cent of the hard drugs that come into France from the Far East come through Russia now. And Russians have always been very, very adept in any black market, as I expect you know.'

I asked if the fourth monkey's name was Vasily. I knew by now there were four and I'd worked out that if they got their money and split it four ways, they'd get about £300,000 each.

She told me that the fourth monkey was younger than the others, like he could almost have been one of their sons. They bullied him and babied him, first one, then the other. They called him Vasya, but this was short for Vasily. He was quiet and small. When the others argued and shouted, he seldom joined in. Valentina said: 'He has a sweet face.'

It was this Vasya who took me to empty my shit pail. I could tell it was him from the way he handled me, more gently than the others. He tied my blindfold on and then put the bucket into one of my hands and took the other arm and guided me out of the room.

I could see light seeping through the blindfold as we went along a corridor, past Valentina's cell, then we went down one step on to a different level and into a smelly toilet. Vasya moved me forward. 'Go on,' he said in French: 'empty your pail.'

He was holding me all the time, so I had to do this with one hand, and I thought, I could drop the fucking bucket and everything will spill over our feet. So I did it as carefully as I could. I tried not to breathe as I took the lid off. I wondered if all the scrunched-up celebrities would block the drains.

After Vasya had pulled the chain, he took the bucket from me and rinsed it out in the toilet bowl. I didn't know whether Alexis or the others would have bothered to do this. While he was rinsing, I lifted my head and felt a breeze on my face, coming from my left, so I knew there had to be a window in this toilet. I wanted to put out a hand, to feel how large the window was, but I didn't dare. I said in French to Vasya: 'Does Valentina have a bucket in her room, or do you let her use the toilet?'

'She uses the toilet,' he said, 'except in the night, when she must use her bucket.'

I wanted to go on with more questions. I wanted to say to Vasya, 'Do you let her wash and take care of herself? What's happened to her hair, to her smart dress, to her white shoes . . . ?' But I could hear Alexis and Todorsky very near us, so I just took my bucket in silence and let Vasya march me back to my room.

It was a long time before I could move my slate. When I did, the sun came in, high and dazzling. Valentina said we ought to walk through Switzerland again, but I explained to her that we had to do some manual work. I told her to move her mattress near to her bit of the iron pipe and then we would take it in turns to try to loosen it, from both sides of the wall. And she was really pleased with this idea. She saw that if we could remove the piece of pipe, we would have a secret spyhole through which we could talk. Whenever the monkeys came back, we could replace the pipe and they'd never know what we'd done.

My bit of the pipe had a right-angle in it, so I tried lifting the long end and turning it, like you turn a wheelbrace when you're getting a wheel off a car, but it wouldn't move. On her side, Valentina got a long rusty nail she'd found on her first day, and with it she tried to gouge away the plaster round the pipe-end, to loosen it in the wall.

The wall had a surprising grip on it. It was like the whole structure of that wall had settled down around this useless, forgotten piece of iron. I said to Valentina: 'This is like trying to extract the sword Excalibur from the stone!'

We gave up for a while when the monkeys – Vasya and Todorsky on their own – returned with our food. What we had today was just potatoes and onions in a kind of thin brown gravy and I thought of Grisha looking at the restaurant menu in the Place de l'Alma and seeing twenty-five different delicacies, including quail, and Valentina saying the restaurant was no good. Now, like me, she ate every bit of this disgusting onion and lumpy mash and then waited silently in the dark, as if a second helping was going to appear. Of course, nothing else came; no one in this kidnapping group had got the idea of *pudding*.

It was late in the day, getting bluish and dark through my sky hole, when we were able to go back to our work on the pipe. I searched my cell for a nail or something to gouge with, but I couldn't find anything. I wondered what the monkeys had done with my Sabatier knife. And I felt, when I remembered this, a kind of disappointment at the loss of my Concorde notebook – not about the thing itself, but about all my unfinished theories that would never be brought to any conclusion, but just stay floating out there, like forgotten bits of arithmetic, lost in space and time.

I told Valentina about this. I said I'd been writing everything down for weeks and now it was all wasted. I heard her sigh and she said: 'I feel for you, darling. Since I've been in here, I've come to believe my book will never be finished.'

I held on tightly to the pipe. I thought, now she's going to tell me that she's been stealing all that stuff from Grisha's book.

'Why?' I said innocently. 'Why wouldn't it be finished?'

'I don't know. Perhaps it's no longer the book I want to write.'

'Haven't Bianquis paid you a lot of money for it?'

'Sure. But I could give the money back. I could just tell them I want to write something else.'

'What would it be?'

'What?'

'The other book you'd write now. What would it be about?'

'I don't know. It hasn't come to me yet.'

There was silence then. I thought, she *will* tell me, she *will* confide in me, but the right time hasn't come yet.

'Perhaps,' I said tentatively, 'your other book would be about Anton?'

'Anton? My father?'

'Yes.'

'Maybe. Yes. Perhaps it would.'

After about another half-hour's work on the pipe, we felt it move. Valentina said that, on her side of it, there was quite a heap of plaster dust, where she'd been patiently gouging out the wall with her rusty nail, but she knew if she just scattered this dust around it wouldn't be noticed. She said that her cell hadn't been cleaned once since she'd been put in it, and because there was no air it was starting to smell.

Then she sighed. 'Why did this happen, Lewis?' she said. 'I keep saying to Alexis, "What got into your head?" To kidnap me is just a crazy joke, a revenge that is so typically Russian, it makes me laugh. But to take you: this is not a laughing matter.'

I told her not to think about this now. Once we'd got the pipe out of the wall, it would be miles easier to hear each other and have proper conversations; therefore we had to concentrate all our energy on this. Valentina said: 'I'm trying, darling, but I'm not a plumber, you know.'

But slowly, slowly, now, the long end of the pipe was beginning to turn. When the long end was at the vertical position, I could have kicked it down if I'd had any shoes, but the kidnappers hadn't returned these. I wondered whether one of them had a son, or a nephew or something, with size six feet.

I was working in total darkness now. I knew the grating noise of the pipe as it turned in the wall could be heard in the quiet of the house, and I just had to hope that Alexis and his friends were sleeping or stoned or not there at all. I'd begun to believe, from the noises of boats that I sometimes heard when my skylight was open, that we were near a river or a canal. I could imagine the monkeys renting a houseboat there, or a converted barge like you saw on the Seine, and coming and going secretly from that.

Now that the pipe was loose in the wall, it was up to me to pull it through. Valentina couldn't do much more from her side, so I told her to lie down and rest. As I pulled and strained, I thought how ironic it was that this important feat of strength had to be achieved by the puniest bits of my whole being – my arms.

And then I felt the pipe come free. It was like a tooth that's finally given up its struggle to stay attached to the gum and the bone. I simply drew it out and it didn't resist any more, but just came out, and I held it in my hands.

I knocked on the wall. 'It's out!' I said. 'It's out!'

'OK,' said Valentina. 'Lie down, darling, and put your mouth close to the hole and I'll do the same and just whisper something to me and I'll see if I can hear you.'

So I laid the pipe aside and settled myself by the hole with my head resting on my left arm. I could feel something warm coming through to me from the other side of the wall and I knew it was Valentina's breath. The thing that I wanted to whisper to her was a confession of my mad, unstoppable love.

We could hear each other perfectly now, just as if we were lying face to face on a bed and whispering in the dark, like lovers do in movies. Except that in the movies there always had to be some kind of light coming from somewhere, moonlight or street neon or a motel sign blinking on and off, or else the screen would be completely blank.

I said: 'Alexis only took me because I was getting close to what had happened. I think his first idea may have been just to threaten me.'

'Threaten you how?'

I described how the face had come to my attic window. I said I still couldn't tell which one of the kidnappers it was, because it had been hidden by this horrible cloth, but I knew that if I hadn't run out to Moinel's apartment this person would have come into the flat and threatened me or even killed me.

'But why, *why*?' said Valentina.

'Because Moinel and I worked out how you'd been taken – from the hospital, right?'

'Yes. It was clever what they did – so easy. But how did you work it out, darling?'

'Just by following every lead, and that was one of them. Moinel knows some of the doctors there and so he could get authorisation to look at the register. And then I went back on my own, because I realised the receptionist we'd talked to was Russian . . .'

'She was the one. No one will tell me her name. But I've come to think the whole idea may have started with her, that she's connected to Alexis in some way. And, suddenly, he thought it would be easy to get rich by taking me . . .'

'So she was at Reception when you checked in?'

'Yes. I checked in with her and then I sat down in the waiting area. Then she went away. I was early for my appointment. One of the other receptionists came by, but she was just on her way to somewhere. She didn't stay, but she said hello to me.'

'And she admired your dress?'

'Yes, I think she did. How did you know?'

'That's what she told your mother on the telephone. Did she look at the register?'

'Oh no. She'd just come to collect something from the desk. Then she left and the Russian girl came back. She told me Dr Bouchain was doing his consultations in a different room today. She asked me to follow her and so I followed her. We walked a long way down some corridors and then she opened a door and said this was the room. But it wasn't the room. It was some kind of a store, and there was a man in there, wearing a white hospital coat. I remember thinking, this guy looks very like poor Alexis . . .'

'And then . . . ?'

'The Russian girl gave me an injection, in my arm. I was still awake after it, but very sleepy. I remember they put me in a wheelchair and then wheeled me out back into the corridor. I wanted to ask where Bouchain was, but I couldn't speak. That's all I can recall, darling. I suppose they put me in a car or a van or whatever it is they've got. When I woke up, I was here, in the dark.'

We were silent for a bit. Neither of us moved and I supposed Valentina could feel my breath coming through the hole, just as I could feel hers. It was odd to think of our two invisible breaths meeting in the space where the pipe had been, but just passing each other and travelling on.

After a while, I got up from the floor. I'd suddenly decided that now was the moment when I was going to give Valentina her present – the thing she'd never before held in her hands. I told her I was fetching something for her and then I'd try to pass it through the hole into her room. She said: 'What is it going to be, Lewis?' And I said: 'Wait.'

I fetched Elroy from his position on the mattress. I untied his string, so that I could still mark out my floor measurement to the skylight, then I lay down again and said to Valentina: 'Reach into the pipe hole as far as you can. Something's going to come through to you.'

I put him into the hole head first and helped him along the

little tunnel by pushing his feet. As I felt him arrive on the other side and get pulled out by Valentina, I thought, I was right when I used to long to be as tiny as him.

At first, she didn't say anything. I guess she was trying to figure out what on earth Elroy was. Then, gradually she would feel that he was a kind of doll with a face and limbs and everything and even start wondering whether he'd come from the Palais Royal toy-shop. I waited, with my face very near to the hole. Only after a long time went by did Valentina say: 'What's his name?'

'Elroy,' I said. 'He's a Royal Marine.'

What I remember most about the days that followed were all the hours I spent listening to Valentina's voice telling me about the past. It was like her whole life was being gathered in and brought back from all the far corners of the cold earth where it had once been and distilled in the darkness of her cell and poured into my ear through the funnel in the wall. It was like I was learning in a short space of time more than I'd been taught in nearly fourteen years of existence.

'You know, Lewis,' she kept saying, 'I think this is boring for you, hearing about all these things which are past and gone. Why don't we talk about the future?'

I said I didn't want to talk about that. I knew there might be no future. Valentina must have known this, too, deep inside her somewhere, but she'd just decided not to admit it.

She told me the person in her family she most resembled was her grandmother, Zoya, Anton's mother. She said: 'Zoya was fat and greedy, like me. Her idea of paradise would have been to own a pâtisserie shop. But paradise never came.'

Zoya lived in Leningrad, where Anton was born. She lived there all her life, including right through the siege of the city which began in 1941 and lasted nine hundred days. During all this time, there were no trains and no trams and no light.

Food was so scarce, people ate up all the dogs and cats and rats and all the sparrows and starlings of the city. They made soup from book bindings and glue. When someone died, as 900,000 people did die, bits of their bodies were often eaten in secret, in the lightless rooms. Buttocks were considered a delicacy. Zoya and her neighbours kept themselves alive for two weeks in the winter of 1942 by making a stew out of four crows. Into this stew they put morsels of a road-mender, who had died on the stairs.

I asked Valentina whether, if we were starving and I died, she'd slice off slivers of my bum and make a casserole with them, and she said: 'Darling, I can say no, never, I would never, never, do that, I would rather die. But the truth is you do not *know* what you are capable of doing, until that moment – of starvation or self-protection or whatever it is – arrives. People say they know, but they do not. If you had told Zoya, when she was young, that one day she would eat pieces of a road-mender's body, she would have said that was impossible. But when the moment came, this is what she did.'

I said that if I was starving and Valentina was dead, I would definitely eat her. I asked her if breasts were a delicacy.

She said: 'Well, I don't know. Perhaps not. Perhaps there is too much fat in them, what do you think?'

I said I thought they might taste of cream. Then I added: 'The only thing I'd like to have to go with you, Valentina, would be a bit of sugar.'

She told me about the ship frozen in the Neva river at the time of Zoya's cannibalism. All through the siege, this ship kept going with a radio broadcast, run from the ship's generator. It called itself Radio Leningrad. It tried to bring people news about the war and news about where food was to be found and when the siege would end. Valentina said: 'Zoya told my father that these broadcasts were the things that people most looked forward to every single day. A voice that talks to you, even if you can't see it, like we can't see each other now, can give you hope, even if there really and truly is no hope at all. And do you know what those broadcasters used to transmit between the programmes, Lewis? They found a metronome and put it by the mike and just let it tick, on and on. And Zoya said that when you switched on your radio and heard that metronome, you knew that the ship was still there in the river and that the city was still alive.'

I wanted to write this down, about the metronome, in case I ever forgot it. I thought, there must be hundreds of thousands of piano teachers all round the world, setting up their fucking metronomes, who don't know what a heroic function it once performed. If people knew the history of the world better than they do, they might have different attitudes towards all kinds of things, including cannibalism. But I couldn't write anything down because Alexis had stolen my Concorde notebook. I knew it was Alexis because he was the only one who understood a bit of English.

He first began to get agitated around this time. His agitation and the Siege of Leningrad were sort of linked in my mind, like Alexis was going mad and planning to kill us and cut us up to put in a stew.

Valentina told me he was getting restless because no response had come to his ransom demand. He'd demanded that Bianquis pay ten million francs, in cash, to be handed over at the refreshment kiosk in the Parc des Buttes Chaumont on a certain day. Now that certain day had passed and no one had come there. No money. Nothing. The request had just been totally ignored.

'So,' I said, 'what's Alexis going to do?'

'Well,' said Valentina calmly, 'he's threatening to kill me. But he knows he's not capable of killing me. That's why he shouts and screams. You see, he's never really got beyond adolescence. He dreams stupid dreams and deludes himself about what he can or cannot do. He's forgotten how well I know him.'

'Will Bianquis pay the money in the end?'

'Look, darling, ten million is a lot. Nobody parts with that kind of money if they don't have to. They will stall. They will hope Alexis will crack and let us go.'

'Why don't you pay it?' I said. 'Why don't you just tell

303

Alexis how to get into your safe and let him take all your jewellery?'

'You think I have ten million francs' worth of jewellery, Lewis?'

'I guess . . .'

'Well, I don't, darling. Nowhere near that. More like one million, if that.'

'You could give him a bit of money as well, couldn't you?'

Valentina sighed. 'I could,' she said, 'but why should I? I've earned every penny of this money. I've worked for it for fifteen years. Why should I let Alexis just help himself?'

'If you die, the money won't be any good to you.'

'I'm not going to die! If I thought there was a risk of it, I might tell Alexis to take the money and let me go. But I've told you: there's not the least probability that that will happen.'

I said moodily: 'I think Bianquis should just pay.'

'It's a lot of money. But I think something's happening out there. It may be to do with you, I don't know. They've asked Alexis for more time, for another week, while they try to put the money together. But he doesn't like this delay. He's got dreams of what he will do when he's rich. The delay is making him frightened.'

I said that when I was frightened I quite often played chess, sometimes just in my mind or sometimes with a real opponent or with a computer. And Valentina seized on this and said: 'Chess is a good idea, darling. It might calm Alexis down. Alexis was like you when I lived with him – only in that one respect, of course: he could reduce his anxiety by playing chess. And he often won. I don't know why, when his mind is so wild, but he did.'

We drifted off the subject of Alexis and on to the subject of Stalin, whom Valentina called 'another madman with a chess player's cunning mind'. She told me that Anton and Olga (Mrs Gavrilovich) had met in the queue to pay their last respects to Stalin's dead body. She said so many people were in that queue that seventeen of them were crushed to death during the days the coffin was open for public viewing.

I asked why, when Stalin had done such terrible things, Russians wanted to come and look at him. Valentina said: 'You can understand why, can't you? They needed to get proof. Proof that it was over. Proof that he was lying in the velvet coffin and that they were still alive.'

'How did Stalin die?' I asked.

'Well, you know, he had a terrible death. Very, very slow, like death was torturing him. He had a cerebral haemorrhage, but it didn't kill him straight away. It made him suffocate, agonisingly slowly, in his own blood. They say his features turned dark and his lips black. It took him four days to die. But of course when Maman and Papa saw him, the morticians had drained some of the blood and made him appear normal again, and, anyway, I think Maman and Papa hardly noticed how he looked. Papa used to say: "I made this pilgrimage from Leningrad to Moscow and I thought it was to say adieu to Stalin. But it wasn't. It was a pilgrimage to find your mother." Imagine. You're in a queue of a million people and you look round and you see your future wife standing right behind you.'

'Was Olga beautiful then?'

'Yes. She had beautiful eyes, especially. And hair very thick and dark. She worked in Moscow at that time, in a shoe factory. She always says the first thing she noticed about Anton was what a poor condition his shoes were in. She wondered if he'd walked all the way from Leningrad!'

I remembered the shoe coming down on my book then, on the steps in the theatre foyer, and how the mark left on Paul Berger's copy of *Le Grand Meaulnes* had bothered me. I said to Valentina: 'How did Alexis know about the Meaulnes business?'

I could hear Valentina move on the other side of the wall. Lying there, with your face near the talking funnel, could make your body get stiff and quite often we broke off and went for walks. Mostly, we walked round Switzerland. We became sort of fond of these Swiss walks, with their cow bells and their wood-choppers and their sunsets over the mountains. But sometimes we went to other places and walked there. One of these places was London.

'The difficulty I have with Alexis,' said Valentina, after she'd settled herself down in a new position, 'is remembering to treat him like a stranger. I was married to him for more than a year. I used to wash his hair. I'd listen to his poems in the middle of the night. And so I find, still, after all this time has gone by, that I tell him things without meaning to. I should have told him nothing about you, but it never, never, occurred to me that he would try to harm you. I just said that I had become . . . very fond of you, like you could be my own son, or something, the son Alexis wanted and I never had, and that I had given you a musical box and was helping you with your translation of *Le Grand Meaulnes*. I don't know why I told him these things, but I just did, and now I'm so sorry, Lewis, I'm so sorry . . .'

'Don't cry, Valentina,' I said. 'Tell me about the *café-charbon*. Who came there? What was it like working in the café?'

I heard Valentina blow her nose. I asked her if she was blowing it on a torn-up bit of *France Dimanche* and she said she was. Then she said: 'When I was a child, I used to love the *café-charbon*. We had an old cart then, with a pony. Imagine a pony on the streets of Paris! Nowadays, it would be killed by a BMW in about one week. But not then. And Anton would let me sit on the pony, sometimes, when he made his deliveries. And when you're a child, the only life you know is the one you've got, and so that's the life you love. It's the same for us all. Children try their best to love what they're given. But then later, when you can see beyond that life, you realise what poverty is, what drudgery is, what boredom is. I would look at my mother and father and think, how can they stand it? For all these years and years, this life of the *café-charbon*! How can they not see how pitiful it is? And I vowed, Lewis, I vowed to myself that I would find some other life. I didn't know what, but I vowed nevertheless.'

'And you did.'

'Yes. Thank goodness, I did. But maybe, you see, if I hadn't met Alexis—'

We had to stop this conversation there because we heard the monkeys coming back. I hoped they were bringing us a meal, even if it was a stew made from crows.

Food was on our minds quite a lot of the time. The only thing about the *café-charbon* Valentina seemed sad to have lost was the griddle pan on which she and Olga used to make *croque-monsieurs*. And on one of our walks round London, when I asked Valentina where she'd been she said she'd had tea at Brown's Hotel and dinner at the Caprice. When she told me where these places were, I pointed out to her that this wasn't a proper walk, but all she said was: 'I *walked* from Brown's to the Caprice, darling. This meant going down Albemarle Street, crossing Piccadilly and into Arlington Street. It was raining, but I didn't take a taxi.'

I didn't know London as well as she did. I just knew the bits of it I'd been taken to see, like the Houses of Parliament and Buckingham Palace, so mainly I just walked between these two places and back again, through St James's Park.

I didn't go down into the Tube and risk coming face to face with any untalented buskers. And, anyway, I couldn't remember which Tube lines ran where, except that the Northern line went up to Hampstead and Hugh had once taken me there when I was about ten and we'd flown our bird kite on a wooded hill. I kept this place in reserve, for when I'd run out of other walks. I knew it might be difficult to imagine myself there alone, without Hugh and the kite.

I remembered that the Houses of Parliament were by the river, so when I'd gone round them and into Westminster Abbey and looked at a few tombs and out again, I started walking along the Embankment, going east, where there were loads of new buildings alongside the water and the dome of St Paul's in the distance.

307

And it was weird, the minute I arrived there, how clearly I could see everything and smell the river and hear the engines of boats. All I was doing was going round and round my cell and sometimes tapping on Valentina's wall, but this imaginary London got such a grip on my mind, it was like I was a movie camera going along and getting everything into itself on film. The light seemed amazingly clear, so that there was a kind of shine on things, and as well as *seeing* these things I was also *composing* them into frames and going in and out of close-up shots and wide shots, and this felt like such a brilliant thing to be doing that my heart started to beat wildly.

So then I sat down for a moment, on the floor of my cell and on a conveniently placed municipal bench, looking out along the water. I tapped on the wall and said: 'Valentina, do you think being a film director might be a good career?'

'A film director, did you say?'

'Yes.'

'Is that what you want to be?'

'I don't know. I just suddenly thought it up.'

Valentina didn't say anything for a moment. Then she said: 'It's odd you should mention that. Do you know where I was on my London walk?'

'Where?'

'I was just going along Kensington High Street and I thought, I'll look in at the Odeon and see what movies they're showing this afternoon. Perhaps this is some kind of sign, darling, about your future life?'

The house was quiet, so we took the pipe out of the wall and lay down to rest, after pounding the hard pavements of London, and I asked Valentina how her 'future life' as a writer of medieval romances had come into her mind. And she told me again that she never would have thought up the idea of becoming a writer if she hadn't met Alexis.

'At the time of the café,' she told me, 'when I was eighteen, nineteen, that kind of time, Papa and Maman used to take me to some Russian evenings they had up at Montmartre.

'They were held in one of the old *guinguettes*. They used to clear away some tables and there would be dancing to the balalaika and that kind of thing. I think they were shabby places and the vodka they served was very poor quality, but I liked that Russian music very much and being with Russian people always made Anton and Olga happy. Strange, you see? They hated Russia in a way, but I think they were always homesick for the language.'

'Were you homesick for the language?'

'No. Remember I was three when they brought me here. I spoke Russian with them, but French at school and with everyone else. For me, Russian was the language of the family, that's all. But anyway, it was at one of those *guinguette* evenings that I met Alexis. All the others at those dances were shopkeepers or taxi drivers or café owners like us, or factory people, but suddenly there was this thin, serious young man and he told me he was a poet, and in a very short time I lost my heart to him. It wasn't that I loved him. What I loved was what he *did*. And all I wanted to say to him was: "Take me away."

'We got married. But he couldn't take me away from anything or to anywhere, because we had no money, nothing, and I had to stay on and work in the café just like before, while Alexis earned his few little beans from his poems, published here and there, in small-circulation journals.

'And I soon realised that this life would just go on. On and on. Alexis had changed nothing. So I thought, if he can write, so can I. But I will write something that a *lot* of people want to read. Alexis's poems were so *Russian*, so much about suffering and prisons and grey skies. And I knew I didn't want to write about these things. You see how terrible our history is? I've given you a little flavour of it, haven't I? And I didn't want to write about my own life, either. Because what was in my own life except work in the café and seeing my father struggling backwards and forwards from the coal cellar with his sacks of coal? Who would have read a novel about these things? No one.'

I started to say that Dostoevsky had written about suffering and poverty in *Crime and Punishment* and so many hundreds of thousands of readers had read it that it now had the status of a 'world classic', but Valentina wasn't listening. She began to describe to me how she'd started going to libraries and researching details about life in the Middle Ages, when chivalry was still a word that had meaning and handsome men used to ride around with hawks on their wrists. She said: 'It was when I read about these hawks that I knew I had found my subject. My first hero was a falconer. That book sold ninety thousand copies.'

We lay in the dark for a while. I knew Valentina wanted me to say something about this falconer, but nothing came into my mind, so we just lay there, without talking. I'd moved my mattress up to the pipe hole, so that I could be comfortable during our conversations, and now I rolled over on to my back and stared up at the invisible roof. I'd forgotten if it was day or night or what the sky might be doing if I got up and moved the slate.

After about five minutes of silence, I heard Elroy come slithering through the hole towards me. He was Valentina's now, but she'd sent him on a mission into my cell.

Every day, when there was light and when the house was silent, I stood on the table and chair and worked on the slates until my arms ached too badly to continue.

Valentina had passed her rusty nail to me, stuck into Elroy's uniform, and I was trying to use this as a lever, to work the pins loose from the wood batons. As I worked, and I could feel the adjoining slates begin to move, a plan of escape came filtering very slowly into my mind, but the plan depended not only on the size of the hole I could make in the roof, but on other factors, whose outcome I couldn't know. Any one of these other factors, if it went against me, would render my plan unworkable.

Where the first slate had moved and rain had come in, one

of the batons had gone brittle and pulpy along about five or six centimetres of its length. This gave me the idea of taking out a section of baton, so that, if I could remove the slates above, I'd eventually create a hole wide enough to climb through. But although it would be relatively easy to smash the pulpy section with the iron pipe, I hadn't solved the problem of how I was going to cut through the undamaged wood on either side.

Valentina knew I was working on an escape hole. She seemed to like the idea of the hole, but not the idea of climbing out of it. It was like she saw making the hole as just a way of passing the time. Whenever I mentioned getting out on to the roof, she said: 'Lewis, the roof is dangerous. What you must not risk is your life.'

I knew we had to be on the third floor of a house. When the monkeys went quiet, I decided they were on the ground floor. At night, sometimes, I heard someone moving about right underneath me and so I assumed one of them probably slept there, and once or twice I woke up and knew, without being able to see anything, that Alexis was standing right outside my door; I could hear the little gasp in his breathing. And then I'd wait to see what he was going to do. But he never did anything. He just stood there, listening and gasping, and then he went away.

One morning, he heard us talking through the wall. Valentina was telling me how Anton and his regiment, fighting under Zhukov, were never allowed home on leave during the whole war. They just had to fight on and on and on. The only way a man could get home leave was if he was so badly wounded he couldn't hold a rifle. She said: 'That's why the Russian army never gave up, you see. Even in temperatures so low, the wounded would die of frostbite in fifteen minutes if they were left out in the snow. There was no way out of the war for any of them – except to win it. And you know, Lewis, people talk about the German soldiers being brave, and I think they were: they had to endure that terrible cold as well and their uniforms were thin and inadequate. But Anton used to say to me, "Valya,

I will tell you the truth of the war on the Eastern Front and that is that no one fought like we fought! No one anywhere else on earth!" '

I was about to say that, from the sound of all this, the war fought by the Brits in Western Europe was just a relatively puny thing compared with what the Russians endured, when I heard Alexis shout: 'You hear, Lewis? You learn? You don't look down on us any more?'

What terrified me wasn't his sudden shouting, but the idea that he was going to come into my cell and see the pipe out of the wall and order the hole to be blocked up. I grabbed the pipe and, as quietly as I could, began inserting it back into the wall. While I was doing this, I said: 'I've never looked down on anyone else's army since I saw this programme about Caen, when the British stopped for a tea break and let a German tank get into the city and start blasting it to smithereens.'

There was a silence. I knew Alexis wouldn't understand the expression 'smithereens'. I didn't understand it either, not exactly. Then I said: 'Will you play a chess game with me?'

I could hear him gasping. Valentina said nothing. Then Alexis said: 'You play chess, Meaulnes?'

'Yes.'

He laughed his high laugh and said: 'English chess?'

I had the pipe back in place. I could feel Valentina take hold of her end of it and settle it back into position. I waited. Alexis was still laughing. I wondered whether poets had a universal tendency to laugh at their own jokes. I'd never met any poets before.

'I usually play for money,' he said.

'I haven't got any money,' I said. 'You took it all.'

This made him laugh even harder. 'I will consider your proposal,' he said. Then he went away.

To get Alexis to play chess with me was one essential part of my escape plan. Another essential part of the plan was to win at least one of the games, so I decided not to mention this to Valentina. I wouldn't know, until we'd played the first game, whether I was capable of winning against Alexis or not. What I did think was likely was that Alexis *would* agree to play with me. Being a kidnapper had to be almost as boring, on a day-to-day level, as being the kidnapped. The prime qualitative difference between the two forms of existence was a difference of light.

But Valentina and I fought boredom in loads of peculiar ways. When we next removed the pipe, I said to her: 'Put your ear very close to the hole and close your eyes and listen.'

I got my sifflet du chasseur and began to be a bird. I still didn't know which bird I was, but I thought Valentina probably couldn't tell the difference between a chaffinch and a robin, so this didn't really matter.

After a long while of listening in silence to the whistling, she said: 'Darling, how are you doing that? It brings tears to my eyes.'

'Practice,' I said.

'Who taught you?'

'No one. I just picked it up.'

When I was tired of being this anonymous bird, I gave my mouth a rest for a while and then tried to be a lark, by letting more air come between my tongue and the sifflet, so that the sound was more shrill and on a two-note scale.

Valentina liked my lark. I don't know whether she'd ever heard one in her life, but she said, 'That is just exactly and completely like a lark, darling!' Then she asked me to tell her about Devon and the dunes and our house near the sea, where she'd never been. She kept reassuring me that I'd be back there again very soon, but somehow no part of me wanted to believe this. What I wanted to believe, I found it impossible to express.

I described our house, which wasn't particularly beautiful, just old and ordinary and painted white, with wallflowers growing by the front door, and a tamarisk hedge at the bottom of the garden and a clothes line that ran from the kitchen wall to a wormy apple tree. I said that I'd always lived there and that the cellar was full of toys I'd had when I was small, which Hugh and Alice somehow couldn't bear to part with. I said: 'I go and look at them about once a year. I don't know who they're being kept for.'

Then Valentina said an odd thing. She said: 'Well, you know, Alice isn't so old, darling. Thirty-seven isn't old. She could have another baby if she wanted to. Perhaps they're keeping the toys for that day?'

'No,' I said.

We were silent for a bit. And then, in the silence, I thought, yes, after all, that could turn out to be it, Valentina has put her finger on it: this unborn kid is the future. Except that nobody can say for sure who its father will be. It could be born with short sight. Or wings.

But Hugh will believe it's his. In time, my chess set will be given to it. Hugh will teach it how to interpret the standing stones of South Devon and how to recognise the cry of the lark. Reams of information that it never asked for will be poured into its ears. It will be taken on the Northern line to fly its kite on a windy hill. Hugh will tell it that happiness is no bigger than a shrimp in a rock pool, but it will try nevertheless – as I had tried – to love England and to love its life.

The next morning, the kidnappers let me take a shower. When they said the word 'douche', I had difficulty believing I'd heard right. One of the things I'd begun to dream about was the bath in the attic at the rue Rembrandt. In these dreams, I heard that old whistler in the next room and I remembered the tune he'd been whistling had been slow and sad, like a sort of lament.

Vasily took me to the shower. He was the one who did most of the menial stuff and he was in a bad mood that day. He put on my blindfold, and then shoved me along the corridor and down some wooden stairs to the next floor. He told me, in French, that I smelled like a rat. I asked him how he knew what a rat smelled like, but he didn't answer. I slipped on the stairs and fell and he yanked me up, then pushed me into the shower room and locked me in.

I took off the blindfold. The room just had a tiled floor with a drain in it and a rusty shower head coming out of the wall. There was a tiny window, big enough to contain one pane of frosted glass. Vasily hadn't given me any soap, but I found some on the floor by the drain. Everything in there, including the soap, felt cold.

I took off my clothes. They looked and smelled like a health hazard and I wanted a hospital nurse to be there to take them away and put them in the incinerator with all the blood-stained gauze and burn them to ash. But there was no nurse and no incinerator, so I decided to wash my underpants and socks and T-shirt. I just took them with me into the shower and soaped them and trod on them and rinsed them and soaped them and trod on them again. I knew that, in the dark, they'd take hours and hours to dry, but I didn't care.

Bits of you get sore if you don't wash. Your arse feels like it's been cut open with a medieval sword. And then when you can soap it and let the warm water just run and run on to the wound, it's the most soothing thing you could ever have imagined.

I stayed in the shower till the water ran cold. There was no towel, so I just stood there, calling for Vasily and shivering. And then, when he came in, he wasn't wearing his monkey mask. I don't know if he'd forgotten to put it on or he expected me to take a shower with my blindfold on, or what. He came in, carrying an old threadbare towel, as if nothing was wrong and then he realised that I was staring at him. He threw the towel at me and ran out, but it was too late: I'd seen his face.

I dried myself on the towel and squeezed out my wet clothes. All I had to put on now were my trousers and jacket and in the light of the shower room I could see how dirty they were. With these on, with no shoes, I looked liked a métro beggar, the kind of pitiful kid who doesn't sing or anything, but just sits there by the wall, holding out his hand. I thought, well, never mind, they're probably going to kill me now anyway. I know who Alexis is and now I've seen Vasily's face, so I'm in exactly the same amount of danger as Valentina. And then I thought how odd it was that the face I'd seen had been so soft, so sort of babyish and kind, yet it was the sight of this baby face that had diminished my chances of staying alive. I could hear Shukov and Todorsky yelling at Vasily. I thought, they'll probably yell for hours, or even get in a fight; maybe they'll even kill poor little Vasya and I'll be in this shower room till night time, till they've drowned his body in the river.

But Todorsky, wearing his mask, took me back to my cell. I carried my wet clothes and laid them out to dry on my chair. I decided that when the house was quiet again, I might risk putting them on the roof in the sun.

Later that day, after we'd eaten some tough meat with oily white beans, a knife came through the pipe hole. It was an ordinary dinner knife, but, unlike the one I'd been given, it had a serrated edge. Valentina whispered: 'If they ask for it back, I think we'll have to give it back, so try it now. See if you can make any impact on the batons with it.'

Moving my table and chair and locating the loose slate took me approximately sixty seconds now. As usual, when I turned the slate, a slab of sunlight fell in. And I could make it bigger. Two more slates had been loosened enough to pivot on their pins.

I calculated the distance between the cuts I was going to make in the baton, not by how wide my body was, but by how wide Valentina's hips might possibly be. I had to guess at it. I held out my arms and tried to imagine them going right round her.

The knife wouldn't operate like a saw; moving backwards and forwards, it only snagged the wood on the downward movement, so this was how I had to work, as if I were pulling the knife through a blade-sharpener. After half an hour's constant friction, I'd made a cut in the wood about two millimetres deep. It wasn't difficult to work out that to saw through the baton in just this one place would take me approximately seven hours, and already my arms felt as if they'd been doing crucifixion practice. But I made myself go on. I laid my underpants out on the slates in the sun and kept sawing. I thought, my life and Valentina's could be saved, not by jewellery from Cartier, but by a piece of cutlery.

By the time night came, I was exhausted. A river of pain began to run from my right hand to my shoulder and up into my neck. I said to Valentina: 'Do hostages ever get given paracetamol?'

She was in the middle of telling me about Nikita Khrushchev, who became the President of the Soviet Union after Stalin died. She said Nikita Khrushchev had a fat, smiling face, and because of this face of his, people trusted him. She said: 'If you ask for a pain killer, they will wonder why you're in pain. It might be better just to endure it.'

Then she told me about what she called Khrushchev's 'maize craze'. This 'maize craze' was the thing that finally drove Anton out of Russia. Valentina said it broke the remaining bit of his Soviet heart.

Apparently, Nikita Khrushchev went on a visit to Idaho in the United States some time in the 1950s. He was taken on a tour of the maize fields there, and when he saw all this plump maize growing under the Idaho sun he decided it was the ideal crop to grow back home to solve the food shortages. So he ordered maize to be planted in vast swathes right across the country, including on Anton's farm. Anton used to refer to him as *kukuruznik*, which meant 'maize freak', but the farmers soon saw that the maize wasn't growing. It wasn't like that fat Idaho maize; it was dry and thin. The air was too cold for it.

Valentina said: 'My father used to go out in the middle of the night and look at his maize crop in the moonlight. It should have been as high as his shoulder, but it barely came up to his waist. He'd grown potatoes before and his potatoes had been all right, snug under the soil, and he knew what he could see in the moonlit maize: he could see hunger and ruin.'

In the dark of my cell, it didn't seem difficult to picture Anton standing in the maize field with the moon glimmering down, except that what I imagined it glimmering down on was his white hair, and then I realised that all this had happened so long ago, his hair wouldn't have been white, but still dark, like it was when he met Olga in the queue to see Stalin's coffin.

I said to Valentina: 'You once told me you stood in the maize.'

'Yes. I did. I looked out of my window one night and I saw Anton there in the maize. So I went down and joined him. The maize was taller than I was. I didn't know it was no good. But I was only three.'

And I tried to picture her then: this plump little girl, wearing some kind of bright dress, feeling small among the scratchy green stalks.

She told me it was that same autumn, when the maize cobs had failed to ripen, that Anton and Olga joined the official visit by the Collective Farmers of the Lovat River Valley to the wine co-operative in Provence. They took Valentina with them because they knew they were never going to come back.

I said: 'How could they be sure? How could they know they weren't going to be found and arrested?'

'They couldn't,' said Valentina. 'What they did involved a great amount of risk. But sometimes, in a life, risk is inevitable, Lewis. I expect you will discover this.'

I almost said that I knew it perfectly well already and that my escape plan had quite a high risk element to it, but I didn't. When the time came, I wanted Valentina to believe that my plan was flawless.

We were quiet for a while and I began to think that Valentina had gone to sleep, but then she suddenly said: 'I took a risk, in my recent life. I counted on something that didn't happen. And now, I've realised – since I've been here – that I will have to pay some price for it.'

I knew what she was talking about. She was talking about

Grisha's book and how she'd believed that his life of Catherine the Great would never be published outside Russia, but I didn't let on.

'What price?' I asked.

I heard her turn over on her mattress. 'It's too complicated to explain, darling,' she said.

'Try,' I said.

'No, I can't explain it all. It had to do with the pressure I was under, from my publishers here and in the States and in London, to produce a book every two years or so. I knew that one day I would run out of stories . . . and this is what has happened.'

I said: 'But your book's almost finished.'

'It's almost finished, but now it will never be *completely* finished. If I get out of here, I'm going to renegotiate everything. I think Valentina Gavril has written her last Medieval Romance.'

She said she wanted to go to sleep then. It was like she was on the very brink of telling me the truth and then something held her back.

The following day, just after I'd been with Vasya to empty my shit pail, Alexis came into my cell. He was wearing his monkey mask.

He got Vasya to stick a light bulb in the overhead lamp, then he pulled my table out from the wall until it was under the light and told me to sit down. Vasya brought in a second chair and placed it opposite me. Then Alexis went away.

I looked up at the roof baton, where I'd been sawing away at it with the knife. If you examined it closely, you could see there was a cut in it, but I didn't think Alexis was going to be staring at the roof; I knew that he'd decided on a game of chess.

His chess set was very beautiful, made of ebony and ivory, the pieces heavy and sort of stained and worn away by the hands of the players. I was sure the set had come from Russia.

Probably, Russia was the place where the most fantastic chess sets in the world were made.

Alexis sat down and we began setting out the pieces, like we were old friends who played a game every evening.

'White or Black, Meaulnes?' he asked.

'I don't mind,' I said. 'But if I win, I want something.'

He said nothing to this at first. He said he preferred to play Black. Then he just stared at his side of the board intently as he prepared it, like you see biological researchers staring at a row of tiny little tubes. Sometimes, before a game of chess has begun, you can start to see invisible moves in the minds of the chessmen, and I knew this was what was happening to Alexis now.

Then, suddenly, he looked up. 'What is it you want?' he asked.

I said: 'I want my notebook back.'

'Notebook?'

'It's got a picture of Concorde on it.'

'You fly on Concorde, rich boy?'

'No. Can I have my notebook?'

Alexis looked up. It was impossible to tell what his face was doing behind the monkey mask, but I could see his eyes fixed on me. 'First, you have to win,' he said.

Suddenly, I felt nervous. I hadn't felt it a moment before, but now I did. I looked at Alexis's hands, with their long pale fingers ready to swoop on his opening move, and I thought, I won't win against hands like that: there's too much knowledge and practice in them.

I was playing White. I made one of my favourite openings, pawn to king four. Without the least hesitation, Alexis did the same, pawn to king four.

My concentration didn't feel good. I thought, I must go for a fast knockout, or else I'll lose it, so I brought my queen out straight away: queen to bishop three. Alexis allowed himself a laugh. I wanted to say, 'That's against the rules; you've got to keep quiet.' But I didn't. I just watched Alexis rush out his knight and my crude attempts to checkmate early were parried so easily, it was embarrassing. In less than ten minutes, my queen was hustled to the edge of the board. Without my queen, I knew, and Alexis knew, that I couldn't go on. I felt kind of stunned and stupid. I hadn't lost a chess game so fast and so idiotically for years.

I knew Alexis was grinning behind his mask as he put the beautiful chess pieces away. 'Next time you will win,' he said, 'but we don't have any notebook. We found a knife, that was all. You will have to ask for something else.'

I thought, when the game was over, Alexis might forget about the light in my cell and leave it on. But he didn't. He sent Vasya in with a cloth and the bulb was taken away.

I wanted to describe the game to Valentina, to tell her that the *presence* of Alexis had unnerved me and see if she could give me any tips about how to beat him next time, but I didn't dare take the pipe out of the wall, because I could hear the monkeys chattering near us. They were talking in Russian, so I couldn't understand a word, but I knew they were discussing the game, saying what a transparent chess player I was. From time to time, Alexis laughed his laugh like an animal cry.

Valentina knew I hadn't won. She knocked on the wall and said: 'Lewis, don't be downhearted, darling. Everybody who plays Alexis says he is hard to beat.'

'Thanks,' I said.

I felt tired, but I didn't want to lie down and snivel over my loss of the chess match, so I decided to go for an imaginary walk round London. It was raining on the Thames, pocking the surface of the water. The faces of the Embankment joggers were wet and their hair was slicked down by the rain and their legs were muddy. I crossed one of the bridges and felt the wind come blustering round me, trying to blow me off the bridge and down into the grey-green river.

I was making my way towards the Festival Hall, where I had once been taken to a concert by Grandma Gwyneth when I was nine or ten. I could remember having tea in some airy interior space, which was occupied only by light and waitresses and plastic chairs.

Then we climbed up miles of wooden stairs and came out at the very top of the auditorium and looked down at the grand piano on the concert platform, far away. Grandma Gwyneth had said: 'What we're going to hear, sweetheart, is a piece called *Rhapsody in Blue*, by an American composer called George Gershwin. Here it is, you see, in your programme, *Rhapsody in Blue*, and it's one of my favourite pieces of music of all time.'

The two of us went to the concert on our own; Bertie, Hugh and Alice didn't come. Sometimes, she did this: took me on 'treats' of her own devising. She wanted me to like the music so much, she kept looking at me all the time they were playing it, to see if I *was* liking it. What I said to her afterwards was: 'I didn't like it at first, but it got better.'

Now, on my imaginary walk, I went into the Festival Hall and sat down in a plastic chair. There was a smell of stale coffee in the air. And opposite me, on another chair, Grandma Gwyneth was sitting, wearing a coral-coloured bit of knitwear and a tweed skirt, and she was crying her eyes out into a tiny little hankie. The thing I found myself wondering was, why was it that she and Bertie always had hankies available whenever they were needed, and nobody else ever did?

I stopped my walk then. I hadn't gone at all far. I sat down on my chair and felt sick with sorrow at all the anguish I was causing. I thought of Alice, searching for me in the deep dark of Notre-Dame. I thought of Moinel ringing our apartment bell and asking for me and knowing that I'd broken my promise to him. I thought of Violette cleaning my empty room and feeling afraid and wondering which, if any, of the spirits she should talk to.

And then I thought about Hugh, with Bertie and Gwyneth, travelling to Heathrow in a taxi they couldn't afford, and just watching the fields of the West Country going by in silence and knowing that, until now, their lives had been relatively happy compared with some, or even compared with most, but now that happiness was finished and gone.

I tried to reassure everybody. First of all, I said: 'I had to find Valentina. This was the one and only important thing I've done in my life.' I wanted to add: 'When you're older, you'll understand this,' which was a thing people said to me all the time, but then I remembered that Gwyneth and Bertie were quite old anyway, so it wasn't really appropriate. I left this alone and just said: 'But I'm going to stay alive. I'm going to get out of here. I've got it worked out. The only thing I refuse to do is leave without Valentina.'

They all looked at me in silence. They were in a little semicircle in front of me and I could see them struggling with all their individual sad thoughts. But I knew that only Moinel and Violette cared about Valentina and the others didn't really mind whether she lived or died.

For most of the next night, I worked on the baton. I'd cut it right through in one place and so I began straight away on the second cut. I knew the dinner knife and I were in a kind of race, now, with the delivery of the ransom money. The knife had sliced its way through the equivalent of about seventy-five thousand beef steaks. Its serrated head was tiring and beginning to bend.

Only two slates were still attached to the bit of baton on which I was working; the others round them were loose and just held down by their own weight. I had a collection of slate pins in my pocket. And I was now able to stick my head out into the night.

I described to Valentina the things I could see. I said: 'There's an orange glimmer in the sky quite far away on the left and I suppose that's Paris, but I think we're sort of in the country, here, because I can't see any other buildings or hear any traffic.'

'Can you see the road?' asked Valentina.

We knew there was a road leading to our place because we

sometimes heard cars or vans coming and going, but I told her that with only my head out in the air I couldn't see anything on the ground, just the tops of things.

'The tops of what?' she said.

'Trees.'

She began to speculate on what this house was and who owned it. She said it couldn't be derelict, even though our rooms and the shower room were old and dirty, because it had electricity and hot water. She thought it had to belong to a relation of one of the kidnappers, to someone they could trust completely. 'And Alexis,' she said, 'has no relations. He used to have an old mother who worked in a newspaper kiosk, but she died. I think she died of cold in that freezing little kiosk. So it must be some relation of Todorsky's or Shukov's. Someone once told me Leo Todorsky had a cousin who was a concert pianist, but I never believed it. I think probably the whole family are criminals and dealers.'

I said I thought there was water near by. From time to time, not often, I heard a noise like a boat's engine. I thought it could be one of those old canals that nobody used much any more.

The moon came up while I worked and I noticed that it was getting towards full. Ingrid once informed Carl that girls of sixteen were more 'cosmic' than boys because their periods were influenced by the movements of the moon, and when Carl told me about this alleged cosmicness I said Ingrid was talking complete and total crap. But now, when I looked at the moon, I thought, there's something about the way it is that reminds me of Valentina.

She was sleeping. She said she was tired because she'd been walking around Manhattan, from her publisher's apartment on Park Avenue right down to a Mexican restaurant on West 13th Street. She'd seen a pair of cops on roller blades. She said the sky was red, fading to green. A white limo went by her and she knew Al Pacino was inside it. She said: 'It gave me an odd feeling to be in New York City with no money.'

324

To keep myself awake and make my arm carry on working, I tried to go through my chess game with Alexis and work out how he'd parried so easily. My first chess teacher had been an actor, who used to do baby-sitting for Hugh and Alice for about a pound an hour. His name was Julian. I was meant to put my light out and go to sleep at nine, but I never did. I used to stay up with Julian and eat sultanas and play chess, and one of the first things he told me was: 'Never play a game just once; play it a second time in your mind. That way, your defeats are never wasted.'

It was difficult to keep track of time. The number of days that had passed since I'd woken up in this attic and vomited on the floor could have been ten, or twelve, or more. It could have been fifteen. In movies about prisons, people nearly always scratched little lines into the wall to make sure they knew when Wednesday was coming round again or when snow would begin to fall. Sometimes, you had a scene where they looked at all the lines and worked out that it was their wedding anniversary or Christmas Day or something and started to cry. I could have made some marks with Valentina's rusty nail, but I hadn't done it. Part of me had become uninterested in time.

Valentina said she knew that autumn was coming. She said she could hear it in the wind. And she told me she longed to be in Paris again, walking along with Sergei in the fresh autumn air, seeing the new season's fashions coming into the shops, watching the roses in the Parc Monceau begin to fade and the chestnut leaves turn brown, seeing the tourists depart and the Parisians return, looking forward to winter in the most beautiful city on earth. And I imagined her there, with the sunlight falling on her blonde head and on Sergei's auburn coat. I thought, when it's the two of them together, it's like there's no Arthur Miller, just two Marilyns.

A new thing was that Valentina sometimes sang to me through the pipe hole. She had quite a beautiful voice. I imagined the monkeys on their other floor, hearing her singing and stopping to listen and sometimes recognising the tunes, because what she mainly sang were old Russian songs she'd learned from Olga and Anton. Some of them had words and some didn't, or else they once had and Valentina had forgotten them. Most of them were love songs and when I asked her to translate the words, she'd say things like: 'Well, this man is a train driver. He's making a comparison between his woman's body and the embankments and cuttings his train is passing through.'

Then one afternoon, when I was resting from my work on the baton and half asleep on my mattress and the autumn wind was gusting around the slates above us, Valentina hummed a tune that I suddenly recognised. I said to her: 'That was the tune I heard in my bathroom – the one the whistler whistled.'

She stopped humming. 'I don't think so,' she said.

But I was sure. Ever since Grandma Gwyneth had begun my musical education by taking me to hear *Rhapsody in Blue* at the Festival Hall, I could remember pieces of music in my mind. I told Valentina to sing it again, and this time she put some words to it.

'That was it,' I said. 'I know it. That was the song.'

'Lewis,' she said, 'nobody in France knows that old song. So whoever was in that room – if there was anybody in that room – could not have been whistling that.'

'Why not? Because it's Russian?'

'Yes. It's Russian. It's from the 1930s, and it was my father's favourite song all his life. The singer is a stork. He is making a nest on a high factory chimney, out of reach of any human hand. And if you are thinking of laughing, please do not. It's a song about persecutions.'

I said I wasn't thinking of laughing. I said I'd remembered that the singer of *It's not easy being green* had been a frog. Then I said: 'I know what's in that room, Valentina. Apart from the bed, it's all the old stuff you used to have in the café. There's the Wurlitzer you've turned into a safe, but there's also an awning up there and a Dubonnet ad and stacks of chairs and an oven. So it's obvious who was whistling, isn't it: it was Anton.'

'Don't be silly, Lewis,' she said.

I didn't feel like saying anything more. I just lay there and pulled my blanket over me. Now that this autumn wind had come, it felt cold in our rooms.

After a few moments of silence, in which I felt myself start to fall asleep and then just pull back from it, like from the edge of a lake of warm sand, Valentina whispered: 'He's buried in the Cimetière de Montmartre.'

'Where he's buried wouldn't make any difference,' I said.

'But I just don't believe that was what you heard, Lewis. You've got it muddled in your mind.'

I said: 'If it wasn't Anton, who was it, then?'

'It was no one. That room is always kept locked. You were tired after your journey from England. I remember, that evening, you were very tired and confused . . .'

'Later, I was tired. Not then, when I heard that whistler.' And I whistled the tune, so that Valentina could see that I recognised its phrasing and could reproduce it more or less exactly. As I whistled, I wondered how the words fitted in and whether the stork's nest was vandalised at the end of the song, or if it survived.

When I finished, Valentina said: 'Why would Anton whistle to you – and not to me?'

'Easy,' I said.

'Why?'

'He was warning me. And I don't care whether you believe me or not. He was drawing my attention to the fact that one day I was going to have to save your life.'

The first time I climbed out on to the roof, it was raining. It was the middle of the night and you could smell this new rain on everything around, as though it had made the landscape exhale. Even the roof slates were exhaling.

I made my way up to the ridge, just above the gap, and

crouched there, like an actual monkey, with my eyes darting nervously around. The rain was so soft, it made a kind of gauzy bandage round every point of light. Except there weren't many points of light. Our house – or farm or whatever it was – seemed to be way out on its own somewhere, with a thick line of trees to the right of it and an old empty meadow sloping away from it towards a flat horizon.

I monkey-walked to the gable end of the roof and looked down. From here, I could see the road or track we'd heard the cars on. It ran past the house and meandered away up the meadow and I had the feeling that, at the top there, it joined a proper road. I waited, to see if something would come along, and after about ten minutes I saw yellow headlights, blurred by the gauze of rain, go slowly past, and so I knew that was where we'd go when we made our escape, to that road.

In Devon, I was forbidden ever to hitch lifts, but this was what we would do – hitch a lift back into Paris and back into our lives. I pictured us waiting on the road for a car to come by. We stood there, hiding in the shadow of some trees, holding hands. The only thing I wished I had, besides Valentina's hand in mine, was shoes on my feet.

But there was a problem: it felt high, that roof – too high, too much on its own in the black sky, as if, when you left it, you'd fall down and down into nothing at all and go on falling for ever. Behind me was a smudge of Paris light, only dimly orange in the rain and miles away, but there nevertheless, patiently waiting for us, and I wished I was on the other end of the roof, looking at that and not at the darkness below me and the tall trees. I couldn't see, from where I was crouching, any way of getting safely to the ground.

I stayed still, poised on the gable-end like a bird, thinking about Didier and the air balloon that came towards him and his father through the brightening sky. It seemed to me that, in some way I might never have the philosophical insight to explain, Didier had brought me to where I was, squatting on the roof ridge, with all this deathly space underneath me. But he hadn't explained to me how to get down. I wanted to yell at him: 'Tell me how to get out of here! You said you could fly, but you never told me what you really meant. I need to fly now, but I can't, because you never showed me how.'

I felt really angry and pissed off with him. And not just about the flying. The thing that pissed me off more than anything was the idea that, when everything was over and Alice and I had gone back to England, he would probably forget us. He'd go on with his life with Angélique; he'd buy her ugly dresses at the market and sometimes take her roller-blading on Sundays, and he'd never think of us. And I just couldn't stand this thought. Because I knew for certain that all through our lives we'd remember him.

I was getting wet up on the ridge, but it wasn't cold and I considered taking off my clothes and letting the drizzle wash me clean. When you're a hostage, water takes on a different significance. Then I was deflected from doing this by the sound of a door opening and an outside light being switched on. I didn't move. I wanted to drop down below the roof line but I knew I couldn't do this soundlessly, so it was better to stay still. Nobody looks up at their own roof, not unless they think there's something unsafe up there, or unless they're old Grisha with his head in the clouds.

After a moment, I heard a car start up. I knew it was a Citroën 2CV from the rattle that engine has. It reminded me of waiting in the school playground for Alice to remember me and drive over.

Then I heard something I didn't expect: it was a woman's voice, shouting in Russian. She sounded really angry and I waited to hear which one of the kidnappers she was angry with, but nobody answered her. She slammed her door. The Citroën's lights came on and the car was driven up the track towards the road. I saw it bounce and lurch, just like Alice's 2CV used to do, and I thought how odd it was that every single car in the world had become more advanced and smooth and sophisticated except this one crazy model.

At the road, it turned left, driving towards the Paris light. I watched it until it was out of sight and then I made my way silently, gripping the wet surfaces with my hands and toes, back to my hole and fanned the slates back into position above me, like closing a cunning little door.

I didn't tell Valentina that I hadn't been able to work out a way of getting down from the roof. I just described what I'd been able to see and that there was a road not far away. In the last few days, Valentina hadn't been on any walks and I knew this was a bad sign, a sign that she was depressed.

She started to talk about a dream she'd had. She'd been in Rome in the dream (Valentina always dreamed in this international kind of way) and looking at Raphael's tomb in the Pantheon. And through the hole in the Pantheon roof had started to come a great mass of birds.

These birds were black, like starlings or crows, and so many thousands of them came fluttering in that they began to fill up the whole gigantic space and Valentina knew that if she stayed where she was, looking at Raphael's tomb, she'd be suffocated by them. The thought of being suffocated by birds was terrible, but when she tried to walk away she found she couldn't move from the spot. 'And what I realised,' she said, 'was that I was going to die. I stood there and accepted it: the birds were Death and the person they'd come to get was me.'

I was silent for a moment. Just hearing her tell the dream had made me shiver. Dreaming it must have been quite bad. I said airily: 'What you thought were birds in the dream weren't birds at all, or Death, or anything like that; they were Yves St Laurent dresses. Some of the dresses were black and had feathers attached to them, which is why they looked like birds, but in fact what you dreamed was the number of designer outfits you're going to be able to afford before you snuff it.'

After the rain, it got hot again. I could feel this heat coming through the slates and I could smell it in the sweat on Alexis's body.

He was getting anxious again. He took me to empty my shit pail one morning (he said Vasily was ill) and as he pushed me along the corridor, I could hear him gasping more agonisingly than usual and I could feel his arm shaking. He said to me in French: 'I want you to know, if those people try to get clever, if they try to crap on me, I will kill Valentina and I will kill you.'

I was going to be sort of smart-arsed and say to him: 'I don't know why you wanted me to know that, Alexis,' but I didn't. I needed information, so I asked him if Bianquis had promised him the money.

'Yes,' he said, 'promised. But if they think they can trick me, those rich cunts . . .'

'When? When's the money going to come?'

'I'm not telling you, Meaulnes. All I'm telling you is if they don't pay up, you and Valya are dead!'

'Merci beaucoup,' I said. And then he hit me across the back of my head, so that I lurched forward and the shit pail fell out of my hand and bounced on the wood floor, and although I couldn't see anything through my blindfold I knew it had to be spilling all that remained of its contents that hadn't been soaked up by the famous faces in *France Dimanche*.

I felt really angry that Alexis had hit me. It was the kind of anger I'd felt about that stealer at school, only magnified about a hundred times. I regained my balance and turned round to punch him in his shrunken stomach, but he knew exactly what I was going to do and grabbed my arms and wrenched them down. He held me pinioned, so close to his trembling body that I couldn't move. His hands were bruising my arms and I could hear the gasp in his lungs very close to my ear. And all I could think about was trying to get away from him. So I spat at him, with as fat a gob of spit as I could dredge up out of my dry mouth, and there was a split second's pause as the spit landed somewhere on his shirt. Then he kicked my feet from under me and let me fall.

I tried to get up. I knew I was sitting in a puddle of urine. Then I heard Valentina start to yell at Alexis through her door and it was at this moment that he went completely wild, kicking out at the overturned bucket and beating his fist on the wall and screaming in Russian. It was like he was screaming about everything in his life, everything in his world, like he was tearing open his lungs and his heart and letting all the anger and misery come deluging out. You couldn't tell, after a minute, whether he was screaming or crying or both, or what. He was just making sounds, and they were like no other sounds I'd ever heard in my life.

Later, I said to Valentina: 'Do you think that's what people heard in Leningrad, that winter when the siege was on and they knew they were dying – a kind of noise like that?'

'Not specially, darling,' she said. 'In Russia, that is what they hear all the time.'

We didn't see Alexis again for two days. I wondered if that woman I'd seen getting into the Citroën was taking care of him.

I climbed out on to the roof again, and on this night the moon came and went behind streaky clouds and revealed to me something I hadn't found the time before: at the back of the house, between it and the thicket of trees, was a barn.

I hadn't discovered it because it was quite small and low, and to see it you had to edge *down* the roof, nearer to the gutter line. It was one of those places that looks as if it's been built in a day, as if the farmer just decided in the night, 'I'll put a barn there tomorrow', and then went and bought a lot of corrugated iron and some old wooden posts and some nails and erected it without anyone noticing. But this farmer had been quite lazy. He wasn't like Hugh, worrying about views and windows and ways of laying brick; he hadn't wanted to lug the sheets of iron one centimetre further than he had to, so he'd put his barn as near to the house as possible.

I calculated that the distance between the wall of the house and the barn was about 1.5 metres. To get on to the barn roof from the lowest point of the house roof involved a drop of approximately three metres. The corrugated iron would have some give in it: it would be more springy than concrete or slate; and the sheets had been laid almost flat, just tilting up slightly to the left, so that the rain could run down and away. Once we'd landed on the roof of the barn, getting to the ground would be easy, because the barn was full of hay and broken bales of it had spilled out all around. All we'd have to do was let ourselves fall down on to the hay.

I crouched on the roof, looking at the barn for a long time. The moonlight shone on the iron ridges of its roof. The question of shoes bothered me. I knew the hardest thing would be trying to steady ourselves on the slates, poised for the leap, and that this would have been far easier wearing trainers. Grip and steadiness were *prime* and we'd both be hampered, because presumably all Valentina had with her were the white sandals she'd worn that day she left to have lunch with Grisha. And I imagined her naked feet, with their beautiful convex toenails with just a vestige of red nail polish remaining on them, standing where I was now, trying to grip the slates, and her whispering to me in the dark: 'Hold on to me, darling. Don't let me go . . .'

The next time I saw Alexis was the night of the storm.

He was calm. The storm had come in at dusk and now it was exploding and flashing right over our heads, and in the midst of it Alexis was calm and quiet. It was like the storm was grumbling and protesting for him and allowing him to be still.

He came into my room with Vasya and they inserted the light bulb and set up the chessboard. I didn't know what time it was, but I knew it was quite late, like ten o'clock or something, and I thought, perhaps Alexis is really afraid of the storm and he wants to play chess all night to distract himself.

He was wearing his monkey mask. His hair that came down to his shoulders looked cleaner than the last time I'd seen it and I thought, I expect that Russian girl, whoever she is, has been cooking him meals and sucking his cock and lying in the bath with him, shampooing his hair.

As he set out the pieces, he said in French: 'What d'you want, Meaulnes, if you win? Your Concorde book? Exploding Peanut Theory: very clever!' And he laughed his girl's laugh. What the laugh said was that he knew my chances of winning were completely useless.

I let a long moment pass. The last time we'd played, Alexis had said he didn't have my notebook, but I made no reference to this. I knew he lied about everything; Valentina had told me he did. What I said was: 'I don't expect I'll win. But if I do, I want Valentina.'

Both Alexis and Vasya raised their heads from the board and stared at me through the holes in their monkey masks.

'Oh yes?' said Alexis. 'She belongs to you like your notebook?'

I said: 'No. What I mean is, I want you to let her sleep in this room, just tonight, while the storm lasts. That's all.'

'So you're afraid of the storm? You want your "mummy"?'

'Yes.'

Alexis and Vasya both laughed then and said something in Russian and then laughed again. I didn't look at them. I just concentrated on setting out my side of the board and, as I put each piece in place, tried to imagine the chessmen like an army, like my troops, about to begin their fight for my freedom.

I knew Alexis wouldn't agree to any request of mine yet. He liked to keep you waiting for everything – even for water. Only when the game was over would he refer to it.

Like last time, Vasya hung around, watching us. He brought in a third chair and sat at the table, staring at the board, before either of us had made a single move. I hoped his eyes wouldn't go wandering up to the roof and notice that one section of baton had been cut through and wedged back in place with folded newspaper.

We were about to begin, when Alexis snapped out some command in Russian to Vasya and he got up obediently and went out. He went sort of slowly, tearing his eyes away reluctantly from the vacant board, and so I knew he was playing his own game in his mind and the chances of him looking up at the roof were small.

He came back with a half-full bottle of whisky and one glass and put these near Alexis. Valentina had told me that drinking whisky could sometimes make Alexis mellow and kind and sometimes make him cruel and you never knew which of these moods was going to come.

When he poured some out, the smell of the whisky reminded me of being in Scotland, with my Scottish grandmother, Annie, who lived alone in Edinburgh and spent most of her money on bingo and booze. She always asked for 'small' drinks, which she sometimes called 'wee' drinks – 'Hugh, dear, will you pour me a wee whisky?' – but she had so many wee ones that the quantity she got through became immense and not 'wee' at all. And she smelled of this whisky and her rooms somehow smelled of it, even her bedroom, and I suppose this was why we saw more of Gwyneth and Bertie than we did of her. When I asked Alice if she missed her, she said: 'No. Never.'

This time, as I waited to begin, I didn't feel nervous. My mind was concentrated and cool. I knew Alexis wouldn't expect me to repeat my pawn-to-king-four opening, so this is exactly what I did. Alexis hesitated. I saw him surveying the centre and I expected him to try to crowd me out there like last time, but he didn't. He just pushed a pawn one square forward on the flank: pawn to king's knight three.

I thought, that's interesting, he's leaving me the centre, so I started to grab it, with pawn to queen four. Automatically, Alexis developed his bishop with bishop to knight two. And I was just getting happy with my dominance of the centre, pushing my pawn to king's bishop four, when Alexis tipped his monkey mask up above his mouth, took a long gulp of whisky and then just lazily pushed his central pawn to queen four.

I kept my body very still, surveying my big centre and not wanting to relinquish it. I could hear the storm continuing, noisier than ever, and I thought, imitate the storm, persist in the centre. So I kept on pushing my pawns, but, each time I pushed, Alexis blocked and after about a dozen moves I realised my king was vulnerable, with a Black knight and a Black bishop moving steadily in.

This was the kind of moment in a game where you either panic or else, because you've almost accepted defeat, a weird calm comes over you and you become reckless, like a tennis player charging and volleying. And this is what happened. I just experienced this icy calm and remembered a thing Julian used to say about pawns: 'If you push them, it's for life'; and I thought, that's it, I've just got to keep pushing, even now. It's for life.

I threw another pawn forward. Alexis paused, wondering what on earth I was doing, then snicked out my pawn sort of daintily, as if he was taking a sugar lump out of a china bowl. Next, I gave up my knight, and even though I didn't look up I knew both Alexis and Vasily were staring at me, thinking, what kind of chess is this? But Alexis grabbed it, as I knew he would. He grabbed it fast and greedily, like the computer would have done. He was snapping up lots of material and enjoying this and it was like he didn't notice, until he saw my queen land on rook six, until it was almost too late, that his king was exposed.

It was a race then. Alexis began rushing over everything in sight to defend his king, but I had enough men left and I was their steel-cool commander-in-the-field. I got to checkmate in ten moves.

There was a silence in the room. Vasya was staring at Alexis, like he couldn't believe this had happened. Alexis finished the

whisky in his glass and got up. I thought he might kick over
the table or something, but he didn't. It was as if he was
mellowing out with the whisky and didn't really care. He said:
'I will ask Valya if she minds sleeping near to your shit bucket,'
and he went out.

I was left alone with Vasily, who seemed to be in shock. He
said to me in French: 'Who taught you to keep pushing pawns
like that?'

'Somebody called Julian,' I said. 'Long ago.'

He was laying the chessmen carefully in their wooden box.
Next door, I could hear Alexis talking to Valentina in Russian.
I sat in my chair, waiting.

Vasya went out, taking the chess set, and switching off the
light as he went, and after the brightness of the unshaded bulb
the darkness in the room seemed absolute, like it used to feel
when I was a kid. I was never afraid of it exactly, but I used to
get angry with it, it felt so pointless. I once said to Grandma
Gwyneth: 'What's it *for*?' And she said it was for the birds, so
that they could rest their throats before morning.

I stayed still, resting my brain after the chess game. I could
hear the storm continuing in a circle, not being able to make
up its mind to move away, but the rain had stopped. Part of
me was thinking about how slippery the slate roof would have
become after this torrent of rain and the other part was
thinking, if Valentina comes and sleeps in my room, I'm not
going to attempt any escape, not tonight; I'm just going to lie
down beside her.

I don't know how long I sat on the chair in the darkness.
What I remember next was that my door was opened again
and the light was snapped on and Alexis was there, still wearing
his monkey mask. He looked round for me on the mattress
and seemed surprised that I was still sitting at the table. 'Go to
bed,' he said. 'Valentina is coming in a while.'

'When?' I asked. 'How long?'

'Go to bed. Go to sleep. Then she will come.'

I reckoned he was lying. He didn't have to do anything for

337

me or give me anything, even though I'd won the game. He could make any old promise and not keep it. And he liked taunting me. He thought I was a rich, spoilt kid whose brilliant future was all mapped out. He probably had moments of wanting to drown me in a rock pool. At my age, so Valentina had told me, he had a job as a cemetery sweeper at Père Lachaise. The thing he hated most in the cemetery was the bindweed that grew everywhere and stuck to your arms.

I got up slowly and lay down on my mattress. The damp and cold from the roof seemed to begin seeping through into the room now and I felt as cold as I'd been on my first night in here, when I'd puked on the floor. I pulled my blanket round me and lay with my eyes open, listening.

The house had gone quiet, like the monkeys were down-stairs, and no sound came from next door. Tentatively, I tapped on Valentina's wall, but no answering knock came. I put my ear close to the wall, but there was nothing to be heard, only the storm fretting on and on above us, moving near and moving away, then moving near again, like something that wanted to go somewhere but couldn't find its way.

I was almost asleep, as if in the cradle of the storm, when my door opened and I saw, from the light in the corridor, Vasily and Alexis both standing there. They came in and switched the light on again and I had to shield my eyes from it. Then they began to move things around in my room. They lifted the table and put it and the two chairs against the back wall, behind me. They stuck my shit pail under the table. Then they went out and came back, dragging a mattress, and laid this down by the far wall, where the table had been.

I sat up and watched them. They did everything in silence, with their masks still on, and when they'd put the mattress in place Alexis turned to me and said: 'In chess, if I lose, I always pay my debts.' Then they switched off the light, took the bulb out of its socket and went out, but they didn't close my door and I could hear them standing outside and talking.

I'd been cold, but now a weird burning feeling welled up in

me and I could hear my heart pumping. I sat still, holding on to my knees.

After a few minutes, Alexis came back and behind him was Valentina. He led her forward into my room and she stood there, peering at me in the dark, and Alexis looked at me and said, 'Here's "Maman",' and then he closed the door and bolted it shut.

She came and knelt down by my bed. I couldn't really see her, only feel that she was there, and I reached up with my arms outstretched, like kids reach up with their eyes all wide, like they know the world is going to be given to them there and then. I held on to her and pressed my face into her neck and kissed her and breathed her in and I could feel her arms going round me and clasping me to her, my chest to her breasts and my face into the soft hollow of her shoulder.

She rocked me and she let me cry. I felt her hand on my head, stroking my hair. I thought, I'm going to stay like this for ever and I'm going to cry for ever, and I knew that no moment of my life had ever been like this one. I couldn't say anything. The power of speech had drowned inside me. All I could do was just hold on to Valentina and weep.

The storm finally went away and when I opened the gap in the slates, a pallid sliver of moonlight came in, like a ghost that had been waiting there for a place to haunt.

By this ghostly light, Valentina and I looked at each other, and when our eyes had readjusted themselves in the grey shadows we saw that all our rue Rembrandt smartness had completely gone and what we resembled now were street people with no home. 'Darling,' said Valentina, 'did you ever see an old movie called *The Mudlarks*? About the river children by the Thames? Well, you look like one of those mudlarks, you know!' And she laughed.

She was still wearing the black-and-white dress. In the moonshine, all I could really see were the white bits and the white plaster on her broken arm, but the sight of that dress, which had been there at the centre of all my anxiety and all my longing for so many days and weeks, somehow choked me. I stared at it. It was creased and filthy and the hem of the skirt was torn and hanging down. I said: 'Your dress is a bit dirty, Valentina.'

'My dress, darling?' she said. 'Oh yes, so it is.'

She began to laugh unstoppably then. And it wasn't a hysterical, frightened laugh; it was her old infectious laugh that was sort of filled with lightness. I joined in and we fell on to the dusty floor, holding on to each other and flailing about with laughter, like morons. I wondered if Alexis could hear us and, if so, whether this laughter would piss him off and he'd rush in and take Valentina back to her cell. But no one came to the door, and when we'd recovered from our giggling we sat side by side on my mattress, with our arms round each other and our heads leaning in together. Round Valentina's head was tied the 'Ypres' scarf and it was sort of lolling down over one ear, like a slipped bandage. I knew she'd put it on because her hair would be dirty and there might be too many grey bits coming through for her liking, but at the back of her neck some little blonde wisps were straggling out and I reached up and touched these and stroked them between my finger and thumb, and the touch of her hair was as soft as I'd always imagined it to be.

After all our conversations through the pipe hole, we seemed to have run out of things to say. We just sat there and the moonlight got brighter as the storm clouds began a kind of race across the horizon, reminding me that the night was passing and that all my planning was coming to its moment of crisis. Before the morning came, while Alexis and Vasily slept, I knew that we had to climb out on to the roof, make our daring leap across to the barn, tumble on to the hay and walk to our freedom up the road. Except I didn't want to move. It was like I no longer believed in my plan. The hours I'd spent sawing through the batons, patiently moving the slates on their pins – they all seemed really futile, like the imaginings of a film-maker who hasn't got the plot properly worked out.

What I wanted to do was stay there, just exactly as we were for a while, and then slowly, slowly, let myself fall on to the mattress and, as I fell, take Valentina down with me, and without speaking, without saying a single thing, and almost without her noticing what was happening, lift up the skirt of her torn dress and fit myself inside her and rock her gently, like a parent rocks a child, to calm her and soothe her and love her into darkness and into sleep.

And so this, in my ghostly cell, where the light was seeping out as the moon moved away down the sky, was what I did. And when Valentina understood what I was doing and what I felt, instead of turning away from me or pretending to be shocked or insulted or that any of this was strange she just let me come into her, and she held me and let me kiss her ear and her neck, where the blonde wisps of hair lay curled.

And when it was over, she lay on her back and put my head on her breasts and still held me to her and I knew she was smiling, I mean laughing almost, amused, like she was remembering something funny or crazy from long ago. The thing she could have been remembering was the boy-lover of Catherine the Great. She stroked my hair and after a little while she whispered to me: 'Darling, now I know all your secrets and you know mine, and all that matters is that we keep them safe.'

'Yes,' I said. 'That's all that matters.'

I went to sleep and when I woke up it was almost morning.

When I saw that I was lying with Valentina, with my head on her shoulder, I longed to just stay there and not move, but I also knew that if we didn't try to make our escape now, we'd never make it at all. Part of me didn't want to make it at all. If I could have lived in this room with Valentina for the rest of time, that would have been OK with me. But I knew this wouldn't happen. I knew that when the ransom money arrived,

341

Shukov or Todorsky would be sent into our cells to kill us and our bodies would be buried under the trees.

I woke Valentina and said to her: 'The time's come. We've got to go now.'

She opened her eyes and stared at me. I was leaning on my elbow looking down at her and she stared up at me gravely and then reached up and stroked my eyebrow with her finger. 'Lewis,' she said, 'do you know what today is?'

'Yes,' I said, 'it's the day when we put my plan into operation.'

She smiled. 'I've been keeping track,' she said; 'ever since I was brought here, I've been counting days. It's the sixteenth of September.'

'That's my birthday,' I said.

'Yes. I know. That's what day it is.'

I lay still for a moment. Then I gently touched one of Valentina's breasts and felt it there, large and soft and warm under my hand, and she didn't move or push my hand away. What she said was: 'Happy birthday, darling.'

I thought, if I leave my hand on her breast one second more, I won't be able to move away from her. So I got up and began carrying the table and chair to the centre of the room. When they were in place, I climbed up and removed the baton and took off the slates. When I stuck my head out, the sky above me was grey and flat, but I could see, far off, way beyond the horizon of the meadow, a line of yellow light brimming up above the earth.

I listened. A long way away, a dog was barking, but apart from this, everything was silent. It was odd, in that silence, to think that I'd been alive for fourteen years and that now, today, I was no longer a virgin.

I looked all around. And suddenly I could see, beyond the trees, something faintly glimmering, and I knew it was the river or canal where the boats sometimes passed. And I thought, instead of burying us, they might just tie stones to our feet and drown us there, and we'd lie in the mud and waterweed through all the autumn and winter and the fish and the snakes would come and nibble us away and by spring we'd be gone.

I climbed down again and back into the room. Valentina was retying her 'Ypres' scarf round her hair, and today she tied it like Russian peasant women do, winding the ends right round her head and knotting them at the back. This task was difficult because she couldn't lift the arm in the cast very high.

I stood by the table and said: 'Valentina, the time's come now. We've got to make our escape.'

She finished knotting her scarf and held out her hand to me. 'Darling,' she said, 'come here. Listen to me. I know you've made this wonderful, daring plan and that you've worked so hard on those batons. But it's no use asking me to climb around on the roof. I just can't do it, Lewis.'

'You've got to do it,' I said. 'Look, it's almost light. We can't stay here discussing it. All we have to do is lower ourselves down towards the guttering and then jump on to the barn roof. It isn't difficult . . .'

'I'm too afraid of roofs, Lewis. I always was. And you know, I believe this whole thing will be resolved, probably quite soon, and then Alexis will release me.'

I went and knelt down by Valentina. Above us, I could sense the patch of sky getting lighter all the time. I took hold of one of her wrists and gripped it. 'He won't release you, Valentina!' I almost shouted. 'I don't know why you've never been able to admit this! Even if he can't bear to kill you himself, one of the others will have to do it.'

'No, darling. They will get their money and disappear; that's what will happen. I'm sure they have it all planned. Russia has changed so much now. They will go back there and no one in France will hear from them again. But they haven't even hurt me, Lewis. Don't tell me they would risk killing me.'

'They *have* to kill you! And me, as well. Because I know who they are and I've seen Vasya's face. So don't keep sticking to your stupid argument, Valentina. You're wasting time and every minute you waste could be crucial.'

She let me pull her to her feet. Then she drew me to her and held me against her for a moment. 'Lewis,' she said, 'why are you so passionate about everything?'

'I'm not,' I said. 'I'm just passionate about you. And I'm not going without you. Either we both leave or neither of us goes. If we stay, all my work on the roof will have been in vain. And in a few days' time, we'll die.'

We stood there. I thought, either we'll stand like this, holding each other for the bit of time remaining to us, or Valentina will decide to agree to my plan.

She agreed to get out on to the roof and then see if she could let herself try to inch down it. She said: 'I just don't know, until I'm out there, what I will be capable of.' Then she added: 'Of course, if we do get back to Paris today, like you've planned, darling, I'll take you to lunch at the Plaza.'

I could feel the seconds and minutes passing. I let go of Valentina and climbed out. The light on the horizon was welling up, brighter and brighter. And the air was still, like the storm had never occurred.

I had to help Valentina out. Her arm in its plaster hampered her. In this glimmer of early morning, I saw that her skin, which had always been a kind of golden colour, had paled in all the weeks of darkness.

She held on to me tightly and I put my arm round her waist, and it was as if I was lifting her out and back into the world. She blinked up at the light, and when she felt the fresh air on her face she said: 'Oh God, I'd forgotten that, Lewis: that lovely smell of the earth.'

We sat on the roof, holding on to the ridge, and looked around us. Valentina seemed stunned to see the things that were there: sky and poplar trees and the meadow lying under a white mist. It was like she'd arrived in China or some place she never knew existed.

I knew we shouldn't talk, because voices out in the air can travel so far, so after I'd let her stare at the landscape for a bit

I just whispered to her that we had to climb down the roof now and get ready for our leap. She looked over at where the corrugated top of the barn was and I knew she was thinking that it seemed too far away, because her eyes suddenly focused on it, like a camera lens trying to swivel into close-up, and I felt her body go rigid and tense.

'I can't do it, Lewis,' she whispered.

'Yes, you can,' I said. 'You've got to. There's nothing else. It's this or death.'

But she still didn't believe me. And I felt choked now. I thought, what if I'm wrong? What if I'm putting her through all this, when in a week's time she'll be released just as she believes? My heart was thumping. I stared around helplessly, as if I thought a ladder or a rope might suddenly materialise in front of my eyes, but the only thing that materialised was the sun coming up, warning me that minutes were passing, and then I felt a kind of calm, like I'd felt in the chess game, anchor me to my plan. I'd made a choice, taken a decision, and now I had to follow it through. I heard Didier say: 'Not to choose is also to make a choice, Louis,' and I knew that while we stayed there, hesitating, not choosing, Alexis and Vasily could be waking up and climbing the stairs and unlocking the door to my cell. And then everything would be lost.

I touched Valentina's hand, indicating she should watch what I did and follow me. Then I let go of the ridge and lay on the slates, half turned towards them, moving myself sideways, not straight down, but tacking across the roof, digging in with my fingers and with my heels. I didn't look down; I focused on the slates, counting each one as I climbed lower . . . seven, eight, nine . . . eleven . . .

I looked up. Valentina hadn't moved. I held out my hand, beckoning her towards me, and I watched her slowly, awkwardly, lower herself from the ridge. I shifted my position, improving my grip, and waited for her. The sun was up now and across the roof I saw our two shadows fall, so instead of watching Valentina's body with its broken arm trying to cling on to the roof and move down it, I shifted my gaze and watched the shadows and just waited patiently until her shadow came level with mine and then merged with it as she reached the point where I was and I put out my arm to steady her.

She was breathing hard. There was sweat on her face. The black-and-white dress was rucked up almost round her waist and I could see her knickers, made of creamy silk, torn round one edge. 'God,' she said, 'I'm so frightened, Lewis. We weren't made to cling to the tops of buildings.'

'You're doing fine,' I said. 'We're almost there.'

We stayed where we were for about a minute, holding on, getting our breath. We were only a few feet from the gutter line and when I looked down I could see the barn roof much nearer now. But this was going to be the hardest bit. Instead of clinging to the slates, we had to turn, force ourselves to turn and face outwards, standing upright over the void. And then we had to fly.

I delayed a little longer. I laid my head on the slates and looked at Valentina. What I wanted to say was: 'My whole future is you. There's nothing anywhere in any shape or form in my future life except you. I don't know why this has happened to me, but that's the way it's always going to be.' But I thought I would say this later, when we were in a more comfortable position, when we were sitting down at a table in the restaurant of the Plaza Hotel. So all I did was smile and stroke Valentina's arm, and then I gathered all my strength and all my courage and I turned away from her and round towards the sunrise and leapt outwards and felt the air underneath me buoy me up away from the pull of gravity and land me, still upright, on the corrugated iron roof of the barn.

I let myself topple forwards. The iron was rusty and harsh on my bare feet, but it didn't buckle or split. A feeling of elation began stabbing at me, stronger than anything I seemed to have known. I wanted to yell, 'I did it! I did it!' I wanted to dance about on the iron like a voodoo spirit. So I turned and got to my feet and began to wave wildly at Valentina. I waved and waved, with both my arms. I saw her above me, smiling . . .

Epilogue

Today is the first of November.

The clocks have gone back by one hour, which means that it's going to get dark by about five in the afternoon, and that suits me fine. I prefer it when there's no light in the sky.

At school, I spend a lot of time looking out of the window, watching the line of sycamore trees at the end of the playing fields. These trees are having a really horrendous time: the wind just whips them and torments them hour after hour and whole branches have broken off and lie around underneath them in the grass.

I find it pretty hard to give my attention to what the teachers are saying. I'd honestly rather look at these trees. 'Lewis,' the teachers sometimes say, 'are you with us?'

Quite often, I get brought in to see the headmaster, Mr Quaid. This is because I've stopped doing any homework except Maths. The harder the Maths gets, the more I like it. But the other subjects seem pointless. My ability to interest myself in the structure of biological photocells, or in standards of living in Latin America, or in the priggish character of Tom Tulliver in *The Mill on the Floss*, diminishes with each day.

Mr Quaid tells me he understands this, but feels disappointed by it. He's quite nice to me. He doesn't bollock me or threaten me with expulsion. He just looks at me sadly and reminds me that I'm on my GCSE track this year. He says I used to be one of the 'high-flyers' of Beckett Bridges School.

Sometimes he gives me Nescafé, made by his secretary, in a white china mug. I can't stand Nescafé. He waits for me to make some comment about being a high-flyer, but I find it really difficult to think of anything to say. From his office window, you can see the very tops of the sycamore trees, so I look out at them and try to drink the coffee, which makes my stomach burn. And after a while, Mr Quaid says something like: 'Well, Lewis, what is the answer to all of this?'

One of the things I don't know the answer to is where Valentina is buried.

I keep asking Alice and she keeps saying she doesn't know. 'I've told you,' she says, 'I don't know, Lewis.' As if knowledge were finite and couldn't be acquired. As if what's in her mind now is all that's ever going to be there.

I figure that if Anton was buried in the Cimetière de Montmartre, Valentina would have wanted to be buried there, somewhere near him. But the Cimetière de Montmartre might be full up by now. They might have left some room in Anton's grave to put Mrs Gavrilovich in, but not Valentina as well. So where is she? Once or twice, I've come near to calling up Mrs Gavrilovich and asking her, but then when I get the phone in my hand, I hesitate.

I imagine the apartment in the rue Daru and Mrs Gavrilovich sitting in it. She's eating her little cakes and giving crumbs to Sergei, who lies across her feet. She's staring at her icon. She's gone into her own sorrowful world and she doesn't want to be disturbed. And I respect that.

People won't leave me alone, though. They think my being silent is sinister, sort of weird, so they try to get me to talk to them. I've been found a counsellor, whose name is Daniel. He lives in Sidmouth, so I think the people he mainly counsels are retired. He probably sits in their bungalow gardens, on their patio loungers, counselling them while they stir their tea and check their bingo numbers.

But actually, I quite like him. What I primarily like is the fact that he knows virtually nothing about me. He wears crazy ties with fish or sunflowers or leopards on them and he has wild hair, a bit like Grisha's. He's about forty-three and he lives alone, without even a pet.

He makes me talk about it, though, and this I don't like. He says I have to get the facts completely straight in my mind. And only then, in time, will I learn to stop taking responsibility for it. I tell him: 'It was my idea to try to escape by climbing on to the roof, so I *want* to take responsibility for it. That is my existential choice.'

Talking about it brings such a mass of pain into me, it's like I'm the one who's fallen and hit the ground. So I say it all very fast, as if I'm sending in a report from a war zone, with the enemy getting nearer and nearer. I say: 'I'm standing on the roof of the barn. I look up at Valentina and she smiles at me and then we see the helicopter. It comes out of nowhere, like out of the sunrise. It's a police helicopter. It just comes roaring in, right above Valentina. And that's it.'

'That's what?' says Daniel.

'That's the moment. She's distracted by the helicopter and the revolving blades are creating this down-draught like a wind. She can't hang on to the slates any more. And I see her body begin to slide. She reaches out with her good arm, but she can't get a grip on anything. Her arm just flails around in the air, like she was waving at something. And then she falls.'

And when I've said all this, I can't speak for the next ten minutes or so. I'm just completely exhausted.

One time, I say to Daniel: 'Hugh needs counselling, you know. He probably needs it more than I do.'

'What makes you say that?' Daniel asks.

'Because he's taking responsibility for everything too.'

'In what way?'

'He thinks he never should have let Alice and me go to Paris on our own. He thinks if he'd been there everything would have been different.'

Then I describe how Hugh is since we got back, like how he talks in whispers a lot of the time and how he's become completely and totally obedient to Alice and tries to do all the shopping and everything, to save her the trouble of moving from her desk. And like how he sleeps in the spare room, not in Alice's bed, and plays Mahler symphonies late at night, drinking red wine.

Daniel asks me if I think everything would have been different if Hugh had been there and I say: 'No. Not for me. It wouldn't have made any difference at all.'

There's a long silence, while Daniel's thin fingers fiddle with his leopard tie. And as always when there's a sudden silence, I feel myself moving away from whatever place it is I'm in and returning to Valentina. Quite often, I'm in her bedroom at the rue Rembrandt, lying among the cushions while she strokes my hair, but not always. Because I can find her anywhere. I could be walking along by the bouquinistes, or sitting in the rue Poncelet, watching the bustle of the market. I could be down in the métro or under the catalpa trees at Jussieu or looking at the green parrots in the bird market. I could be in the kitchen feeding Sergei, or in the dining-room eating lunch or up in my attic playing my musical box. But she is always with me. I can smell her. She is so close to me, I could reach out and touch her.

'What about Alice?' asks Daniel, when this silence ends. 'What do you think she feels about what happened?'

I sigh. I don't like being made to leave Valentina to focus on Alice; it hurts my head. I say to Daniel: 'Look, I don't know Alice any more. And she doesn't know me. And that's just how it is, and it's always going to be like that.'

'Why?' says Daniel. 'Why's it "always going to be like that"?'

'Because,' I say, 'it just is.'

Even with Daniel, I get tired of talking. I get tired pretty fast. I can't be bothered to explain to him that Alice and I have totally different interpretations of the same period of time. Or that sometimes when I look at her here at home I know she's miles away in her mind, in the same place as I am: she's back in Paris with her lover.

I'd rather just be quiet and look at the things in Daniel's room – his photographs of the sea, his collection of cactus plants, his black venetian blind – or be on the bus going home.

The bus is good. No one says anything to me. I just ride along, watching the day being overtaken by the night. And sometimes I find myself smiling. The thing I'm smiling at is the knowledge that there's one thing about Valentina and me that Daniel will never know. Never, ever. No one on earth will know it. It's her secret and mine and it's safe with me.

One night, about one o'clock or something, I go downstairs to make a glass of malted milk. Malted milk is meant to still your brain and make you sleep like a child, but it doesn't. It just lets you lie there wondering when this lovely sleep is going to come. But I like it anyway.

I'm about to go into the kitchen, but then I stop outside the door because I can hear Alice and Hugh in there, talking. I thought they were in bed in their separate rooms, but they're not; they're sitting at the kitchen table, talking about their marriage, and I can tell that Hugh is crying. I listen for a bit, then I can't stand to stay there a moment longer. In fact, I can't bear to be in the house with them any more. So I take one of the old waterproof coats from near the back door and let myself out into the garden.

The wind is tearing at the trees. I wouldn't mind lying on the lawn and staying awake all night, listening to everything moving in the wind, except that it feels cold out here, so I walk right down the length of the lawn and go into the hut.

The smell in there is really nice. Hugh thinks the best things about the hut are the dinky wooden porch he erected round the door and the way the windows fit so brilliantly and the cockerel weather vane on the roof. But he's wrong: the best thing about it is the smell. He and Bertie put in a wide shelf, made of pine, which is meant to be Alice's desk, and it's like the pine they used is really still a pine tree and this foresty smell in the hut comes from the sap which still bleeds out of the wood in several places.

Not one single time has Alice taken work out here or sat at this desk, but now I lie down under it and cover myself with the gardening coat and stay there till morning.

Bertie and Gwyneth come back to stay for a while.

When Gwyneth sees me, she starts crying and says: 'Oh Lewis, thank God it's over.'

Not just her, but everyone, including Daniel, thinks it's all sliding nicely away out of sight, into the past, and becoming history. But I will never let it be over. I will never let it become history. I'm like the bison who, in the core of his being, can remember the Great Plains and knows that he was once right there, in what – to him – was the most beautiful place on earth.

Bertie offers to play chess with me, but I tell him I've lost interest in chess. My chess set is packed away in its box, in a cupboard. I never want to see it again.

'What do you want to do, then?' Bertie says. 'We can do anything you like.' So I ask him if he can drive me to Exeter and lend me some money and he says, 'Absolutely. Why not?' So we go on our own and walk around Exeter until we find a big toy-shop. And I spend thirty-nine pounds on a fantastic battery-operated car with flashing lights and a remote-control horn, and Bertie and I go and try it out on a piece of derelict ground and we both agree that it's seriously excellent. Then I wrap it up and take it to a post office and send it to Pozzi. I enjoy writing his little name on the label: Pozzi Babbala.

On the way back home, we stop at a Happy Eater and order eggs and sausages and I explain to Bertie who Pozzi is and where he lives, in that building made of mosaics, and about the village in Benin. This is the greatest amount of talking I've done for a long time and Bertie listens very attentively.

But then he admits he can't remember where Benin is, so I

draw a map of Africa on one of the Happy Eater napkins and sketch in Benin, very small, next to Nigeria. The shape of Benin is like a bunch of flowers and Violette's village is somewhere low down among the stalks.

Bertie suddenly looks up from this drawing and wipes his mouth and says: 'You know, Lewis, if they hadn't rescued you, I just don't know how any of us would have survived.'

The police only found us because of Moinel. Alice says I should write and thank him for saving my life, but I can't see it like that. If Moinel had known nothing, that helicopter would never have come out of the sunrise.

But he knew the link to the kidnappers had to be the Russian receptionist at the hospital and he made Carmody focus on her. I know her name now. It's Sonya, like Sonya Marmeladov in *Crime and Punishment*. It was Sonya I heard shouting the night they drove off in the Citroën 2CV and it was Alexis she was shouting at.

She was Alexis's girlfriend, but she betrayed him in the end. Carmody broke her down with his interrogations. He just went on and on and on at her until she cracked. She held out for seventeen days and then, after that row with Alexis, she made a plea bargain with Carmody and told him everything. If Sonya and Alexis had had the row two days earlier, if Moinel had kept silent, Valentina would still be alive.

I've begun a letter to Grisha. I'm writing it in French: *Cher Grigory . . .*

I start by telling him how good I think his book is. Alice once said writers are like children: what they long for is unadulterated praise.

Then I say that I understand why he prefers looking at the sky to looking at people and explain that I feel the same way now. I describe the sycamores beyond the playing fields. I add: *There's also a walk I make, over the cliffs and down to the sea. My father, Hugh, always wants to come on this walk with me, but I hardly ever let him. The reason I like looking at the sea is that I know what lies beyond it: France.*

I keep the letter in a drawer and add things to it from time to time. One of the things I add is that I often dream there's a bird on my own neck, trying to fly me into some kind of future. I tell Grisha it's a mathematical bird and the future that it's flying me towards is logical and clear and cold and bright. The language I'm going to speak there is one that only a few people can understand.

On a Sunday night, I decide to end the letter and post it. And after a week or so, I start looking forward to getting a reply. The post to and from Russia takes a long time, but I know that one day a reply will come. And this will become a part of my life now: writing to Grisha and receiving news about the Moscow sky.

And so November just goes on and becomes December and Alice and Hugh start buying Christmas presents, and I buy nothing for anybody. I just can't see how people could be interested in this Christmas shit any more. I say to Daniel: 'When I hear them playing carols in the shops, I want to gun down everybody in sight.'

And as Christmas comes nearer, being in my room makes me edgy. It's full of things which remind me of Christmases gone by, when I was a boy and knew nothing and thought the only function a metronome could ever have, as long as the world lasted, was to keep time. I lie in bed and stare at the room and at my old self in it and I say aloud: 'The day has come when you and I have to part company.'

So I tell Hugh, I don't want to sleep in there any more; I want to sleep in the hut. At first, he says it's too cold, too uncomfortable, a stupid idea. But I make Daniel talk to him about it, and after that he changes his mind. He puts a mattress in there, under the desk, and a greenhouse heater and a paraffin lamp. He asks me what else I'd like.

I tell him I don't want anything, just a blanket. I say I

358

imagined all along that he was building the hut for me. And this pleases him somehow and he touches my shoulder and smiles.

So that's more or less where I live now, separate from the house, separate from Alice and Hugh. It's getting pretty cold as the winter goes on, but I don't want to move. I'm going to try and stick it out because I'm far more content in there, on my own. By the flickering paraffin light, which reminds me of the light in the attic room of François Seurel, I do my mathematical calculations and the numbers go forwards and onwards, taking me with them through time.

And on certain nights, when it's very dark and still, something amazing happens to me. If I close my eyes, I can dream myself back into my attic cell and reach out and find, very near me in the wall, the hole through which I can feel the warm touch of Valentina's breath.

And then, after only a moment or two, I hear her laughter and a feeling like happiness comes into me and is mine.

Acknowledgements

I would like to thank the following people,
without whose knowledge and assistance
this novel could not have been written:

Frank Willis for his knowledge of the Russian language;
Jean Bourdier for his information about French police procedures
and his patient correcting of my French syntax;
David Norwood for his invaluable help with Lewis's chess problems;
Commissaire Yves Jobic for his guidance on police intervention;
Claude Jonis for his generously undertaken additional Paris research;
David Gentleman for his marvellous Paris watercolours,
which inspired many of the trails I followed on the ground;
and Penelope Hoare, editor and friend, who, as always,
helped to make this a better book than it once was.

A **WSP** READING GROUP GUIDE

The Way I Found Her

Rose Tremain

ABOUT THIS GUIDE

The suggested questions are intended to help your
reading group find new and interesting angles and
topics for discussion for Rose Tremain's *The Way I
Found Her.* We hope that these ideas will enrich your
discussion and increase your enjoyment of the book.

Many fine books from Washington Square Press
include Reading Group Guides. For a complete listing,
or to read the Guides on-line, visit
http://www.simonsays.com/reading/guides

DISCUSSION QUESTIONS

1. In the book, Lewis is geographically distanced from his father and emotionally distanced from his mother. Does any character (or characters) in the story take on a surrogate parental role for him? How?

2. What factors contribute to Lewis' strained relationship with his mother? Is it simply teen angst connected with entering young adulthood, or is it something else? How is this shown in the story?

3. Several times in the novel, Lewis reflects on his ideas about how he perceives things. This manifests itself in several ways, including the different perceptions he and his mother have about Valentina. How do you feel leaving Devon for Paris has changed Lewis' perceptions, and in what ways?

4. Didier and Baba both play significant roles in Lewis' life during his time in Paris. What characteristics do you think he finds in them that he doesn't in Alice or Valentina? Would it be fair to say that Didier and Baba are from a different world than Alice and Valentina? Why?

5. Lewis and Valentina both share a desire to transcend their situations—Lewis wants to abandon family life on the coast of Devon for the romance of Continental Europe, while Valentina hopes to never return to the life she led as a poor Russian immigrant. As a popular writer, does Valentina ever succeed in burying her immigrant girlhood? At the novel's end, did Lewis succeed in any transcendence of his own?

6. Among the posh rooms of Valentina's Paris apartment is the cluttered junk room where she secretly stows away things that belonged to Anton, her father. How does this represent the way she views her past?

7. At different points in the book, Lewis mentions that his father said he should think of his life as a rock pool and his quota of happiness as tiny little shrimp in the pool so he would never be disappointed. In what ways does Lewis adhere to his father's advice?

8. In most of the novel, Lewis lives in a world of imagination, whether he is living out the lives of characters from the books he reads, or the imaginary walks he takes during his abduction by Alexis. In the last chapter, Lewis is older. How would you characterize the older Lewis, and how has he changed?

9. The reader is never fully aware of the exact details of Alice's relationship with Didier or Valentina's ultimate fate. What effects does this have? What does it lead you to believe about the two incidents?

10. In the last chapter, what is the significance of Lewis' sending the remote control car to Pozzi and keeping in touch with Grisha?

11. Does the formulaic logic of mathematics, in some way, become a substitute for something Lewis has lost during the course of the novel?

ROSE TREMAIN is the author of seven novels,
including the bestselling *Restoration*, which received the
Sunday Express Book of the Year Award in 1989, was shortlisted for the
Booker Prize, and was made into an Academy Award®-winning
film in 1995. *Sacred Country* won both the James Tait
Memorial Prize and the Prix Femina Etranger in France.
Ms. Tremain lives in London and Norwich, England.

35215731R00208

Made in the USA
Middletown, DE
24 September 2016